CRITICS AND READERS PRAISE

ENIGMA

"Bestseller Coulter is at the top of her game in her 21st FBI thriller . . . Twists and turns galore in both investigations ensure there's never a dull moment."

—*Publishers Weekly*, starred review

"A master of smooth, eminently readable narratives."

—*Booklist*

"*Enigma* is a new seductive and menacing thriller that sets new standards to judge thrillers. It's a thriller most people would like to finish it in one sitting. It is intense and packed with action and inventive fantasy Catherine Coulter is known for. This must be next on your reading list if you love to read thrillers."

—*The Washington Book Review*

"As always, I was on the edge of my seat. *Enigma* is another great suspense thriller!"

—L. Brennan

"I just finished *Enigma* and it was superb. You had me going until the last epilogue. What an incredible, complicated plot. Without a doubt your FBI stories are my favorite reading."

—H. Brown

"I LOVED *Enigma* and couldn't put it down! I had to pace myself so I wouldn't finish too quickly as I hated to see it end. I've read all the FBI and the Brit in the FBI series and I can't wait for the next one."

—B. Kelley

"I just finished *Enigma*. You've done it again! A fabulous read with enough twists and turns to keep the adrenaline meter on HIGH! Congratulations on another success. I really enjoyed this book and can't wait for the next."

—N. LeComte

"I give *Enigma* five stars. I couldn't put it down. Another page-turning thriller."

—A. Konieczka

"I loved *Enigma*! I tried to pace myself to make it last but was not successful. I had to finish it this afternoon. Fantastic job and as usual, I can't wait for the next one."

—S. Burian

"*Enigma* was wonderful! Your descriptions and how the scenes play out are fantastic. Thank you again for writing a wonderful story, bringing everything together and making me lose sleep because I couldn't put the book down."

—C. Storzum

CRITICS AND READERS PRAISE

INSIDIOUS

"Coulter keeps the two plot lines equally engaging—and the reader guessing—all the way to the satisfying resolution of each."

—*Publishers Weekly*

"Two very intriguing mysteries . . . you can't go wrong with a Coulter book, as she has proven time after time."

—*RT Book Reviews*

"Catherine Coulter knows how to weave and web incredibly heinous crimes that make you think and shudder."

—*Mrs. Leif's Two Fangs About It*

"You outdid yourself on this one. The best one yet. I had a very hard time putting it down. I had to take my wife to the doctor today and while I was waiting, I was getting almost to the end of the book. I was so engrossed in the story that I did not realize my wife was leaving."

—T. Muller

"Wow! I finished *Insidious* last night. I didn't see that [ending] coming. Great job of keeping me and all the other readers in the dark. Keep up the great novels. I can't wait for the next one."

—D. Riker

"I could not put [*Insidious*] down. Both of your story lines were well thought out and the characterizations were so thorough I could picture each person and their attitude in my mind. You gave us enough to try and figure out the villain but twist it just enough that we might be close but not close enough. You write such compelling stories."

—S. Lavalais

THE FBI THRILLERS

A BRIT IN THE FBI THRILLERS
(WITH J.T. ELLISON)

CATHERINE COULTER

ENIGMA

POCKET BOOKS

New York London Toronto Sydney New Delhi

Pocket Books
An Imprint of Simon & Schuster, Inc.
1230 Avenue of the Americas
New York, NY 10020

This book is a work of fiction. Any references to historical events, real people, or real places are used fictitiously. Other names, characters, places, and events are products of the author's imagination, and any resemblance to actual events or places or persons, living or dead, is entirely coincidental.

First Pocket Books paperback edition August 2018

POCKET and colophon are registered trademarks of Simon & Schuster, Inc.

For information about special discounts for bulk purchases, please contact Simon & Schuster Special Sales at 1-866-506-1949 or business@simonandschuster.com.

The Simon & Schuster Speakers Bureau can bring authors to your live event. For more information or to book an event, contact the Simon & Schuster Speakers Bureau at 1-866-248-3049 or visit our website at www.simonspeakers.com.

Manufactured in the United States of America

10 9 8 7 6 5 4 3 2 1

ISBN 978-1-5011-3810-2
ISBN 978-1-5011-3811-9 (ebook)

ACKNOWLEDGMENTS

To Angela Bell, FBI, who always hooks me up with the experts I need.

To Special Supervisory Agent Joshua Wilson, of FBI CARD team—child abduction rapid deployment—for detailed information on their procedures. If I got everything right, you can reward me by wearing a billboard: *Enigma* on both sides. If I got anything wrong, you can punish me by wearing a billboard with *Enigma* on only one side.

To Karen Evans, my brilliant, funny assistant and right side of my brain. Your name will live forever as the Queen of Nothing Is Impossible. May our synergy continue into the misty future.

Whenever science makes a discovery, the Devil grabs it while the angels are debating the best way to use it.
—Alan Valentine

PROLOGUE

People couldn't move out of his way fast enough, some of them even crossed the street to avoid getting too close to him. He realized, on some level, that what was going on in his head was making him look and act crazy, but he couldn't help that. Maybe the blur of his thoughts, the dizziness, the weakness he felt would get better. His brain tripped away from that thought so fast he couldn't catch it long enough to consider what it meant.

At least he'd managed to get what he needed from Morley's Gun and Sports. He'd broken in, found the AR-15 he was looking for displayed on a wall, and was aware enough to wrap it in a bag along with the Remington cartridges so people wouldn't see he was carrying a rifle. And he'd found some hunting clothes on a display table, grabbed up chinos, shirts, boots, and socks. It had felt strange to be putting on real clothes, clothes that sort of fit. He'd left his green drawstring pants, smock, and slippers on the floor.

He put one foot in front of the other on the street, focused only on moving on. He waved down a passing bus and held out the money he'd stolen to the bus driver and let him pick out what was owed. The bus was a gift. Maybe he wouldn't be too late. He sat down, breathed slowly in and out, and whispered his mantra over and over so he wouldn't forget: *I've got to save her; I've got to get to her in time.*

1

Dr. Janice Hudson clutched Savich's arm, her words tumbling over one another. "Thank goodness you were home, Dillon, and you came. Listen, I was outside weeding my impatiens when I saw a man ring Kara's doorbell. She opened the door and he started yelling at her, waving his arms around, and then he shoved her inside and closed the door. I heard her scream."

"Did he see you?"

"No, no, he didn't. He's a young man, Dillon, unkempt, baggy clothes, and he had a long package under his arm. I thought it could be some sort of gun." He wanted to tell her that was unlikely, but he'd known Dr. Janice Hudson all his life; she'd been a close friend of his grandmother's. She'd also been a psychiatrist for more than forty years, and he could only imagine what she'd seen in that time. He'd trusted her instincts enough to drop everything and run over when she'd called him.

"I called 911, too, but I don't know how long it will take them to get here. You have to help Kara, she's such a sweet girl. Like I told you, she's pregnant; the baby is due in one week. She's been renting the house for nearly six months and—"

She drew a deep breath, got herself together. "That's not important. Dillon, when I saw his face, and the way he moved, stumbling and weaving when he stood in place, he seemed severely disturbed, probably medicated. Every now and then he screams at her—there, listen!"

It was a young man's voice, a mad voice overwhelmed with panic. *"You've got to understand! You have to come with me; we have to get away from them. I know they're coming and they'll take you. You've got to come away with me before it's too late!"*

"Who will take her? Before what's too late? He sounds paranoid, delusional. He's been yelling about the baby, ranting and cursing about some kind of gods, making no rational sense. He hasn't said who those gods are, but I'm frightened for Kara, especially if he's armed. I've dealt with people as disturbed as he is too many times in my life not to be. Dillon, you've got to help her, now."

Savich turned to see a police car pull up, a Crown Vic behind it. Two officers piled out of the squad car, and behind them Detective Aldo Mayer, a man other cops called Fireplug behind his back, hauled himself out of the Crown Vic, looking harassed. Savich could let Mayer deal with this. Mayer had experience, and he'd clearly been close when the call came in. Savich saw him wave to the two officers and motion them over.

The man screamed at them through the front window. *"I know they sent you, but how did they find me so fast? It's too soon! You stay away, I've got a rifle. Stay back!"*

He pushed the barrel of an AR-15 assault rifle out from between the drapes and fired. The cops scrambled for cover as bullets struck the side of the Crown Vic and the patrol car. There was silence again, except for the sirens in the distance.

"Dillon, they're not cops to him, they're here to take him to the people he fears. If he snaps, he might hurt Kara and the baby. His paranoia is out of control, he'll do whatever he thinks he has to do." She leaned into him. "I know a way you can get into Kara's house without anyone seeing you. What do you say?"

Another cop car pulled up to the curb, the officers quickly taking cover. Detective Mayer shouted through a bullhorn, "Sir, we're not here to do you any harm. There's no reason for anyone to get hurt. We can talk, we can figure this out. Tell us the problem, tell us how we can help you."

"Don't lie to me! I know who you are. They found me and sent you. I can beat them, at least for a little while. Leave or I'll kill you, all of you if I have to! Do you understand me? They don't know everything. I figured it out; I fooled them! I got away from them. Get back!"

Savich heard tears bubbling in his shattered voice. And a deep well of madness, and fear.

The man screamed, *"I'll kill everyone to stop them, do you hear me? I'll kill all of us!"*

He fired off another half-dozen rounds through the small space between the tightly pulled drapes. A front tire on the lead patrol car burst, and bullets shattered the passenger-side window of the Crown Vic, sending Detective Mayer to his belly.

They couldn't return fire, they had no idea where Kara Moody was.

The distant sirens were closer now, and soon there would be pandemonium in the street. Savich would lose his chance. Dr. Janice was right: He had no choice. The man was unpredictable and dangerous, and he had an assault rifle. Savich felt the familiar weight of his Glock on his belt clip and hoped he wouldn't have to use it. He saw Sherlock's beloved face, remembered Sean's manic laughter when he'd beaten his father at a new video game, and prayed he wouldn't take a bullet. Savich said to Dr. Janice, "Tell me how to get in the house."

As she spoke to him, Savich texted Metro detective Ben Raven.

Urgent. Come to 2782 Prospect Street.
Hostage situation. Mayer here. Bail me out.

Savich heard the man yelling again, his panicked madness giving way to something like determination, and acceptance. *"I mean it! It has to stop. I won't let them hurt her. Leave. Tell them they can't have her!"*

Savich climbed over Dr. Janice's fence and dropped onto Kara Moody's side yard. There were only three high windows on the near side of the house, no chance the man would see him. Savich pushed through a planting of red petunias and white impatiens, cut through a huge star jasmine that covered a root cellar door at the back of the house. Dr. Janice had lived next door for fifty years and knew the original owners had dug out the space to use as a bomb shelter, something from another age.

He moved the jasmine away, saw the moldy wooden door Dr. Janice had described to him. It wasn't locked. The rusted handle creaked and groaned as he pulled it open and looked down at rotted wooden stairs that disappeared into blackness. He pulled out his cell phone to use as a light, and carefully stepped down the stairs until he felt the rotted wood begin to give way, and jumped, knees bent, to the dirt floor. He felt a rat carcass crunch beneath his boot, breathed in stale, nasty air, cooler than outside, and nearly coughed, but managed to hold it in. He doubted anyone had been in this shelter since the Nixon administration. His cell light haloed spiderwebs draped from open beams, crisscrossing the space, and more rodent carcasses littered the dirt floor. Jars were lined up on warped wooden shelves, covered with mold, dirt, and spiderwebs. Straight ahead another set of sagging wooden stairs led up to a door. Dr. Janice had told him it opened into a closet in the second bedroom, the baby's room.

He thanked heaven for small favors when the stairs held his weight. He tried the narrow door at the top. It was locked. He grabbed the wooden rail to steady himself, reared back, and slammed his shoulder against the lock. It held. He reared back again and this time he kicked it, nearly lost his balance, and felt his heart do a mad flip. The door popped open. He prayed the man hadn't heard him.

He shoved the door slowly outward, pushing aside cardboard boxes stacked against it, until he had enough of a path to pass. He eased the outer closet door open slowly and looked into a room painted a light blue. A bright mobile with the name *Alex* hung over a crib, and next to the crib was a rocking chair with a blue throw and a dresser painted with Walt Disney characters. Everything was ready for the baby's arrival.

He stepped quietly into the hallway, guessed he was thirty feet from the living room when he heard the man screaming at the cops again. *"Bastards! They sent you, didn't they? But they don't want me dead, not yet at least, so he told you not to kill me."*

Savich heard Kara Moody's voice, soft and low, but he couldn't make out what she was saying. She sounded controlled, trying to keep him calm. He prayed she could hold herself together a bit longer. It might help keep the man from shooting her . . . and then possibly himself.

Savich held his Glock at his side and walked as quietly as he could through the updated kitchen toward an arched opening to the dining room. The L-shaped living room was beyond it, and he saw Kara Moody first, her ankles and wrists duct-taped to a chair, her long straight dark hair straggling around her face. A burgundy Redskins T-shirt covered her big belly and her loose white cotton pants. Her narrow feet were bare. She was in her midtwenties, and pretty. Her eyes were fastened on her feet, trying to avoid the man's eyes, and his attention. Savich moved forward, saw the man standing by the window in profile, the assault rifle held loosely at his side. Savich wondered where he'd gotten hold of that killing machine. He was swaying back and forth. Was it from stress or drugs? Probably both. He'd sounded young, but still, Savich was surprised to see he was no older than twenty-five, slight, maybe one forty, and no taller than five foot nine. There was a light beard scruff on his narrow face. He might have been good-looking if rage and fear weren't contorting his face. He wore a wrinkled shirt over baggy chinos that looked like he'd lived in them since he'd escaped from wherever he'd been held, from the people who'd probably been trying to take care of him. Were they the gods he was running from, the gods he believed had found him so quickly and sent the police to bring him back?

Savich flattened himself behind the dining room wall, next to the arched opening, and calmed his breathing. He heard Detective Mayer's voice on the bullhorn trying to reason with a man who had no tether to reason, offering to provide him whatever he wanted if he didn't harm Ms. Moody.

The man screamed, *"You're a liar! I don't believe you, not a word! I won't let you take me, or take her. Do you hear me?"* He let out a high, mad laugh. *"I will not let you win!"* He screamed the words again, wailed them. Then he stopped, turned to face Kara Moody, and whispered, *"I don't know what to do. I've got to figure this out. I want what's best for you, I do, only not how you'd think. But maybe it doesn't matter now."*

He began shaking his head, and his free hand tugged at his hair. He was ready to break and yelled, *"What am I going to do?"*

Kara Moody raised her head, and Savich realized she knew as well as he did it was crunch time and she had to try. "Please listen to me. Please tell me who you are and why you want me to go with you. Go where? Who is after you? After us? Can't you see I'm pregnant?"

He ran to her, leaned forward, cupped her chin in his hand, and jerked her face up. *"Of course you're pregnant. Why do you think I came? Did you call them? Did you tell them I was here?"* He stopped again, shook his head, as if trying to straighten out his thoughts. *"No, you didn't call them; I didn't let you. I had to tie you up, you know that, don't you? You'd have run before I could convince you to come with me. Wait, then who called them? I don't understand. I don't understand!"*

Savich couldn't act, the man was too close to her, his face nearly touching hers, close enough to kiss her. Her voice remained amazingly calm as she whispered into his face, "No, I didn't call them. I don't like them, either. I don't want them to get near me. Who are you? Have I seen you before? Were you in Baltimore?"

"Baltimore," he repeated, as if trying to make sense of it.

He reared back and screamed at her, spittle flying, *"I'm an enigma. He keeps telling me that's what I am, that is what we are. I can't let them take me, can't let them take you! It's evil, a monstrous evil!"* He shoved himself back away from her.

"Drop the gun now!"

The man whipped around at the sound of Savich's voice and yelled, *"No!"* He jerked up his rifle, screamed, *"How did you get in here?"*

Savich fired, hit the gun, and sent it flying out of the man's hands, skidding across the oak floor to fetch up against a chair leg. The young man howled and lunged toward Kara, his hands outstretched. Savich fired again, striking him high in the shoulder. He flinched, but it didn't stop him. His hands were reaching toward her big belly. Savich took careful aim and fired just as Kara lurched back in the chair and it toppled over. The bullet blew a cloud of blood from the man's head, and he jerked backward at the impact. But it had only grazed him, and he whirled around again to face Savich. He looked confused, like a child being disciplined for something he didn't understand. He licked dry lips, whispered, *"I don't understand. You're not a god. They don't want me dead. Who are you?"* He grabbed his shoulder when his brain finally recognized his pain, and he staggered, tears streaming down his face. He slammed his other hand to his head, and brought it down again, stared at the blood streaming between his fingers. He made a small mewling sound, his eyes rolled back in his head, and he fell on his side to the floor. He was out.

Savich pulled Kara's chair back up, saw she was all right. "Hold on." He knew everyone had heard the shots. He raced to the window to see a newly arrived SWAT team jogging toward the house, their weapons at the ready, bulletproof shields in front of them as they prepared to rush the house. He heard Mayer's voice shouting, "Go, go, go!"

As if choreographed, a dozen cops rose up from behind their police cars to fan out behind them. Savich threw open the door, raised his creds in the air through the opening, yelled, "FBI! The shooter is down! It's over! The shooter is down!"

It was as if they didn't see him, hadn't heard him, as if they were guided missiles set on their course. They kept coming. Savich understood the adrenaline rush, knew their training had hardwired them not to stop until they got to Kara Moody.

He yelled again, "FBI. Dillon Savich! The man is alive but he's down! Don't shoot! It's over!"

The SWAT team leader stopped, raised his hand. "Is that you, Savich? Dillon Savich?"

It was Luke Palmer, twenty-year veteran, a man he'd met a couple of years before at the gym, a man he knew was scary good at his job.

"Luke, yes, it's me, Savich! He's down, unconscious! Ms. Moody is unhurt."

"But how did you— Never mind." Luke turned, spoke to his team, then shouted to the cops surrounding the house, "Stand down! It's Agent Dillon Savich. The shooter is down!"

There were shouts in return, and Luke yelled out again, "It's over! Stand down!" He and his people lowered their weapons and were soon all in the house. Luke paused a moment and shook Savich's hand. "Nice work."

Detective Mayer roared through the open front door, yelled, "What do you mean it's over? Savich? What is the fricking FBI even doing here?"

Savich looked over at Mayer, a man who relied on intimidation to get his way, a man who liked to enforce rules but only if they didn't apply to him. He'd always disliked Savich, called him a glory hound to his face and who knew what else behind his back. What would Mayer call him now? Savich didn't care. He turned back into the house. He'd deal with Mayer later.

He saw Luke and his SWAT team had already secured the man's rifle and clamped his wrists in front of him with flex-cuffs, even though he was unconscious. Savich supposed the bullet that had grazed his head had knocked him out. He hoped there was no more serious damage. A team member began applying pressure to the shoulder wound and another pressed a bandage against the man's head. The bullet wound in his shoulder looked to be through and through, hopefully not too serious.

Savich went to Kara Moody. A Metro officer was cutting the duct tape from around her ankles and wrists with a pocket knife. She gasped in pain when her wrists were freed. The officer gently pulled her arms back in front of her and began rubbing her wrists.

Savich went down on his haunches in front of her. "Your shoulders should stop hurting soon, and in a couple of minutes you'll have your feeling back."

Kara stared at him, licked her dry lips. "You shot him twice. He's not dead, is he?"

"No, he's not dead. You don't know who he is?"

She shook her head, a hank of sweaty hair stuck to her cheek. "I've never seen him before in my life. He said he wanted to save me from something, but when the cops arrived he thought they were here to take him, and take me, too—somewhere, he didn't say. He was mumbling, shaking, and a couple of times he staggered." She stopped talking, took a breath. Then she attempted a smile. "I know who you are—you're Dr. Janice's friend, Dillon Savich, the FBI agent. She's told me about you. She told me she was glad she had at least one friend at the top of the food chain, someone who kicked big butt."

He started to say something about Sherlock kicking big butt, instead he said only, "Yes. Dr. Janice called me."

"If she hadn't, I might be dead. Thank you."

He smiled, still feeling the rush of adrenaline pumping through him. "I'm as relieved as you are that we're both still alive." He looked toward the unconscious young man. "I'm glad he's alive, too."

Savich felt her eyes on his face. "He looks so young. Why me? Why did he come here, to me?" Her breathing hitched and a lone tear streaked down her cheek. She tried to raise her arm, but it still hurt too much. Savich wiped the tear away. She said against his hand, her own hands on her belly, "Thank you for our lives." She looked over at the still figure. "He is mad, isn't he?"

Savich saw the living room had filled with cops, most of them shooting looks at him. He turned back to Kara. "He seemed to be." He noticed how hard she must have pulled against the duct tape that bound her ankles and wrists, hard enough to leave angry furrows. "Now you need to get back to thinking about yourself and your baby. There's nothing more to be afraid of. The police will find out who he is and why he came here to you." Savich hoped that would be true, that Mayer would chase it down.

A paramedic came to look at Kara. "Are you all right, ma'am?"

She managed a nod.

"How does he look?" Savich asked, nodding toward the young man being loaded onto a gurney.

"The shoulder doesn't look bad. The bullet tore through fat and muscle and exited. There's always a lot of bleeding from scalp wounds, but his skull seems intact. We don't know why he's unconscious, though. We need to get him to a CT scanner right away." He gave Savich a salute. "He was either very lucky or that was good shooting," and he ran after the departing gurney.

Savich heard Mayer shout his name. He rose and turned to see Fireplug charging him like an enraged bull. He didn't want to have to deal with Mayer now, with everyone's adrenaline still running high, with violent emotions still boiling below the surface. He didn't want to have to punch him out, say something he'd be sure to regret later. Then again, maybe not. No, he had to keep a lid on it. Where was Ben Raven when he needed him? Savich straightened, looked at Mayer straight on, and kept his voice calm. "Detective Mayer, you'll be pleased to know Ms. Moody is all right."

"I don't care if you live here, or if a neighbor called you! It doesn't matter. You had no right to enter her house!"

Savich imagined hurling Mayer through the window, watching him land on his face in the rosebushes. But that wouldn't do. Savich turned his back on Mayer and helped Kara Moody stand up. She sagged against him, and he held her up, began rubbing her back. Her belly was as big as Sherlock's had been right before Sean was born. He realized he'd rubbed Sherlock's back just that way.

He heard Mayer's furious voice. "I'm going to see you brought up on charges, you pushy bastard, you interfered in a police matter. You've got no defense."

Before Savich could figure out how to answer Fireplug, he heard Detective Ben Raven's voice shouting, "It's all right, Aldo! Pull yourself together. Savich checked with me first!"

Savich thought that sounded good, even righteous.

Mayer whipped around, his face red, his pulse pounding in his neck. "Don't try to protect him, Raven! He shouldn't be here and neither should you! I was over on Wisconsin when the call came in, I was first on scene. I don't even know how he got into the house without any of us seeing him."

Savich said, "Dr. Janice Hudson, whose house is directly next door, called me because I live on the next block. She was a psychiatrist for nearly half a century, and she was certain he was on the edge, that there wasn't time to wait. She knew a back way into the house."

Raven grabbed Mayer's arm before he could move on Savich. "Use your brain, Aldo, calm down! The hostage is okay. The shooter is down. We won. We all won. Isn't that victory enough?"

There was stone silence from Mayer. He sucked in a breath and stepped back, shook off Ben's hand. "This isn't over, Savich."

"It should be, Detective," Savich said. He sent a nod to Raven and said to Kara Moody, who'd been staring at Mayer, obviously confused, "When's the baby due?"

She looked at the man's blood on the oak floor, knew she could have so easily died, Alex could have died. But they hadn't. She gave Savich a big smile. "Well, actually, soon now. I've been in labor for the past ten minutes."

2

NEAR PENNINGTON GAP, VIRGINIA
MONDAY MORNING

U.S. Federal Marshal Chan Michaels was chair-dancing to "Heathens" by Twenty One Pilots to keep himself alert as he drove the marshals' big black van. He liked the pounding rhythm, liked the video even more because all of it was shot in jail. He wondered if Liam Hennessey, who actually preferred to go by his moniker, Manta Ray, knew that. Sure he did; the dude wasn't stupid, anything but, from what Chan had heard. When the Pilots finished, Chan turned down the sound to listen through the wire cage to whatever it was his fellow marshals Otter and Benz were saying.

They were talking sports, of course, this time, basketball. He heard Manta Ray laugh at something Otter said, a nice, inviting laugh. Amazing, really, coming from a psychopath. Chan had dealt with enough of them to know they could make you forget how seriously scary bad they were when they laid on the charm. The federal prosecutor must have done a happy dance when Manta Ray accepted a plea bargain rather than wait a year for a jury trial. Who knew what would have happened if there were women on the jury? Even men seemed to be drawn to Manta Ray until they found out who and what he was. If he wasn't out to kill you, you had to like the guy.

Otter said something Chan couldn't make out, probably more basketball talk, even though it was baseball season, and he tuned them out. He was happy enough to let the Warriors rule the basketball kingdom as Otter insisted, but he didn't really care. With him, it was always all about football and the Redskins. He heard Benz say to Manta Ray, "You're what, thirty-three?"

Benz knew better than that. The less said to a prisoner while being transported, the better. But Benz was nearing retirement, and he didn't pay much attention to the rules anymore. He'd transported thousands of prisoners over his long career, seen about everything, and now, he did what he wanted.

Manta Ray said in his smooth voice with its hint of the Irish from County Cork, his birthplace, "I turned thirty-four in jail last week. One of the lady guards brought me a chocolate cupcake with a candle on top. She couldn't light the candle, it was against the rules, she said, as if I'd stick it in her face and try to escape, and she rolled her eyes. Her name was Monica. She was cute, and she liked me. I told Monica to take the candle off the cupcake and lick it." Manta Ray gave them a big white-toothed grin.

Otter snorted out an embarrassed laugh. Benz said, "I saw a prisoner stick a lighted match in a guard's ear once, all he could reach. No one knew how he'd gotten hold of it."

"Did he manage to hurt him?" Manta Ray asked.

Benz said, "The guard outweighed him by fifty pounds. He punched him in the ribs a couple of times, put him in the infirmary. After he got out, he spent two weeks in solitary."

"A good story." Manta Ray lowered his voice. "Me? If that guard had tried that on me, I'd have stuffed my birthday cupcake up his nose and held his mouth closed. Imagine, death by cupcake." He gave an easy laugh, only this time Chan felt gooseflesh rise on his arms. He heard Otter take a sharp breath. Manta Ray freaked him out. He was young, new to the federal marshal's service. Chan imagined he hadn't heard a lot of talk like this before.

"Now there's a visual," Benz said, and yawned. Nothing a prisoner said could touch Benz. "I hear you have a big-time lawyer. Why'd he plea bargain you out?"

Chan was surprised Benz would ask that. That was over-the-top even for him. Sports talk was one thing, maybe even the cupcake story, but talking about his case, that was just plain unprofessional. Chan started to say something when Manta Ray said matter-of-factly, "Bowler, my lawyer, was afraid I'd get the death penalty, even though it was Marvin who killed the bank teller, not me. But hey, if you're there to play, you have to pay. Me? I don't believe in violence."

Benz said, "Yeah, right. One of your priors was for stomping your girlfriend. You broke three of her teeth and her jaw."

Chan pictured Manta Ray shrugging. "Bitch hit my

kid. I didn't like it." He fell silent. Chan had heard the federal prosecutor say the guy had three or four kids with different women. No wives. How would those kids grow up carting this guy's genes around?

There was silence in the back of the van. Chan didn't think it would last. Benz was shooting off his mouth because he was bored, and Otter was only following his lead.

Sure enough, Benz picked it up again. "Your buddy Marvin Cass got his brains blown out at the bank, but you got away, even with a bullet in your side. I was impressed reading that, even if the FBI found you later in that flophouse in the warehouse district in Alexandria. They didn't find any of the jewelry or money you stole from the bank safe-deposit boxes, did they? You had the grit to hide it first. That impressed me, too. Tell me something. Now that you're about to spend the next thirty years in lockup, maybe you want to change your mind, clear your conscience? Tell us where you hid all that fine stuff you stole?"

Manta Ray laughed, tut-tutted. "Are you conspiring with a prisoner, Mr. Federal Marshal? You want a share to fill out your retirement?"

Otter gave another nervous laugh, said, "Of course he isn't, but I bet you could still get less time if you told the FBI where you hid all of it. Why haven't you?"

"Ah, lad, an excellent question. Of course there's an answer, there's always an answer. Maybe you'll find out soon enough." His Irish was riding high, so thick it was like he'd left Ireland the week before.

Chan looked in his rearview, saw Manta Ray had leaned back against the van wall and closed his eyes. Actually, he'd wondered about that, too. Why hold on to the loot if it was going to cost him thirty years in prison?

Benz said, "In thirty years, I'll probably be underground. But thirty years is a long time, a very long time. I plan to spend it fishing the Great Lakes and playing a lot of golf courses. I'll be free to do what I want when I want. I could have sex every night until I croak, what with Viagra. But you? Sorry, buddy, you're screwed."

Chan would have told anyone but Benz to shut up by now, but he didn't want to start an argument, didn't want Manta Ray to hear that. So he decided to mind his own, maybe listen to the Pilots again and chairdance some more. But first, right now, he couldn't help but listen.

Manta Ray said, "You think I'm going to go without sex for thirty years?" He laughed, only this time, his laugh was nasty, with an edge that made Chan's skin crawl. "We'll see about that, won't we?"

Silence again. This time it lasted.

They had less than an hour before they reached Lee Penitentiary, the high-security federal prison in Pennington Gap, Virginia. Chan couldn't wait to hand Manta Ray over to the prison staff. He looked in the rearview, saw Benz reading a novel, Otter staring through the mesh cage out the front of the van.

Finally, Chan saw a flash of the huge white concrete penitentiary tower in the distance through a small gap between two low hills. Nearly there. He turned the big black Chevy van off the interstate onto the narrow two-lane road that led to Lee. Only two miles to go. Chan glanced into his rearview, saw Manta Ray was awake, leaning forward, focused. On what? His dark eyes dominated a strong high-cheekboned face that was movie-star good-looking, no doubt about that. But Chan could see that someone would forget the good looks, if he looked long enough into Manta Ray's eyes and saw the blackness behind them. It looked to Chan like his lips were moving, like he was chanting silently. Was he meditating or trying to cast some kind of a curse? Chan felt a stab of fear, shook his head at himself. Manta Ray was a seriously scary man, and he'd seen a lot of scary in his ten years as a U.S. marshal.

Chan drove carefully as the road narrowed over a short bridge, the stream beneath running high because of the recent heavy rains. Once off the bridge, the oaks and maples grew so lush they nearly met over the road. It was beautiful country, endless rolling hills dotted with small towns, cattle, sheep, an occasional white house, and more trees than you'd care to count. That day the sky was a clear shining blue, the air sweet and warm. He'd never minded the prisoner runs to Lee— except maybe this one. He didn't want to think about it, but he was uncomfortable in the same van with this prisoner. He was a bottomless pit of mean covered with a coat of slippery charm. He wanted this run over.

Chan smoothly followed a bend in the road when he saw a motorcycle on its side across both lanes, the rider down beside it, unmoving. He braked, threw the steering wheel over just as a man burst from the trees and ran toward them, dressed in commando black, mask, and army boots. A dark metal canister shot through his open driver's-side window, an inch from Chan's face, and slammed against the passenger door.

A flash bang.

Chan only had an instant to throw the van into reverse and lay on the gas before a ferocious bright light blinded him and an incredible blast in the enclosed space deafened him. The whole van shook with the force of the concussion. It knocked him senseless for a moment. When his brain was working again, his world was spinning and his body bowed forward in pain. He lost control. The van shot backward off the road, its rear end slamming hard into an oak, throwing Chan sideways. As his head lashed back, the airbag exploded in his face.

He heard Otter and Benz yelling, moving around. Then he heard the back window shatter under a rain of bullets, and heard another flash bang crash into the van. He heard Otter yell, heard another huge explosion, then he heard groans. At least Manta Ray wasn't going anywhere in his three-piece prisoner's suit, his feet shackled to the floor of the van.

Only Chan could get them out of here. He pushed away the airbag and swiped his shirtsleeve over his tearing eyes, trying to clear his vision. He got the engine turned over again, but the van only lurched to one side on its rear wheels. It had to be a broken axle.

He heard another canister slam into the van through the shattered back window. Chan knew it wasn't another flash bang when he heard it hissing out some kind of aerosol and heard Benz and Otter wheezing and coughing. The gas would get to him through the wire cage in seconds.

Chan pressed the power button on his sat phone, punched in the emergency number and yelled, "We're down! We're down! One mile from Lee! We're down!" He felt the world fading, and there was nothing he could do about it. He watched smoke rise in a skinny gray funnel from beneath the hood as the sat phone dropped from his hand.

He heard someone's voice outside the van, shouting orders. How many were there? It didn't matter, nothing he could do mattered anymore. Chan wondered if the gas, or whatever it was, was going to kill him. He didn't want to die, he wanted to stay with Liddy and the kids—

3

CRIMINAL APPREHENSION UNIT, CAU
HOOVER BUILDING
WASHINGTON, D.C.
MONDAY AFTERNOON

When Savich invited Special Agent Cam Wittier to move over to the CAU from the Criminal Division, there was no question in her mind it was a good move, though her chief had cursed Savich out for stealing her. She knew it was going to be an easy transition for her since she already knew most of the CAU agents and liked them, and they seemed to like her and think she was a good addition. She'd long admired the unit and what they did, just as she admired CAU chief Dillon Savich, occasionally even wished he wasn't married to her kickboxing partner, Sherlock. She did wonder, though, if he would have invited her into the unit if she hadn't managed to solve the Starlet Slasher murders two weeks before in L.A. She wasn't about to float that question. She doubted she ever would.

It was twelve thirty on a bright Monday afternoon in July, an oven outside, but inside the Hoover Building the AC was pumping along fine. It was officially her first day in her new unit. She'd left the personnel department only a few minutes ago and paused a moment in the doorway, uncertain. All five agents working in-house looked up from their computers and their cells, stopped their conversations, smiled at her, waved, welcomed her. Shirley, the unit secretary, hugged her and showed her to the desk of Special Agent Dane Carver, who'd recently transferred to the Los Angeles Field Office, with his professor wife and baby daughter. L.A. was a meaty assignment in the bank-robbery capital of the country, but Cam preferred the CAU. She spoke to everyone, listened, laughed. She didn't see Sherlock, but she did see her new boss, Dillon Savich, through his office windows, alternately speaking on his cell and typing on his laptop MAX. He looked up, smiled at her.

She was soon drinking a mug of black coffee and leaning over Agent Ruth Noble's shoulder reading a report from Walt Monaco, SAC of the Richmond Field Office, about Liam Hennessey, aka Manta Ray, and his escape from the U.S. Marshals only a mile out from their destination—Lee Penitentiary in Pennington Gap, Virginia, the high-security federal prison.

He'd escaped only three hours before, and Monaco had already mobilized the local FBI office and coordinated with local law enforcement to begin the manhunt.

Agent Ruth Noble looked up and put her hand over her cell phone. "Give me a minute, Cam, then we can discuss this mess. It's my son Rafe—he's suffering girlfriend problems."

Cam nodded, waited until Ruth punched off. Though she wasn't a stranger here in her new home, she knew better than to rush into things like she usually did back in the Criminal Division. *What happened? Let's get this moving; let's go!* She said with an easy smile, "Girlfriends can be tough. What'd you tell Rafe?"

"I told him to speak to his father." Ruth gave Cam a fat smile. "I told him his father knows everything about girls—well, just about everything, can't overdo—and he should do whatever his father says. Now I'll call Dix, warn him, so he'll have time to come up with the right approach."

Cam laughed. She liked Ruth, knew a bit of her history. She'd married the sheriff of Maestro, Virginia, and become a mother to his two teenage sons. Ruth, she'd heard, had a target group of local informants in her back pocket, most gathered when she'd been a detective with Metro. It was one of her informants who'd called to tell them where Manta Ray was hiding in Alexandria on the day of the robbery.

Savich stepped out of his office. "Cam, welcome to the CAU. I'm glad you're here." He raised his voice to get everyone's attention. "As you know, we have a situation. I sent all of you Walt's report on Manta Ray's escape. Come into the conference room, I've got some new information, and we need to go over what happened."

Ollie Hamish, Savich's second-in-command, asked, "Where's Sherlock?"

"It's her yearly physical, and yes, I ordered her to keep it with the promise I'd fill her in on everything later."

When everyone was seated around the CAU conference table, Savich said, "Walt is in charge of the local manhunt. He and his people in Richmond are gearing up to cover all the roads for Manta Ray and the men who took him. Marshal Chan Michaels, the driver of the transport van, told officials at the scene he wasn't sure how many men staged the escape. He and the other two guards were incapacitated almost immediately by a flash bang and some sort of knockout gas. So our only physical evidence is what's left of the flash bangs and the housing for the chemical agent they used. They're trying to identify it now.

"Liam Hennessey, or Manta Ray, as he calls himself, had only one known cohort, Marvin Cass, and he was killed during the bank robbery. Other than this one robbery, to the best of our knowledge, Manta Ray has operated on his own."

Cam said, "That was the Second National Bank of Alexandria, Virginia, right?"

Savich nodded. "Manta Ray was busy dumping the contents of the six safe-deposit boxes into a dark brown leather bag when his partner decided he wanted some cash. He ordered a teller to fill up a sack for him, but she was too slow. He shot her in the head. Cass and Manta Ray ran out of the bank, fortunately without shooting anyone else. But the teller died en route to the hospital.

"Two FBI agents were near enough to be at the scene only a few minutes after the alarm tripped. In the firefight, Cass was killed and Manta Ray was shot in the side, but he escaped on a motorcycle, drove a circuitous route through some alleys where cars couldn't go." He sent a nod toward Ruth.

She said, "One of my informants called me, said this guy who'd just escaped had staggered, bleeding like stink, into one of the ancient buildings in the derelict warehouse section in Alexandria. Dougie's always reliable, so I called the agents involved and they went out there.

"Gotta say, Manta Ray was worth the three hundred bucks I paid Dougie, even if he spent it on drugs and Wild Turkey."

Savich picked it up. "Manta Ray was bleeding pretty bad, but he managed to hold himself together long enough to hide what he'd taken from the safe-deposit boxes before the FBI got him. Agents haven't been able to find any of the stash, and believe me, they've torn that warehouse apart. Manta Ray refused to talk. Ollie?"

Ollie said, "From what Walt wrote, today's escape was flawlessly planned and executed. As you said, Savich, Manta Ray usually acts alone, and look what happened the one time he didn't. His partner killed that bank teller. One question is, how was he able to hire anyone to break him out while he was locked up inside Northern Neck Regional Jail?"

Savich said, "Manta Ray's lawyer, Duce Bowler,

springs to mind. The bank robbery happened less than a month ago, but on the advice of Bowler, Manta Ray accepted a plea bargain. Thirty years to avoid the death penalty. Duce Bowler's name is the only one that appears on the visitor sign-in.

"Here's a big question: Manta Ray rifled only six safe-deposit boxes and maybe that was all the time he could afford, but why those particular boxes? The six owners reported only jewelry, cash, and papers that could easily be replaced, nothing unusual. But someone went to a lot of trouble to break Manta Ray out, and you have to wonder if it had something to do with what was in those boxes. Was one of the box owners desperate enough to get back whatever it was Manta Ray stole to break him out to get it? Four of the six box owners are old bank customers, and they look solid, but the other two could do with a closer look. We'll be repeating those two interviews."

Ruth raised her hand. "Dillon, I've been thinking about Walt's report. It took the driver, Chan Michaels, and the other two guards about thirty minutes to come around after they were pulled from the van. That had to be true for Manta Ray, too. They must have loaded him in a car and driven him out of there quickly, knowing the roads would get dangerous for them real fast. I wish we knew how many were involved in breaking him out."

Savich said, "Chan Michaels saw a man down in the middle of the road beside the motorcycle and he heard someone barking orders, but he was fading fast and disoriented from the flash bang and the gas bomb. The whole breakout was over in a couple of minutes.

"Michaels also said he believes Manta Ray knew what was coming, based on some of the things he said and his body language. He was ready. So did Bowler tip him off?" Savich shook his head. "Walt told me it was a good enough operation that he'd be happy to hire whoever planned it to come work for him."

Ruth tapped her fingertips on Manta Ray's prison photo. "The dude looks seriously hot, even in prison orange, I'll give him that, but underneath that sexy smile? The black of a rotted tooth." She let that hang a moment, then added, "Three of us had a flash bang blow up in our faces last November in San Francisco. We couldn't hear, couldn't see, felt like someone had thwacked our heads with an ax. I don't think Chan Michaels and the other guards had a chance after that. Still, the whole thing makes us look like Keystone Cops."

Ollie took a swig of his coffee. "We should have deported Manta Ray—Liam Hennessey—back to Ireland, let them put him in that Belfast prison, what's it called? The Maze? By the way, do any of you know where he got the moniker, Manta Ray?"

Savich said, "We'll ask him when we get him back in custody. Let's get back to the people who freed him. He was in prison, so how did he make contact with whoever planned this? His only visitor was his lawyer, Duce Bowler, the obvious go-between. Walt asked us to interview him even though he's well aware that

Bowler knows he has attorney-client privilege and won't say a thing. He'll claim Manta Ray could have gotten word to the outside some other way. What other way? All he has to do is shrug that question off, and trust me, he will."

"But Bowler's got to be right in the middle," Cam said.

Savich nodded. "I'm going to set MAX onto opening up Bowler's life like an oyster. We'll begin with his client list."

Ruth said, "Poor MAX won't find any pearls inside."

There was a spot of laughter.

Savich said, "Ruth, you and Ollie will pay lawyer Bowler a visit this afternoon, get a feel for him, see what you make of him. Before you leave, drop by my office and take whatever MAX has dug up on him. Maybe you'll have some ammunition.

"Now, there's something big I've saved for the end, something none of you know about yet." He sat forward. "A teenager by the name of Kim Harbinger was heading back from a camping trip in the Daniel Boone National Forest in Kentucky less than an hour ago. She spotted three men in the parking lot, heading into the forest. She believes Manta Ray was one of them. The forest is about a two-hour drive from Pennington Gap, so the timing's about right. We're paying attention to her because Kim's dad is Chief Harbinger, of the Pennington Gap Police Department. She'd seen photos of Manta Ray in his office, thought he looked like a rock star, and that's why she remembered him.

She called her dad immediately. Chief Harbinger called Richmond FBI, and Walt called Mr. Maitland to ask for more manpower. I told Mr. Maitland we're lucky to have the perfect agent with us to track Manta Ray down in that forest, if he's in there. As to the number of men who broke Manta Ray out, we still don't know, but if the teenager is right, it was the two men who went into the forest with him.

"New York SAC Milo Zachery sent down one of his crew yesterday to work a case with the Criminal Division—Special Agent Jack Cabot. I know him quite well. He's an ex–army ranger with experience in special ops, an expert in survival and surveillance techniques in the wild. He's perfect for tracking these guys, and I've already hijacked him. I was thinking about which of you to partner up with him. Cam, as I recall, you spent some of your formative years hiking around in national parks with your parents. And you hiked and camped throughout college. Isn't that right?"

"Yes, I did, but—you're picking me, Dillon?" The agents around the conference table would have had to be deaf not to hear the excitement in her voice. She nearly bounced out of her chair.

"Yes, you. Come to my office and we'll talk. The rest of you, carry on. Text me your ideas."

4

Executive Assistant Director Jimmy Maitland, Savich's boss, stuck his head in Savich's office as Cam was on her way out the door. She gave him a blazing smile. Maitland could tell she was itching to get past him, so he only said, "Welcome aboard, Agent Wittier. Good luck."

Maitland's eyebrow went up as he watched her nearly run through the unit. "She's a good addition, Savich. She looks so happy and excited; if I didn't know better, I'd think you'd given her a paid vacation to Paris."

Savich waved his boss to a chair. "Knowing Cam, she prefers this assignment to climbing the Eiffel Tower, as amazing as that sounds. I told you about the teenager who spotted Manta Ray. Cam will be partnering with Jack Cabot, flying with him to the Daniel Boone National Forest. They'll go in after him and whoever's with him."

Maitland said, "Cabot's a great choice, but that's quite an assignment for a new agent in your unit. I suppose Agent Wittier's already had her trial by fire, though, in the Starlet Slasher case in L.A."

Savich nodded. "I think she has the skill set to handle it, after what she showed us in L.A." He smiled. "She'll realize soon enough she's teamed up with Tarzan-with-brains, and I hope they'll figure out how to use each other's strengths, guard each other's backs. Better than plunking her down at a desk here in the CAU, wondering how she fits in."

"And knowing you, you wanted to see if you could get Jack to transfer from Milo Zachery's kingdom in New York to the CAU, right?"

"Of course not, I don't want Milo after my head. Well, okay, maybe. Milo does owe me one. It's not a bad idea."

"You think that teenager really saw Manta Ray? Saw him walking into that forest?"

"I'm sitting at about eighty percent on that, maybe higher because it would be a smart move to get Manta Ray tucked away from the manhunt going on outside. They could be planning to take their time in the forest until things cool off, even have prepositioned food and equipment waiting for them, and a planned meet at some designated pickup point later. It was really bad luck for Manta Ray and his men if they were spotted by a teenage hiker." Savich grinned. "Now I've talked myself up to ninety percent."

Maitland sat back in his chair, swung his leg. "My real reason for coming is to let you know Detective Aldo Mayer's captain called me about the Kara Moody incident you were involved in yesterday. Ramirez said he had to promise Mayer he'd call me to calm him down. We agreed there would be no formal complaint from Metro about your, ah, interfering in a local police matter. It turned out well, after all." Maitland shrugged. "If it had gone down differently I'd have to keep them from hanging you by your feet, but this way, no worries. Hard to bring charges against the guy who walked out of that house helping a pregnant lady in labor. That's all over YouTube this morning, you know that? One of the neighbors posted the video before the media even arrived. Has Kara Moody had the baby yet?"

Savich grunted. "A baby boy, Alex, born late last night, healthy, six and a half pounds."

Maitland gave him a big grin. "From what Captain Ramirez told me, your only problem is with Mayer. He's not too happy with you, thinks you made him look like an idiot. Maybe it's best to keep your distance from him for a while."

"No problem, if I can keep Sherlock from taking him down in a dark alley, locking her knees around his neck, and reminding him of the importance of good manners. She isn't happy with him right now."

Maitland laughed. "What a visual. You're going to see Moody and the baby?"

Savich nodded. "Yes, and Mayer's got no say in that."

"Do you know if Metro has identified the guy?"

"It's Detective Mayer's case, sir; it's not my business."

Maitland arched a brow, said nothing. He rose. "Whatever you say, Savich. Keep me in the loop, all right?"

"I have no plans to get involved."

"Right." Maitland gave him a salute and left his office, heading over to speak to Shirley.

Savich watched Maitland weave his way out of the unit, speaking to each agent, asking questions, nodding, and he wondered again, *Why was that young man so desperate to take Kara Moody away from that house? Why did he call himself an enigma?*

5

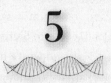

ANDREWS AIR FORCE BASE
CAMP SPRINGS, MARYLAND
MONDAY AFTERNOON

Special Agent Jack Cabot finished his preflight inspection by walking around the white FBI Skylane 182 with its distinctive blue stripe. He patted the fuselage, stood back a moment, and admired the shine. The Skylane was as clean as his dog, Cropper, after Jack washed him along with his SUV. He walked to the top of the airstairs and slid on his aviator sunglasses. It was a bright, hot afternoon, with only a slight breeze. The humidity was the killer. He wished he had a garden hose to spray himself down.

He looked out over the busy airfield. Andrews was always hopping, the noise at times just short of mandatory-earplug levels. He looked down at his watch thinking Agent Wittier was now officially late when he noticed a long-legged woman striding purposefully toward him, a banged-up backpack slung over her arm, a fleece sweatshirt tied around her neck. She wore lightweight dark green Polartec pants, a green-checked Polartec long-sleeve shirt, and well-worn hiking boots. So this was Agent Wittier, his partner on the assignment. At least she knew how to dress for their mission.

He wondered why he'd been assigned a female agent, truth be told, rather than an ex–special forces type like himself. There was nothing like field experience in holiday destination spots like Kabul to train for locating and bringing in dangerous hostiles hunkered down in the desolate hills. Maybe she was ex-military, or maybe she was as wily and mean as his ex-mother-in-law.

He had to admit Agent Wittier's straight-on, take-no-prisoners stride as she walked toward him fit her hard-ass camping clothes and the Glock on her belt clip. But his image of her changed when he saw her short blond wavy hair tangling around her face in the hot breeze. He could tell from twenty yards away she was pretty. He'd bet her eyes were laser-sharp on him behind her aviator sunglasses.

Cam looked at the man staring down at her with his arms crossed easily over his chest. She'd wondered what an ex–special forces cowboy from New York would look like, and he fit the bill. Special Agent Jack Cabot looked tough and chiseled and military, no beard scruff on his tanned face. His dark hair was cut short. He was taller than she was, which put him over six feet, and younger than she'd expected, maybe early thirties. He was wearing a dark Polartec shirt and had his Glock clipped on his belt, as she did. His boots looked like they'd clomped over a great many gnarly miles. He was buff, but not a muscle-bound yahoo who liked to pretend he sprinkled nails in his Cheerios instead of blueberries. He didn't look like he snarled very often. She could deal with him.

Then Cam looked past him at the tiny single-engine airplane, shocked at how small the propeller was, small enough to stir her guacamole with the blade. She was surprised to feel her stomach churn like a greasy ball. Until that moment, she hadn't thought much about the flight. Of course she'd flown noncommercial before, with only the occasional butterfly flitting in her belly. But this white-winged miniature box, this big toy, was going to transport them to Kentucky? A stray bird could knock it out of the sky. She'd grill the pilot, make sure he knew what he was doing, maybe ask him if he had any Valium.

Jack was aware of her scrutiny, both of him and the plane, and gave her a wave. "Welcome aboard. I'm Jack Cabot and you're Agent Wittier."

She nodded, licked her lips. "Yes, Cam Wittier. Nice to meet you. Where's the pilot?"

"You're looking at him. I guess that makes you the copilot."

The greasy ball in her stomach took a bounce nearly to her throat, this time with a dash of nausea. "You're flying us to Daniel Boone National Forest?"

Jack wasn't deaf—he heard the touch of panic in her voice and he'd seen that look before from soldiers who could walk through gunfire without hesitation but turned white when they boarded a helicopter. He'd talk her down, let her see how competent he was. He nodded to her, checked his watch. "I've finished my pre-flight inspection. We're good to go. Two hours unless we hit a lot of bumps. There'll be some, since we'll be over the Appalachians. Nothing to be concerned about."

Cam looked at the step that led up into the belly of the little white death trap. She cleared her throat. "I've never flown in a single-engine before. It's—very small. It's got only one engine."

"One good engine. Trust me, that makes all the difference. You get airsick?"

"Not on a reasonable-size plane, but this?" She looked at his beautiful baby and gave a convulsive swallow. "That one engine—good or not—it goes out and we're toast."

"Nah, I'm a glider pilot. I'd find somewhere flat to land. No worries. I was expecting you sooner. We have to move out now if we want to get to the national forest well before dark." He saw her place one tentative foot on the step, gulp, then take another slow step. He tried for a bit of distraction. "We're dressed pretty much the same, partner. We could be twins if you weren't a blonde."

She looked him up and down. She wanted to ask him about his pilot's license but decided he could take it the wrong way. She sucked it up, got right in his face, and tried for bravado. "Twins? Nah, I'd have kicked you out of our mom's womb."

He grinned. "I won't crash us, I promise. I've been doing this a long time. Toss your backpack with mine in the back and come up front." He pulled the clam-shell door closed, secured it.

She wanted to tell him he wasn't old enough to have that much experience. Was he counting flying toy planes when he was a kid? Jack pointed to the copilot's seat. "Sit down, and I'll seat-belt you in." He handed her headphones. "Press this button and we can speak to each other." He reached into the back again to make sure her backpack was secured.

Cam watched him ease into the pilot's seat, a tight fit for a big man. He fastened his own harness and began flipping switches. She listened to him speak to the tower, a lot of numbers and letters, an alpha and a tango thrown in. The tower seemed okay with what he said, and answered back with some more garbled letters and numbers. Okay, he talked like he knew what he was doing, and the guy in the tower didn't seem concerned. When they got clearance and began to taxi, Cam sucked in air and smoothed out her fists. He looked over at her, grinned. "You've got nothing to worry about, I promise; I'll get you there without a problem." Then he frowned. "Well, if we don't get too much turbulence—just kidding, sorry," he added, see-ing her face go white.

They waited on the tarmac behind three small single-engine aircraft for their turn to shoot up into the sky in this oversize white coffin. Jack gave her another look, saw she was holding herself as stiff as a frozen pizza. "You'll feel better once we're airborne, trust me." And then they were moving faster and faster on the runway, and the plane smoothly lifted into the sky. Cam's breath whooshed out and he saw her lips move, imagined she was giving herself a pep talk. Or maybe she was praying.

As they slowly gained altitude, Jack said, "I guess if we get into trouble up here you won't be taking over."

"Trouble? What do you mean trouble? What kind of trouble?" Her voice came out in a croak, and she realized she sounded like a pathetic wuss. She cleared her throat and tried again. "Agent Cabot, it's a perfect summer day, only an occasional billowy cloud in the sky to keep you from seeing where you're going. So far I don't see any SAM missiles below to shoot us down, no bows and arrows, either. So don't disappoint my parents; get us there in one piece."

"Yes, ma'am. I'll do my pitiful best."

He banked the small plane, perhaps at a steeper angle than he could have, saw her jaw clench, straightened out again, and headed due west. Washington soon disappeared behind them, and suburbs sprawled out below them, surrounded by the beautiful rolling green hills of Virginia.

The small plane hummed smoothly, no kicks, or lurches, no flashing red warning lights. Cam breathed more easily and thanked heaven her nausea went away.

She pressed the comms button again. "I guess I was expecting to meet up with a guy with *Spec Ops* tattooed on his arm, maybe a skull with a bullet in its mouth on his neck."

He shot her a grin. "My mama made me promise no tattoos until I'm forty-five. I guess she figured I wouldn't be tempted, even drunk, to want a tattoo by that age."

"At that age, your wife would probably shoot you. Now, I'm told you're an expert at survival and all, but my boss, Agent Dillon Savich, didn't say whether you leap tall buildings."

He laughed. "Hey, Wittier, I'm proud of you. It's hard to crack jokes when you're terrified. You doing better?"

"No, but I'm sucking it up, and insulting you helps."

"You'll be fine once your brain accepts you're in expert hands, namely mine. Yes, give me a bottle of water and the sun, and I can find an anthill. Leap tall buildings? Three stories is my personal best. But the truth is, I'm not nearly as tough as my ex-mother-in-law."

"I've never had a mother-in-law, but yours sounds iconic."

He laughed, checked his compass, his altimeter, his airspeed. All okay. Lucky for Agent Wittier it was a beautiful day to fly. She was still on the pale side, time to take her mind elsewhere. "Tell me what you bring to the table."

Cam was quiet a moment, shrugged. "Not much, I'm afraid, except for a decent brain, for what that's worth. I've been in the outdoors a fair amount of time, mainly when I was a kid, but in college, too, groups of us, hiking, white-water rafting. I know my way around a campsite. I've never been in the Daniel Boone National Forest, though."

"They tell me you've got more than a decent brain, did some strong work in L.A."

She perked up, preened for a second, then shrugged again. "That was a team effort."

"Yeah, it always is, but you were the lead. I hear you nearly got your head blown off but managed to save your partner's life. Tell me about it."

Was he really interested? The small plane gave a bump, sending her heart into her throat. Who cared if he was interested or passing the time? She started talking, giving him the highlights of the Starlet Slasher case, from her first meeting with the LAPD detectives to the night she tracked down the serial killer with her partner, Detective Daniel Montoya. She told him about her parents, the actors.

Her story gave Jack a good idea what she was about—competent, able to think outside the box, maybe a bit too fearless. Telling him what happened had the added benefit of bringing color to her cheeks. "A good win. Okay, Wittier, so you've got a brain, you can hike, you wore the right clothes. Do you have any other useful skills?"

He didn't sound hopeful, and that sent her chin up and thinned her lips. Good. Having her pissed off at him was better than having her scared.

"My friends in college called me a ninja camper— in and out of a campsite faster than well, the Flash, no muss, no fuss."

"Ninja camping? Is that a military term?"

"It sounds like it should be—but I guess it isn't manly enough. I can shoot straight. And I'm good at fixing mechanical problems, like busted fuel pumps on cars. I could help overhaul the engine on this plane if we got knocked out of the sky by a pissed-off goose. If you're wounded, I can stitch you up without hurling on you."

They hit some bumps, making the plane lurch and bounce. Cam looked down and wished she hadn't. She saw nothing but tree-covered hills below those billowy clouds. Jack said, "We'll be through this bit of air in a moment. Close your eyes, sit back, and hum James Bay's 'Let It Go.' "

She spurted out a laugh and closed her eyes and heard the song play in her head whether she liked it or not. They were through the turbulence soon enough. Jack checked his cruise speed—145 knots—and made minor adjustments to the elevator and rudder trim. "Okay, you can open your eyes. I guess I saved us. It's time to talk about what's going to happen when we land. I already spoke to Wayne Duke, the Cumberland District park ranger who will be our guide in the national forest. Chief Harbinger of the Pennington Gap PD will be meeting us when we land at London-Corbin Magee Field."

"I hope he'll have all the gear we'll need with him, like bivvy bags, a portable stove."

"Not a problem—he'll provide whatever we need. We're going to keep the team small—the two of us,

Wayne Duke, the park ranger, and Chief Harbinger. The other park rangers will help us as lookouts. The chief is assigning four of his deputies to cover major exit points from the forest, and he's coordinating with other local law enforcement to patrol outside the forest, both west and east, on the lookout for anyone who doesn't belong there. Hey, look down. Is that beautiful, or what?"

Cam looked out the small window again, saw the endless chain of rolling tree-covered Appalachian hills below the thinning clouds, the occasional small town, and homesteads set far apart on the rich green land. A single road cut through them straight as a knife.

Jack checked his watch. "The field is just inside Kentucky, about thirty miles from the entrance we'll be using into the national forest."

Jack had already been slowly descending. "There's Magee Field coming up."

Magee was a large expanse of tarmac cut into the land in front of a row of flat-roofed white single-story buildings and a pair of hangars. A trio of single-engine planes was lined up in front of the largest building. Cam saw a couple of guys in overalls talking, paying them no mind. Other than that, the place looked deserted. One of the men with a rooster tail of white hair finally looked up, shaded his eyes, and gave them a little wave.

Jack had his flaps down, and Cam's stomach did a flip as the ground came up to meet them. She decided to be heroic and keep her eyes open. The Skylane angled smoothly downward, already lined up with the end of the runway, bumped once, twice, and settled, its wheels solid on the tarmac. Jack turned and taxied to a stop beside the other three aircraft, cut the engine.

She was quiet for a moment, settling like the plane, taking big easy breaths until her heart stopped kettle-drumming in her chest. She turned to Jack as she took off her headphones. "We're on the ground, and we're in one piece. Good job, Cabot. I forgot to ask, do we have parachutes on board?"

He laughed. "The FBI could only afford one so we'd have piggybacked."

She rolled her eyes, watched him go through his shutdown checklist.

"We made good time. No particular headwind. You did good, too, Wittier."

"I'll admit to some white knuckles. I was wondering if I'd make it to heaven if we crashed into one of those cloud-covered hills."

"Lots of people are jumpy about small planes their first time out. You'll be fine when we fly back. You ready to dance with the devil when we catch him?"

"Looking forward to it."

Jack opened the door, grabbed his backpack, and hopped down the steps, Cam behind him. She stood a moment, content to breathe in the clean warm air and feel the gentle breeze ruffle her hair and dry the sweat from her forehead. It was so quiet, so peaceful with the engine off, and only trees around them, enough to build a city.

Jack pulled out his cell, then slid it back into his shirt pocket. "No need to call, that's Chief Harbinger there, in that big honker black SUV coming toward us. Amazing timing."

"I texted him as soon as we had a signal."

He hadn't seen her do that. They watched a big man dressed for the woods climb out of the SUV. He shouted, "Welcome to Magee, outpost of the brave." A very pretty young girl scooted out the passenger door and stepped around to stand at his side. His daughter, Kim Harbinger? Why had the chief brought his teen-age daughter with him?

6

Savich stood beside Dr. Grace Wordsworth, a tall, thin black woman with white wings in her hair and glasses over intelligent eyes, looking down at the young man lying on his back. A single blanket was pulled up to his bandaged shoulder and an adhesive strip covered the scalp wound where Savich's bullet had grazed his left temple. He was bone-white and lay utterly still, the slow rise and fall of his chest his only obvious sign of life. Savich saw his uninjured arm was handcuffed to the metal bed frame, an IV line in his wrist.

Dr. Wordsworth checked his pulse, put her stethoscope over his heart, and straightened. "At least our John Doe is breathing easily on his own. But he hasn't helped us much in figuring out why he's in a coma. His CT scan was perfectly normal—no evidence of hematoma or brain contusion. We've looked at his cerebrospinal fluid with a lumbar puncture, and again, there was no evidence of bleeding, or of infection. By the way, Dr. Avery, the consulting neurologist, said John Doe's irrational behavior yesterday sounded like delirium to him, not a psychiatric illness. Something else—a metabolic problem or something toxic—may be to blame. He has some abnormal central reflexes that point to something affecting his entire nervous system. So you can relax if you were worried his head wound put him in this condition. The bullet probably concussed him, sure, but this is something else entirely." She glanced down at her watch and its large digital readout. "We may know more after they fit him in for his MRI in a couple of hours."

"Something else? Could he have overdosed on a drug?"

"Our usual toxicology panel showed a trace of Haldol in his system—that's an old antipsychotic drug—but nothing else he shouldn't have taken. As I said, there was only a trace, which means he hadn't taken any therapeutic dose for upward of three or four days. But there are a lot of drugs and supplements out there we haven't tested for yet that can cause neurotoxicity. We've sent a sample of his blood to a facility with a specialized mass spectroscopy unit to try to identify any drugs we might have missed. We'll have to wait for the results. Some kind of drug effect is a real possibility. His blood tests show his bone marrow is suppressed, and his liver shows signs of injury for some reason. So I have a medical mystery on my hands, and no history to work with. Have you made any progress identifying him?"

"Not yet."

"Take a look at this." Dr. Wordsworth carefully lifted

John Doe's handcuffed wrist and pulled at a loose plastic wristband. "It looks almost like a conventional hospital ID band, but it's not ours. I've never seen a psychiatric facility put such a bizarre tag on a patient, though. It doesn't make sense. Even at a private institution, there ought to be some sort of comprehensible patient identification on it, the name of the facility, much more than this. There's a handwritten date on it—also strange. It's Saturday, two days ago, perhaps the day he escaped? His last treatment date?" She looked up at Savich, shook her head. "Perhaps they changed out his wristband each time he had a treatment. And look here, in small letters, *E 2*. Nothing else."

Savich stared at the wide pale yellow plastic strip. Saturday most likely wasn't the date he entered the facility, so Dr. Wordsworth was probably right, it was the date of his last treatment. But for what? And what could *E 2* mean? Savich felt a tug of memory, and then it was gone. "Can't help with that," he said. "I've checked with Metro. They've had no inquiries from any psychiatric facility about our Mr. Doe. Nor does Metro know who he is. His fingerprints aren't in the system."

Dr. Wordsworth checked the IV infusion set, made a minor adjustment. "Isn't that unusual? Your not being able to identify someone?"

"It only means he's never worked for the government, been in the military, or been arrested. I tried the facial recognition program, missing persons country-wide, but without any luck." Savich wondered if Mayer had done the same.

Dr. Wordsworth said, "Our staff have been contacting all the medical facilities and psychiatric hospitals in the District, in Maryland, and in Virginia. None of them have claimed him so far. If he was in a small facility or with his family, we'd expect them to be all over this. And then I ask myself, why would a family—especially a family—put a wristband like this on him?"

Savich said slowly, "It could be he escaped from somewhere, Doctor. He thought he had a mission, and it involved a woman who's just given birth upstairs. Why her in particular, I don't know yet."

"Everyone here knows you saved Ms. Moody from John Doe."

He said nothing, only shook his head.

"There's something else you have to see." She pulled back the thin blanket that covered John Doe's arms. "Look at the needle tracks on his arms. You might think he was a big-time drug addict, but those scars aren't anything like the scars of a drug addict. They're carefully placed and well cared for, with no sign they were ever infected. There's no way a drug addict could do that himself. And look up here at his neck and under his collarbone. He's had large-bore catheters placed there, such as we use for people who need long-term venous access for their treatments, or for dialysis. These scars are the result of medical care, though for what I have no idea yet."

The hospital loudspeaker paged Dr. Wordsworth to the ER, stat. Savich quickly gave her his card. She tucked it in her pocket, shook his hand, held it a moment. "Agent Savich, I'll let you know if the head MRI shows anything unusual, and I trust you'll call me if you find anything that can help me. I can see you care about him. You want to know who he is and what all this is about as much as I do." She looked again toward John Doe, shook her head, and was out the door.

Savich looked down at John Doe. He looked so very young, helpless. He now clearly remembered him saying *I'm an enigma*. Was that what the *E* stood for? And the *2*? Was there another enigma who came before him? Savich pulled out his cell and called Ben Raven at Metro. "Ben, are you in the field?"

"Yep. A beating, domestic. I hate these. What's going on?"

"Do me a favor. I'm worried about our Mr. John Doe from yesterday. He's still in a coma, completely helpless. He claimed someone was out hunting for him, that they wanted him back, and Kara Moody. If he's right"—he didn't want to sound ridiculous, so he only said—"it's possible someone doesn't mean him well. Could you assign an officer to him?"

A pause, then Raven said, "This is your gut talking, Savich?"

"Yes, that and a couple of odd things, inexplicable things about him."

"I'll check with my lieutenant, get a guard cleared

with hospital security for a couple of days." Savich could
see Ben's grin as he said, "Guess you didn't want to ask
Mayer?"

"Not in this lifetime. Can you get him here as fast
as you can?"

"Hang on."

Savich looked at John Doe as he waited for Ben
Raven to come back on the line.

"Okay, it's a go. We already have an officer on premises. He'll be right up. Officer Tommy Sharpe is his
name."

"Thanks, Ben." Savich punched off. He wished
John Doe were FBI purview. Even more than that he
wished he'd had the foresight to turn on the recorder
on his cell phone when he'd been in Kara Moody's
house. With the urgency, the adrenaline rush, he simply couldn't remember exactly what John Doe had
said.

Savich pulled up a chair close to John Doe's bed and
texted Cam for a status report. Her reply came back:

**Still alive, about to land at Magee Field in Ken-
tucky. Cabot appears competent, at least he
hasn't crashed us yet. Sick sense of humor.**

Savich grinned, texted back,

**Let me know when you've reached the national
forest. Give me your take on Duke and Harbinger.**

Then he texted Jack much the same thing, not expecting an answer from the air, and punched off. He slipped his cell back into his pocket and studied the needle marks that ran up and down John Doe's arms. *What's wrong with you? Do you need some kind of drug that can't be swallowed in pill form? What drug?*

Savich looked up when he heard Detective Aldo Mayer's familiar voice at the door. "What are you doing here?"

7

BOWLER, BOWLER, AND BOWLER
CORNER OF K STREET SW AND 17TH STREET NW
WASHINGTON, D.C.
MONDAY AFTERNOON

Duce Bowler's law offices on the fifth floor of the older, nondescript Blackthorn Building were a surprise. Agents Ruth Noble and Ollie Hamish stepped into an eighteenth-century French drawing room, with gilt sofas and chairs and classic paintings on the pale yellow walls, the three windows framed with floor-length gold brocade draperies looped open with long golden cords. Even the reception desk was eighteenth-century gold and white, with graceful curved legs, the desktop holding only a state-of-the-art computer monitor, a keyboard, and two phones. There were no clients waiting in modern dress to spoil the effect.

Ruth and Ollie crossed the expanse of glossy oak floor toward a tall, lanky young man dressed in a black suit, white shirt, and gray tie, who was rising from his gilt chair behind the desk. He smiled uncertainly at them. "Good afternoon, sir, madam. I am Kendrick. I'm afraid no one is free to assist you. May I set up an appointment for you?"

Ollie wouldn't have been surprised if they'd made Kendrick wear a wig and knee pants. "We're here to see Mr. Duce Bowler, Kendrick. I don't see any clients waiting. Business is bad?"

"No, sir. An appointment is necessary, particularly on days when Mr. Bowler is prepping for a court case."

Ruth handed Kendrick their creds and made introductions. "We'll see him now, Kendrick."

"You're really FBI agents? You look so nice, I wouldn't have guessed. Well, never mind that. Mr. and Mrs. Bowler are in the conference room." Kendrick looked at his watch. "He might be taking a break. I took him his bear claw a couple of minutes ago. Maybe I could ask if he can spare the time to see you."

"Just show us the way, Kendrick," Ollie said. "Now would be good."

Kendrick looked flustered, as if he didn't know what to do, but he shrugged and led them down a long pale-gray-carpeted hallway past a series of niches in the walls, each with a bust of a famous eighteenth-century Frenchman, beginning with Louis XV and Voltaire, each labeled with their dates of birth and death.

"Those wigs must have been hot," Ollie said. "Makes my scalp itch to look at them."

Kendrick turned, grinned, and pointed to the last bust set in a place of honor: Marie Antoinette. "This one's Mrs. Bowler's favorite, and the only woman. Mrs. Bowler says she wore enough perfume to float a boat. They didn't bathe much back then. Mrs. Bowler also said the real Marie Antoinette didn't have that much bosom."

They passed a half-dozen gilt-edged doors, heard voices as they passed. Kendrick said, "All the doors are closed because Mrs. Bowler likes everyone to keep themselves private, clients and secretaries included. The world has ears, Mrs. Bowler says."

Kendrick opened a set of double doors, stepped into a conference room, and announced, "Mr. Duce— ah, Mr. and Mrs. Bowler, two FBI agents are here to see you. I'm sorry, but they insisted."

A thin, basketball-tall man rose, a half-eaten bear claw in his hand, sputtering as he wiped his mouth. "Kendrick, what is this? These agents did not call to request a meeting. I have nothing to say to them." He waved a thin hand at piles of papers on the table. "I'm very busy, Kendrick. Take them away."

Ruth smiled. "Mr. Bowler. Mrs. Bowler?" She introduced herself and Ollie. They handed over their creds, waited, saying nothing more until Mr. Bowler, scowling, handed them back.

Mrs. Bowler said as she rose, "My husband does not have time to speak to you. He's preparing for a very important court case. You do understand, don't you, that he is not obliged to speak to you?"

Ollie nearly spurted out a laugh. Mr. Bowler was a good six feet six inches, and his wife and partner topped out at no more than five feet, her head barely reaching his armpit. She was about the same age as her husband, early fifties. She was dressed as elegantly as her husband, both of them proud products of Barneys, if Ruth didn't miss her guess. Unlike her husband, Renée Bowler wasn't holding a bear claw.

Kendrick said, "I'm sorry, Mr. Bowler, but they were insistent, sir." Kendrick, no fool, slipped out of the room quickly, closing the double doors behind him.

Ollie said, "We're here to speak to you about Manta Ray—Mr. Liam Hennessey. You are his lawyer, isn't that correct, Mr. Bowler?"

Bowler drew himself up and threw his head back, trying to intimidate, but he couldn't pull it off, what with his pale eyes darting back and forth between Ruth and Ollie. Still, even though they could tell he was worried, he kept his voice calm and professional. "I was Mr. Hennessey's lawyer, but I no longer represent him. Like every other citizen of the District, I heard it on a news bulletin when he escaped federal custody. Incredible incompetence on law enforcement's part, I have to say. I did my best by him, a prison term rather than a lethal injection, but that was enough. I've washed my hands of him, removed him from my client list, and I will have nothing more to do with him. So I have nothing more to say to you, either. Now, if you don't mind, I have work to do."

Ruth saw a sheen of sweat glisten on Bowler's forehead. She pulled out her stone face and said, in a voice colder than an ice floe, "Mr. Bowler, you will either speak to us here or we will escort you to the Hoover Building. The venue is up to you."

He stared at her for an instant, a deer in the head-lights, before looking at his wife. Despite her size, Ruth recognized at once it was Mrs. Bowler who drove this bus. Maybe more rottweiler than bus driver, even in her four-inch stilettos.

Ruth turned to her. "You are aware your husband was the only one listed as visiting Mr. Hennessey at the Northern Neck Regional Jail. We've checked the video cams, of course, and there was no doubt it was your husband who visited him on several occasions. Only your husband could have brokered a deal between Mr. Hennessey and whoever arranged Hennessey's escape. We suspect it was in return for the contents of the six safe-deposit boxes he robbed a month ago, isn't that right?"

Bowler's forehead continued to shine with sweat while Mrs. Bowler examined the bright pink polish on her thumbnail. Then she frowned a bit. Had her nail polish chipped? Ruth watched her toss her bobbed blond hair. "Surely you have some understanding of lawyer-client privilege, Agent Noble. Shall I recite the statute to you both, Agent Hamish? Mr. Bowler had no role in Mr. Hennessey's escape from federal custody. It would be unethical for him to answer any questions about his conversations with his client. You need to leave now."

Ollie said pleasantly, "If Mr. Hennessey and Mr. Bowler were conspiring to set Hennessey free, there is no privilege, Mrs. Bowler, as I'm sure you know. Mr. Bowler, your firm isn't in financial trouble. You, personally, do very little criminal work. The question I have is why you would accept carrying out anything as dicey as this since you had to know we'd come knocking on your door. I doubt you'd want to risk leaving a financial record, so I would guess you'll claim your work for Mr. Hennessey was pro bono. Tell me, did whoever put you up to this threaten you, or perhaps know about something you would rather no one found out about?"

As he spoke, Ollie handed Mr. Bowler a sheet of paper. "You'll recognize these two names because they're your clients. Both of these individuals are under investigation for money laundering for MS-13, the Salvadoran drug cartel. The federal prosecutor seems to think you were involved, and he's working hard to nail it down. That doesn't put you in a very good position. Disbarment, prison—more than enough to motivate you to cooperate with us. If you do, we're sure the federal prosecutor would be willing to close his file on your involvement.

"Now's the time to show good faith. Who were you really representing, Mr. Bowler? Who paid you to broker a deal with Liam Hennessey?"

Mrs. Bowler said, contempt in her voice, "There are no charges against us, and if there ever are, they'll be proved groundless. We are a reputable firm."

Ruth ignored her. "Mr. Bowler, you have to know that when we apprehend Mr. Hennessey, he will tell us in great detail how you helped facilitate his escape. He will throw you under the bus without any hesitation. And if he should die instead, you can be sure we'll investigate you until we find every piece of dirt hidden under your expensive carpets. We'll investigate your clients until they realize you are a liability. I doubt your Russian clients, in particular, will be pleased with you, and I hear they're not known for their forbearance."

Mr. Bowler's Adam's apple worked frantically above his Gucci tie. Ruth leaned forward. "You wouldn't do well in prison, Mr. Bowler. You are not a young man. You wouldn't be able to defend yourself against the predators. For your own sake, you should tell us the name of the person who hired you to broker the deal with Hennessey."

Mrs. Bowler laid her small hand on her husband's arm. "Ignore her, Duce." She whirled back to face them, her palms flattened on the table. "You will listen to me, Agent Noble. My husband did not broker any deal. Hennessey is a resourceful man. He obviously had ways to reach his cohorts on the outside. My husband had nothing to do with Mr. Hennessey's escape."

The double doors flew open. "Mother? What is going on here? What is Kendrick going on about?"

Ollie and Ruth turned to see a young Amazon stride into the conference room like a force of nature. She was six feet tall, with long dark brown hair clipped away from her face, strong sharp features, not above thirty. She was the image of her father, and the third Bowler listed in the firm name. They'd know quickly enough if she was her mother's daughter.

Ruth knew exactly who she was, but she asked, "And who are you?"

"I am Magda Bowler." A sculpted eyebrow went up. "And you are?"

Ruth and Ollie introduced themselves and put their creds in her outstretched hand. She studied them closely, handed them back. "Why are you here?"

Ruth said, "We are questioning your father about his arrangements with Manta Ray—Liam Hennessey."

"You are wasting your time. We no longer represent Mr. Hennessey. I'm sure my parents already told you that. I came in to put an end to your harassment."

Ruth smiled at her. "Trust me, you do not know what harassment is." She flashed a look at Mrs. Bowler. "There are no nail salons in prison, Mrs. Bowler. As I'm sure you already know, the person who hired you is dangerous. You and your husband will want to think about this very seriously, before it's too late."

"Too late?" Magda Bowler planted herself in front of them, hanging on to her control by a thread. "I don't like your threats, especially after you've already proven yourselves incompetent by letting Hennessey escape."

"Magda, come here!" Her mother's voice drew her up short. So Mrs. Bowler did drive the family bus.

Ruth and Ollie watched Magda Bowler walk stiffly to stand between her parents. The three of them stared silently after Ruth and Ollie as they left the conference room, shooting death rays between their shoulder blades. Ruth said to Ollie as they walked past Marie

Antoinette's bust, "Mr. Bowler's ready to break. He's scared."

"You know what I think?" Ollie gave Kendrick a wave as they walked out of the offices, to the elevator. Once inside, he said, "I don't think Mr. Bowler ever believed his off-the-books client would be able to break Manta Ray out of federal custody. Are all three of them in on it? It's hard to imagine that Mr. Bowler acted by himself. You're right, Ruth. If any of them break, it'll be him."

She pulled out her cell, dialed Savich. "If that's true, Ollie, we should get some surveillance on Bowler. Who knows? Maybe we shook him up enough so he'll schedule a meet with whoever hired him."

8

Kara Moody could hardly believe how giddy she felt when she held her son, Alex. Suddenly everything made sense; her life had purpose. She was happy, excited about the future. She hadn't felt anything like it in a very long time.

In the past year, her life had flown out of control, and she'd floundered and questioned everything, turned herself into an emotional fruitcake. She could admit it to herself without rancor because none of that mattered now. There was no doubt in her mind her decisions to keep Alex and leave Baltimore were the best decisions she'd made in her life. She had no friends who really understood her choices. As for Aunt Elizabeth and Uncle Carl, they only saw she was alone and pregnant, and treated her like a scandalous teenager from thirty years ago. They'd wanted her to have an abortion, as did most of her friends, and she'd broken with them, no choice. As for her mother, she now lived in Oregon with her husband and two children, and they rarely spoke. Kara couldn't imagine her caring one way or the other.

So she'd taken it all on her own shoulders, made some calls, found a part-time job at the Raleigh Gallery in Georgetown, packed up her Honda, and headed south. In addition to her savings, she had a small inheritance, enough to afford the rent on the house in Georgetown. And to her surprise, she soon found buyers for her own paintings through the gallery. Her art career had seemed to flourish with each week Alex grew inside her.

Dr. Janice Hudson, her next-door neighbor, had been with her, her coach through the long labor, there to cheer when Alex was born. Dr. Janice had whispered to her when she'd first held Alex in her arms that she'd just come through the most profound experience granted to humans. She should never forget she was in charge of two people now, she and no one else. And Dr. Janice had contacted her boss at the Raleigh Gallery, and now she had three huge bouquets of flowers, with congratulations to her and Alex.

Alex. Her beautiful boy had a mop of dark hair, the same shade as hers, the same shade as her father's had once been before the cancer had taken him so quickly. She'd named her son Alex Ives Moody, after her father and her grandfather, both good men who'd encouraged her to stay the course as an artist, both gone now. It saddened her that they'd never see her miracle, that Alex would never know them.

She found she couldn't look away from Alex's bassinet even though it was empty for the moment. A nurse had come in to take him for an ultraviolet-light treatment to prevent him from getting jaundice, she'd told Kara, which sounded scary to her, but the nurse had assured her it was a common treatment that couldn't hurt him, she wasn't to worry. It had only been ten minutes and she already missed him. She loved having him in her room, not ten feet away from her, ready for her to feed him, sing to him, tell him she would love him with all her soul forever.

She looked up when a nurse came back into her room with Alex in her arms. "He's asleep, the little angel. The treatment went fine, he slept right through it. Let him sleep for a while more, Ms. Moody, say thirty more minutes until he wakes up by himself. He'll be ready to eat by then." She carefully placed him in his bassinet. "Can I get you anything?"

"No, thank you. You're sure he's all right?"

"He's perfect." The nurse nodded, smiled at her, and left.

Kara sat up on the side of her bed, her feet dangling, staring at the bassinet. She wanted to hold him now, watch him smack his lips as he had that morning when she'd sung him a Scottish ballad, but she forced herself to wait a bit longer. She thought instead about the series of Tuscany vineyard oil paintings she'd very nearly finished for the reception area of the Alonzo Group's new Washington office. Exactly what they wanted, one of the VPs told her, and she'd basked. She thought about all the portraits she'd paint of Alex. Life was good.

The terror she'd been through the day before came

unbidden into her mind. She couldn't escape it, not yet, sitting duct-taped in that chair, helpless, terrified she'd failed to protect her baby, because she'd been alone by her own choice. But he couldn't hurt her now. He was in a coma on the third floor, a nurse assured her. They called him John Doe because he'd had no ID on him. Kara knew she'd have to speak to the police again, tell them everything she could remember, but not now. She looked over at the bassinet again and smiled. Alex was sleeping the sleep of angels.

She slipped out of bed and walked quietly to his bassinet. She leaned down to lift the light blue blanket nearly covering his small face, to look at her gift from God.

9

"I asked you what you were doing here." Mayer's voice sounded calm enough, and that was a nice change. Maybe he wasn't going to draw his weapon.

Savich rose. "Good afternoon, Detective. I'm here to see how John Doe is doing."

"He's in a freaking coma, that's how he's doing." Mayer took a step forward, stopped. "You could have learned that from a telephone call."

"You could have called as well. So why are you here?"

"What's it to you? It's my case, not yours. I'm here to see if he's come around. The mutt's got a lot to answer for. First off, I'd like him to tell me his name."

"No one has contacted you about him yet?"

"Nope, no one, not a mental institution, or lockup, not his family. He doesn't look homeless, so someone will come to claim him; they always do."

Mayer walked to the bed and looked dispassionately down at the motionless young man. "He looks almost dead. It might have been easier if you'd killed him. I see a bad future for him if he wakes up. Look at those needle marks on his arms. He's already fried his veins, and now he's looking at a long stretch in prison if he's competent enough to stand trial. Have they told you anything about all the tests they're doing on him?"

Savich started to tell him there was no way John Doe had been shooting himself up, but decided to drop it. "No, only a trace of an antipsychotic drug left in his system."

Mayer turned at a voice he recognized outside the room. He listened, then rounded on Savich. "What is Officer Sharpe doing up here? You did that, didn't you? Arranged for a police guard for this guy?"

"Actually, Ben Raven arranged it."

"But you called Raven, didn't you? You had no right to stick your freaking Fed nose into my business. Why are you even here, really? Playing the glory hound again?"

Savich pictured Mayer in the fetal position on the floor, hugging his gut. He said easily, "I wondered why you haven't interviewed me, asked me if I'd heard anything John Doe said that might help identify him."

"If you knew anything, you'd have shouted it to the cameras. Besides, who gives a crap what a crazy man rants? He was obviously off his meds—I heard him screaming about the gods this and the gods that, but none of it made any sense." He paused a moment, thrust out his chin. "Everyone could see that. When I speak to Ms. Moody, I'm sure she'll agree."

"He certainly appeared distraught, and yes, con- fused, but don't you want to know why he seems to have broken out of a mental institution to rescue a pregnant woman from someone? And no one has claimed him?"

"Nah, he wasn't there to save anyone. He's crazy. Look, I've got dead bodies piling up, Savich. Dead bodies with names, with families who need justice. This guy? When the folks from his funny farm arrive, they'll tell us everything we want to know. They'll have a thick file on him, count on it." He shot Savich a look of cold dislike. "I can see you're not going to give up on this; why, I don't know. It's not like you Feds don't have enough of your own crap to deal with." He frowned, then shrugged. "Okay, I did speak to Ms. Moody, but she said she'd never seen him before, that he wanted to take her away but she couldn't figure out why because he was too confused. When the police showed up, he got frantic, made no sense at all. So I think he picked a random house to invade. That's it. Nothing more, zip, nada. And if he ever wakes up, he'll get carted back to where he came from, or off to prison in shackles, and this will all be over."

"Suppose it wasn't a mental institution. That tag around his wrist could be from somewhere else. Some-place as far off the grid as he is."

"Oh, come on, get real. Now you're talking conspir-acies? You're making something out of the rantings of a crazy guy. Why are you really here, Savich?"

"Probably the same reason as you. I want to know who he is, what he is. I want to know what happened to him."

Mayer looked down at the still face. For an un-guarded moment his defensive anger fell away. He said in a low voice, "He's so bloody young. What, maybe twenty-two, twenty-five? So yeah, I want to know what happened to him, why he fell off the rails." So Mayer was more concerned about this young man than he'd let on, but he wasn't about to show that to Savich. Didn't he realize he already had? Mayer shook his head. "You said you want to know *what* he is. What do you mean by that?"

"To be honest, Detective, I don't know what I meant."

"Well, it really isn't any of your business anyway, is it? And you're wasting taxpayer money, Metro money, on a guard without a reason."

"I heard him say some very odd things. I think there's more going on here than his delusions. I'm wor-ried the people he escaped from—" He paused, shook his head. "A couple of days. I'd like to keep him safe for a couple of days."

Savich looked down at the plastic wrist bracelet, then back over at Mayer. "Detective, what do you think of when you see or hear the word *enigma*?"

Mayer scowled at him, shrugged again. "What's this with word games, Savich? Everybody knows *enigma* was the code the Germans used back in World War Two. There was a movie about the Brit guy who broke it."

"Look at his ID band, Detective."

"What? You think this *E* stands for *enigma*?"

"Possibly. An enigma can also be a person or a thing that's mysterious, puzzling, or difficult to understand," Savich said slowly. "John Doe called himself that—an enigma."

That gave Mayer pause, but only for a moment. "So what? Who cares? You think he's a member of some kind of cryptology club? Some secret group? Get real, Savich. We'll probably find out what he meant when he said that and laugh." He drew himself up and leaned toward Savich. "In the meantime, I want you to stay away from him. He's none of your concern." Mayer grunted, turned on his heel, and walked out of the room.

A police officer stuck his head in the room after he left. "Agent Savich? I'm Officer Tommy Sharpe. It's a pleasure to meet you." He looked over his shoulder. "Detective Mayer isn't happy." Tommy didn't sound particularly concerned.

Savich shook his hand. "Officer Sharpe."

"Call me Tommy. Everybody does, even the dudes I arrest." He paused, then added, "I wish they wouldn't." Sharpe wasn't exactly green, but close, maybe a couple of years out of police academy. He looked strong as a young bull, and had a kid's face the passing years would never change.

"All right, Tommy."

Sharpe walked into the room and stood beside the bed. "I hear he's the guy you took down yesterday in Georgetown. Doesn't look like he's going to be a lot of trouble to me. Can you tell me what to expect? Why you think he needs a guard?"

Savich said, "I don't have anything specific in mind, but I do know he was scared some people would be coming after him."

"And you don't think that was because he's crazy?"

Savich smiled. "I don't know if *crazy*'s the right word for him, but we'll see. I'd rather listen to my gut than be sorry if this thing doesn't end well. I'd appreciate your sticking close to him, not letting anyone near him you haven't vetted first."

Sharpe nodded. "He's very young."

"Yes, he is. About your age."

Sharpe gave him a big grin. "Nah, I've got at least two years on him."

Savich gave Officer Tommy Sharpe his cell number and took the elevator to the maternity floor. He showed his creds at the entrance to the maternity-unit security guard with the name Ray Hunter on his name tag. Ray's head was topped with a crop of bright red hair, and he looked bored. A red eyebrow went up when Savich showed him his creds. "Any trouble here, Agent Savich?"

"No, I'm here to see a new mother, Kara Moody." Savich looked at his name tag again. "Why, Ray? Have you had any problems on the floor?"

"Not since last week when an ex-husband tried to take his kid out of the unit by himself without checking with anybody. The infant security bands were still on the baby. Obviously the guy didn't know the procedures to follow. The alarm went off and everything shut down as it was supposed to, the elevators, stairwells. It was a mess until we got him talked down and the baby back safe in his mother's room." He shook his head. "It's sad we have to be here to guard a maternity ward against people out to steal babies, but it's a strange world."

Savich gave Ray a salute and set off toward the nurses' station to ask for Kara Moody's room number. He heard loud voices down the hall and someone was screaming.

It was Kara.

10

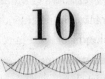

Cam stepped forward, shook the chief's big hand. "Chief Harbinger? I'm Agent Cam Wittier. This is Agent Jack Cabot."

They handed him their creds, watched him nod as he looked them over and handed them back. "Good to put faces to names. My name's Quinn, but everybody calls me Chief. Just Chief. You okay with that?"

"Not a problem, Chief," Jack said.

Chief turned, took his daughter's hand. His voice was both irritated and admiring. "And this is my daughter, Kim. I think you know my daughter spotted Manta Ray and his two compadres walking into the national forest. We'll be dropping her off at the London Ranger Station, where we'll be picking up our guide, Head Ranger Wayne Duke—we call him Duke. I thought it might be useful to give you a chance to speak with Kim on the way over. In fact, she insisted on speaking with you in person, even said her lips were sealed after she came up with that idea. She's just like her mom. I've learned from harsh experience it's easier to cooperate."

Kim rolled her eyes and quickly stepped forward, a huge smile on her face, showing beautiful white teeth. She had a long blond ponytail and bright blue eyes, only a bit darker than Sherlock's. Her cutoff jeans and sleeveless white shirt showed off her tan and a fit body. High-tops and heavy white socks polished off her presentation, a teen who spent a lot of time outdoors.

"It's a pleasure to meet you, Kim." Cam shook her hand, handed Kim her creds. Jack did the same. It was a show of respect that made the teenager's eyes widen with pleasure.

Cam nodded toward Chief Harbinger. "When I was your age, Kim, I never got away with giving my dad ultimatums. I've always thought it was a pity." Kim grinned at her father like a sinner who'd cleaned out the collection plate.

"I didn't, either," Jack said. "My parents kept me so straight-arrow, joining the service was like a vacation."

He looked so badass, everyone laughed.

Chief raised an eyebrow straight up. "She's lucky it was a good idea," he said, and gave his daughter the stink-eye.

"In any case, Kim," Jack said, "we're pleased you'll be able to tell us about Manta Ray. His real name's Liam Hennessey, and no, I don't know where he got that moniker. First we want to know why you're so certain it was Manta Ray you saw."

Chief looked at his watch. "Hold off on the questions until we get on our way to the London Ranger Station. As I said, we're hooking up with Head Ranger

Wayne Duke there, and meeting up with Harry Morsi. He sells most of the outdoor equipment in Pennington Gap. He's bringing along everything we'll need for several days, and nothing we won't. Kim, Harry will be driving you back home."

"Or I could go in with you, Dad. You know I'm a really good hiker; I know the forest. I could—"

"Kimmie, that's not going to happen. Now I expect you to keep your word."

Cam watched Kim finally nod, but she didn't look happy. The girl wanted adventure, but it wasn't going to happen this time.

Chief turned back to Cam and Jack. "One of Duke's men will be driving us to East Branch Road, where we'll head into the forest, hopefully before sunset. Since we'll be in the woods, even the quarter moon won't give us much light, so we'll have to stop before long and pick up their trail tomorrow morning."

"Give me a minute," Jack said, and moseyed over to a man in overalls who was wiping his hands on a rag, looking the Skylane over. They had their heads together for maybe two minutes before the man nodded, and they shook hands. When Jack was back, he said, "My baby is in good hands. No worries."

Chief gave a little wave at the man in the overalls. "Hank Withers is as trustworthy as they come, seems to know everything there is to know about planes. Can't say it hurts that it's an FBI plane—he knows if something happens to it on his watch, he'll be dog-paddling in the crapper."

Cam took one last look at the Skylane. "It'd be nice if your baby would grow up a bit while we're gone, like twenty feet longer with an extra engine or two."

Jack patted her arm. "Trust me, I have a feeling that when we get back you'll be happy to hop on board."

They stowed their backpacks in the back of the SUV, piled in, Cam in front with Chief Harbinger and Jack in the back with Kim. Chief pulled out of the airfield onto a two-lane blacktop. "If I'd turned right, we'd end up in Corbin. But we're going on the main road to the London Ranger Station." He shot her a grin. "Which doesn't meant anything to you. Okay, Jack, Cam, fire away. Kim, answer their questions."

Jack said, "First, Kim, tell us why you're so certain it was Manta Ray you saw walking into the forest."

Kim leaned toward him. "I'd seen this guy's— Manta Ray's—wanted poster in Dad's office and remembered thinking what a waste because he was so handsome. My friend Pam and I, we'd just come out from East Branch Road. We'd spent the morning with some kids from town, hiking and picnicking. We were driving on the dirt road leading out, and I saw him plain as day, with two other guys. One of them was handing Manta Ray a dark wool cap. I couldn't believe it. I guess I must have sucked in my breath because Pam assumed I knew them and started to stop, and I panicked, told her to get out of there fast. I called my dad right away." She paused a moment. "I didn't even think about snapping their photo until later. Sorry."

Jack said, "That must have been a moment, but you kept your head. You did good, Kim."

She beamed at him. "For a minute there, I thought they knew I was watching them and I nearly peed myself. But now I don't think they were paying any attention to us. They were focused on getting into the forest."

Cam pulled out her cell, found a photo of Manta Ray, and handed it to Kim. "This is the man you and Pam saw?"

"Oh yes, that's him." She sighed. "He's so hot, plus the poster said he's from Ireland, even has an Irish accent. What a bummer he's a criminal."

Jack said, "You said they were going into the forest. Did they have any kind of gear with them?"

"Nope, they didn't have any camping gear or backpacks. The two guys with Manta Ray were carrying small blue gym bags that looked brand-new. That was it, not even water bottles."

Jack knew there wasn't underwear in those gym bags, there were weapons.

Cam said, "I don't suppose Manta Ray was still wearing prison orange?"

"No orange. He had on jeans that looked so stiff they had to be right off the rack. His plaid shirt and hiking boots, too, everything looked brand-new. I guess he didn't know you never start on a long hike in brand-new boots."

"And the two men with him?"

"Nothing special. Long-sleeve shirts, jeans, and

those wool caps. Their clothes weren't new, but not ratty, either."

Cam wondered if they were experienced hikers, if they could handle the wilderness, or if they were city raised, like Manta Ray.

Cam said, "We assumed they'd be picking up gear and supplies once they were inside the forest, at some predesignated drop. That's got to be what they did, then. They had Manta Ray's escape well planned."

Chief said, "Kim, give Jack the folder."

Kim was sitting on it. She pulled it out, opened it. "Dad had me meet with Leo Pruitt, our local artist, to get these sketches done. Mr. Pruitt doesn't spend much time on the planet, usually all he paints are rocks and bears, but he tried. They're not bad, pretty right on, really, even though I only saw them for a few seconds." She handed Jack a pencil drawing. "He didn't draw Manta Ray; no need to." Cam turned in her seat to look at the drawing in Jack's hands. It showed a heavyset man with dark beard scruff and a buzz cut.

"This man was taller than Manta Ray, and he looked hard and tough, you know? Like a thug."

"Manta Ray is a bit over six foot," Cam said, "so this man was maybe six foot three?"

Kim nodded. "Yes, he was big. He looked like he worked out in a gym, maybe used steroids. He had big, thick legs that stretched out his jeans, and I remember there was a small tear over his left knee."

Jack looked down at the drawing. "Too bad he was wearing sunglasses."

"Yes, but Mr. Pruitt nailed them, though. The lenses were square, perfectly square, with black frames, and they looked weird. He's the one who handed Manta Ray the cap before he put on his own, so I saw his hair. It was dark brown."

Chief called out, "Did you see him walk, Kim? Did he seem old? Young?"

Kim twirled her ponytail around her busy fingers while she thought about it. "I only had a fast look at the three of them, but he didn't seem as old as you, Dad."

"Thanks, kid. So late thirties?"

She nodded. "I guess so. And he was tanned, at least his face was."

"Show us the second man," Jack said.

She pulled out a second drawing. This sketch looked pretty rough. It showed a slender face covered with aviator sunglasses and a dark wool cap pulled low, hiding all the hair.

Kim said, "This guy was lots shorter than the big guy and Manta Ray. Maybe five foot eight, same as me. He looked like he might be in charge, though; well, that was the impression I got. He kind of swaggered, took the lead, expected the other two to follow him. But there was something different about him, the shape of his face, his really sliced-thin cheekbones." She shrugged. "I thought first he might be foreign, Hispanic maybe, but I've been thinking about him a lot, and here's the thing." Kim leaned in close. "I'm not so sure it was a he. It might have been a she."

That was a kicker. Jack said, "A woman?" He looked

down at the drawing. Impossible to tell. "Why do you think that?"

"Well, I'm not a hundred percent sure, but what happened is I turned to sneak a look at them as we were driving away. They were moving out fast, with her in front of the two guys. Even though her jeans were loose I got a good look at her butt. It wasn't a guy's butt, it was a girl's."

Chief looked at her in his rearview. "Nice timing, Kim, you couldn't have done that better." He grinned at her as he turned the SUV onto a short paved driveway toward a low redbrick building nestled among maples, oaks, and larches. "This is the London Ranger Station, where we're meeting Duke." Chief checked his watch. "And Harry should be here any minute with the camping gear. Grab your stuff and I'll give you an overview while we're waiting." He pulled out a map of the forest, spread it out on the hood of the SUV. "You see the forest runs along the Cumberland Plateau in the Appalachian foothills of eastern Kentucky. You can see the roads for vehicles, trails for bikes, hikers, and horseback riding, and the stretches of private property. We're going to avoid all the visitor areas because we hope Manta Ray and his group will do the same. One of Duke's rangers will drive us to where Kim saw them last—on East Branch Road. It's about five miles from here. Duke will go over all this in more detail when he gets here."

They looked up to see a young man wearing a John Deere ball cap, jeans, and a cotton shirt climb out of a red Ford F-150 and wave to them. The chief folded the map, stuck it in his pocket. "That's Harry, right on time."

Harry Morsi introduced himself and walked them over to the bed of his truck, piled high with the gear he'd brought. "Didn't know how heavy you'd be packing, so I brought pretty much everything. I've got two light MSR backpacking stoves with fuel canister lines, my newest lightweight Nalgenes along with a water-filter system so you can drink from the streams without worrying about giardia, bivvy sacks, three lightweight sleeping bags with ground pads. Duke told me there was no rain in the forecast, but in case it does rain, here are some lightweight rain jackets, extra socks. A couple of tarps you can build a shelter with if it rains and the ground's wet, some lengths of nylon and bungee cord to fasten down the tarps if you need them. I've got instant oatmeal, freeze-dried eggs, dried fruit, nuts, and some freeze-dried carbs."

Jack said, "Chief, you brought along a good set of binoculars and your sat phone, right?"

"Wouldn't forget those," Chief said. "And I've got my scoped Remington, the 7600 pump-action in the SUV. It's accurate and dependable, fast follow-up shots."

Jack nodded. "It's a fine rifle, and I hope we don't have to use it." He looked toward Harry's truck bed. "Harry, we appreciate all your trouble, but we're not going out there to relax and get comfortable. We'll be traveling as light and fast as we can. And I don't expect we'll be out there for very long."

11

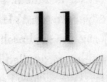

WASHINGTON MEMORIAL HOSPITAL
WASHINGTON, D.C.
MONDAY AFTERNOON

Savich ran into Kara's room, Ray Hunter the security guard and a nurse from the front desk on his heels. Kara was standing by the bassinet holding a bundle of blankets and towels in her hands, staring down. She wasn't screaming now. She was silent, frozen.

"Kara?"

She slowly turned, raised blank eyes to Savich's face. "He's gone, Dillon. I don't understand. Alex is gone. I wanted to tell the nurse but I couldn't stop screaming. The nurse who took him for an ultraviolet treatment, she didn't bring him back. She brought these." Kara handed him the blankets. Three hospital towels were twisted together inside the blanket.

The alarm sounded as Philly Adams, the nursing supervisor, came running into the room and slowed, calmed herself. She looked at Kara, at the nest of towels in the blanket, realized exactly what had happened, and went into command mode. "I understand Alex is missing, Ms. Moody. Ray will put all our procedures into motion. There's the alarm. That means the elevators and stairwells are in lockdown. Hospital security will be here any moment. As you know, Alex has a radiofrequency tag fastened to his umbilicus and another tag around his ankle. I will have the nurses check all the rooms. We will find him, Ms. Moody." She looked at Savich, eyebrow arched, and he introduced himself.

Savich ignored the alarm, the sound of voices, running feet, the faces peering into the room. He put the blankets down in the bassinet, took Kara's arms in his hands to steady her. "Tell me what happened, Kara."

He watched her draw on the strength she'd showed at her house with John Doe. "One of the nurses came to take him for his ultraviolet treatment. She said it was to help prevent his getting jaundice. When she brought him back, she told me to let him sleep for a while longer before feeding him."

Philly said, "Ms. Moody, Alex wouldn't have had an ultraviolet light treatment. It's used for babies who already have jaundice."

Savich said, "How long ago did she supposedly bring him back?"

"About ten minutes. I sat on my bed looking at the bassinet for a while, but I wanted so much to hold him. I had to see him, speak to him, and so I came over to the bassinet and lifted the cover away from his face, but he wasn't there." Her voice caught. "Dillon, it was towels, just towels."

Savich said, "Kara, the nurse who brought him back, what was her name?"

"I—I don't know, I didn't recognize her, never saw her before. She was very professional, very nice."

"What did she look like?"

"She was wearing a cap, so I couldn't see her hair, and glasses, narrow with black frames. I remember thinking that style didn't look good on her. She had on a white lab coat over a nurse's uniform. She was in her midthirties."

Savich said, "Picture her in your mind. Was she heavy? Slender? Fit? Anything unusual about her you can see?"

"She was slender, tall, maybe five foot eight. I think she had a bit of a limp, like she'd hurt her left foot and couldn't put her full weight on it."

"Anything else you can remember about her?"

Kara shook her head.

Ray Hunter had come into the room to stand beside Philly Adams.

Philly placed her hand on his arm. "What's happening, Ray?"

Ray said, "Our security chief, Oslo Elk, has contacted the CARD team and Metro, and spread all his people around the exits. The supervisory agent said there'd be two agents on-site real soon along with some FBI agents from the Washington Field Office." Ray added to Kara, "CARD stands for the Child Abduction Rapid Deployment team. They're a special FBI unit, and they're experts at finding missing babies taken from hospitals."

Chief of Security Oslo Elk rushed into the room,

quickly introduced himself to Savich and Kara, and said to Philly Adams, "The security log shows one of your night-shift nurses, Polly Pallen, checked into the unit using her key card forty-five minutes ago."

"Polly? She wasn't scheduled. Wait a second." She was on her cell, nodded, punched off. "One of our nurses, Abby Hinton, said Polly wasn't here, but she saw a nurse in the unit she didn't recognize a few minutes ago. She didn't think much about it, thought she was a traveler—a visiting nurse—or a temp."

Kara stared at Philly Adams. "You're telling me you let a strange woman loose with our babies? You didn't double-check that she should be here?"

Philly looked devastated. "I'm sorry, but we were busy and Abby assumed I'd been notified. It shouldn't have happened, but we're doing everything we can."

Kara looked like she wanted to leap on Philly Adams. Savich put his hand on her arm.

Chief Elk said, "Then the woman must have gotten hold of Polly Pallen's key card. We'll try to reach nurse Pallen to be sure, but it's a good bet. Let's hope she didn't get out of here before the alarm locked all the doors, and that includes the rear stairwell the personnel use. Agent Savich, you want to come look at some video with me? I've seen it once already. I'm hoping you'll see more. We've got cameras on all the stairs. We can see if that's the way she left the floor."

Three nurses stayed with Kara. Before Savich left with Chief Elk, he took her arms in his hands and forced her to look up at him. "I know you want to scream at everyone here who was supposed to keep Alex safe. Believe me, they're all doing their best now. I want you to keep faith and trust we will get Alex back."

As Savich walked down five flights of stairs with Security Chief Elk to the hospital security office off the lobby, he wondered if the media scanners had already lit up like Christmas trees. There would soon be chaos. Elk was saying, "We have eight cameras on the floor, two in the main stairwell, another two in the personnel stairwell. There aren't any cameras in the patient rooms, so we won't see the woman actually taking the baby. Damnation, I hate this. It's the second time it's happened on my watch. We got the other baby back okay, but this time it looks like a real pro job, and tell me why go to all this trouble to take that particular baby?"

John Doe knows why. He tried to stop it, tried to save Kara. Savich had wished John Doe were FBI purview. Now he was. Kidnapping was a federal crime, and Alex and John Doe were connected now, one case. Detective Mayer wasn't going to like being told that at all.

"All ready, Chief," the surveillance tech said, so excited he was nearly bouncing up and down in his chair.

Elk said, "Gilly is showing us three separate feeds on each of the monitors on the maternity floor, in the elevators and in the stairwells. He's taken the feeds to fifteen minutes before the alarm went off. Fast-forward, Gilly, let Agent Savich see the routine."

Savich heard the door open behind him but didn't look around.

They watched Ray Hunter, the security guard, check visitors onto the maternity floor and look over staff IDs, watched the public and staff with their carts and equipment enter and leave the elevators. Nurses passed the cameras in the hallways, going about their business, pushing linens and medication carts and computer monitors into and out of patient rooms.

They saw a nurse in black-framed glasses and a surgical cap walk down the hallway toward Kara's room. She looked relaxed, at home. She was tall, slender, in her midthirties, exactly as Kara described her. She went into Kara's room, emerged soon carrying what appeared to be Alex wrapped in blankets. When she reappeared ten minutes later, she was carrying Alex back into Kara's room.

Chief Elk said, "She knows where the cameras are, did a good job of avoiding them. I think she left Alex in the empty room next to Kara's then picked him up. Watch."

A minute later she was carrying Alex to the rear personnel door, sliding in the key card, and stepping through, the door closing behind her. Fast and slick.

They watched her walk quickly down five flights of stairs and exit the stairwell into the lobby near the east door.

"Switch to the cameras at the east exit and the parking lots," Elk said.

Gilly pressed a few keys on his keyboard to bring up the lobby feeds. They saw her step into the women's room and a few moments later, step out, the nurse's uniform, glasses, and cap gone, carrying Alex. A man in his midthirties, tall, as fit as she, and dressed just as casually in a shirt and chinos, met her in the lobby and walked beside her as she cradled the baby, his hand on her shoulder. They walked out the east exit, the picture of happy new parents.

"Give me a minute and back that up," Savich said. "I want to see their faces better."

Gilly brought it back to when they were nearer the camera and zoomed in on their faces. Savich took several pictures and uploaded them to the CAU. "That's probably good enough to run through facial recognition. Maybe one of them is in the database."

Gilly brought up the camera outside the east exit, and they saw them again, a man and a woman carrying a baby directly east onto Parker Street. Kara was right, the woman did favor her left foot, only a bit of a limp, barely noticeable. They paused at the intersection, and an old dark blue Toyota SUV pulled up. They climbed in and drove away.

"Any chance of making out that license plate? Another camera?" Savich asked.

"No, that's the closest we can get to them from our property," Elk said, "but there should be Metro cops covering Parker Street. I'll call in that car, get an Amber Alert started. There are a couple of banks along that street with security cameras. Maybe that will help."

Savich turned to see Sherlock standing beside the security room door. "The chief's right. It was slick," she said. "The woman knew enough about nursing to fool the staff and Kara, stole the right key card and knew how to use it, and she and the man were out of the hospital as quickly as humanly possible. Now the question we have to answer is why. And what does it all have to do with John Doe?"

"I love your brain," Savich said, touching his hand to her cheek. "You're only here one minute and you cut right to the core. I want you to speak to Kara, see if she's remembered anything more, any details at all. The CARD agents should be up there soon. At least we know what they look like, know the woman who stole Alex has a limp.

"Chief Elk, you're coordinating the search with the Metro cops? And dealing with the media?"

"Yeah, no choice there."

As Savich and Sherlock left the security office, they heard Elk on his cell calling the public relations department.

Savich and Sherlock saw the CARD agents when they opened the stairwell door onto the maternity floor, speaking with Ray Hunter. CARD Agent Constance Butler, a honed and fit woman with cropped gray hair, spotted Savich, nodded, and introduced herself. The other agent, Bolt Haller, came up, shook their hands. "I understand you've been looking at video with Chief Elk. He's started things rolling on the Amber Alert on Alex and the blue Toyota SUV. Tell us what you saw, Agent Savich, then we'll speak to Ms. Moody."

"I'll leave you to it, Dillon," Sherlock said. "I'm going to go see Kara."

12

BOWLER, BOWLER, AND BOWLER
CORNER OF K STREET SW AND 17TH STREET NW
WASHINGTON, D.C.
LATE MONDAY AFTERNOON

Ruth went with her gut and parked her Fiat across from the Blackthorn Building. She watched the staffers pour out, ready for their Monday-evening rituals. She ducked down when she saw the Bowlers' receptionist, Kendrick, walk out, pause on the sidewalk, and look around. A classic red Mustang pulled up and Kendrick got in. Ruth saw a flash of blond hair and sunglasses at the wheel.

Mrs. Bowler and Magda came out a couple of minutes later, both carrying briefcases, Magda obviously arguing with her mother. About what her daddy had done? Or what the FBI could possibly do to them? They disappeared into the garage beside the Blackthorn Building, and drove out a couple of minutes later together in a dark blue BMW. They weren't arguing any longer, both staring out the windshield as Mrs. Bowler carefully eased into traffic. Ruth wondered exactly what they knew. How complicit were they?

Duce Bowler came out thirty minutes later, alone,

his head down, carrying a briefcase. It looked to Ruth like he was talking to himself, shaking his head, even nodding. Was he trying to decide what to do? Or had he already made phone calls, made all the arrangements? He disappeared into the garage, came out driving a new dark gray Lexus GS F. Unlike his wife, he screeched into traffic, ignoring honking cars, obviously on edge. Good. It was still powerfully hot, even after five o'clock in the afternoon. His windows were rolled up, the AC doubtless on high.

Ruth pulled smoothly into traffic, three cars behind Mr. Bowler's Lexus. She soon realized he wasn't going home to Bowleigh, Maryland, he was going to Virginia. She was pleased she'd listened to her gut and started the surveillance early.

Thirty minutes later she was in Alexandria, following Bowler down King Street, past Market Square, and left onto Queen Street. He pulled into a public parking garage and luckily, Ruth managed to squeeze her small Fiat between two SUVs curbside. She watched Bowler come out of the public garage, cross Queen Street, and walk into Bilbo Baggins restaurant with its famous bright yellow facade and red awning.

She called Ollie, told him where Bowler was. "He's still alone. I'll bet you he set up a meet in a nice public spot. I'll call you in fifteen minutes or when whoever he's meeting gets here." Ruth punched off, waited a few more minutes, and slipped into the restaurant after him. It was cool and dark inside, filled to brimming with happy-hour workers and tourists, loud with conversations and laughter. Through the endless shuffle of waiters among the closely packed tables, she spotted Bowler at the bar, hunched over what looked to be a martini. She slipped into the restroom hallway and stood watching him and whoever came through the front door. Minutes passed. It was nearly six o'clock. Could she have been wrong? Was Bilbo Baggins simply one of Bowler's favorite watering holes, his place to de-stress after a difficult day? This day certainly qualified. He consulted his watch, swiveled on his barstool, and, like her, looked back at the front door, then down at his watch again.

A back booth cleared and Bowler was fast off his barstool to claim it. Ruth walked to the end of the bar to get a better view of him. She ordered a Belgian blond ale and looked toward him now and then. Ruth was good at surveillance; she was patient and she didn't miss much. She watched him tapping his fingertips on the table as more time passed, occasionally sipping his martini, and rarely looking away from the front door.

Ruth punched in Ollie's number. "Still no sign of the person he's supposed to meet. Bowler's getting antsy, starting to look angry. I don't need backup yet, and yes, I'm being careful, he won't see me. I'll check back in in fifteen minutes."

Ruth took another sip of her beer. She heard a male voice close to her right ear. "Hi, my name's John Murphy. I'm a local, not a tourist. Can I buy you another Belgian blond?"

Ruth looked no-nonsense in her black pants and

white shirt, her Glock hidden beneath her black jacket. No cleavage, no lipstick. He deserved a smile. She turned on her stool and gave him one. "Hi, John. You look like a nice guy, but alas, I'm married and waiting for my husband." She waggled her wedding ring at him.

Murphy gave her a salute and a mournful smile. "Then you'll never know why you should drop the old man." He turned away.

She appreciated an optimist. Ruth thought of her husband, Dix, and smiled again. She pretended to take another sip of her ale and looked again at Bowler. Ten minutes later, she was on the point of checking in with Ollie when Bowler stood suddenly, threw a twenty-dollar bill on the table, and wove his way through the packed restaurant toward the front door. She watched him punch a number in his cell, listen, then punch off. No doubt in her mind now, Bowler was angry. He'd been stood up. He'd never know how much of a bummer that was for both of them.

She slipped out after him, jaywalked behind him toward the public garage. She peeled off to go to her car, then changed her mind and followed Bowler into the garage. There was no attendant, only ticket machines. It was dark and hot, the air sluggish, a few people coming and going. She kept her distance, stayed to the far side of the garage, followed him to level two, to his Lexus. An older couple was walking twenty feet ahead of Bowler. She heard someone whistling, a scrap of conversation.

The lights went out in the garage.

13

Four people were hovering over Kara Moody when Sherlock walked into her room, Dr. Hamshaw, who'd delivered Alex, Philly Adams, and two Metro detectives. One of the detectives was asking Kara a question, but she only shook her head back and forth, hugging herself as she rocked in her chair, tears rolling down her cheeks. Sherlock introduced herself, showed her creds to everyone. Dr. Hamshaw said to her, "I gave Ms. Moody some Versed to calm her. Unfortunately she's more sensitive to the drug than most and it's nearly blanked her out. She'll be doing better in a few minutes." She leaned down and took Kara's pulse, checked her pupils.

Sherlock studied Kara's blank face, the streak of tears she couldn't seem to control. Her dark hair was hooked behind her ears, hanging loose to her shoulders. Her eyes were blue, not unlike Sherlock's, but darker, turbulent, her lashes absurdly long. She was twenty-seven, a lovely young woman despite her swollen eyes. Sherlock didn't think the injection had really deadened her pain. She asked to be left alone with Ms. Moody and waited until the four had filed out. She went down on her knees beside Kara's chair, took a Kleenex out of her pocket, and wiped the tears from Kara's face. She took her hand and said slowly, "Kara, I'm Agent Sherlock. Dillon Savich is my husband. You and I met briefly at the hospital yesterday." She waited.

Slowly, Kara turned drugged eyes to her face. "I remember you, your red hair. It's beautiful, your hair. You and Dillon are both agents?"

"That's right. We work together." She leaned close, squeezed her hand. "Versed is a wonderful drug, but too much of it and you're floating off with Peter Pan, not tethered to the world. Do you know where you are, Kara?"

Kara frowned at her and whispered, her voice thin, insubstantial, "I don't see Peter Pan, but yes, this does feel a little bit like never-never land, kind of filmy and blurred. I was hoping for a peaceful green island, blue ocean all around it."

Kara looked away from Sherlock, toward the window.

Sherlock said quietly, "Alex will need you soon, Kara, and that means you have to come back; you have to be ready to take care of him. He'll need you just as I need you now."

Kara looked back at Sherlock, ran her tongue over her dry lips. "Imagine, you're Dillon's wife. I remember now, you saved so many people that day at JFK. I've never been a heroine."

"You're wrong about that, Kara. Both Dillon and I

admire you immensely. You were alone and a madman forced his way into your house, yet you were calm and focused because you knew you had to be to protect Alex. And then you went into labor."

Sherlock felt Kara squeeze her hand, a small movement, but she felt it, just as she heard the whispered thank-you. She felt compassion mixed with hot fury. She couldn't imagine what she would have done if someone had stolen Sean—out of the hospital nursery where even she, a hard-nosed FBI agent, had trusted everyone to keep him safe.

Sherlock leaned in. "Kara, it's time to say goodbye to never-never land and bring yourself back to me. Blink your eyes, that's it, and don't look away from me. You have to help me find Alex. Can you tell me what happened?"

"Yes, I can do that." Kara shook her head to clear her brain. Sherlock saw her fingers pulling on a loose thread of the afghan spread over her hospital gown.

She told Sherlock about the nurse who'd come in to take Alex, how she'd come back carrying Alex and laid him in the bassinet. "She assured me everything was fine, he was a champ, and he even slept through the treatment and he was still sleeping. I should be patient and let him sleep, and she left.

"I tried to be patient, but I couldn't wait, you know? Well, maybe ten minutes and then I had to see him, had to hold him. I'd let him sleep if he wanted to. So I got out of bed and walked over to the bassinet to get him." Her voice fell off a cliff, her breathing hitched.

Sherlock squeezed her hand to bring her back. "The nurse, she was carrying him?"

Kara nodded. Another tear slid down her cheek. "How could she do this? How could anyone do this?" She fell silent, twisting her hands, whispered, "I was so happy. Alex was healthy and he was mine. Even that awful thing that happened to me, that crazy man, none of it mattered. Everything was about Alex."

She went still, began shaking her head back and forth. Then she whispered, stumbling, as if saying the words aloud would make her believe them. "Alex wasn't—he wasn't there. It was a pile of blankets and towels, but Alex wasn't there."

Sherlock wanted to hug her, to weep with her, but she managed to keep her voice matter-of-fact. "Stay with me, Kara. The nurse who took him, had you seen her before?"

"I didn't really look at her or at her name tag, but I do know I hadn't seen her before."

Sherlock brought up a photo on her cell phone from the security video Savich had uploaded to the CAU. "Is this the woman?"

Kara stiffened all over. "Yes, that's her. How could she? She was nice; she was friendly. How could she steal my baby? Who is she? What's her name?"

"We'll know soon who she is. You told Dillon she had a limp."

"Yes, it was slight, like she'd hurt her left foot."

"Kara, the FBI CARD team is in charge now. They're experts; they specialize in finding babies stolen out of hospitals. Trust me on this: there are no better people in the world to help us find Alex."

Kara Moody didn't look like she believed her.

Sherlock wondered how much to tell her, then decided Kara deserved the truth. She looked up to see Dillon and Agent Haller in the doorway, obviously listening. For how long? Dillon remained silent, nodded to her.

Sherlock turned back to Kara. "Kara, this wasn't some sort of baby kidnapping ring. There was a reason Alex was taken, and we believe it has something to do with John Doe, the man who forced his way into your house yesterday and is being guarded now downstairs. Did he tell you anything that could help us, anything you could understand?"

"Wait, wait—Alex was taken because of him, that poor, crazy young man? I don't understand."

"We don't, either, yet, but we'll figure it all out. I need you to think back, Kara. Tell me what you remember."

"I've tried to piece together what he said, but it was all so garbled, so bizarre. I do know he was afraid of someone, and at the same time he was furious. He hated this person or these people. He wasn't there to hurt me or Alex. He believed he was saving us from something." She looked at Sherlock. "I'm sorry but there's really nothing more. Did that help?"

"Yes, it did. Kara, who is Alex's father?"

14

Kara Moody lurched back as if slapped, then lowered her head, her dark hair curtaining her face. Sherlock pulled Kara's hair back and hooked it behind her ear again, leaned forward, and took her shoulders in her hands. "Come back, Kara, look at me, talk to me. This is critical. Tell me about Alex's father."

Kara raised her head, licked her lips again. "I'm not back in never-never land, Agent Sherlock, it's that I don't know who he is."

That was unexpected. Sherlock said, "You mean you were with more than one man at the time?"

Kara shuddered. "No, no, nothing like that. Here's the truth. When I found out I was pregnant, I couldn't believe it, even argued with the doctor. I had no idea how it happened. He sort of scoffed and asked me if it was an immaculate conception. But it was true; I wasn't seeing anyone. The doctor tried to pinpoint the date I got pregnant and I remembered my friend Sylvie Vaughn's party, at her place in Baltimore. It was a catered birthday party for her husband, Josh. When I woke up the morning after the party, I couldn't remember how I got home. I was ashamed, thought I must have drank too much, maybe passed out. I called Sylvie to apologize, but she said she'd bet a lot of guests didn't know how they got home. She told me not to worry, I hadn't taken off my clothes and gotten up on a table to dance. But the thing is, I don't remember getting drunk, only a couple glasses of wine."

"How many people were at the party?"

"Thirty, maybe more. I didn't know most of them, but Sylvie's right, everyone was having a great time, lots of booze."

"Do you remember leaving your wine to go to the bathroom? To dance?"

She raised her eyes to Sherlock's face. "I must have, because I came to believe I was roofied."

Sherlock tightened her hand on Kara's. "Yes, it sounds like you were. Back up, Kara, start at the beginning. Tell me what you remember from that night."

Kara closed her eyes, trying to focus. "I arrived at Sylvie's condo, greeted a few people I knew, met a few new people, some single guys, some guys with dates or wives, all Josh's friends. I remember wishing Josh a happy birthday. He kissed me and hugged me, and I wanted to kick him because he tried to put his tongue in my mouth. I got away from him as soon as I could. I never liked him much, and he was already getting drunk." She stopped, looked utterly vulnerable.

"You're doing very well, Kara. Go on."

"I woke up in my own bed the next morning, and

three weeks later I was told by my doctor that my nausea wasn't from a lingering flu. I was pregnant."

"Did you call the police?"

"And tell them what? I'm pregnant and I think I was roofied because I don't remember anything? No, I didn't."

"Did you tell your friend Sylvie?"

"Again, and say what exactly? Sylvie, I need to know the names of all the guys at your party because I think one of them roofied me and I'm pregnant?"

That's exactly what you should have done. And called the police. Nine months have passed. Would your friend Sylvie even remember who was there?

"Kara, when you woke up the morning after, was there any sign you'd had sex?"

"No," Kara said slowly. "And later, when I found out I was pregnant, I wondered how it could have happened at the party, since there were no signs. Unless the man washed me when he was done." She shuddered. "The thought of that is so creepy, so humiliating. I wanted to find him and kill him, but of course there was no way I could even identify who he was."

"Did you tell your friends, your family, you were pregnant?"

"No, not at first. But then, of course, I started showing and I had to tell them. I had two close friends at the time, one of them Sylvie Vaughn. I told them the truth, that I'd been roofied. Sylvie was upset I hadn't told her right away, said she could have checked out the men at the party, and I thought, yeah, and how would you do that? My other close friend, Brenda Love, she's a textile artist, urged me to have an abortion, put it all behind me, and get on with my life. Like Alex didn't mean anything."

"Did your friend Sylvie Vaughn also urge you to have an abortion?"

Kara shook her head. "Sylvie's great; she's more of a listener and always supportive. When I told her I wanted to keep the baby, and really pushed her for her opinion, she finally said if she were standing in my shoes, she'd keep the baby, too. The baby would be mine, all mine, and this faceless donor—that's what she called him—could go hang himself. I loved her for that.

"As for family, only my uncle Carl and aunt Elizabeth live close by Baltimore, in Mill Creek. Let me just say they weren't particularly supportive. They insisted I have an abortion. Even if I weren't Catholic, Agent Sherlock, I would never have aborted the baby. I wanted him. I had a part-time job at a modern gallery in Baltimore to help support my painting, and I'm a good salesperson. I knew I could get another job easily enough, so I packed up my Honda and moved here to Washington. I got a job right away at the Raleigh Gallery in Georgetown and I've met some really nice people. And of course Dr. Janice, my next-door neighbor. She stayed with me during my labor."

Kara looked wrung out. Sherlock patted her hand. "Dr. Janice told me you're an artist, a neo-impressionist she called you."

"That's close enough," Kara said, and added with

an exhausted smile, "I'm all for reality if I can blur it around the edges a bit."

"Did she tell you Dillon's grandmother is Sarah Elliott? She and Sarah were very good friends."

Kara's mouth gaped open. "*The* Sarah Elliott? Really? That's amazing. I wonder why she didn't tell me."

"Maybe she believed what you were doing was more important and you didn't need any comparisons. Dillon whittles beautiful pieces, and his sister, Lily, does the *No Wrinkles Remus* political cartoon in the *Washington Post*."

That small excursion had distracted Kara for maybe three minutes, but reality snapped her back. "How are you going to find Alex?"

Sherlock took Kara Moody's face between her hands. "We already have a good start. We may know the name of the woman who took him very soon now. I will personally speak to Sylvie Vaughn. Now, we need a sample of Alex's DNA, so there'll be no doubts we've got the right baby when we find him. Yours, too. An FBI tech will be here to collect it soon."

"Alex has lots of black hair, thick as mine. I brushed it yesterday with a tiny brush a nurse gave me. There's probably some hair on the brush. Will that do?"

"That's perfect. I need your friend Sylvie's information."

Kara gave her Sylvie Vaughn's address, email, and cell phone. "Unless she's moved, she'll be there."

Sherlock said, "Have you called Sylvie, told her about Alex?"

Kara shook her head. "No, I can't. I mean, there's nothing she could do."

Sherlock got Brenda Love's information next. She stood, put her small tablet back in her pocket. "It's time for you to meet the CARD agents now, Kara. Special Agents Haller and Butler are here to tell you what's been done so far and what their plans are. There's an Amber Alert out for Alex already." She paused a moment, leaned down. "I can't imagine my own son, Sean, being taken. You're being very brave, Kara, and you're smart. Talk to them about what happened in Baltimore, what happened yesterday with John Doe. Anything could help. I will make sure you know everything that's happening."

After she'd introduced Kara to CARD agents Haller and Butler, she met Dillon outside Kara's room and walked to the elevator, no longer on lockdown.

Sherlock said, "I wonder what the kidnappers want. Not money, but what?" She pressed the elevator button. "Whatever it is they want, you know as well as I do that it involves John Doe."

"And he can't tell us," Savich said. "I wonder if Kara's friends can help us find out how Alex's kidnapping is connected to him."

15

**PUBLIC GARAGE ON QUEEN STREET
ALEXANDRIA, VIRGINIA**

Ruth nearly stumbled in the sudden pitch black. She righted herself and held perfectly still, pressed against a car door. No mystery here: This was a setup, Bowler the target. She heard an older man yell, "Hey, who are you? What are you doing? If you want money—" His voice hitched and she heard him groan, but that, too, was cut off. A woman screamed, went silent. Ruth knew the older couple she'd seen walking in front of Bowler was down, maybe dead.

Ruth punched in Ollie's number, whispered, "Back up now, Ollie! It's an ambush! I'm in the public garage across from the restaurant. I don't know Bowler's status. Hurry!"

She held perfectly still, straining to hear any movement, breathing, anything at all, but it was silent now. She shouted into the darkness, "FBI! Mr. Bowler, keep hidden! Don't make a sound! Agents are barricading the garage entrance and exits!"

Silence.

How far out were the nearest agents and police? Ruth panned the darkness with her Glock waiting for her eyes to adjust to the pitch black, breathing as lightly as she could. She sensed no movement in the still air. She hoped the older couple was alive, hadn't paid with their lives for being in the wrong place at the wrong time. There was nothing she could do for them right now.

Ruth made a decision, shouted, "Mr. Bowler, you realize now the person you were supposed to meet at the restaurant set you up. Come toward my voice. You need to tell me who hired you, and the assassin will have no more reason to kill you."

A bullet struck a car fender right behind her. So the assassin wasn't gone. He'd fired toward the sound of her voice. She dropped to her knees and crawled behind a van beside her. Another bullet rang out, this one not as close, then a third bullet struck the wall two cars away, sending concrete shards flying.

A man's voice called out, "Hey, bitch cop, I don't hear any backup. Hey, you leave now and I'll let you live."

Ruth aimed her Glock toward his voice and pulled off three fast rounds, then two more, lower down, to each side. She heard three pings off cars and glass shattering. And the fifth shot? Could she have hit him? There was no sound of a gun dropping to the concrete floor, no moan. She didn't move.

Where were the agents? The police? She had to keep the assassin pinned down, keep him from finding Bowler. Then she heard a beautiful sound, faint at first, sirens coming closer. Ollie had called the Alexandria police. She heard their cars screeching up to the garage, knew they were blocking the entrance. She heard shouts.

Then, to her horror, lights flooded the garage.

Ruth yelled, "Get those lights off!"

She heard footsteps, a shout, then a single shot.

The lights went out again, and a score of flashlights came on to light the garage. But Ruth knew it was too late.

They found the older couple, thankfully not dead, but both unconscious, struck on their heads. She felt the pulse in their throats, slow and steady.

An Alexandria police officer yelled, "I found one. He's dead."

She'd failed, the assassin had killed Bowler. Ruth ran past the couple to where the police officer knelt. She looked down at a slight young man sprawled on his back behind a black Toyota, a bullet through his heart, a .357 Magnum on the concrete floor beside his right hand.

Ruth's heart jumped into her throat. It had to be the assassin, which meant Bowler not only had a gun, he'd been close enough to the assassin when the lights came on to kill him.

She yelled, "Mr. Bowler! The assassin is dead, you're safe. You can come out now!"

Duce Bowler wasn't in the garage.

16

HOME OF BEAU BRECKENRIDGE MADDOX,
FOUNDER OF GEN-CORE TECHNOLOGIES
BALTIMORE, MARYLAND
LATE MONDAY AFTERNOON

Lister Maddox stood listening at the door of his father's bedroom, his hand raised to knock. He heard Hannah's sweet, patient voice cajoling his father to take his new medicine, promising him it tasted like peppermint, and didn't he love peppermint? It was indeed new to him, a medication Lister had formulated personally to supplement his father's infusions. His prayer, now his litany: *Please let this one work.*

He slowly turned the knob and stepped into the King's Bedchamber, an exact replica of the King's Bedchamber in Restoration House in Kent, England. The high white sculpted-plaster ceiling was set off by a black-and-white japanned cornice celebrating Charles II's visit in 1684, and the walls below it were hung with gold silk damask. An antique ornate lacquer cabinet stood beside a mullioned window and a small harpsichord, its raised lid and gracefully curved sides painted with classical scenes. His father's four-poster bed dominated the large room, with rare Polish needlework draped over its top and hanging over the sides, its medieval scenes all shades of blue. The four carved bedposts were covered in black silk damask, the counterpane strawberry silk bordered with gold. The walls were covered with copies of the original portraits in the King's Bedchamber, of men and women dressed in seventeenth-century lace.

Lister remembered his first visit to Restoration House when he was a child, his father holding his hand as he led him from one magnificent room to the next, weaving tales about Charles II and Queen Christina of Sweden, and stories of the endless violence that had erupted near and within its walls, violence that had seeped into the very walls, leaving ghosts tied to this house—could Lister feel the stain of them? Lister hadn't ever felt any ghost stain or seen a ghost in Restoration House, but his father said he had once, and he reveled in the telling of it. There'd been many visits, blurred together now, but he did remember it was in this house his father had given his small son antique Murano glass worry beads on his eighth birthday to keep his small hands occupied, worry beads very much like those held in his hand now.

Hardly anyone could tell the difference between the original King's Bedchamber and his father's re-creation, one of two rooms he'd built faithful to the original in England. The Willows, as his father had named his jewel, resembled Restoration House on the outside, too, with its three stories of dark red brick and the beautifully maintained English gardens surrounding the house. His father had elected to set the Willows in Anne Arundel County on the Patapsco River, only a fifteen-minute drive from the company he'd founded, Gen-Core Technologies, in the Carroll-Camden Industrial Area. The Willows was the crown of the whole wealthy enclave, standing in the middle of a large lush private park, the gardens surrounded by ancient thick oak and maple trees, with a high stone wall surrounding the property to keep the curious away. The back of the Willows fronted the river, and a rich, thick lawn sloped down to the water's edge. As a child, Lister had dangled his feet in the water off the wooden dock while his flamboyant father entertained him, his mother, and their friends with his dives off the high platform at the back of his yacht, powerful dives, his form perfect. At least his mother had had the chance to live in this amazing house for a couple of years before she'd died, a skeleton in a morphine haze.

Lister shuddered now, remembering her claw of a hand dropping away from his when she breathed her last breath. He'd wondered over the years why his father hadn't been at his wife's deathbed, but he'd never had the courage to ask.

The Willows was large, well over ten thousand square feet, and his father would never know Enigma 3 was already in a room in the south wing. He'd decided against taking the baby back to the Annex, the bleak building near Gen-Core he normally used for his research. It was too dangerous to use now that Enigma 2 had escaped and Quince had failed in his assignment today. He'd threaded his worry beads endlessly between his fingers until Burley and Quince finally delivered Enigma 3 to Ella Peters, the pediatric nurse who would be his constant attendant twenty-four hours a day, even sleep in the same room with him. Ella owed his father her life, and she knew that he, his father's son, was working to help him, and was owed her loyalty in turn. It wasn't until much later his father told him how he'd stopped Ella's abusive husband from killing her. A pity, his father had added, Ella's husband was killed driving drunk a week later. Yes, it would all work out, everything would be back on track soon. Quince would remedy his failure.

Lister stepped forward into the King's Bedchamber, his low boots loud on the naked oak planks, his father having refused to cover the floor because there was no carpet in the original.

His father was no longer the powerful figure who'd ruled Gen-Core Technologies brilliantly and with ruthless efficiency for more than thirty years. The once renowned genetic scientist was now sitting in a wheelchair, facing Lister as he walked toward him, no expression on his face. Hannah Fox, once his lover for more years than Lister could remember, was now his nurse. She never left his side, hovered over him, always touching him, kissing him, speaking to him as if he understood what she was saying. As she watched Lister approach, she held up the empty syringe, a smile on her still-striking face. "How long will it be before we know?" She left the words *this time* unspoken.

Lister picked up his father's hand, remembered how strong it had been, how that hand had clasped his as a child, making him feel safe. He whispered, "Maybe by tonight."

Lister always spoke in a whisper around his father, but Hannah didn't. She said in a normal voice, "That soon?"

"It's a new formulation, so I'm not sure, but if it acts, it should act quickly."

Hannah raised her eyes upward as if she was praying. He knew she loved his father. It would take one of their deaths to separate them. Would the new formulation make a difference? Maybe, maybe it would. He wanted desperately to tell his father what he'd set into motion, what he hoped to accomplish, that there was still hope for him, but his father wouldn't understand him, of course. But maybe soon, things would change, at least a bit. Lister walked to the wheelchair, leaned down, and kissed the cheek of the impossibly handsome man who sat there, his face wrinkle-free, not looking a day over fifty. "Hello, Father."

There was no response.

"I've come to give you my weekly report on the status of our business." Lister pulled a small tablet out of his briefcase and began his weekly recital. His father never looked away from his son's face as he spoke.

17

Cam walked behind Ranger Wayne Duke in the gathering twilight. She knew Duke was forty-five, but he looked older, his face darkly tanned and seamed from all his years outdoors. He was a no-nonsense man, built lean like a runner and tough as an old boot, always ready, she imagined, to deal with a bear or a drunken tourist. He wore a Beretta snug in a clip at his waist, his Remington 7600 slung over his shoulder next to his backpack. He seemed at home with his weapons and with the forest. When he raised his hand and turned back to speak to them, his voice was judge-calm and low, his Virginia drawl soft and smooth as butter. "We've got to make some assumptions if we're going to hope to pick up their trail. We're all agreed they're going to be heading north, as far away from civilization as they can make it on foot." He pointed to a small snaking trail that forked off to the right. "If they peeled off here, they'd be heading into low hills, open scrub, and sparse trees. Not a difficult hike, at least along the ridges, but they'd be exposed there, so I'm thinking

they're going to be moving closer to the drainages—
the creeks—for tree cover. It's tougher terrain, but I'd
take that trade-off. There's a trail leading down to the
creek a bit farther up.

"Chief tells me you're an ex–army ranger, Jack, so
you're welcome to lead out if you want. Chief, you and
Agent Wittier stick close to me. Once we get to the
creek, we'll want to spread out. What you want to look
for is boot prints, broken branches, displaced rocks,
any sign of their passing. There aren't many hikers
where we're going, so anything fresh you see is probably them."

Jack said, "You take the lead, Duke. You know the
lay of the land. I think you're right they'll be heading
for overhead tree cover, to avoid line-of-sight surveillance."

"Let's move out then." As they fell into line behind
him, Duke said over his shoulder, "It's about five miles
along a meandering creek up to Highway 490 and 89.
They might try to make the five miles tonight, make it
less likely local law enforcement patrolling roads would
catch sight of them, but maybe not. If we can find their
tracks near the creek before dark, we can keep after
them, but even with the quarter moon tonight it'll still
be too dark to see anything. We'll probably have to
wait until first light."

Jack said, "At least they have no idea anyone's behind
them. That's why we opted out of any helicopters overhead to help us spot them. With any luck, we'll be a
surprise."

Duke pushed a branch out of the way. "Daniel Boone is mostly a wide-open forest, a lot of pretty clear terrain, with gentle, low-country slopes that top out at about twenty degrees. Most of the deeper woods are around the creeks. We can be at the creek in about thirty minutes, if we move fast. That's where we'll set up camp."

They hiked in silence, the only human sounds they heard were their footsteps and their own breathing. Duke moved faster as the dusk deepened. At least the temperature was falling, cooling off from the heat of the day. They followed the troughs of the rolling hills into thickening woods until Duke raised his hand. "The creek is ahead, down that incline. I know we'd all like to keep going, but there's no point in pushing on now. They have three, maybe four hours on us. This is as good a spot as any for the night. We're open to the sky, but there won't be any rain tonight, so we don't have to worry about shelter. We can even use the camp stoves, but after tonight we'll have to be more careful. We can't risk being spotted."

Soon each of them had their bivvy sacks rolled out, their pads and lightweight sleeping bags inside, laid in a rough circle.

Jack set up the two camp stoves with fuel canisters, watched the small gas flames flare to life, something that always made him feel at home. Chief announced it would be chili and rice for dinner. As long as there was ketchup, Jack was good to go. He put a small pail of water on for coffee.

They sat in a row on a fallen log eating their chili and drinking their instant coffee as it slowly turned pitch black around them. Duke picked up his headlight, adjusted its stretchy band, and slipped it over his head. "That's better. I wouldn't want to miss any of this fine gourmet chili."

They laughed, slipped on their own headlights.

Chief took a final drink of his black coffee, shuddered. "Too bad there isn't a Starbucks around. It's only out of politeness I call this coffee." He shook out his camp cup. "Tell us about where we're headed tomorrow, Duke."

Duke said quietly, as if he didn't want to alarm any critters nearby hunkered down for the night, "As you know, the Daniel Boone National Forest stretches nearly to Ohio. There are hundreds of caves, dozens of lakes and mountains, waterfalls, gorges, creeks like this one, and hundreds of miles of trails. We have private property, owner-operated farms, private houses, roads, large campgrounds, open fields.

"What's most important is that we get thousands of bikers and campers on any given day in high summer and that plays to our advantage. We'll stay away from those main trails since we know they'll want to avoid people. If we find tracks, we'll know who it is. Still, it's too bad we don't have anything that belongs to Manta Ray or I'd have Milo's hound dog, Cody, out here to track them for us."

Cam said, "Not to worry, Duke, we have our own human hound dog. Jack's as good as Cody, right, Jack?"

Jack grinned at her, his headlight making his face glow like a lit-up pumpkin. "Give me the sun and a footprint and I'm good to go."

"Remember, folks, all this is my best guess."

Chief shook his empty camp cup at him. "Come on, Duke, you've been all over this forest for years. Your best guess is as good as gold. Where do you think they're headed?"

Duke took a last sip of his coffee and wiped out his camp cup. He pulled a butt-curved map out of his pocket, unfolded it, and laid it down by the light of the stoves. "I'll call the two people with Manta Ray his keepers. Let's say the keepers are experienced hikers, but we know Manta Ray isn't, he's a city boy from what you've told me, and that makes him the weak link. Whoever busted him out doesn't want him breaking his neck. So I've ruled out these two wilderness areas, here and here—they'd have to cross a couple of gorges, both rough and dangerous. That's how I came up with following this creek below us, Hellard Branch, to avoid the ridge where there's too much chance of being seen. I'm hoping we can pick up their trail somewhere between here and Highway 490."

They followed his finger on the map. "They'll have to cross Winding Blade Road, then back into scrubby terrain before they reach the thicker tree cover of Denny Branch. It's about four miles from our location."

Jack said, "Manta Ray's definitely out of his element. He grew up on the streets of Belfast, came to the U.S., and made his living on the streets of New York.

Let's hope it's a big problem for them." He adjusted his headlight and rose.

Cam said, "You headed out somewhere, Jack?"

"I'm going to circle around for a while, make sure they're nowhere near here. One thing I learned in Afghanistan was never underestimate the enemy."

18

DANIEL BOONE NATIONAL FOREST
MONDAY NIGHT

"It's dark as a snake pit. All I want is a freaking fire."

Elena's headlight flashed in Manta Ray's direction. "I told you, no fires. The last thing we need is for some ranger to follow his nose and pay us a visit, demand to know who we are and why we're stupid enough to build a fire in a non-designated area. Eat your mac and cheese, Liam."

Manta Ray's headlamp jiggered her way. "Then we'd stick a knife in his gullet, so who cares?" He paused, cocked his head. "Liam? Only cops call me Liam since I hit the States years ago. Why'd you call me Liam?"

Because Manta Ray is too stupid to say out loud. I'm sparing myself. Elena took a bite of the instant mac and cheese Jacobson had picked out for their dinner. It wasn't all that good, but on the other hand, it wasn't supposed to be. She wanted to tell him to stop whining, but remembered Sergei telling her the night before exactly how to treat Manta Ray, as he lay next to her in the darkened bedroom, his hand running lightly over her hip.

Keep him safe, but tell him as little as possible. Don't

get in his face, moy golub, *unless you've got no choice about it. He's smart and he's a ruthless killer. It's our great good luck his partner screwed up that bank robbery. Leave him to me; I'll deal with him.*

She hadn't seen any sign of his smarts yet or his ruthlessness, and for a moment she doubted Sergei when he'd told her not to bother to try to break Manta Ray for the information, but then she'd looked into the Irishman's eyes and seen nothing but a fathomless void. But maybe she could get him to let slip where he'd stashed the small locked metal box he'd taken from Cortina Alvarez's safe-deposit box at the bank. After all, hadn't Elena's mother always told her she had a silver tongue because she could talk anybody into anything, even as a little girl? Elena shook her head. She hadn't thought of her mother in years, not since she'd died with an empty vodka bottle clutched in her skinny hands in her dirty little Moscow apartment.

She looked over at Jacobson. She would have to keep him from trying to beat the crap out of Liam to find out about the metal box, or if Liam chanced to make a break for it. She didn't think he would. He had to know their job was to keep him safe and take good care of him. Jacobson was throwing pebbles into the underbrush. Hadn't he noticed the Irishman's eyes? No, he hadn't noticed, he hardly noticed anything unless he was going to kill it.

She realized Liam was looking at her, and he asked again, "Why'd you call me Liam?"

She dredged up a smile, locked in an admiring look.

"I think Liam has gravitas, better fits a man who hit up a bank in broad daylight." *Give him respect, that's what he wants.* "I'll call you Manta Ray, if that's what you'd like."

"Gravitas? I like that, Elena. Makes me sound important. Liam'll be nice for a while, sure, go ahead."

His Irish brogue had thickened and he gave her a potent smile, a smile she'd bet had nailed a lot of women. She smiled back.

If only this Irish shite didn't hold all the cards. She continued, "I think you would have gotten clean away if your partner hadn't been a moron and killed that bank teller."

Manta Ray shrugged. "Marvin wasn't that much of a moron, usually. He had this one problem: He was addicted to money. He saw it, he had to have it." He raised his camp cup and saluted the silent air. "To Marvin. Goodbye, buddy. Too bad you couldn't take it with you."

"Take what? The money?" Jacobson asked.

Manta Ray nodded, said matter-of-factly, "Marvin Cass already had lots of money, a couple of million stashed with his mum. Now she's rich. I wonder if she'd rather keep all of it or have her son back."

"From the sound of him, I bet she'd vote for the money, no question," Jacobson said. He took the last bite of his mac and cheese, swallowed. "Cass got you shot. How come you're not pissed about it?"

"He paid the highest price, poor old bugger."

Jacobson said, "I heard Cass had a habit of starting

bar fights he couldn't win, regularly got the crap beat out of him. Seems he wasn't much into self-control."

Manta Ray said, "Ah, you've heard of him then, have you? No, Marvin was a spur-of-the-moment kind of guy. In most things. But he told me he was planning a trip to Belfast and he wanted me to come with him, show him where I grew up, show him the Maze prison, where I vacationed for five years." He shrugged. "Who knows? Maybe when you're dead, you can still dream, you think? Marvin can still dream about Belfast."

Jacobson seemed to think about it, then shook his head. "Nah, dead is dead and that means you're nothing anymore."

Elena wanted to tell them they were both idiots, but she said, "Cass is dead, but you're not, Liam; you were tough enough to survive, but we do owe him." She raised her coffee cup. "To Cass. Without him none of us would be here."

Manta Ray saluted her with his empty coffee cup, gave her another drop-dead-gorgeous smile. "Right you are. It's one of life's lessons—you do what you've gotta do."

She heard a snort from Jacobson, shot him a look. He was ready to stick his oar in, the ignorant fool. He stared at Manta Ray, flexed his big hands. "It's a lesson I know well," he said, "so don't think I'm not going to teach it to you all over again if you give me a reason."

Manta Ray grinned at him. "I don't take well to threats, mate, never have. Last time somebody tried to teach me what to do was in the Maze. They had to wash his brain matter off the wall next to my cell."

"Shut up, Jacobson, you're not in charge here." *Do you think you're going to scare him after he survived five years in that hellhole in Belfast?*

Manta Ray looked between the two of them, the muscle and the brain. It amused him to let Elena believe she was in charge. He saw she was watching him now, to see if he'd say more, respond in some way, maybe snap Jacobson's neck for her? He was good at reading people, knew she was looking for an angle, a way to get him to open up to her. Jacobson was as easy to read as a child's book, a tool that could kill without hesitation and with some skill, nothing more. But Elena was still a mystery. He appreciated their breaking him out of that marshals' van, but he knew he had to be careful while in the control of people he knew nothing about. Torture wasn't their plan, or Jacobson would have been at him already. Here was Elena, actually trying to gain his trust, and wasn't that a good laugh? Why not let her try, use her to find out what he could? When they were finally out of this godforsaken wilderness, then he'd do what he wanted with her.

He stayed quiet, drawing Celtic letters with his finger in the dirt. He accepted a second helping of mac and cheese from Elena. It was bad, as bad as the prison food he'd eaten for the past month in Richmond, but he shoveled it down. When he was finished, he decided it was time to feed the animals. He smiled at Jacobson and Elena. "You guys did good, getting me away from the marshals this morning. Really good."

"I planned it," Jacobson said. "I'm thinking you could return the favor, tell us where you hid the crap you took out of that safe-deposit box."

Elena wanted to pull out her Beretta and shoot Jacobson in the mouth. The buffoon wanted to take the lead? Did he honestly believe Manta Ray would give up the information that was keeping him alive because he asked him to? She said, "The boss was impressed you didn't tell the FBI where you'd hidden the stuff, very impressed."

"Relieved, more like, whoever your boss is." Manta Ray shrugged. "The FBI were never a threat; they can't break free of their own stupid laws and rules." He spread his arms wide. "I love America." Once again, the killer smile. "Anyway, it was a good job, mates. If you want to make this a lovefest, why don't you tell me what the plan is? So we picked up all this camping stuff waiting for us in a car boot just outside the forest and now we've hiked to a nice spot by a creek. Are we going to see the boss tomorrow?"

Elena said, "No, not tomorrow. Consider this a camping and hiking vacation. All you need to know is that we'll keep you safe from the FBI."

"So we're marking time in the forest until the heat is off? Not a bad plan. How long?"

"I'll let you know," Elena said.

Manta Ray hadn't expected she'd tell him any more.

He said nothing, took off his boot and his thick sock, and aimed his headlight at his foot.

Elena frowned, leaned toward him. "What are you doing?"

"My heel hurts."

Jacobson was emptying a small bag of peanuts into his mouth. "What do you mean it hurts?"

"It's red, and it hurts to touch it. I'm getting a blister. Why didn't you get the right size boot?"

"It is the right size," Elena said. "But you never can be sure about a fit unless you try the boots on and walk around in them for a while. Jacobson, give him the first-aid kit."

Jacobson gave her a look but got the first-aid kit out of his backpack, tossed it to Manta Ray. Elena watched Manta Ray gingerly rub Neosporin on his heel, press some gauze over the blister, and wrap an Ace bandage over and around his foot to hold it in place.

It was all she needed, an infected blister. She'd intended to keep their pace slow, no reason not to, since they were trying to kill time anyway. He was looking at his foot, turning it this way and that. She couldn't believe it, but even his feet were beautiful, like Michelangelo's *David*. She remembered the first time she'd seen Liam's photo, remembered her hormones had come to attention. He was a looker, no doubt about it. She bet he had phenomenal success with women.

She gave Liam a bright smile. "It's been a long day. Your heel will be better in the morning. Get some rest."

He started to open his mouth but decided against

it. He eyed the sleeping bag. No way did he want to zip himself into that skinny confining coffin. No, he wanted to stretch out and fall asleep by a nice cozy fire. He ended up lying on top of the sleeping bag. He watched Elena pull off her boots, crawl into the sleeping bag. He went over in his mind how he would deal with the boss. He knew he was the golden goose. If the boss forgot that, he was the biggest fool alive.

The air was still and warm. Jacobson was snoring. Manta Ray closed his eyes and remembered himself as a young man of eighteen, at home in the underbelly of Belfast, and for a moment felt the glow of exhilaration. And the winning, he'd loved the winning, and seeing the faces of those who knew he'd bested them, even if he had to beat or bludgeon a few to make them understand. And of course the money. His mum had complained about where it came from but she took it anyway. Then he was nabbed after beating a stupid copper and sent to the Maze prison, where real hunger was only a small part of the endless misery. *Liam Ryan Hennessey, you are hereby sentenced to five years imprisonment at the Maze prison, commencing immediately.*

He could still hear the gavel bang down, hear his mum weeping.

19

Kara Moody had no more tears, not even anger toward the people who'd let that woman steal Alex. It hadn't helped trying to fan her rage at the hospital, against fate, against God, against anyone she could think to blame. She found herself floating in a kind of blackness, with nothing to hold on to. Every few minutes a nurse came in to sit with her, repeating endlessly how the FBI would bring Alex back, and she pretended to listen, nodding her head occasionally. But deep down, she wondered if she would slowly dissolve into that blackness and let it carry her away. She stared across her room at the empty bassinet, Alex's bassinet. Dr. Janice had been there, sitting with her, staying close, saying little. Of course everyone knew Alex had been kidnapped, because of the Amber Alert, and Dr. Janice had fielded calls for her.

It was late, but she couldn't sleep, didn't want to sleep really, so finally she got out of bed, pulled on the ancient pink robe Dr. Janice had brought her from home, slid her feet into her old tatty rabbit slippers, and slipped out of her room. The hallway was empty, the nurses' station thirty feet away. She saw a maternity ward guard, not the same one who'd let them take Alex, but another, younger man who looked bored. She waited until he went to the break room and slipped down the stairs to the third floor.

When she stepped onto the floor, she realized she didn't know what room John Doe was in. Then she saw a policeman down the hall, his seat tilted back against the wall, a magazine in his hand. She watched him awhile, decided he wasn't going to go relieve himself anytime soon, and walked up to him. He saw her coming from the corner of his eye and became immediately alert, his hand going to the gun at his waist.

"Officer, I'm Kara Moody. I'm the woman the man in there tried to save." *I'm also the new mother whose baby was stolen.* She couldn't say those words aloud, couldn't get them to even form in her mouth. "I'm sorry, but I don't know his name."

Officer Ted Rickman, night shift, said, "No one does. They're calling him John Doe." He eyed her up and down. "What are you doing here, Ms. Moody? It's after midnight."

"I know he's unconscious, but I need to see him. However crazy he seemed, he believed he was saving me and my baby from something. May I see him?"

Rickman saw the empty shock in her eyes. He couldn't begin to imagine what she was feeling. He knew there was no husband in the picture, knew this young woman was alone and here she'd had her baby stolen right out of the hospital. Rickman slowly rose and walked through the door. He nodded, pointed to the unmoving man on the narrow hospital bed. A dim light shone from a single lamp. Kara stared at him, whispered, "He's not moving."

"No, he's not. He's in a coma." Officer Rickman thought of his own two small children, remembered the joy at their births, couldn't imagine what he'd do if something had happened to them. Rickman's cell rang. "Excuse me."

Kara walked slowly to the bed and stared down at John Doe, the man she'd believed was crazy, who wanted to take her away to protect her. But from what? From whom? Whoever it was, he'd cared enough about her and her baby to risk his life for them. She saw Officer Rickman still on his cell, standing in the doorway, watching her as he listened. Did he think she'd lost it? She didn't care. She pulled up a chair, sat down beside John Doe, and studied his young face. There was still a bandage around his head, and his beard scruff had grown. Odd, but he looked somehow familiar to her now, but how could that be? He was breathing normally, evenly, looking peacefully asleep. When he'd forced his way into her house and tied her to the chair, she'd seen only a terrifying monster, not this motionless, slight young man who couldn't be more than twenty-five.

Kara lightly touched her fingers to his cheek. His skin was warm through the stubble. She couldn't remember the color of his eyes. Blue, maybe?

She stroked his hand and said quietly, "I've heard that people in a coma can hear people talking to them. Do you hear me? Do you know who I am? I wish I could remember exactly what you said, but so much of it didn't make sense to me, and I was so scared."

She sat silently, stroking his hand, studying his face, a handsome face, really. She let it come pouring out of her, how she'd been in labor even at the house and about her beautiful boy she'd named Alex, after her father. She told him about her father, what he'd been like and how much she missed him. Kara felt tears running down her cheeks, hadn't even realized it until she tasted salt. She swiped the tears away with her fist. "I'm sorry about crying, but Alex is gone. Someone stole him. He's just gone. Was it the people you were trying to protect me from? You've got to wake up and help me. I don't know what to do. I wish I knew your name at least. Won't you wake up and tell me?"

There was no movement, no sound except his slow, even breathing. She swiped her eyes again and began to lightly rub her fingers over his cheek. She talked about music, her art, how she'd painted a field of wild flowers during a rainstorm, about what she was planning when she and Alex were together again. She talked until finally, she laid her head against his shoulder and fell asleep.

She was standing in the middle of the field she'd painted, the rain cascading down over her, the only sound that of the raindrops splattering against her and hitting the earth. Then there was a sound rain wouldn't make, but there it was—something niggled at her consciousness, something that wasn't quite right. She blinked away sleep and slowly raised her head toward the door. It was closed. Nice of Officer Rickman to give her so much privacy. She heard footsteps and then the door slowly opened. He was coming to check on them. She relaxed, laid her face back down on John Doe's shoulder.

Officer Rickman didn't say anything, so she slitted her eyes open and saw a man she didn't recognize, slim and military fit, easing his way into the room. He was wearing surgical scrubs and a mask over his face. At the sound of his footsteps, Kara realized he was wearing loafers, not the soft-soled shoes the nurses wore. He held a syringe in his hand.

This man wasn't here to help her; he was the enemy.

He was looking at her, frowning, and she quickly closed her eyes, heart pounding, readying herself. She heard him walking toward the bed, slitted her eyes again, and saw him raise his hand to inject something into the IV tubing tethered to John Doe's wrist.

Kara jumped straight up, grabbed the pitcher off the bedside table, and hurled it across the bed at him, yelling at the top of her lungs. An arc of water splashed on the man, and the pitcher hit him square in the chest. He leaped back, cursing, but came at her. She reared back and smashed her fist into his chest, sending him reeling off-balance, and the syringe went flying. She grabbed a chair and kept yelling, screaming, until finally he cursed and ran from the room.

When Savich and Sherlock burst into John Doe's room fifteen minutes later, Kara was still holding him pressed against her. Two nurses, an orderly, and two security guards were trying to reassure her the danger was over, that she could let him go, but she was refusing, repeating over and over he wasn't safe, until she saw Sherlock.

Sherlock made her way through the crowd, held out her hand to Kara, and gently pulled her away. She held her close, whispered, "It's all right now, it's over." She eased her back. "Tell me what happened, Kara."

Kara drew a steadying breath. "A man came into the room dressed like a doctor or a nurse. Sherlock, he was holding a syringe in his hand and he was going to inject something in his IV line. I knew he was going to kill him. Officer Rickman never came. Where was he?"

An excellent question. Sherlock cupped Kara's shocked white face between her hands, kept her voice calm, matter-of-fact. "But you stopped him, Kara. You saved him, all by yourself. You are very brave. When John Doe wakes up, I'll tell him all about how you saved his life."

Sherlock saw Dillon on the phone and looked around for the Metro night guard, Rickman. She asked the night nursing supervisor checking John Doe's vitals, "Have you seen the police officer assigned to guard John Doe?"

Nurse Ellerby cocked her head. "I don't understand. You didn't know? He got a phone call an hour ago, said he was told to go home, that he was off duty because John Doe was an FBI case now. He stopped by the desk to tell us Ms. Moody was with John Doe."

Savich came over to Sherlock and Nurse Ellerby. He knew who had called off the guard. He felt such rage at Mayer it was a good thing for Mayer that he wasn't there. He'd bet Mayer had been watching baseball, drinking a beer, when he'd decided this was how he'd get back at Savich, not a thought in his head about John Doe's safety.

Of course Mayer hadn't called Savich, but he had to know he could be in real trouble if he didn't make any effort to contact him. Savich scrolled quickly through his emails. Sure enough, there was a late email to him from the CAU secretary, Shirley, informing him Detective Mayer from Metro had awakened her, told her she needed to let Savich know that since John Doe was an FBI case now, he was pulling the Metro officer off guard duty.

Savich was still so angry, his hand was shaking as he punched in Jimmy Maitland's number. It was nearly two o'clock in the morning. Maitland answered on the third ring, sounding like a bear pulled out of hibernation. "What's the matter?"

Savich told him what Mayer had pulled, and what had happened, which brought Maitland straight out of bed. Maitland's anger was legendary, and Savich found it calmed him knowing his boss would see Mayer got what he deserved. Should he suggest that a firing squad sounded good? If not a firing squad, then a solid street fight, nothing off-limits. Maitland asked for more details, then said, "I'll have two agents guarding John Doe around the clock, beginning now."

He looked up to see Kara and Sherlock standing over John Doe, Kara holding his limp hand. He heard her say, "He's so very quiet." She looked over at Savich. "When that man came in I saw he wasn't wearing rubber-soled shoes and knew something was very wrong. And that the police officer was gone."

Sherlock hugged Kara to her side. "Believe me, that won't happen again."

Sherlock saw Dillon slowly nod. She saw the pulse pounding in his throat, knew something bad had happened that had made him really angry. It had to do with the missing guard.

20

DANIEL BOONE NATIONAL FOREST
EARLY TUESDAY MORNING

Cam heard a noise, only a slight rustling sound, and instantly awoke, her Glock in her hand. She looked through the netting of her bivvy sack into the darkness and made out a man's shadowed face inches from her nose. She almost screamed.

"Morning, Special Agent, it's me, Jack. Time to rise and shine."

She wanted to clock him for scaring her. "I could have shot you, idiot." She couldn't see his expression in the dark, he'd turned away to wake up Chief and Duke. There was an urgency, a near crackling of energy in him, and she felt herself responding to it. Jack turned on his headlight. "I've checked; there's no one nearby," he said. "Safe to use these now. There'll be enough light in about fifteen minutes to look for their tracks."

After an oatmeal and coffee breakfast and a quick wash in the cold creek, they moved out along Denny Branch, slowing now and then to walk upslope in search of tracks. Even close to the creek, where they believed Manta Ray's group should have passed, they had to slow enough to study the terrain for any sign of another human's passing. They finished off their breakfasts with power bars and drank from their canteens as the temperature slowly climbed under a brilliant morning sun. They saw deer, a fox, and three squirrels staring down on them from a dogwood branch, but no tracks.

At eight o'clock straight up, Jack peeled off one more time away from the creek and upslope into the trees. He saw a set of boot prints and a crushed shrub. He felt a surge of excitement, called out, "Come look."

They gathered around Jack, saw the boot prints heading east. "They've been walking up here, parallel to the creek."

"I wasn't expecting that," Duke said. "Still, I guess it makes sense. It's an easier route, with enough cover to reduce the chance of being seen. You're right, Jack, they're going east, up toward the ridge. I hope they don't hook up with a hiker trail. What made you come this far up, Jack?"

Jack never looked up from the tracks. "We should have seen their tracks by now if they'd been hiking along the creek." He shaded his eyes, looked upward. "I can't see them going all the way up to the ridge, though, unless they have to for some reason we don't know." He pointed. "See how one set of prints is weighted on the right foot. I think Manta Ray is limping in those new hiking boots. The other two tracks show an even stride, and they're taking their time." Jack looked over at Cam, grinned. "We're going to catch them."

Duke had walked ahead, studying the tracks. "My

guess is they passed here before dark last night. They
had to come down close to the creek to get a quicker
crossing over to Indian Creek Road—that's Highway
490. They'll have wanted to get over it as close to dark
as possible, less chance of being seen. Once they got
past there, they'd be in less-populated country, and
that's where they'll have stopped for the night." Duke
rose, wiped his hands on his pants. "If we hurry it up,
we'll get to Highway 490 in about fifteen minutes."

"Let's make it ten," Jack said. "From here it'll be easy
to keep the tracks in sight." He took the lead, jogging at
a smooth, steady pace.

Ten minutes later, they reached Rockcastle River,
and once across, they reached Highway 490. They
saw one car cruise by but no one else, no campers,
no hikers, only a lone doe leading her fawn across the
road.

Jack pulled out the sat phone, handed it to Duke.
"Time to contact your rangers, tell them we've tracked
them to the highway and we'll be picking up their
trail on the other side. Chief, go ahead and check in
with your deputies, tell them we're going to be moving north from the highway. They need to focus their
patrols on the roads they can get to north of here."

After Chief and Duke took turns with the sat
phone, they crossed the highway to find the trail again.
It was the same kind of terrain, shrubby, with sparse
trees, an occasional maple thicket. They walked along
the creek, where the trees and vegetation grew thicker.
Still no tracks.

Cam realized she'd stopped hearing any birds or small animals, only the rustling wind in the trees. It was as if they sensed something dangerous in their midst and were lying low.

Suddenly Jack held up his fist, stopped, went down on his haunches. Cam crouched down beside him. Duke nearly ran into her. "What? What is it?"

"Something's not right. Breathe in the air."

He was right. Cam breathed in deeply and smelled something dark and rancid that grabbed her by the throat. She whispered, "It's blood."

Duke pointed. "Over there, under that scrub oak."

They found a young man, lying on his back, covered with oak leaves and a couple of stray small leafy branches. They knew he was dead before they pushed the leaves off his gray slack face.

"He's not more than twenty," Chief said. Out of habit, he touched his fingers to the pulse in the boy's neck. There was nothing. He crossed himself, said a prayer.

Cam picked up broken sunglasses that lay near his curled left hand. She said, "They stabbed him in the heart and covered him with leaves."

Jack said, "And left him to be scavenged by animals. Didn't want to take the time to bury him."

Duke found his wallet in his back pocket. "James Delinsky, twenty-one, from Richmond, Virginia. His student ID's from Virginia Tech."

Cam leaned down and closed his lids. "I'm sorry, James," she whispered. "I'm so very sorry."

Chief was already back on his sat phone. He handed it to Duke to describe the exact location. They were near enough to the highway for his deputies to come in on foot. There would be no sirens, no helicopter for Manta Ray's group to hear.

Chief handed Jack the sat phone. "This really is sick, pisses me off. No reason to kill anyone; he was just a kid."

Cam looked up at Jack. He was staring down at the young man. Jack's face was expressionless, but she knew he was deeply angry. If Manta Ray had appeared at that moment, she wondered if Jack would kill him without hesitation. She wondered what she would do.

"Wrong place, wrong time," Chief said. "My nephew, Billy, is about his age, loves to hike around here. It could have been him." He added, "Standard procedure is to stay with him until our people arrive, but not this time. The best thing we can do for this young man is to find his killers." He pulled out his sleeping bag and laid it over James Delinsky. He placed rocks on the sleeping bag to keep the animals away.

Chief was frowning. "Too bad we can't plan on killing Manta Ray. I'd sure like to save the taxpayers some money."

Cam said, "Sorry to say but this is bigger than Manta Ray, Chief. We need to find out who's behind Manta Ray and get them all."

They pressed on toward the northwest, crossed Park Cemetery Road up into Horse Lick Creek. There were tracks there, where the group had stopped to fill their canteens. Duke said, "Look. Manta Ray is really limping now. He took off his left boot, waded in the water to cut the pain. I don't think they'll be able to stay in this rough terrain for much longer. They'll have to move back up over the hills—it's the easiest way north."

Duke took off his sunglasses and looked east, then spread his map on the ground. "Here we are. I think they'll cut off where the creek bends here and climb up over Bethel Ridge to avoid the main road. That'll eventually get them to Gravel Lick Creek. It's tough going at first, but then it eases up."

They moved quickly toward the ridge, over terrain that was rough and steep at first. Boulders and rock faces bordered crevices and deep gullies gouged out as if by a giant's hand. The rising heat sapped their energy. Cam wondered if Jack was part mountain goat as she struggled to keep up, sometimes jogging, sometimes crawling, aware only of her own hard breathing and the crunch of her boots on the rocky ground.

Jack gave a low whistle and gathered them around a set of Manta Ray's erratic tracks, showed them where he had stopped and sat down, forcing the other two to wait for him.

"We're gaining on them every minute," Jack said. "We'll see if we can spot them from the top of Bethel Ridge. What's beyond the ridge, Duke?"

Duke said quietly, "The small town of Sandy Gap, and an elementary school."

21

Sherlock and CARD agent Connie Butler made good time to Baltimore through the heavy traffic. Connie zipped her bright red Mini Cooper into an upper-middle-class neighborhood in the Mount Clare section and parked across the street from a Victorian town house painted white with green trim, its blue window boxes filled with red and white petunias. Sherlock had spent the driving time filling Connie in on everything they knew about John Doe's break-in at Kara's house on Sunday and the attempt on his life the night before.

Connie Butler cut the engine and turned to Sherlock, smiling. "And here you are ready to go again on about three hours' sleep."

On cue, Sherlock yawned. She pulled a small thermos out of her briefcase, took a long drink of Dillon's rich black special brew, and basked in the feel of the caffeine zinging through her bloodstream. "That'll pick me right up. I'm fine. Tell me, what's your bet about what we're going to find here?"

Connie said, "Sorry, Sherlock, it's possible Sylvie Vaughn knows something about Alex's kidnapping. I know you're convinced John Doe is also connected, but I've got to tell you I'm not ready to make that leap even though someone tried to kill him last night. One thing I find strange is that Kara was in his room at all, given she claims she never saw him before he broke into her house on Sunday. Do you know what that's all about?"

Sherlock knew Connie was a twenty-five-year FBI veteran, five of them with the CARD team. She'd seen most of everything, Sherlock imagined, and yet she was having trouble getting her mind around how much more this case was than a simple kidnapping. Many of the pieces seemed unrelated, Sherlock would be the first to admit that, but to her, they would eventually all tie together. She just didn't know exactly how yet. She said slowly, "I think Kara feels some kinship to him since Alex was taken. It's a pity John Doe wasn't coherent enough to tell her what kind of danger they were in. I've never believed in coincidences, Connie, and our situation is loaded with them. My gut is shouting that Sylvie Vaughn isn't as innocent as Kara believes she is about what happened to her nine months ago. Will you play that idea out with me in there?"

"Of course. Look, if it turns out Sylvie Vaughn is involved in any of this, she wasn't ever Kara's friend and she deserves whatever comes. You want to take the lead, or should I?"

Agent Connie Butler looked like a grandmother, her gray hair cut short, no muss, no fuss, no makeup on her pretty face, ready to pass out homemade cookies to the neighborhood kids. Sherlock grinned at her. "Why don't I start and you can jump in."

Connie unfastened her seat belt. "Fair enough. There's a Jaguar parked in the driveway. Kara told you Vaughn works from home, right?"

"Yes, and that's her car. Sylvie Vaughn writes a Monday/Thursday women's fashion blog—what women should wear to make them look good given their budget, fashion tips, makeup, the right hairstyle, you get the idea. She does a once-weekly YouTube production. Kara says she never appears on-screen; she's the voice in the background. She brings on women of all ages and body types to model clothes she's selected for them that make the most of their assets. She's big on emphasizing everyone's assets. She gives advice depending on their age and the impression they want to make, and so on. Kara says she's very popular."

Connie said, "Now *that* I knew. Kara told Bolt Haller and me about her show at the hospital. It's called *Cycling Madness*—I know, weird name, like those book titles that have nothing to do with what's inside the covers. I watched a couple of the shows on YouTube yesterday. She's good, Sherlock; she's been on for a couple of years now and still growing."

"I should have done that myself," Sherlock said, and nodded toward the door. "Kara said Josh, the husband, drives a BMW and works for an investment firm, Ely and Briggs. Did Kara tell you she'd met Vaughn by chance when she came to a showing of Kara's painting at the gallery where she worked in downtown Balti-more? That they became best friends very quickly?"

"Yes, she mentioned it. Are you thinking Sylvie Vaughn had a motive, that she made friends with Kara on purpose?"

"Maybe. I don't know. But I do know Kara didn't accidently get pregnant at her party. Let's go see what she has to say." As Sherlock clicked open her seat belt and opened the car door, Connie's cell rang. Sherlock turned to see her looking at the screen. "Gotta take this. Go ahead, Sherlock, I'll be right after you."

Sherlock expected Sylvie Vaughn to be a walking advertisement of good taste and appropriate fit and style, in short, to have made spectacular use of her assets. Instead, a very tall, stick-thin woman, in her midthirties, opened the door, dressed in capri black tights and a short stretchy black top that showed every muscle and bone. She wore her straight dark hair parted on the side and falling lank on either side of her long face to her shoulders, and glasses too big for her thin face. Sherlock blinked, smiled, and introduced herself. "Sylvie Vaughn?"

"Yes." She looked down at a thin wrist sporting both a black Fitbit and a black iWatch. "I'm working. It's very early. I'm sorry, but who are you and what do you want?"

Sherlock introduced herself, handed Sylvie Vaughn her creds.

She raised a black eyebrow. "FBI? What is this? I don't understand—oh, you probably want to speak to my husband, Josh. He's not here. He's at work, an invest-ment firm, no doubt fast-talking a hapless client into buying God only knows what. Did he get himself into trouble?" She sighed. "All right, come in and tell me what my lamebrain husband has done."

Sherlock looked back to see Butler still speaking into her cell, her tablet in one hand, writing as she lis-tened. "My partner will be along shortly."

Sylvie stepped back, waved her in. "I'm in dire need of coffee. I'll get you a cup, too." Sylvie Vaughn waved a hand around the living room. "Don't mind the mess, the housekeeper is coming this morning, bless her well-paid heart. I didn't even make up the bed, not that I ever do, such a waste of time."

Sherlock stepped into a white world filled with dark blue furnishings, from dark blue draperies to dark blue scatter rugs on the floor. Clothing, underwear, shoes—from sandals to six-inch ankle breakers—covered every surface. Dozens of magazines were piled up next to a dark blue easy chair with several, hope-fully empty mugs piled on top.

She smiled at Sylvie. "I love housekeepers."

Sherlock watched her shove away sample fabrics stacked on a dark blue leather chair, frown, and rub her finger over a damp-looking stain on its arm. "Have a seat. I'll get us some coffee, and you can tell me how much I'm going to have to put out on a lawyer this time. Please tell me he didn't kill anyone."

"Not that I know of," Sherlock said, and watched Sylvie stride out of the living room. Sherlock waited where she was, getting a feel for the place. She wondered what Josh the fast-talking husband thought about this room. Not a minute later, Sylvie returned carrying two mugs. Before she could hand over one, Sherlock pulled out her cell, called up John Doe's photo. "Do you recognize this man?"

22

Sylvie looked closely at the photo. "He looks like he's asleep. Please don't tell me he's dead."

"No, he's not dead. Do you know him?"

"No, I've never seen him before. Why? Who is he?"

"He couldn't be a friend of your husband's? Perhaps one of the neighbors?"

"No, or I'd have seen him." She thrust the mug at Sherlock. "I hope you didn't want milk or sugar. I'm out of both." She looked around the large living room with a dispassionate eye. "You're lucky I work in the back, otherwise there wouldn't be anyplace to sit. Now, what do you think Josh has done?"

Sherlock took a drink of the coffee, so strong she wondered if she'd sprout hair on her chest. It was delicious. She toasted Sylvie with her mug. "Thank you. I'm not here about your husband. I'm here about Kara Moody, one of your best friends, I believe. She moved to Washington, D.C. five months ago?"

Sylvie sat forward. "Is Kara all right? I haven't spoken to her in ages. We email, sure, but only short, weekly updates on what we've been doing. Is something wrong?"

"Kara had her baby, Alex, on Sunday."

Sylvie sat forward, smiling hugely. "Good for her. I wondered why I hadn't heard from her. Alex is healthy? Beautiful? Kara is, so I imagine he's adorable."

"Yes, he is. I understand you met Kara at the gallery where she worked, that you became close friends very quickly."

Sylvie beamed. "And isn't that great? Never happened to me like that before. But Kara—she was special, and I saw it right away. You know what else? She has a great sense of style, and a nice figure. I was always trying to get her on *Cycling Madness*, my YouTube show, to model clothes for me. I knew she'd look great in whatever I put her in, but she wouldn't."

Sherlock said, "Yes, she is lovely. Do you remember why you were in that particular gallery that day, Ms. Vaughn? The day you met Kara for the first time?"

Sylvie watched a pile of magazines slide off the arm of the sofa and land on top of some underwear. Then she smiled. "Oh, I remember now. I wanted to buy a painting for my mother."

"She liked a particular painting at that gallery?"

"I don't remember, to be honest. After I met Kara, I forgot about my mom's painting. Can you please explain to me why you're here and asking me these questions about Kara?"

"Actually, Ms. Vaughn, I'm here to ask you what you

know about Kara getting drugged at your house nine months ago at your husband's birthday party."

Sylvie's thin shoulders went board straight, but she didn't say anything, only looked down into her coffee mug as if the coffee would give her an answer. Slowly she looked back up at Sherlock. "Kara didn't tell me until she was nearly five months along that she was pregnant and what she thought had happened to her at my party.

"I didn't want to believe it until I remembered that some of the men there were friends of my husband's, and I didn't know them. So I started thinking about which of those guys drinking too much and shoveling down my excellent hors d'oeuvres would stoop that low, but, honestly? I couldn't think of anyone. I asked Josh and he acted all macho until I punched him and told him I was serious. He said sure, most of the guys were horndogs, but none of them were into roofies. I believed him.

"I'm pretty good about inviting couples—I like the balance—but it was my husband's thirty-fifth birthday, and as I said, he had some of his own friends here. A couple were single, a couple divorced and on the make, if you know what I mean. There was lots of booze and dancing and general drunkenness; that's how Josh likes his parties. We don't have problems with the neighbors calling the cops because I always invite them, too, and they're all couples, probably drink more than the other guests.

"Look, there were so many people in and out, having a good time, I couldn't keep track of everyone. Mostly I spent my time with the women, giving them free advice on what they should wear to Great-Aunt Maud's funeral or to a college commencement for nephew Peter. It was a very long night. I remember not seeing Kara after ten o'clock, figured since she wasn't a big drinker and she hadn't liked any of Josh's friends, she'd gone home.

"When she called me the next morning to apologize, I was surprised, I really didn't understand why. Kara rarely drank too much and so I told her not to worry about it; there were so many happy drunks weaving in and out of the house, some of them didn't leave until the booze ran out. I asked her if she was ill, a hangover, you know? But she said no, and then she hung up." Sylvie leaned down and picked a slinky white top off a solid dark blue rug. She frowned at it, tossed it toward a chair, where one sleeve hooked around the chair arm.

"So now, instead of calling me and telling me about her baby, Kara sends the FBI? She doesn't think it was my husband, does she? Sure, I saw the way he kissed her, but he was accounted for all night. I honestly don't think he could do something that despicable, and he was so drunk I had to pour him into bed at nearly three o'clock. He demanded I sing him 'Happy Birthday' again. He was snoring by the end of it."

Sherlock and Sylvie looked up to see Agent Butler standing in the open doorway to the living room.

Sherlock made the introductions, Sylvie offered coffee, which Butler refused, and told her just to toss the magazines off a rocker and take a seat.

Sherlock said, "Ms. Vaughn can't remember any man at her party nine months ago who acted at all suspicious. Correct, Ms. Vaughn?"

"That's right. I suppose you'd like me to give you a list of all the single men Josh and I can remember were here?"

"Yes, that would be fine," Sherlock said. "Here's my card with all my contact information. As soon as possible, please."

Connie handed Sylvie her card as well. "When was the last time you contacted Kara?" They watched Vaughn toss the cards on top of a bright pink vest.

"It's been a week. I told Agent Sherlock we usually emailed back and forth, kept each other up-to-date. She told me her painting was coming along really fine, and she sounded very happy and excited about the baby coming. She also said she really liked her job at the Raleigh Gallery, that the owner was going to give her a show." She paused. "Kara had her baby; his name is Alex. He's beautiful. I don't really understand why you're here."

Sherlock rose, Connie followed suit. "Ms. Vaughn, Kara's baby, Alex, was kidnapped yesterday from the maternity ward at Washington Memorial Hospital. I believe Kara's being roofied at your party may have something to do with why Alex was kidnapped."

Sherlock saw it, a flash of fear, of knowledge, in Sylvie Vaughn's eyes. It was gone so fast she wondered if she'd imagined it.

Sylvie stood, straight and thin as a post, her long arms at her sides, her hands fists. "Is that why Kara hasn't called me? You told her I could be responsible for her baby's kidnapping?" She was breathing hard. "None of this makes any sense to me." She looked down at either her Fitbit or her iWatch, tough to tell. "I'd like you to leave now. I've got deadlines. I can't imagine you have anything else insulting left to ask me."

Sherlock handed her another card. "Call me, Ms. Vaughn, if you decide to talk to us." She paused, then added, "As Kara's dear friend, it would seem to me you'd want to do everything you could to help us find Alex."

Sylvie took her card, gave Sherlock a long look, and tossed it on top of a pair of leopard-print tights. She walked on their heels to the door, closed it behind them. They heard the dead bolt snap into place.

"Pissed her off but good," Connie said. She gave Sherlock a sideways look. "Maybe she does know something."

"Yeah, she ain't no poker player."

As they walked down the stone steps from the town house to Connie's Mini Cooper across the street, Sherlock veered off, said in a loud voice, "I want to take a look at this beauty. It's a Jaguar, maybe six years old." Connie watched her lean in and look at the interior, keeping up a running commentary as she walked to the other side. A moment later, Sherlock rejoined her at the curb.

"Why don't we hang around for a while, maybe down the street a ways so she won't see the red car. Let's see if she goes anywhere."

Butler raised a brow. "I trust if she leaves she won't see the GPS tracker you put on her car."

Sherlock grinned at her. "Only another cop would have noticed. It is a nice car."

"For a second there I wondered why you were talking so loud, but then I realized it was for her benefit." Butler cranked up the car. "I'll pull over down the street, but I would guess you're not going to want to stay long. And I bet we're not going to be interviewing Josh Vaughn today after all. You're probably wondering what I was doing on the phone. I've got something to tell you you're not going to believe."

23

The devil was jabbing his pitchfork into his heel. Manta Ray didn't remember hurting this bad when he was shot in the side. Jacobson's antibiotic salve hadn't helped a bit, and the bandages made it hurt worse. Manta Ray sat on a rock between a gnarly maple tree and a mess of spiny shrubs. Jacobson and Elena stood over him.

"Your heel hurt?"

Not like Jacobson cared, the *stupid ass.* "Yeah, real bad."

"Let me take a look." Elena squatted beside him, waited until he got his sock off, thinking he was whining like a little girl until she lifted his foot onto her thigh. It looked much worse than it had that morning. It was nasty now, raw and open, probably infected. Not good. Elena called to Jacobson to give her the first-aid kit.

She dabbed on more antibiotic cream and flattened down the last three gauze bandages. He moaned a couple of times, stiffened up. She took a new white T-shirt out of his backpack, used her Ka-Bar to cut it into strips. Then she doubled two strips and stretched them like an Ace bandage around his foot and heel, tight as she could, tying it at his ankle. She gave him four aspirin, handed him his canteen. She watched him pop the aspirin, lean back against the warm rock, and close his eyes. She'd done the best she could, but she had to face it—Liam wouldn't be hiking anywhere. And that meant she and Jacobson wouldn't, either. She didn't have a problem with lying around for a while, after all, they were in no hurry.

Elena rose and looked around her. Bethel Ridge was a magnificent spot. It was a clear day and she could see miles and miles in all directions, mostly tree-covered hills and creeks winding like ribbons through the land. Farther in the distance she saw a few small white houses and horses grazing in pastures. They'd stopped under a small stand of trees for shade against the bright afternoon sun. Too bad they couldn't stay here, but Elena knew they couldn't. They'd have to make their way down to Clover Bottom Creek and camp in the trees until Liam's heel dried up. They'd be protected there, no one would see them. Boredom would be the problem, and trying to keep Jacobson under control. She'd have him make a crutch for Liam, keep him busy for a little while. She'd have to call Sergei, tell him about Manta Ray's heel being too raw for him to move much, let him know they'd have to stay put for a while rather than continuing on northward toward Interstate 64, where he'd arranged for their pickup.

Manta Ray said, "You know what I want? I want to

get back to civilization. A nice hotel, a bathtub filled with hot water instead of these pissy cold creeks, and a john with a pile of magazines, with the swimsuit issue on top. Do you think there's a hotel in that town over there? What's the name of that Podunk?"

"Sandy Gap, and there's no way we're going anywhere near that town. We're going to stay out of sight. That young hiker, well, that was a mistake. We don't want a repeat of that, or worse."

"If you guys had bought the right size boot, this never would have happened."

Elena took a deep breath for patience because what she really wanted to do was slit his throat with her Ka-Bar. "They are the right size. I told you the problems you get when you don't try on boots. You've never hiked, you have city-boy feet. We're going to go back down to the creek, where there's plenty of cover and stop there, wait for your heel to get better." She wasn't about to admit it had never occurred to her he could get a blister. She never would. Maybe someday she'd tell Sergei and they'd have a good laugh. "We'll have to stretch our supplies a bit, but we have enough."

She thought Jacobson would speak and shook her head at him. Surprisingly, he kept his mouth shut. But not for long, she knew, no, never for very long.

She rose, dusted off her pants. "Jacobson and I will help you, but you're going to have to suck it up until we get back down off this ridge. We'll give the aspirin another few minutes to kick in."

Manta Ray thought that was about right. He looked over at Jacobson leaning against a boulder, chewing on a twig, looking back at him like he was a loser. Manta Ray reminded himself to kill the stupid bully once they were out of this hellhole.

He grinned up at both of them, his saviors, his guards. He might be their prisoner, but they were his ticket to freedom and money, more than he'd originally planned on. Their boss obviously badly wanted or needed that box he'd slid into his leather case along with everything else from those safe-deposit boxes. He wished now he'd opened it so he'd know exactly what kind of money to demand, but once he'd escaped to the warehouse in Alexandria, all he had time or energy for was to see the box was safe and to stay alive.

"Elena, you said no one could be looking for us, so why move at all? Why not camp here? We got a great view. Jacobson can hike down to the creek and get us fresh water when we need it."

Patience, patience. Her mantra now. "You know the answer, Liam. Even though there's a bit of tree cover up here, someone could spot us—" The sat phone rang. Elena jumped. Their ironclad rule was no communication unless it was critical. That meant something had changed, something was wrong. The two men watched her dig the phone from her backpack and walk out of sight behind a pile of boulders.

Manta Ray said to Jacobson, "Is that your boss?" *The one I've got by the short hairs?* "I wonder what's got Elena so concerned?"

Jacobson shrugged, pulled out a power bar, and ate it in two bites.

Manta Ray watched him, the pain in his heel down to a dull throb now after the rest and the aspirin. He said, "Hey, if we stay up here you need to give me one of your knives. I could take care of the next stray hiker. You got that first guy clean, though, I'll give you that."

Jacobson puffed up a bit. "Yeah, my old man taught me how to do it right. The kid was still wondering what was happening when he was dead."

"No muss, no fuss, that's the way to do it. I just didn't like having to stand back and watch somebody else have all the fun. By the time anyone stumbles over him, there'll be nothing left but bones and a wallet."

Jacobson shrugged. "The boss didn't want anyone dead, but hey, there he was, staring at us, and you could see he was going to talk to the first ranger he saw. What could I do?"

"That was good of you to leave his wallet so they'd be able to identify him."

"Yeah, I've got the milk of human kindness running in my veins."

Elena came back, put the sat phone into her backpack. She'd heard him. "The kid wouldn't have said anything, all you had to do was use your brain and let me do the talking." *Idiot.* She'd told Sergei about the murder, though she hadn't wanted to. Deep down, she knew he'd kill Jacobson without hesitation. She knew he wouldn't do anything to her, not ever.

Jacobson said, "Was that the boss? Is there a problem?"

She ignored Jacobson, looked down at the mess of boot prints. She started to tell him to break off a branch and sweep the area, but stopped. It didn't matter. What mattered was moving out of there right away, fast.

She pulled out her map, found the easiest way to Clover Bottom Creek Road. When she knew exactly how to get there, she said, "Get yourself together, Liam. Wrap another couple of socks, your T-shirt, or your shirt, anything you can find around your foot to protect it. We've got to move. Jacobson, there's no time to make him a crutch. You're going to have to help him across the ridge and down to the road. It's not going to be easy, but we don't have a choice."

Jacobson took a step toward her. "Come on, talk. What's wrong?"

"FBI are here; they're already in the forest. They'll have a tracker with them, maybe one of the rangers. The boss says they found out where we entered the park; how, he didn't know. That means they've probably already found our tracks, since we didn't take the time to hide them. We have to move. We've got to be down to the road in"—she looked down at her watch—"three hours and it's not going to be easy to get down there if Liam can't put any weight on his heel.

"Jacobson, toss all the gear and the backpacks in that mess of shrubs over there. We won't be needing them any longer. We'll keep one weapons bag, the binoculars, and the sat phone. Get it together, we're out of here in two minutes."

Manta Ray cocked his head to one side, said in full-blown Irish, "And just how, girl, did your boss find out the FBI are after us?"

Elena stuck her favored Walther PPK into her waistband. "The boss hired people to keep an eye on the Feds and local law enforcement outside the forest. One of them probably got a ranger to tell him what was happening. But what he doesn't understand, and I don't, either, is how they knew exactly where we came in."

She looked over at Liam. He was wrapping his T-shirt, then his shirt around his heel. When he finished tying off the shirtsleeves, he stood, put a bit of weight on the foot, and nodded. "Not bad. All those bandages, my foot looks like a painting of an old guy with gout I saw in Dublin once."

Jacobson was looking at him like he'd like to kick him. He knew it was too soon to leave the forest; the manhunt outside the forest was still way too heavy.

"Jacobson, help him. We're out of here."

24

Duke picked up a bloody alcohol wipe sticking out from under a rock. "Blood's dry, but still fresh enough to smell. I'd say they've got maybe an hour on us, not more. Looks like they shoved all the bloody bandages under these rocks, didn't bother burying them." He studied the rest of the debris. "Manta Ray's heel is bad, from the looks of it, and they stopped here to treat him. And someone was hungry." He pulled a bio bag out of his pocket and put the half-dozen bloody wipes and the power bar wrapper inside, tied it off, slipped it back in his pocket.

Jack said, "I hope it's really hurting him." He went down on his haunches and studied the boot prints on the rock-strewn ground. "Looks like he's disabled. You can see they were in a big hurry to leave this spot. I'll bet the big guy had a shoulder under Manta Ray's arm, helping him. If so, that's going to slow them down. Look at those tracks, they're headed across the ridge down to where, Duke?"

"To Clover Bottom Creek. It doesn't make sense, why, all of a sudden, are they in a hurry? With Manta

Ray's bad heel, why wouldn't they stay here? There are enough trees for protection, not many people hike this way."

"But they wouldn't know that," Chief said. "Maybe it was their plan all along, cut across the ridge and head down to the creek. There's lots of cover there, a good place to stay put for a while."

Cam said, "They didn't even take the time to make Manta Ray a crutch. Why not? Even with the big dude helping him, it's going to be tough getting him across the ridge and flat-out dangerous climbing down to the creek."

Duke said, "If it were me, I'd have stayed here."

Jack scanned the area, said to himself more than anyone else, "Why wouldn't they believe they're safe here?"

Duke said, "They've got to have a sat radio. Maybe someone called, told them that young hiker they murdered was found. They'd be worried the forest would be full of dogs and law enforcement soon."

Cam turned away from an incredible limestone cliff in the distance, her head cocked to one side, and said slowly, "No, that's not it. There hasn't been time for that to get out. Their not staying here couldn't have anything to do with the hiker's murder."

Jack said, "Look at the smaller boot prints." He rose, followed them. "She's walking quickly away from the other two, going behind this boulder, and she stops. Then she turns right around and walks back. She's pacing. Why?"

Cam studied the tracks. "As Duke said, they've got to have a sat phone. I'm thinking someone called them, told them to move out, to leave the ridge fast."

Jack was frowning. "How could this someone who called them know anyone is looking for them?"

Chief said, "Duke and I both told our people, but who would they tell? Not some criminal mastermind who came around asking questions, that's for sure."

Duke nodded. "Still, this site shows us they made some big decisions up here, and it was quick. Chief, how about calling your guys, having them focus their patrols on Clover Bottom Creek Road."

"Even if they do know we're after them," Jack said, hiking up his backpack, "I think we can catch them before they get to that road."

They set out along the ridge, with incredible views in all directions, Jack in the lead. He moved quickly, but always with an eye on the tracks. The sun was brutal overhead. Soon Cam was sweating from the pace Jack set. She focused on keeping her breathing smooth and steady.

Suddenly Jack stopped, leaned down, and picked up a small piece of paper.

They gathered around him. "Look at this, one of them tore open an aspirin packet and a piece fell off."

Cam said, "So, they stopped because Manta Ray is hurting, despite the help, hurting enough for more aspirin."

Chief said, "Good, the bugger's miserable."

Duke sniffed the air, dropped his voice to a whisper.

"They've got to be close. Let's keep it as quiet as we can."

They started down the barren eastern side of the ridge strewn with rocks and gullies of all sizes, gouged out by rainwater running down into the creek drainage. Jack paused as they approached some thick scrubs halfway down the ridge. "Look, Manta Ray fell, took the big man with him. You can see the woman's gone down on her knees to help them up." He saw a mishmash of boot prints that cut away from the overgrown shrubs, toward less steep and dangerous terrain. Jack picked up their tracks quickly, saw they were moving slowly, cutting back and forth to stay on as level ground as possible, but steadily downhill.

"They stopped here again," Jack said. "Take a look."

As Chief leaned down to study the tracks, a shot rang out, clear and loud in the still air. Chief grabbed his side and dropped to his knees.

25

Savich and Sherlock found Kara Moody and Dr. Janice sitting in the crowded hospital cafeteria. When Kara saw them and waved, they saw hope leap into her eyes. Dr. Janice had a hold of Kara's hand, squeezed it. "Hello, Dillon, Sherlock. Kara and I have been having some lunch. Please join us." She paused. "Have you learned anything?"

Sherlock leaned down, hugged Kara, whispered against her cheek, "We've got some good leads, and there are things I need to tell you. Things are coming together, Kara." It wasn't too much of a stretch.

Savich took Dr. Janice's hand. "Is that bagel smeared with cream cheese?"

"Almost," Dr. Janice said. "It's nonfat, but I can almost convince myself it's the real thing. Better for old stomachs, I guess."

Dr. Janice had been a fixture in Savich's life for as long as he could remember, and she was getting up there in years, no way around that, but he didn't like being faced with that reality.

Kara scoffed. "Listen to you, Dr. Janice. I'm counting on you to be around with me to celebrate Alex's twenty-first birthday."

Dr. Janice laughed. "My dear, you can count on it. I might need Alex to carry me to the cake, but I'll be there."

Savich left Sherlock with Kara and joined the cafeteria line to fetch both of them tuna salad sandwiches. Sherlock settled back in her chair and studied Kara's face, taking stock. She was pale, her eyes red-rimmed, but with Dr. Janice's help, she was holding it together. She was wearing jeans and sneakers and a large white shirt with orange and yellow paint smears on the cuffs that Dr. Janice had brought her from home. "We went to your room on the maternity floor, and the nurse told us you'd come to the cafeteria with Dr. Janice. Kara, I hope you got some sleep after we left last night."

"One of the FBI agents escorted me back to my room, and a nurse forced a sleeping pill down my throat, so yes, I slept okay." She didn't tell Sherlock about the nightmare at dawn that jerked her out of sleep, sweating and terrified. She dredged up a grin. "I know they would have discharged me already. I heard one of the nursing supervisors talking about it. But after all that's happened I guess they want to make a show of support rather than push me out, afraid I might sue them. And the thing is, I really don't want to go home—I can't. Not yet. Not until I have Alex back." She shook her head at herself. "And there's John Doe. If he wakes up, I want to know." She picked up the half of her ham sandwich she hadn't touched, looked at it like she'd never seen it before, took a small bite.

"Sherlock, Dr. Janice and I were discussing the man who tried to kill John Doe last night. As I told Agent Haller, I can't say he's the same man in the video who helped kidnap Alex. He was wearing a surgical mask last night.

"Who are these people? Why did they try to kill John Doe? I saw his arms, Sherlock, all those needle marks. What did they do to him?"

"I told you we're going to find out, Kara. Let me tell you about our interview with Sylvie Vaughn."

Dr. Janice said, "Would you like me to leave now? This is all confidential, isn't it?"

"Please don't go," Kara said, her hand on Dr. Janice's arm. "I want you to hear everything. Please."

"You're free to stay, Dr. Janice," Sherlock said. "And free to jump in with any questions you have."

"All right, but I don't know how much good I'll be to you."

"Let's get started then. Kara, are you absolutely sure you never saw John Doe before he burst into your house on Sunday?"

"No, I already told you that. Why are you asking me again?"

"Bear with me. Think back, Kara. Is it at all possible

he was at Sylvie Vaughn's birthday party for her husband nine months ago?"

"It's possible I didn't notice him with everyone moving around from group to group. What about Sylvie? Did she recognize him?"

"When Agent Butler and I visited her this morning, she claimed she'd never seen him before."

Kara studied Sherlock's face. "But you didn't believe her?"

"Let me say she's a person of interest until proven otherwise. I'll know a lot more about Sylvie Vaughn very soon now."

"You told me not to contact her, not to tell her about Alex or his kidnapping."

"I'm glad you didn't. I wanted to be the one to tell her."

Dr. Janice said slowly, "You wanted to catch her by surprise, see her face, her body language when you told her?"

"That's right."

"And something alerted you?"

"I think so, yes."

Kara dropped the half sandwich to her paper plate and leaned toward Sherlock. "I can't believe that, really. We were so close. She was shocked, wasn't she? Really worried about me?"

"She did say that," Sherlock said. She took Kara's hand. "But Dr. Janice is right. I felt something was off; something didn't sound quite right. I'm sorry, Kara.

"Within three minutes of our leaving, she made a

call to another number in Baltimore. We'll know soon who that number belongs to. I asked her to send us a list of the guests at the birthday party nine months ago. She emailed a partial list to Agent Butler, and Agent Butler and Agent Haller are calling them.

"Agent Butler and I left a GPS tracker on the underside of her car. Wherever she goes, whoever she sees, we'll know about it. Until then, we all have a lot to do." She saw Kara looked bewildered and scared, wondering if one of her best friends had betrayed her. "Kara, could you help with that guest list? We could give you and Dr. Janice their names and photos and let you see the transcripts of their interviews. That might help us."

"Yes, of course I can do that," Kara said. Sherlock heard the new energy in her voice. "Dr. Janice, are you in?"

"I think it's a fine idea. Bring on the list." Dr. Janice raised her bottle of water in a small salute to Sherlock, knew she was helping keep Kara busy and focused outside herself.

Savich set down her tuna fish salad sandwich in front of Sherlock and handed her a bottle of water. "I heard you adding to the group looking at the partygoers."

Sherlock smiled at him, lightly nudged his shin with her booted foot. "You heard right. They're both on board."

Kara said slowly, searching Sherlock's face, "But if Sylvie did know about it, if she did set me up, then our entire friendship was a lie. It would mean she knew I was going to be drugged, maybe she knows who John

Doe is." She was shaking her head back and forth. "It's still so hard to believe. I mean, Sylvie was one of my best friends in Baltimore. Why would she do something like that?"

"All good questions. We'll have the answers soon, I promise you, Kara," Sherlock continued, matter-of-fact. "One of the theories of the case has been that the kidnapper might be Alex's father, the man who roofied you at that party. It's common enough, child abduction by a parent, especially by a parent who has no hope of custody. We know now that isn't the case."

She drew a deep breath. "I have something to tell you Kara, something that might be difficult for you, something Agent Butler found out this morning while we were interviewing Sylvie Vaughn."

Kara was staring at her, clearly puzzled. Sherlock saw her reach for Dr. Janice's hand.

"Agent Butler got a phone call from Dr. Franz Benedict, one of our DNA specialists at the FBI. You remember we'd asked him for a DNA profile of you and Alex so we would have a DNA fingerprint to verify Alex's identity when we find him. Dillon had also sent over John Doe's DNA yesterday, asked him to do a rush profile so we'd have his as well, see if we could find him in a DNA database. He happened to notice that some of the DNA markers were strangely similar, something that's highly unlikely, so he ran a paternity index. Kara, it was positive for John Doe.

"Kara, John Doe is Alex's father."

26

"Get down!" Jack yelled, and threw himself on Chief, rolled both of them behind a low outcropping of rock. More shots, bullets ricocheting around them. Cam heard a bullet smash a rock not two inches from her head. Her heart kicked into her throat as she dove behind a boulder to the ground.

Duke was soon on his belly beside her, his Beretta in his hand. He called out, "Is Chief all right?"

"Hit in the side," Jack called back. "I don't know yet how bad it is. Both of you, stay down!"

Duke said, "Sounded like a handgun, from some distance. Did you see a flash, anything to give us their direction, Jack?"

"No. There's open ground ahead, and they've got the advantage of camouflage in those trees and a good line of sight. We're too exposed to move. Stay down, I've got to get the bleeding stopped."

Cam came up on her knees and looked around the edge of the boulder, scanning. Another shot blew apart a small rock a foot from her knee. But not before she saw a flash.

She called out, "Shooter about thirty yards, one o'clock from my position. Not from the ground—maybe from that oak tree." She didn't wait. "Lay down cover for me, Duke."

Duke set down the Remington, raised his Beretta, and fired six fast rounds toward the oak tree as Cam reared up and fired toward where she'd seen the flash of light. Another barrage of bullets came from her left and sent shards of rock blasting like missiles into the air, one striking her arm. She felt a slap of icy cold, then nothing. She pulled back, called out, "Two shooters firing now. From one o'clock and three o'clock. The three o'clock's on the ground, in that knot of maples. Jack? Is Chief all right?"

Chief himself called out, "I'll be okay, Cam, you guys stay down."

Was this a standoff? They couldn't move out, they'd make easy targets. Cam felt a jab of hot pain, stared at the blood streaking down the back of her hand. A spike of rock was sticking out of her arm. She looked over at Duke still hugging the ground, taking quick looks around the big rock in front of him. "Sorry, Duke, do you think you could help me a minute?"

Duke looked back at her, saw the rock arrowed into her upper arm and rolled over to her. "Damn. Sorry, Cam, I didn't even notice, I've been looking out there—"

"I just noticed myself. Pull it out, okay? I've got another shirt in my backpack to tie around it. Duke, do it really fast."

He helped her shrug out of her backpack, pull out a shirt, and rip off a sleeve. His eyes widened. "Cam, what's that over there?"

She jerked her head to look and Duke pulled the shard of rock out of her arm. She felt a brutal shock of pain but kept in the scream. When she could breathe again, she said, "That was good, Duke, thank you." She swallowed bile, steadied herself as he pressed down hard on her arm. One of the shooters must have seen movement, because more bullets struck the rocks in front of them.

Then there was silence.

Cam whispered between gritted teeth, "Do they think they've put us out of commission? Killed one of us?"

Duke said, "They had to have heard Jack tell us Chief's wounded in the side. I don't know what they think about us, the rock shard was an accident."

He tore off the other shirtsleeve, wrapped it tightly around her arm. Despite the pain, she grinned at Duke wadding up the first bloody shirtsleeve and stuffing it along with the bloody rock shard into his bio bag. He said, "Chief's got the first-aid kit in his backpack. Your arm should be okay for a while until we can get some antibiotic for the wound." He knotted her shirtsleeve a bit tighter. "How does it feel, Cam?"

It hurts like crazy, but she said, "I'm good to go. It's been maybe three minutes since they've fired. Manta Ray's safety has got to be their first concern. Do you think they've hauled him out of here? Or do you think they're waiting for one of us to stick his head up?"

"Let's see." Duke hooked Cam's backpack over the barrel of his Remington and raised it in the air.

No bullets. Duke waited a moment, then tossed a rock off into the bushes. Still nothing.

Jack and Chief were listening, too. "You think they're gone?"

"Let me finish here and we'll find out," Jack said. "This might hurt a bit, so feel free to curse a blue streak." Chief let loose while Jack treated the wound. Jack was grinning when he said, "I never heard that said about a mule before, Chief. Your wound isn't bad, through and through, a ridge plowed through the flesh on your side. The bleeding's about stopped. I've had medic training, so I know what I'm doing." Jack wrapped one of Chief's shirts over the gauze bandage and knotted it off, tightened his belt over the padding.

"How does that feel?"

"I'll live. You're a sadist, but you're fast. Thanks, Jack. I owe you."

"I'll keep that in mind." Jack knew they were lucky only one of them had been wounded in the ambush. He said what both of them were thinking. "If you hadn't leaned down to look at those tracks, it would have been worse."

"Yeah, call me Mr. Lucky," Chief said. "My wife's going to blow a fit."

Duke and Cam crawled over to Jack and Chief.

Duke said, "I've been showing them a target for a couple of minutes, no takers. And they didn't fire at me and Cam just now."

"No reason to take any chances," Jack said, never looking up. "Let's stay down until I finish bandaging up Chief and we're ready to go. When we move out, I think it's safer to flank them to the south if we're going to move toward that tree line—" He looked up, spotted the bandage on Cam's arm. He felt a leap of alarm, swallowed. "Tell me what happened."

She saw the fear in his eyes and said quickly, "Nothing much, don't worry. Duke fixed me up."

Duke said, "A rock shard speared her. I pulled it out. Now we need what's left in the first-aid kit. Any alcohol?"

"No," Jack said, "but we've got some more alcohol gauze pads. Hold still." He cleaned the wound with a sterile gauze and water from his canteen. He heard her hiss, but she said nothing, made no other sound, only watched the bloody water run down onto the rocky ground. "Now, some antibiotic ointment and I'll get you bandaged."

When he was done, he studied her face a moment, then looked to Chief. "You guys need to stay here, hidden. Duke and I will track them."

Wrong thing to say. "What? You want me to smack you in the head? Forget it, Jack. Chief is badly wounded, I'm not. I want to get these bastards as much as you do."

Jack looked at Chief, who sighed. "Yeah, you're

probably right. I can move, but I'd slow you down. I'll be fine by myself. Know what I think? These people aren't stupid. I don't think they expected to kill all of us. They wanted to bring one of us down with a serious wound, force all of us to stop. So you guys have to move out now."

Jack nodded. "And they targeted you. Like I said, if you hadn't leaned down the instant they fired, you would have been gut-shot and that would have stopped us in our tracks."

Duke said, "I still think they're headed to Clover Bottom Creek Road, about two miles from here. There's a private airstrip about five miles to the east of there. Now that they know we're behind them, they'll get someone here fast to pick them up and drive them to the airstrip. They could be in Virginia in under an hour."

Jack said, "Then we don't need to track them, we want to get to that road the fastest way you know." Jack saw Chief was holding his side, breathing light, shallow breaths, in obvious pain. "Chief, we'll be back as soon as we can."

Chief didn't like it, but his side hurt like a bitch and he knew he couldn't keep up. "Duke, you need to make some calls on the run, get men to barricade Clover Bottom Creek Road. Go, guys; get those bastards for me."

They left their backpacks with Chief, no more need for them now, and they would move much faster through the shrubs and the twisting terrain without the weight. The pain in Cam's arm eased to a dull throb, one of the benefits of her adrenaline rush, as they hiked as quickly as they could through the rocky terrain.

Twenty minutes later, Jack stopped, raised his fist. They gathered around him to look through the trees down at Clover Bottom Creek Road.

27

They heard a car horn blast three times, then a moment later heard it screech to a halt. Jack yelled, "It's their pickup! Let's move!"

As they burst onto Clover Bottom Creek Road, they saw an old black Chevy Tahoe accelerating fast away from them. Jack ran to the middle of the road, Cam beside him, and fired at the back tires. A rear tire exploded, and the Tahoe jerked hard left, but the driver managed to straighten it out, now riding on a rim, the metal grating and sparking off the rocky dirt road.

They ran after it, still shooting, Jack shoving in another magazine until the Tahoe, lurching madly, pulled around a corner and disappeared from sight.

They ran around the bend to see the Tahoe stopped, facing two sheriffs' Crown Vics blocking the road, four officers standing behind open doors for protection, guns in their hands.

Cam punched Jack in the arm, winced, gave him a big smile. "We've got them!"

They were nearly to the Tahoe when they heard a helicopter.

More police? No, Duke hadn't called for air support. He heard one of the barricade cops shout, "The SUV is empty! Only the driver!"

They heard the helicopter setting down somewhere behind them. Jack shouted, "The truck's a decoy!" and took off running back down the road, Cam and Duke behind him.

Jack rounded the curve, Cam on his heels as Manta Ray and his two keepers climbed into a helicopter that had landed in the middle of the road. The helicopter lifted off as the big man climbed in last, still standing on the skids.

The helicopter hovered, trying to remain steady enough for the big man to climb in, but he saw them, grabbed the doorframe, and fired. Bullets kicked up dirt inches from Jack's feet. He yelled at Cam to take cover, took aim, and fired several rounds. Red bloomed on the big man's shirt and the gun went flying, thudding onto the dirt road.

They watched him try to pull himself in with one arm through the helicopter doorway, saw the outline of someone trying to help him, but his hand was slippery with blood and he lost his hold. He tried to gain purchase on the helicopter skids, but again slipped off. In that instant, he looked down, arms flailing, and met Jack's eyes. He fell, twisting and turning and screaming, forty feet to the dirt road. He landed hard and didn't move. Cam's stomach turned. She wouldn't soon forget that sound. She looked up to see a woman leaning out of the helicopter staring down at them. Or at her dead partner, Cam didn't know which.

Cam would swear she gave them a little wave as the helicopter flew away.

"She thinks she's won," Cam said, and kicked a rock with her boot. It sent a shaft of pain through her arm. She cupped her elbow, her Glock dangling from her fingers. Duke came running up. "The Tahoe driver waited until he spotted us, then he went into his act to get us out of the way." He stopped dead in his tracks, stood perfectly still, staring at the dead man in the middle of the road. "That's—bad."

Jack's hard voice brought him back. "Duke, what's going on back there?"

Duke looked away from the body. "One of the sheriff's deputies knows the guy in the Tahoe. His name is Clyde Chivers, a local. Said he was driving to McKee, that's a very small town down the road, when three people came running out of the trees, stepped out onto the road, and started firing after him. They got one of his back tires, nearly totaled his Tahoe, and he could have been killed. He wants to sue you guys."

Cam said, "Chivers was a tool. I'll give my lucky Susan B. Anthony if they told him much, but still, he's worth talking to. Let's threaten to throw him in an FBI dungeon for fifty years."

Jack nodded toward the dead keeper. "Let me see if he's got any ID on him. Duke, is this the same sheriff we notified about the murdered hiker?"

"Yep. Sheriff Bender in Magee, Jackson County

Sheriff's Department." He looked over again at the dead man sprawled in the middle of the dirt road. "This is more trouble than Bud's seen in a year. He'll arrange for the doctor they use as a coroner to come out and deal with him."

The big man had landed facedown, arms flung out to his side, his right arm no longer dripping blood from Jack's bullet in his shoulder. Jack wasn't about to turn him over. He knelt down and checked his pockets while Cam picked up his Beretta. "Nice weapon. It's older, well used and kept in fine shape. A professional's weapon."

She shoved her hair out of her face, forgetting it was her wounded arm, and winced. "All of it was professional, even the fricking decoy."

Jack sighed, asked Duke for the sat phone. "I can't put it off. Confession time." He turned away to make a call. He spoke, listened, finally punched off the sat. "I told Savich what happened. Maybe we'll be tossed in the FBI dungeon with Clyde Chivers. Let's get Chief to the hospital and you, Cam, you'll have your arm checked."

Cam said, "Duke, if you would see to Chief, I've got to call Ollie to see if he can find out who that helicopter belongs to. I could only make out the first of the tail numbers before it shifted—N382. There will probably be two more numbers and a final letter."

"Good eyes, Cam," Jack said, "but I'll bet those tail numbers are fake, but maybe not all of them. Tell Ollie it's a Robinson R66, white, thin blue stripe. Maybe that'll help." Jack shrugged, cursed under his breath, and kicked another rock off the dirt road.

28

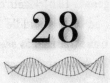

Savich was surprised to be called to his boss's office in the middle of the day. Mr. Maitland's wasn't the largest office in the Hoover Building, nor was it filled with standard-issue desks and chairs. It showcased excellent American antiques Mrs. Maitland had selected. A large glass cabinet stood against a wall, filled with mementos of benchmarks in Maitland's career, framed photos with the great and famous and of his family— Savich's favorite was the one taken last year with Maitland's four sons, all big, strong bruisers, surrounding their mother, who was small and blond but unquestionably the leader of the Maitland pack.

Maitland had asked Savich to have a seat when his longtime secretary, Mrs. Gold, showed Captain Juan Ramirez and Detective Aldo Mayer in. Savich saw it, the look of intimidation on Mayer's face at being called to the emperor's turf.

Maitland shook Captain Ramirez's hand, nodded to Mayer. "Thank you for coming. You know Special Agent Savich?"

"A pleasure, Agent Savich," Ramirez said, and shook his hand.

Maitland did not ask them to sit, nor did he offer coffee. He said, "I asked you to come over this morning, Juan, because your detective here has pulled a stunt that rivals any stupidity I've seen in my long career."

Mayer took a step forward, his face flushed angry red. "Listen here, I pulled off a Metro guard who, I might add, I never approved in the first place." He jerked his head toward Savich. "He did an end-run around me, went to his good buddy Ben Raven, got a police guard assigned to a guy in a fricking coma. A coma? Like we don't even know who he is, much less if he could be in danger."

Savich said quietly, "He would have been murdered last night if Kara Moody hadn't been there to protect him."

Mayer knew this, of course, but it only gave him pause. He plowed forward. "Look, I did everything right, everything according to the book. I notified your secretary that since you claimed the case for the FBI, you could provide your own guards."

His words hung in the tension-filled room. Maitland's voice remained calm as he asked him, "What time did you notify Ms. Needleham?"

"I don't remember, could be it was late, but I'd forgotten about our poor officer, still on duty at the hospital. I only wanted to get him home; he didn't belong there. He never did."

"What time did you call her, Detective Mayer?"

Maitland asked again, still calm but there was a touch of the spurs in his tone. "Well?" Maitland stood tall behind his huge mahogany desk, his arms crossed, looking at Mayer like he wanted to throw him out the window.

Mayer looked down at his feet, then at his captain. "I don't remember."

Savich said easily, "Ms. Needleham, Shirley, emailed me at precisely eleven thirty-three last night. I hadn't checked my email, wouldn't have until this morning, if I hadn't gotten a call that an attempt had been made on John Doe's life."

The only sound was Mayer's hard breathing. Captain Ramirez remained silent, looking straight ahead, not at his detective. Savich continued, his voice as calm as night. "I know you were interested in John Doe, wondered who he was, really, and what had happened to him, just as I was. But because of your dislike for me, Detective Mayer, you put him at dire risk. Are you really trying to justify that?"

Mayer couldn't help himself, it came spewing out. "You proved on Sunday that you're a publicity-seeking glory hound. So you took down a young guy who's certifiably crazy. Big deal. I would have brought him in if you hadn't interfered, if you hadn't wanted the spotlight, the media attention!"

Captain Ramirez took a step forward in front of Mayer. He said formally, "I wish to apologize for my detective's negligence that could have cost a man his life. Agent Savich, what would you like me to do?"

I'd like to break a rib or two myself, or better yet, give him to Sherlock. He said, "Detective Mayer, let me ask you a question. Would you have felt responsible if John Doe had been murdered last night?"

Mayer looked like he'd been shot. "I never thought there was any danger to him! I thought you were just—"

"Just what, Detective?" Maitland asked.

"I thought Savich was throwing his weight around, rubbing my nose in how he could talk Detective Raven into anything. He did the same thing on Sunday! It pissed me off—"

Maitland interrupted him, "Answer his question, Detective Mayer."

Mayer's face was so red Savich was afraid he'd stroke out. No one said a word. Finally, he whispered, "Yes. Yes, I would have felt responsible."

Captain Ramirez said matter-of-factly, "Do you now admit Agent Savich was justified in requesting a police guard?"

Stone silence. Captain Ramirez merely looked at him, waited.

Mayer said finally, "So he turned out to be right, in this case."

Maitland said, "And if Agent Savich hadn't taken a personal interest in this young man, do you think John Doe would still be alive?"

Mayer turned on Savich, but there was nothing more he could say.

Time to end it. Mayer was heaving with anger, with

guilt, with humiliation. He was a man with a long career—a good cop, no, an excellent cop—and he'd finally admitted his mistake.

Mr. Maitland said, "Detective Mayer, you should know Savich didn't call for this meeting, I did. I wanted to hear your apology myself. You have an excellent and fair captain, and he will decide whether to take any disciplinary action." Maitland leaned forward, his big hands splayed on his desktop. "If I were Agent Savich, I doubt I would have behaved as well. I strongly suggest you get over yourself and stop the self-justification because there isn't any." He paused, nodded. "Captain Ramirez, thank you for coming."

When the door closed behind the two men, Maitland said, "I'm thinking maybe Detective Mayer cares more about John Doe than he hates you."

Savich said, "Maybe you're right. But I do know that his hatred of me is hardwired. We'll see what he does now. Thank you for dealing with this, sir."

Maitland came around his desk, sent his fist into Savich's arm. It hurt, but Savich smiled. "I know, boyo, that you would have let it go, but I couldn't. Mayer had to be called out, he had to be brought to book. If there's a next time, I can guarantee he won't be so lucky."

29

IN THE HELICOPTER OVER VIRGINIA

Elena kept her Walther pressed against Liam's side. She was quiet, her mouth seamed, and Liam thought she was probably thinking about Jacobson's perfect-ten swan dive to the road at the feet of those two FBI agents. All in all, in his opinion, it was a satisfying ending for the bully.

Liam turned to her, gave her a white-toothed smile. "Our little vacation in the forest didn't turn out the way you planned, but hey, it had its moments. We're finally going to see the big boss?"

"Shut up." She pressed the gun harder against his side.

He continued to smile. No way would she shoot him, she'd already made that clear. And that made her vulnerable. Quick as a snake, he twisted the gun barrel away from him, grabbed the back of her head with one hand, and pressed the thumb and forefingers of his other hand under both sides of her chin, squeezing fast and hard upward to pinch off her carotid arteries until she sagged against him, unconscious. "Like squeezing a garden hose," he whispered against her temple. "I'm glad you knew enough not to pull the trigger." He kissed her temple. "You owe me, sweetheart. If I'd held you longer, you'd be dead, but I don't want you dead."

The pilot twisted in his seat, yelled, "Hey! What's going on back there? What did you do to Elena?" The helicopter banked, then righted again.

Liam saw him fumbling with a box on the seat next to him. He turned his headset microphone on so the pilot could hear him. "No, mate, don't go for a gun. There's nothing to worry about. She's not dead, only taking a little nap. I didn't want any more trouble from her, and you know women—" He laughed, picked up the Walther from the floor, checked the magazine was full. Excellent. He said, "I've got the gun, but you have no worries as long as you keep flying us where we're supposed to go."

"But why'd you do that, Manta Ray? You didn't have to; she wasn't going to hurt you."

He wasn't Manta Ray now. No, he was Liam, Liam Hennessey. He smiled widely, showing a gold back tooth. For the first time since he was shot, he was in control again. He was flush with pleasure. If he played his cards right, he'd soon be richer than his poor dead partner, Cass, God rest his soul.

Showtime.

He eyed the back of the pilot's head, brought his Irish to full power, falling into the cadence. "Well, laddie, first thing for you to remember is my name is Liam Hennessey. You can call me Liam. I'll admit it: Elena's good, but I'm better. And to be honest, I knew she couldn't shoot me. If I die, her boss's grand schemes go to the grave with me." He lifted the Walther so the pilot could see it.

"Look, mate, I know the lay of the land, probably better than you do. Let's have ourselves a fine chat."

"All they told me is your name's Manta Ray, but who are you?"

I'm your worst nightmare. Liam smiled, gently pressed the Walther to the back of the pilot's neck. He froze. Liam rubbed the muzzle back and forth across his neck. "Don't make me remind you again, mate. I'm not Manta Ray, I'm Liam. And I am the most important man in the world to the boss." He lowered the Walther. "What's your name?"

"Ralph, Ralph Henley. I didn't know you were a mick. Listen, don't kill Elena, the boss would go nuts, shoot all of us. They're lovers, for years now, common knowledge."

"Yeah, I know all about her," Liam said without hesitation. "She's his enforcer and bodyguard and his bedmate."

Henley eyed him, still afraid and uncertain, but at least the crazy bastard wasn't still rubbing the gun against his neck. He had to know if Ralph crashed, he'd die, too. He met Liam's eyes, slowly nodded.

Good, he was starting to accept that Liam was in the know. "You can consider me more like his partner, but I'd be a fool to trust the boss, you know? And she'd take his side. Like you said, they're close and I have to keep the upper hand if I want to stay alive. If I hadn't put her down, the boss would have held all the cards, ended up killing me, burying me deep. Now, I've got a pretty fair chance."

It was fine with him that Ralph was afraid of him, still eyeing him like he was a terrorist. Fear was a great motivator.

Liam knew when to stop pushing, when to let things settle. He sat back and contemplated the unconscious Elena. He had only a couple of minutes before her blood pressure booted up and she came back, maybe woozy for a bit, but mad as hell, ready to fight him. Unlike Jacobson, he wasn't about to underestimate her. He looked for something to tie her up, but he didn't see anything. He pulled a toolbox from under the seat and found mankind's savior—duct tape. He wrapped it around her wrists, her thighs, and her ankles. Then he wrapped her arms to her chest and fastened the tape around the arm of one of the front seats. It kept her forward and steady, and if she twitched, he'd know it.

He smiled, waved at the pilot. "This is only a precaution. She's all right, don't worry. I liked your maneuver back there at the road, that was real impressive. You landed easy, held steady enough to give Jacobson his shot at the agents. Then you rose straight up, nice and smooth and fast. It was well done. Not your fault the big man got shot."

Henley licked his lips, knowing he could be in bad trouble, helping these people escape the cops. He'd seen a man die a horrible death, but still he couldn't help himself. He preened, and Liam saw it, added, "Tell me how you learned to do that."

Henley shrugged, tried to look modest. "It wasn't hard. Any trained pilot could have done it. I was told to be fast in and out, then fly back to the boss's place."

Where is that?

Liam said, "I guess you've worked for the boss for a long time?"

"I'm his pilot whenever he's in the U.S."

"And when he's not, what do you do?"

Liam saw Henley's eyes narrow. He'd taken a wrong step. He said quickly, "Well, of course you fly some bigwigs around." Still, he looked uncertain. Liam laughed. "Do you ever get to fly to New York? That's my kind of town, lots of gorgeous broads, any kind of action you want."

Henley's eyes flickered, his brow smoothed out, and he shrugged. "Yeah, you know how it is. They pay me well, tips under the table, so who cares if I can't understand them?"

Understand them? "I can't, either. Pisses me off."

Henley looked back at him, shrugged again. "Who wants to learn Russian?"

The boss was Russian? "I'm with you on that."

Elena groaned, jerked awake. He leaned forward, stroked her hair. "Shush now, girl, you're okay, I had to close you down for a bit. Don't move now or I'll have to do it again." He leaned closer, whispered in her ear, "Next time I might not pull back quick enough, kill you flat-out. So hold still and don't feel bad I got you. Fact is, you couldn't shoot me, now could you? Might kill me, and then what would the boss have to say to you? And that gave me my chance."

She whispered, "Get this duct tape off me."

"I don't think so, lass. My mum didn't raise a stupid git."

"What are you saying to her? Are you threatening her?"

"No, Ralph, no threats. Elena's getting her brains unscrambled, wanted to know what happened. She's going to be nice and quiet for the rest of our flight."

Still, Henley turned in his seat. "Ms. Orlov, are you all right?"

Elena Orlov? She was Russian, too? Here he'd thought she had some Mexican blood in her. But she didn't have an accent, and Liam had a good ear for accents. He kissed her cheek. "Make Ralph happy, love, reassure him, and then shut up."

She cleared her throat and yelled up at him, "Don't worry, Ralph, I'm good."

"Yes, she is, Ralph." Liam leaned close to her face. "Play nice or I'll throw you out of the helicopter and have Ralph fly me to wherever I choose to go. It's your boss who loses out."

She met his eyes. He saw she believed him.

He said into his headset microphone, "Hey, Ralph, they always speak Russian around you? But you're their pilot."

Henley was shaking his head as he slowly banked left. "They always ask for me, they don't trust their own sisters."

Liam nodded. "But the boss is going to stay awhile. He's got our big deal going down."

"Whatever you're doing with him must be big-time, maybe big enough to get him back cozy again with Putin."

"It goes up that high? How do you know? I thought they only spoke Russian in front of you?"

"Well, his houseboy said something to me before Abram came out and told him to mind his own."

"Abram's one tough cookie."

"Yeah, the boss listens to him, lets him run both his houses, on the Potomac and in Washington."

"Yeah, right," Liam said, nodding. "What did the houseboy say before Abram shut him down?"

"Only that something big was cooking. And then last month, Petrov had me fly him to New York, to the United Nations. He was feeling really pleased with himself, even drank some champagne. He said something about being more important than any of those idiots at the embassy."

The Russian embassy? Liam said, "It's not like he's one of them. He's got his own agenda."

"That's the truth." Henley cut the helicopter down through the clouds, and rural Virginia sprawled out below them, the pastures, trees, and towns south of the maze of highways. They flew northward over bedroom communities, until the jumble of highways spiraled out like spokes on a wheel, all the roads leading to Rome. He said, "You ever been to Petrov's place on the Potomac?"

"No," Liam said, "but I figured I'd see it sooner or later. That's where we're going?"

"Yes. It's nice and private, right on the water, and it's only a short flight from D.C. He wants something from you, right?"

"Oh yeah, he wants something," Liam said.

"What?"

"Maybe he wants me to make him Putin's best friend," Liam said.

30

McKEE, KENTUCKY
TUESDAY AFTERNOON

Cam and Jack climbed out of the Crown Vic in the small town of McKee, population eight hundred souls, and looked up at the biggest building in town, a red-brick three-story wonder boasting square concrete columns at its entry.

"Pretty impressive for a small town," Cam said.

Duke waved his hand. "Well, it's not only the seat of town government, the Jackson County Judicial Center, it's also the Jackson County Sheriff's Department. Anything you need to get done you get done here. Even the three bars in the next block can't compete." He paused, kicked a pebble out of his path. "I sure hated leaving Chief at the hospital. He was cursing a blue streak about having to call his wife. She'll be flying up here, fussing over him, and he hates that. Cam, good thing you got out of there with only some stitches and a sling, thank the good Lord."

"Better yet," Cam said, "the sling makes it look more serious than it really is, and I don't have to worry about calling a husband."

Jack looked around, getting the feel of the town.

McKee was charming, if on the funky side. The short, squat gray store right across from the redbrick monument that housed the jail and courtrooms had a big sign over its window: MR. BILL'S GUNS AND GROCERIES.

They left Duke to chat with the sheriff and were directed by a deputy to the single small, windowless interview room. Clyde Chivers was already seated at the banged-up wooden table at least twice as old as he was, tapping his fingertips on a piece of paper in front of him. He was in his early twenties, skinny as a flagpole, a seedy mustache trying to take root on his upper lip. He looked scared and slightly sick. He met their eyes and tried to manage a look of outrage at this indignity.

Cam pulled out a chair, sat down, eyed him for a moment. "Hey, Clyde, I like the alliteration—Clyde Chivers—your daddy come up with that one? Or is that on your mama's head?"

He blinked, opened his mouth, shut it, then managed, "Nope, it was my aunt Mabel, my mama's sister. She writes poetry." He shut his mouth, straightened his shoulders, and tried to dial up the outrage again. "You're the people who tried to kill me. You wrecked my Tahoe. You should be the ones here in jail, not me."

Jack lounged back in his chair, relaxed and as loose as a lizard on a sunny rock. "Nah, we didn't want you dead, Clyde. Actually, we usually don't want anyone dead. We only wanted to catch the three people you pretended to pick up."

"I don't know about any three people. I was driving to McKee, to see a bud of mine. Why am I here? What do you want? I didn't do anything. You know I was alone, so you have no right—"

Cam sat forward, looked him straight on. "Shut up, Clyde. The sheriff found five crisp one-hundred-dollar bills under your front seat. You going to tell us who gave you the money to pull your little stunt on Clover Bottom Creek Road?"

"I don't know what you're talking about, I didn't do anything, nothin', you hear me?"

Jack said, "Don't waste our time and try to deny it. We're in a hurry here."

"You've got no right to hold me. So I have five hundred bucks, that ain't no crime in my universe."

"There you're wrong," Cam said. "These are very bad people, Clyde. And you helped them escape us."

Clyde Chivers was shaking his head back and forth.

Jack leaned forward. "I don't suppose the guy who called you, who paid you, happened to mention that the three people you helped escape us stuck a knife in a young hiker's heart yesterday? His name was James Delinsky and he was a student at Virginia Tech. They left him for the animals to scavenge. And that means, Clyde, that you aided and abetted murderers. You're either going to confess all your sins and not leave a thing out, or you're going to spend the next twenty years at the Pennington Gap federal penitentiary. Your one and only chance to avoid that future is right now."

Chivers licked his lips as he eyed both Cam and Jack. "No, really, I don't know anything, I—" He tried to shove away from them. Jack leaned over the table and grabbed the front of Chivers's shirt, hauled him out of his chair, and gave him one good shake. "Listen up, Clyde. These are very bad people. They might let you live until you get to prison, but after that? Understand, Clyde, you're what's called a loose end."

Cam said, "And you know what happens to loose ends, don't you?"

"No, that isn't right, no one will hurt me and you can't, either, you—"

Jack gave him a final shake and shoved him back into his chair. "Actually, Clyde, I can do anything I want to you, and probably be awarded a medal for it. As I said, we're talking very bad guys you hooked up with." He looked down at his watch. "You have three minutes."

"I want a deal, yeah, that's it, a deal. I didn't know, I swear I didn't. Give me a deal."

Jack looked over at Cam. "I can't give you a deal, but Agent Wittier here knows the federal prosecutor in charge of this case. Do you think the prosecutor might consider loosening the noose around Clyde's neck if he's honest and up front with us?"

Cam looked thoughtful. "Well, Ms. Cherisse is usually fine with helping people like Clyde here who have a hard time understanding the danger they're in. But, Clyde, you better hope we find these people before they stab you like they did the hiker. He was only a couple of years younger than you."

Chivers was gnawing on his lower lip, looking scared. His hand shook as he picked up the glass of water beside him and drank half of it down. He swiped the back of his hand over his mouth. "Okay, but you've got to believe me. I didn't know anything about these people, not a single thing. The guy said if I did this one thing, they'd leave me alone, but I swear, I wouldn't have done it, except the guy who called me black-mailed me."

Jack rolled his eyes. "Imagine, trying to blackmail an upstanding citizen like you. What about?"

"No, really, it's the truth. He knew about the crop of marijuana in my back forty and he was going to call the sheriff on me. It was either that, or take the five hundred bucks he left in my truck." He puffed up a bit. "I'm not stupid, I checked to make sure the money was there."

Cam said. "Who is the man? Do you know him?"

"He didn't tell me his name, and I didn't recognize his voice. He said he'd heard about my little sideline selling pot and he needed my help, now. He didn't tell me anything about these three people. He told me to drive up and down Clover Bottom Creek Road, and if I saw some people hiking out of the forest, I had to make sure they saw me and then take off like a bat out of hell. I thought, *I'm getting five hundred bucks for punching the gas?* I couldn't believe it when you started shooting at me. You shot out one of my back tires, and I thought I was going to die until I saw the cop cars blocking the road."

"The man who called you. Tell us about him. Did he sound young? Old? Accent? What?"

Chivers thought about that. "He sounded like a regular adult guy, younger than my dad. He did have this accent, not Southern or from Boston, you know how they talk. He sort of sounded like that old series about that English detective in Oxford, Inspector Morse, I think his name was."

"So you're saying the man who called you was in his thirties or forties and had an upper-class British accent."

"Yeah, that's it, and he knew about my crop of weed, and I realized one of my clients must have ratted me out and that's how he got my name. I swear, he threatened me, threatened to call the sheriff. I can't see I had any choice. The prosecutor, she'll believe me, won't she?"

"Yes, she will. Give me your cell phone, Clyde." Cam held out her hand.

"They took it already. Will I get it back?"

She nodded. As she and Jack rose and left the room, she said over her shoulder at the door, "You're free to go, Clyde, if you want to. But I suggest you be very careful. Your cell phone will be with the dispatcher."

Chivers rose straight out of his chair, sputtering. "You can't leave me, it's inhuman. I didn't do anything all that bad, really, don't you see? I mean, my crop helps support my folks. Without me—"

"You could ask the sheriff to keep you in custody if you like." Jack winked at Cam as he shut the door on Clyde Chivers.

Outside in the bullpen Cam retrieved Chivers's cell

phone, scrolled through Chivers's calls with two deputies looking on. She found a blocked call from earlier in the day. "Probably from a burner phone. They don't miss much."

"I know, they're smart. The man who called Chivers, the man in charge, is a Brit? Or was he another underling?"

Cam grinned. "Are we thinking they're so smart because they outfoxed us?"

"I'd like to think they were lucky, but I doubt Savich would agree. I emailed Savich the big man's prints. We'll know if he's in the system soon."

Cam said, "Where are we headed now, Jack?"

"Savich said to come back to Washington. He says he's got a lead on one of the six people who rented the safe-deposit boxes Manta Ray emptied. And he told me the tail number you saw on the Robinson doesn't exist. Agent Lucy McKnight is getting together a list of all Robinson R66 helicopters in the Washington area."

"Did he mention we were fired?"

"He didn't say and I wasn't about to ask him."

31

Savich arrived at John Doe's hospital room twenty minutes after Dr. Wordsworth called him. He spoke briefly to newly assigned guard Agent Wilcox, then stepped in the room to see Dr. Wordsworth checking John Doe's infusion set. Once satisfied, she turned to him and smiled. "Thank you for coming, Agent Savich. Needless to say I've never had one of my patients nearly murdered under my care. It shocks me that something like that could happen here, at the hospital, to someone who's completely helpless." Dr. Wordsworth nodded toward John Doe's second FBI guard, Agent Crosby, standing by the window. "It's a great relief you now have two agents guarding him. Agent Crosby assures me if anyone tries anything more, he will need the emergency room. I called you, Agent Savich, because I promised to follow up with his test results and the bloodwork I sent out." She shook her head. "To be honest here, some of it doesn't make sense to me."

"As puzzling as finding out John Doe is the father of Kara Moody's baby?"

"Nothing could be that strange." She shook her head. "Amazing, really. A man she believes is crazy bursts into her house two days ago, her baby is kidnapped yesterday, last night she saves that man's life, and now she finds out that same man is the father of her baby, a man she'd never seen before." She shook her head again. "She's bearing up so well. In fact, I'm told she spends all her time with him. I hear she thinks of him as a victim, like herself. She never once considered him as her possible rapist."

It was an extraordinary situation. How would it play out? Savich thought of Sherlock's interview with Sylvie Vaughn, and the GPS tracker she'd put on Vaughn's car, and all because of her gut. He'd trust Sherlock's gut any day. "We may know more about what's going on very soon. Doctor, tell me, what doesn't make sense about the test results?"

Dr. Wordsworth took off her glasses, wiped them down on her white coat, set them on her nose again. "As you know, his CT scans and MRIs were normal. The initial abnormal blood tests I told you about yesterday—his liver function tests and blood cell counts—have improved, they're very nearly in the normal range. My neurology consult tested him again this morning, says John Doe's reflexes are improving. His coma is less deep, which means he might regain consciousness soon."

"Doctor, your earring is falling out."

"What?" Her long thin fingers went to the diamond stud nearly ready to fall out of her ear. She smiled, reattached it. "Thank you. I'd hate to lose one of those babies—it was my twenty-fifth anniversary present from my husband." She shook her head, patted the earring. "As I was saying, I was considering a bone marrow biopsy, but I don't want to subject him to anything invasive since he's recovering on his own, and so quickly."

Savich said thoughtfully, "So it seems he's working something toxic out of his system? Have you gotten any information back about any drugs he was given?"

She placed her hand on his arm, drew a deep breath. "That's why I called you. The reference lab found a cocktail of drugs in his system. The first was a natural supplement called quercetin that is marketed as a sort of über vitamin pill. There are claims it reduces the risk of cancer, the risk of heart disease, signs of aging— most medical problems under the sun, really, a cure-all. The FDA has warned there's no proof for any of the claims, but still, it's widely available."

Savich shrugged. "As long as people need hope, some drug will claim to provide it."

She nodded. "That's the sad truth. At least, as far as I know, this supplement can't hurt you. The second drug they found is called epoetin alfa. That's a sophisticated drug that has to be given intravenously. It's produced using recombinant DNA technology, acts like a natural hormone to stimulate the bone marrow to make more red blood cells. Someone has been treating his anemia with it. It can cause some increased blood clotting, but nothing like what John Doe is suffering."

She drew a deep breath. "Now, the third drug they found, they couldn't identify. They do know it's chemically related to a drug called sirolimus, used to treat organ rejection. But the drug they found in his blood is new; it's different. I think the mystery drug is what's been so toxic to him, especially to his nervous system and his bone marrow. That toxicity could be why they gave him the epoetin, to counteract the bone marrow suppression the third drug was causing."

"Aren't there a great many drugs currently being tested that your lab couldn't identify yet? Drugs that haven't been approved or marketed?"

Dr. Wordsworth nodded. "Yes, of course. There are millions of untested and poorly tested compounds out there, many of them owned by pharmaceutical companies and universities. They're often kept jumbled together in what they call compound libraries, in the hope that some of them will be useful as drugs someday." She shrugged. "Fact is, most of them turn out to be ineffective, or toxic, or both. It takes a great deal of money and time and a bit of luck to find one with a valid use and bring it to market."

"And if someone were giving him an experimental drug, an unapproved drug, that might explain his medical condition and why he's improving now he's no longer taking it?"

"Yes, luckily for him." Dr. Wordsworth picked up John Doe's arm, traced her fingertips over the neat line of needle marks. "At first I thought he might have volunteered for some kind of a drug trial, but if he was being given the drug legitimately, for therapeutic reasons, why can't we find anything wrong with him other than what seems to be the toxic effects of a drug?"

She touched a finger to her earring, then shook her head at herself. "That attempt on his life last night, someone with medical knowledge did that. The syringe the murderer was going to inject into John Doe's IV—it was filled with potassium chloride. It would have stopped his heart and killed him, and the murderer knew we would never have found it, even at autopsy. It would have looked like sudden cardiac arrest, death from natural causes."

"And if Kara hadn't been here to frighten the killer off, John Doe could never wake up to tell us otherwise, or about anything that's happened to him."

She took John Doe's hand. "Whatever is happening here, it's way beyond unethical; it's scary. Please find these people before they try again."

32

Henley flew the helicopter in from the south, staying low over the Potomac. As he maneuvered to land on a barren patch near the shore, Liam saw a Hardy 50 motor yacht tied to a wooden dock, not twenty yards from the landing field. It was a boat he knew well, an English boat he'd seen often in the bad old days of his smuggling forays along the Irish coast. It was seaworthy and powerful, but small enough to guide upriver without attracting too much attention. Probably the boss's boat, an easy getaway to wherever he wanted to go.

Henley touched down on the dirt, and Liam watched the rotor blades slow as Henley went methodically through his shutdown checklist. When the blades finally stopped, it was quiet as a graveyard save for the light lapping of the Potomac against the wooden dock. Amazing for a place so close to Alexandria and the millions of people in the metro area. He'd seen no major roads, no close neighbors. It was private.

Henley stepped out and opened their door. He pointed. "Petrov's house is through that mess of trees."

Liam used a Swiss Army knife from the tool kit to cut Elena free from the helicopter seat arm and pulled her out. He winced from the weight he had to put on his heel as he set her down on the skids beside him. He started to cut the duct tape from around her legs to let her walk freely but he chanced to look at her, saw rage in her eyes, and knew in his gut she'd go for him, even with her arms and hands taped together. He was hobbled enough she might well take him down, even with the Walther. And Henley might help her.

"Sorry, love, I know you want to take a strip off me, so you'll have to stay trussed up awhile longer." He patted her cheek, goading her, but she didn't say anything.

He looked toward the Potomac. "Who's there on Petrov's boat?" She turned automatically and he hit her hard with the butt of the Walther. She didn't make a sound, just sagged against him.

"Hey!" Henley took a step toward him. "Why'd you do that?"

Henley was becoming a nuisance. "She's all right. I'm thinking it'd be easier if you carry her. You didn't think you'd be staying with the helicopter, did you, mate?"

"I was told to drop you and take off again."

"Change of plans. Not going to happen. Come and get Elena. Where's Petrov's man? Abram?"

"He'll be meeting us."

Liam saw the moment Henley realized he'd unwittingly given away the farm, and smiled. "Don't feel bad, old man. The only person I could never fool was my da, a right mean son of a bitch. Come on, take her."

Henley lifted Elena in his arms rather than over his shoulder, and staggered. Liam grinned. Elena was well muscled, not a lightweight.

Liam waved the Walther. "Walk ahead of me. If you do anything stupid, I'll blow your head apart."

Henley looked at the Walther, swallowed, gave him a terrified smile. "Ah, you know you never want to kill the pilot."

So Henley thought it would be hard to kill a man who was funny. It was a good point. He smiled. "You're still alive, aren't you?" He waved the Walther. Always careful, Liam limped three steps behind Henley across the scrubby plot of land to a well-worn winding path through a thick copse of trees, full-leafed in midsummer. At the far edge of the trees a green yard spread out in front of them, sloping up to a house facing the Potomac. It wasn't a mansion like some of the houses he'd seen from the air, not pretentious at all, but it wasn't a shack, either. It was elegant in its own simple way, all wood and glass, beautifully weathered, a getaway, designed for the owner and guests to come and go in privacy. And the boss's boat was thirty yards from the front door.

As Liam limped along the flagstone path toward the house, he saw a wide, roofed porch, with two ancient rocking chairs with faded red cushions. Liam couldn't imagine someone like Petrov hanging out there, rocking back and forth, enjoying an evening martini. Everything was silent. He didn't see the man Abram or any other sign of life in the house.

But then the wooden front door opened and an older man walked out onto the porch. He was deeply tanned and perfectly bald. He stood with his arms crossed, his head cocked to one side as he watched them come toward him. He was tall and fit, wearing a white suit, buttoned over a white shirt, white loafers on his bare feet. He wasn't smiling.

"That's Abram?"

Henley nodded.

"Say hello, you idiot."

"Abram, how are you? Is Mr. Petrov here?"

"Yes, of course. Where else would he be?" Abram never looked away from the unconscious Elena in Henley's arms. "He's been waiting. You made good time. I see there's a problem. Mr. Petrov will not be pleased. Bring Ms. Orlov inside. I assume she isn't dead or dying?"

Liam stepped around Henley, aimed his Walther at Abram. "Hello, Abram. I'm Liam Hennessey. Don't you worry about Elena, I gave her a small tap on the head to keep her quiet. Take us to Petrov."

Abram's big hands fisted, then relaxed. He turned on his heel and walked into the house, Henley and Liam following him.

Liam watched him lightly tap on a door, open it, and stick his head in. He heard Russian. Then another man's voice, low and controlled, also speaking Russian.

Abram turned. "Come."

Liam waved the Walther for Abram to precede them and limped behind Henley into a long narrow room with a full bank of wide windows facing the Potomac. He saw dark-stained wooden shelves on two walls, nearly empty, only a dozen or so hardcover books. At the far end of the room stood a big mahogany desk. He watched a man rise when he saw Elena unmoving in Henley's arms and rush around the desk. His voice was sharp, with a clipped upper-class British accent. "What happened, Henley? Is she all right?" He turned quickly to Liam. "What did you do to her?"

"She'll be fine, Mr. Petrov."

"If you've harmed her, you're a dead man."

Liam smiled. "She'll have a headache, but that should be all. You know as well as I do if I hadn't knocked her out, she would have carved out my liver and trussed me up like a turkey for your pleasure. Why should I take a chance of your putting your foot on my neck or locking me up with no food or water until I tell you what you want to know?"

"I am not a barbarian, Manta Ray."

"Call me Liam, Liam Hennessey. My old street name no longer fits me."

Petrov ignored him, waved to Henley to put Elena down on the pale blue brocade sofa. So Elena really was Petrov's Achilles' heel. Liam felt the balance of power shift, and smiled.

Liam hated showing Petrov weakness, but Petrov already knew about his heel, Elena must have told him. He limped to a chair, sat down, and was glad the throbbing eased. He studied the boss. Petrov was in his midforties, not a big man, but he had presence, as if he understood power and how to wield it. Odd impression, that, but there it was. Petrov's forehead was high, his dark hair spearing a thick widow's peak in the middle of his forehead; his hair receding well back on each side. It reminded him of Nicolas Cage's hair, the American actor Liam knew well, having watched his movies at the Old Goddard theatre in Belfast. He had Cage's black eyes, too, but his nose was long and thin, his cheekbones high, and he had very white skin, like he'd never been in the sun. A vampire, the bloody Russian looked like a pretty vampire with Nicolas Cage hair.

Liam said, "I don't speak Russian."

"I wouldn't expect you to," Petrov said, leaving *Because you're an ignorant Irish git* unspoken but clear as day. Petrov turned to Abram. "Take Mr. Henley to the kitchen and give him a beer. And summon Dr. Michaelov. He will examine Elena. And Mr. Hennessey's heel, of course. I will call if I need anything."

Liam heard the two men's voices recede into the distance. He realized he was unconsciously rubbing his heel, and stopped. Petrov was whispering to Elena, touching her face, obviously concerned she might be badly hurt.

"You said you weren't a barbarian, Mr. Petrov. I agree. You are far beyond a barbarian. But for all I know you could promise me the moon for what you need from that safe-deposit box and then shoot me clean between the eyes. Abram could no doubt bury me in that dirt field where your helicopter lands. I took Elena's gun and that means we both have a measure of control. Now we can negotiate."

33

Petrov looked up from Elena's face. He fanned his slender white hands. "You mistake me, Mr. Hennessey. Ours is nothing more than a straightforward business matter. I have held up my end of our bargain. I promised to free you from the federal marshals, and I've done so. I was required to take extraordinary measures to keep you out of the FBI's hands, and I have done so. And now you are here, safe." Petrov waved to Liam's bound foot. "Your foot, the FBI, should I go on?" He paused, then: "And yet you are holding Elena's favored Walther at my chest. I am making you a rich man. It seems to me you would wish to show me a measure of gratitude, Mr. Hennessey."

Liam sat back in the chair, crossed his arms. He liked Petrov, but Liam knew he wasn't a man he'd want to meet in a dark alley. "And what do you think this measure of gratitude should be?"

"Let us say, rather that it would be a simple courtesy for you to confirm for me the name of the person who hired you to rob my safe-deposit box."

Liam cocked an eyebrow, said in full Irish, "My heel

hurts, Mr. Petrov, makes me querulous. Sorry, I'm not feeling very courteous at the moment."

"Even though my own personal physician is coming to take care of your heel?"

"And her, of course." Liam waved the Walther toward the sofa. He heard Elena moan. "She'll be back with you soon, Mr. Petrov. That is my courtesy to you—I didn't kill her."

Petrov gently pulled Elena upright into his arms. He whispered against her ear, "No, don't move, you probably have a concussion."

Elena whispered something Liam couldn't hear as Petrov lightly touched a long finger to the side of her head behind her left temple. "You've got only a lump there. The skin isn't broken. Does it hurt? Can you see me clearly?"

Elena nodded, said something in French, of all things, and Petrov pulled her against him again and slowly rocked her, his face pressed against her hair.

Liam said, "No, I did not kill her, and I am about to bring you your heart's greatest desire. It is you who owes me gratitude. I've decided I want to have enough money to make a difference in my life, but not enough to make you want to hunt me down and cut my throat in my sleep."

"And what do you suppose that amount would be, Mr. Hennessey?"

"Four million dollars and all the jewelry in the safe-deposit boxes."

Petrov never looked away from Elena. "I can get

that amount here by morning. I presume you have other demands to assure your safety?"

"In the morning, that's fine. Only one more demand. After you've given me the four million, you will have Henley fly me, my money, and Elena to wherever I choose. Elena is for my own safety. We'll fly over to collect what you want—I presume it's whatever is in that metal box from one of the safe-deposit boxes I stole?"

"It is. You did not attempt to open the box?"

Liam shook his head, remembered too clearly the awful pain in his side from the bullet whenever he moved.

Petrov whispered something against Elena's ear, in Russian. *"Don't worry, I will let you kill the Irish bastard."*

She nodded, smiled up at him.

Liam didn't like that smile, the sudden pleasure in her dark eyes. What had he told her? It didn't matter, Liam had the Walther. He thought he might go to Morocco. He'd seen movies shot in those vast stretches of barren desert, tribesmen riding camels in their strange clothes. Fez, they called the big town, with its ancient streets and marketplaces. Who cared if the heat could sear off a man's eyebrows? He'd turn up the air conditioning or hire some of those sloe-eyed girls to fan him with palm fronds.

Liam looked over at Petrov and Elena again. He was caressing the back of her hand, speaking quietly to her in Russian. Liam called out, "Elena will be staying in this room with me tonight. Anyone tries to come in and she'll be the first to die. Is that understood?"

Petrov squeezed Elena's hand, nodded. "Neither I nor Abram will give you any problems. But I will give you a warning. If you harm Elena, I will hunt you down to the ends of the earth and your death will be more unpleasant than Jacobson's."

Liam laughed. "A fine threat, but you know, Mr. Petrov, I doubt that's possible." He shrugged. "But it's fair enough. All she has to do is be good, give me no trouble."

Petrov turned back to her. "Don't let him upset you, *moy golub*. You must rest and regain your strength."

"What is *moy golub*?"

Petrov turned dispassionate eyes to him. "My dove."

"Very sweet, mate, but this one a dove? She's more like a viper. I thought for sure she was going to shoot Jacobson. He was a right proper muck-up, that one. I hope you didn't pay him much."

Petrov shrugged. "He was recommended by a contact in Metro, fresh out of jail, needed money. His death was punishment enough for his incompetence. Luckily, there is no way the FBI can trace him to me or to you.

"Tell me, Mr. Hennessey, why are you so distrusting of me? I respect your skills. You did an excellent job hiding the goods. I have done everything I promised to do for you. Yet you still treat me like an enemy rather than as your business partner."

Elena spoke up, her voice sharp. "Sergei is a man of honor. His word is never questioned. There is no reason for you to distrust him."

"Ah, yes, honor among thieves, is that it? I'm glad your boss didn't tell you to pull out my fingernails in that forest, but I'm not going to let either of you give it a go now. What did Petrov call you? His dove? *Moy golub*."

"Don't you call me that, you Irish trash!"

"See, more a vulture." He shook his finger at Elena. "That was rude. I could have thrown you out of the helicopter after Jacobson, opened that little metal box and used it myself, cut out the middle man. But Sergei and I had a deal. So, girl, make nice so I won't have to lock you in a closet. Hey, Sergei, since we're partners and all, tell me what this has to do with Putin."

Petrov went poker stiff. "It has nothing to do with him directly, but Vladimir Putin is a fine man, a great man, exactly the man Russia needs in this time of turmoil. It is your Western press who paint him as a monster, your Western governments that try to slander him, and all those who are loyal to him."

"Guy can't even put on a shirt," Liam said.

By the time Dr. Michaelov arrived, Liam had eaten Abram's lentil soup and a huge hunk of black rye bread, and taken three aspirin. He was tired, but it didn't matter, he could deal with that. He'd learned long ago in prison to keep alert, or get his throat slit.

Dr. Michaelov was a dapper little man, older than Petrov, solidly in his fifties, like Abram. Like Petrov, he was beautifully dressed, in a pale blue pin-striped suit, tasseled Italian loafers on his small feet. Liam thought he looked like a Belfast politician whose house he'd robbed, a smug, smooth-tongued liar who tossed around promises he'd never keep. Liam had made sure he'd cost the lying bugger dearly.

"It took you long enough to get here," Liam called out.

Dr. Michaelov drew himself up, looked down his nose at Liam, and ignored him.

He gave a sharp bow to Petrov. "I was unavoidably detained, Sergei. My apologies."

Liam said nothing as the doctor immediately sat beside Elena and examined her, asked her questions, tested her coordination, and gave her some pills. He stood, again bowed to Petrov, and said in beautifully fluent English with only a whiff of an accent, "Ms. Orlov will be fine. I've given her something for the headache. But she must rest."

Liam called out, "Will she be well enough to travel by tomorrow morning?"

Michaelov turned cold eyes to Liam, looked back to Petrov, his eyebrow raised. Supercilious sod.

Petrov said, "You may answer him, Timur."

"Very well." Michaelov stood stiffly, then said in a voice colder than a Moscow winter, "Ms. Orlov will be well enough by tomorrow to travel, but no more than two or three hours, then she must rest."

Liam gave Timur his heartbreaker smile. "Good to hear. Now come here, mate, and take care of my damned foot."

34

Savich slipped his cell back into his shirt pocket as he sat down on the sofa opposite Jack and Cam. "That was Chief Harbinger calling back. Surgery went well. He'll be back to work in a week. He sounded a bit woozy but managed to curse his surgeon for calling his wife."

Cam laughed. "All bluster. I'll bet he was happy to see her when he woke up."

Jack bit into his third slice of pepperoni pizza, saw that Sherlock was eyeing the last slice in the box, and grinned at her. "All yours."

Sherlock snagged the last slice, waved it at Cam. "Your arm's okay, Cam?"

"Fine, the stitches itch a bit, nothing to worry about." She looked over at Jack, then back at Savich. "Actually, what we were both worried about is whether you were going to dress us down or shoot us."

Savich waved that off. "Stuff happens, so we move on."

Cam said, "We heard from Haller—the Bolt—that you and Sherlock are up to your eyeballs in a baby kidnapping and the attempted murder last night of the unidentified man you took down on Sunday. Can you tell us what's going on?"

Sherlock said, "It's a real puzzle, but the pieces are coming together. It shouldn't be too long now before we know exactly what happened and why. But what's important right now is what's happening with Manta Ray."

Savich picked it up. "You guys did well identifying the helicopter as a Robinson R66. Despite the fake tail number, it's a good lead. Lucy's still working on it.

"Jack, the man you shot who fell from the helicopter was in the system. His name was Arnold Jacobson, age thirty-six, in and out of prison since the age of fourteen. He started with shoplifting, moved on to car theft and breaking and entering, continued up the crime chain to enforcer for some Baltimore loan sharks. He very nearly killed a man in Baltimore and might have gotten away with it, but he had a blowup with his boss, and the boss gave him up. He served a ten-year sentence in Brockbridge Correctional Facility in Maryland, released six months ago. No early parole because he was a troublemaker, ready to stick a shiv into anyone he didn't like. Ollie is looking into known associates, anyone who could connect him to whoever's got Manta Ray.

"Something else you need to know. Ruth surveilled Manta Ray's lawyer, Duce Bowler, when he left his office yesterday afternoon. She and Ollie scared him into calling for a meet with the person who hired him to make the deal with Manta Ray. She followed him into a public garage and he was ambushed. Hard to believe, but Bowler managed to shoot his would-be assassin. At the moment he's in the wind. We have an APB out on him. As for the assassin, his name was Russell Bauer. Like Jacobson, he was fresh out of prison, convicted for nearly killing a man in a bar fight. Like Jacobson, he served his full six-year sentence. We're looking into Bauer's known associates."

Cam was staring at him. "Good grief, Dillon, and here I thought Jack and I were in the middle of the storm. Is Ruth all right?"

"Yes. Bauer knocked an older couple unconscious but didn't kill them."

Jack said, "We should find Bowler quickly. He has no experience staying off the grid, and he's got to be scared to death."

Sherlock said, "Agents are covering Mrs. Bowler and the daughter, Magda Bowler. His cell phone is off, so we can't triangulate his location. But if he uses it to contact them, we'll find him."

Jack said, "He's got to realize we're his best friends right now."

"He's a lawyer," Cam said, and shrugged. "Lawyers don't have friends."

Savich smiled at her. "Now I've got some good news and more work for you and Jack. Of the people who rented those bank safe-deposit boxes, I focused on one in particular—Cortina Alvarez. Have you guys had time to read the initial interviews?"

Cam nodded. "Alvarez—midthirties, a wealthy socialite originally from Mexico, official residence in Washington, D.C., for the last ten years. She claimed she had only jewelry in the box. She provided insurance verification of the pieces."

Savich nodded. "The agents who interviewed her were thorough. They also examined the Mexican public records, verified she was born in Mexico City thirty-five years ago and was orphaned at eighteen, the only beneficiary of her very wealthy parents. She immigrated to the U.S. to attend William and Mary, majored in Slavic literature, speaks three languages. She became a U.S. citizen at twenty-three. She lists no profession, and she travels a lot."

Jack said, "So what made you suspicious of Ms. Alvarez in particular?"

"I had MAX repeat the check on Alvarez in the Mexican public records. Sure enough, there she was, everything looked on the up-and-up, but still, I didn't like the feel of it. I had MAX go deeper."

Sherlock grinned at him and smacked his knee. "Go ahead, Dillon, get some smiles back on these two long faces."

"There is no Cortina Alvarez," he said simply. "The records show her first U.S. passport issued twelve years ago, the background information on her parents, siblings, grandparents, and their addresses and birth and death dates seemingly complete and verifiable. It was so well done, it fooled the interviewers, who believed her legitimate and struck her off the list." He paused a moment, took the last bite of his Dizzy Dan's veggie pizza slice, wiped his hands on a napkin. "It was a near-perfect legend."

Cam sat forward, so excited she almost dropped her pizza. "But why didn't you think it was legitimate?"

Savich shrugged. "It was too pat. I realized I'd seen work like that before by an Italian forger, known in the business as Dr. Perfetto, real name Dr. Antonio Costas, an erstwhile physician based in Milan. He's been in the business for more than thirty years, costs a fortune, but his legends are a forgery gold standard, nearly impossible to break. But independent of the information created for the passport application, MAX couldn't find any prior record of her anywhere."

Sherlock said, "We had a case a couple of years ago that traced back to Dr. Costas. So when he saw it this time, Dillon recognized his style, I guess you could call it."

Savich said, "Actually, in that case, it was Sherlock who picked up on something that didn't feel right. Cortina Alvarez's listed address is the Satterleigh Condominium complex near Rock Creek Park."

Cam said, "I know them. I dated a guy a couple of years ago who owned one of the condos. It's very upscale. Since she claimed to be an heiress, I guess it makes sense Alvarez wouldn't live in a dump."

Savich said, "All her taxes, insurance, and utilities are paid on time, her two-year-old Lexus is housed at the condo. There is sporadic use of credit cards, again, paid on time each month. It appears she's spent very little time here in Washington over the past decade. Her passport destinations are primarily European."

"Which means," Cam said, "she has cars available to her in these locations and drives wherever she wants. She certainly wouldn't rent a car and leave a paper trail."

"Agreed," Savich said. "Cam, you and Jack will pay Ms. Alvarez a visit tomorrow morning. I want to show her muscle. Take her to the Hoover Building, and we'll all have a nice long talk. Here's her passport photo, renewed two years ago."

Jack looked at the sharp-featured face of a woman in her thirties with olive skin, short spiky red hair, green eyes ringed in black eyeliner, and heavy near-black lipstick. She was wearing a black turtleneck sweater and a nose ring. "Says she's five foot six, weighs one twenty-five. She looks like a Goth throwback." He handed the photo to Cam.

Cam studied the photo. "Her hair is dyed or it's a very good wig. With that olive complexion I doubt she has green eyes. Her hair is probably as dark as her eyes and eyebrows." She looked at Savich. "Even this photo isn't real, is it?"

35

"I've run the photo through facial recognition, no matches, which means Alvarez isn't in the database. That is, if that photo really is Alvarez."

Cam picked an olive off her pizza and chewed on it. "Jack, remember Chief Harbinger's daughter had the impression the woman with Jacobson and Manta Ray could be Hispanic?"

"Yeah, sure, but we didn't get any kind of look at her."

Sherlock said, "Okay, but why not her? It would make sense, keep it all in the family so to speak, wouldn't it?"

Savich said, "And that would mean her boss had her set up the safe-deposit box in her name. The question is, who are they?"

Jack took a drink of the Funky Buddha, frowned. "You wouldn't have a Bud, would you, Savich?"

An hour later, Jack walked Cam to the door. "Drive carefully. You sure your arm's okay?"

"Stop worrying, I'm fine."

"Okay, but remember, even though you don't have a broken wing, you're still driving with a lot of missing feathers."

She laughed. "I hope you enjoy Hotel Savich. I hear only the really interesting people are invited to stay here."

"I think it's more to the point that they know I'm pretty much homeless here in Washington." Jack paused, looked beyond her left shoulder. "The guy you dated at the Satterleigh condos, he was a rich guy? Who was he?"

"Derrick Benthurst was his name. His bank nearly destroyed the world economy, but he looked me right in the eye and claimed he knew nothing about it, the lying putz. On the plus side, he had a flat stomach and a nice smile."

"How do you know he had a flat stomach? No, forget that. You didn't get serious with him?"

She laughed, couldn't help herself, and leaned in close. "Derrick was in the process of trying to discover whether he was gay. He was."

He gave her a big smile. "Well, that's enough to make a woman think twice. You're right, what a putz."

"Yes, indeed."

Jack lightly touched his fingers to her blue sling. "I could ask them to let you stay, what with your missing feathers, but there's only one guest bedroom. You'd have to sleep with me or in Sean's room."

She eyed him up and down. "Well, I've got to say

you do clean up well, Cabot, but I sort of liked that black scruff all over your face. Do you snore?"

"Can't say, I never stayed awake to listen to myself."

"Har har. I wonder about Sean. Okay, time to get our brains back to the matter at hand."

Jack said, "Of course you've already read every single one of the initial interviews with the safe-deposit box owners."

She gave him a fat smile. "Sure. And when you're lying in bed alone tonight, you can review Cortina Alvarez's interview. Sleep well, Jack. I sure hope we do something to earn our pay tomorrow."

He stayed on the front porch until she'd backed her white Mazda out of the driveway and disappeared down the street. He walked back into the Savich living room and saw Sean in blue Transformer pajamas, standing next to Savich, his iPad clutched to his chest. He gave a jaw-cracking yawn.

"Papa says I should call you Uncle Jack."

"Sounds good. I already have three nephews. You can be my fourth. It's late, why'd you leave dreamland?"

"I dreamed a big green dragon flew so close to me he nearly burned my ears off and I woke up." Sean yawned again.

Savich lifted his boy into his arms. "Sean wants to challenge you to *Lethal Demon Force*—naturally, it's the advanced version—but I told him he'd have to be at the top of his game to take you on, and that means a solid night of sleep."

Jack smiled at the little boy, his face pressed against

his father's neck, nearly asleep again. He could already see the man in the boy. Jack patted Sean's thick black hair. "That's right, a solid nine hours or I'll zing you good."

Sean gave a little sleep snort.

Sherlock came out of the kitchen, wiping her hands on a towel. "All cleaned up. Hey, I hear Astro." She added to Jack, "Astro's Sean's terrier, a right frightening guard dog, that one. He rarely lets Sean out of his sight here at home. It's late, we should all get some sleep." Astro came tearing into the room, jumped up, and Sherlock caught him in her arms.

Jack looked down at his boots. "Yes, of course. Ah, about the fiasco today, Savich, I—"

"Jack, I'm sure you've played everything over and over in your head already. Tell me the truth—would you have done anything different?"

"No."

"There you go," Savich said. "Do me a favor and take Sean back to bed." He handed Sean to Jack. "I'll take Astro out, lock up, and turn on security."

Ten minutes later, Jack was settled on his back in the middle of a very comfortable bed, reading Cortina Alvarez's interview. When he finished, he turned off the light, stared up at the dark ceiling, and listened to the silence of the night. He saw Jacobson falling again, falling until he smashed onto the dirt road a dozen feet from where he and Cam stood. Jack doubted he'd forget that sound for a very long time.

36

Savich was reading Russell Bauer's prison records when his cell belted out Kenny Chesney's "Noise."

"Savich."

"Raven here. It appears we've got ourselves a full-on Metro/Federal law enforcement overlap."

A black eyebrow went up. "I hope we played nice. Talk to me, Ben."

"I drove over to the Satterleigh Condominium complex this morning to speak to a Cortina Alvarez. Lo and behold what should I see but two of your people driving away. I recognized Cam Wittier. Cortina Alvarez wasn't there. She was traveling again, I was told. One of her neighbors verified your two FBI agents were asking questions about Cortina Alvarez as well. So what's up, Savich? How are we connected? What's the FBI's interest in Cortina Alvarez?"

Had the list of the six safe-deposit owners gotten out? Savich didn't think so. "Ben, could you tell me first why you went to see Cortina Alvarez?"

"And if I do, you'll tell me why your nose is under my tent?"

"Yes, as much as I can."

"All right, I know you won't screw around with me."

"No, I won't, but I can't tell you all of it; things are at too sensitive a point right now."

He heard Ben sigh. "You remember that George Washington student who was murdered six weeks ago? Her name was Mia Prevost."

"Yes, I remember. She was found in her bed, half a dozen savage stab wounds, right?"

"Yes. She was found in her apartment by a girlfriend. We searched her apartment, found fingerprints and some men's clothes in the closet, and thought bingo."

"The boyfriend."

"You got it. But there's more to it, lots more. I'll have to back up. Yesterday, I got a call from the George Washington gym facility, the volleyball coach. They'd gotten around to cleaning out her locker, found some of Mia Prevost's clothes, sneakers, cosmetics, and a small address book. There was only one name in the notebook—Cortina Alvarez and a phone number."

Out of left field. Savich didn't say anything.

Ben continued. "We hadn't known about this particular locker because Mia Prevost used another gym— Five Points Fitness—near her apartment in Carlan Heights. We found everything we expected there, workout clothes, sneakers, hair products. It didn't occur to me she'd have two gym lockers. Yes, I'm an idiot, kick me."

"Only if I could ever go a full day without screwing up. So tell me about the boyfriend. And tell me why you haven't arrested him."

"We're keeping his name under wraps until we can find enough evidence to make it public. You've got to keep this under your hat, Savich. The boyfriend is Eric Hainny's son, Saxon Hainny."

"You mean President Gilbert's chief of staff? That Eric Hainny?"

"The very one. As you can imagine, that makes our case a political land mine. I was allowed to speak to Mr. Hainny at his home in Chevy Chase. He told me, yes, Saxon had dated this girl and brought her over a couple of times. He said she was beautiful and admitted to me that had worried him. When I asked him why, he sort of smiled, said his son was something of a nerd without a lot of social skills. But he alibied his son, said the night Mia Prevost was murdered he and his son were at the Lorenzo Café in Alexandria—you know it, the old Italian place, run by the Lorenzo family? It's a local landmark, always swarmed at dinnertime. When I interviewed the staff who were there that night, no one could be sure whether Hainny and his son were there. They said Hainny does come in often, and he always pays in cash. One waiter couldn't be located, so maybe he was the one who waited on Hainny and his son.

"With Mr. Hainny's permission, I spoke to his son, Saxon, in his presence. Saxon's twenty-four years old, a doctoral student in computer science, a nerd right down to his white socks and pocket protector. My gut said the young guy wouldn't kill a fly. Still, I was ready to snap the cuffs on him, but he started crying. He was distraught over her murder, barely coherent, blamed himself that he hadn't been there to help her. His grief wasn't faked, no one's that good an actor, especially not him. Primo cynic though I am, I couldn't help but believe him. So I was stuck. Until we got this name— Cortina Alvarez. But who knows? Maybe Prevost had just bought the address book and Alvarez was the first name she'd entered. I don't know. So this morning, I drove out to see her and saw your people leaving. Now it's your turn."

"The first thing I'll tell you is Cortina Alvarez doesn't exist."

37

Chief of Staff Eric Hainny sat in his office, staring out his window at the beautiful summer morning. Tourists in their shorts, tugging their kids along, were already stopped in front of the boundary fence, looking, pointing. Did they expect to see President Gilbert in his shorts?

His cell phone sounded out an old-fashioned ringtone. He didn't recognize the number. "Hainny here. Who is this, and how did you get my cell?"

"Mr. Hainny, this is Agent Dillon Savich, FBI. We last met four weeks ago in former Secretary of State Abbott's office."

"I know you, Agent Savich. What is this about?"

Savich had never cared for Eric Hainny, saw him as a power-mongering bulldog in Ralph Lauren suits, overly protective of President Gilbert, a man who luxuriated in the control he wielded over access to the king. He liked to be thought of as a man you underestimated at your own peril. Savich had no doubt he knew the whereabouts of every skeleton in every closet in Washington, and enjoyed using the information whenever it suited him.

"I would like to speak to you about your son, Saxon."

A moment of silence, then Hainny said, "Saxon has already spoken with Detective Ben Raven. There is nothing more to say. How does this involve the FBI? This is a Metro case."

"I have Detective Raven's permission to speak to you, sir. When would it be convenient?"

Hainny drummed his fingers on the paper-strewn desktop his assistant dealt with every afternoon. "This is about my son, Saxon, nothing else?"

"Yes."

"Very well. But not here at the White House. I'll meet you at Rock Creek Park in an hour."

He hung up.

It took Savich fifteen minutes to navigate the traffic on Sixteenth Street N.W. to Rock Creek Park. He parked his Porsche, looked down at his watch. Only ten thirty in the morning, but the park was already thick with families, probably tourists, their kids playing football, throwing Frisbees, enjoying the morning weather before it turned hot and muggy. Savich caught a Frisbee that soared his way, tossed it back to a boy hopping up and down, his friends laughing their heads off when he splatted bubble gum all over his face.

Five minutes later Savich found Hainny seated on a bench in a quiet corner of the park. The area was lined with thick oaks, a small winding creek flowing through them. He was alone, looking straight ahead at the easy-flowing creek. He was dressed in one of his signature Ralph Lauren pin-striped summer suits, this one gray, beautifully cut to hide some of his bulk, with a blue shirt and red power tie. For as long as Savich had known him, Hainny had carried an extra thirty pounds. He was wearing dark sunglasses and Savich doubted anyone else would recognize him as the president's powerful chief of staff sitting in a tourist mecca.

Hainny looked up as he took off his sunglasses, and Savich saw the haggard face of a man who'd lived with something painful for too long and was being forced to face it again. Savich felt sorry for him for a second until the haggard look left his face, replaced by the controlled, cold look of the cunning politician Savich knew him to be. Savich had witnessed firsthand how dictatorial and ruthless Hainny could be, ready to drop-kick anyone who got in his way. He was the president's right-hand man. He saw himself as inviolate.

"Mr. Hainny."

Hainny nodded. "Thank you for coming here, Agent Savich. I think you understand why I would rather not involve any of my staff in this matter or raise any questions." He didn't shake Savich's hand, merely waved for him to sit down.

Hainny looked at the man President Gilbert believed would be the director of the FBI in fifteen years or so. Hainny had to admit he'd been impressed when he'd seen Savich in action the month before. He recognized Savich as a man who would do whatever was necessary if he thought the end was righteous.

Hainny didn't trust men like him. "You informed me you wished to speak to me about my son. I do not understand why, Agent Savich. You said Detective Raven gave you permission to speak to me. However, Mia Prevost's murder is a local police matter, not FBI. What role are you playing?"

"I want your permission to speak to your son, Saxon."

"Again, why are you involved?" He waved a big hand, showing off the Harvard class ring on his pinkie finger.

Savich said deliberately, "You know I can't discuss an ongoing investigation, Mr. Hainny. Detective Raven has held off indicting Saxon, but as it stands, he might be forced to. I believe I can help your son. I want you to tell me everything you can about Mia Prevost and your son's involvement with her."

Hainny looked frozen for a moment. Fear for his son? Savich added, "If it were my son, I would welcome any help you could give me."

Hainny studied Savich, seemed to come to a decision and said slowly, "Very well, although I doubt you can help him. Let me be blunt about my son. Even as a boy Saxon had a brilliant and incisive mind. He often surprised me with some of the uncanny connections he saw in the world around him, and he has applied his talent admirably to his studies. He also likes to talk about Comic-Con to anyone who will listen, he's a die-hard *Star Trek* fan, he speaks Klingon, and, needless to say, he spends a great deal of his time on computers.

"Three months ago, my son asked me to meet his new girlfriend, a psychology major at George Washington. When he walked in with this gorgeous girl I nearly fell off my chair. She was, frankly, completely unlike the very few girls Saxon has managed to date in the past.

"Agent Savich, I've dealt with many kinds of people in my years of public service. Most of them have their own agendas, sometimes laudable, sometimes not. It didn't take me long to wonder about this girl. The second time he brought her over, she showed a great deal of interest in what I do. Of course people consider my job fascinating, and to be honest, many women think it's sexy because I'm the president's gatekeeper, but in her case, I thought perhaps she was simply curious. Still, I wondered if it was because of me she was with Saxon." He shrugged. "It's in my genes to be distrustful. In fact, I'll readily admit I've learned to be paranoid. I'd be stupid if I weren't, in this town. So I ran a check, found she was indeed enrolled in George Washington, in her third year, at the age of twenty-five—a little old for a college third year, I thought—as a psych major. I said nothing about my concerns to my son, but I worried. My son was nuts about her, and she appeared very fond of him as well. I was delighted to see him so happy, but still I worried, something didn't seem to add up." Hainny stopped. Savich saw he'd closed his eyes and was taking a deep, calming breath.

Savich said, "What happened, Mr. Hainny? What did your son tell you?"

"When I heard the news of Mia's murder, I drove

immediately to my son's apartment. He'd just heard about it himself on the local news. He was devastated, out of his mind with rage at what had happened to her, and terrible grief. He said over and over he didn't understand how anyone could hurt Mia. She wouldn't hurt a soul; she had no enemies.

"Saxon told me he woke up in his own bed that morning, but he had been in her apartment the night before. As for anything else, his memory is blank. He didn't know what had happened. He wanted to go to the police right away, but I managed to talk him down, explained he should wait until they contacted him. I knew the media would savage him because of who I am, manufacture a scandal to hurt both of us, and if they could, the president.

"I knew the police would quickly connect him to Mia; he was her boyfriend. They'd been sleeping together, and he'd stayed overnight at her apartment many times. He was in a bad position. He told me he couldn't remember drinking enough to make him pass out. And what would the police think? He'd had a psychotic break? Of course it was my duty to inform the president of what had happened. He was very worried about Saxon. He instructed me to keep him informed but so long as Saxon was not charged, we would have no comment and take no action. I also spoke to Police Commissioner Sturgis, asked him to keep any discussions with my son private if he could.

"Detective Ben Raven, who interviewed Saxon, didn't believe at first that Saxon couldn't remember anything, that he'd blanked out, but a blind man could see Saxon's grief, his depth of feeling for Prevost. We were informed there was no physical evidence that linked him directly to the crime.

"I assume they're now looking at her former associates but not the ex-boyfriend Saxon told me about. It seems she made him up; why, I don't know. So far as I know, they haven't found anyone to build a case against except Saxon. As you can imagine, I'm very worried about my son."

"Tell me, Mr. Hainny, has anyone approached you?"

Hainny gave a snort. "Of course you'd immediately see everything clearly." He looked away from Savich, his hands now fisted on his legs. "I wouldn't be surprised at a demand for money perhaps, but no one has approached me, and it's been six weeks." He looked back. "I don't know what this is all about. All I know is that my son is innocent."

Hainny stood, looked around the park with unseeing eyes, then gave Savich the barest nod. "Here is his cell number and address. I will tell him to expect you."

38

Sherlock studied the passport photo of a pretty young woman with hair same color as her eyes, as dark as night hanging loose around her sharp-featured, intelligent face. Brenda Love was twenty-eight and Kara Moody's other best friend, currently on vacation in Spain. Sherlock had called and introduced herself, told her Kara's baby had been born, then kidnapped out of the hospital, and asked if she could answer questions.

Brenda Love fell silent. Sherlock heard only street noise in the background, alas, no flamenco music. Love said finally, "How do I know you are who you say you are?"

"I can have Kara call your cell and vouch for me. How's that?"

Brenda Love agreed. Sherlock had to admit it was exactly what she would have done. She didn't have to wait long before she was back on her cell with Ms. Love, who told her she was at a sidewalk café across from the

Prado Museum drinking a latte. Sherlock envied her. She and Dillon had managed to walk all over the Prado two years before, taking in the power of Goya's paintings with three-year-old Sean in tow. Sherlock said, "I'm going to email you a photo of a young man. Tell me if you've ever seen him before."

In a moment, Love said, "Got it. He's good-looking, maybe a bit younger than Kara, younger than me. No, I've never seen him before. Why? You think he kidnapped Kara's baby?"

Sherlock cast her rod into the water. "No, that wouldn't be possible, he's currently lying in a coma in the hospital. He's also the baby's father."

Stark silence. "You've got to be kidding me. Kara didn't say anything to me about him." She sighed. "In fact, she said she couldn't talk to me, could only confirm you were FBI and she was working with you and it was okay to speak to you."

Sherlock said, "When we're done here, feel free to speak to her again, Ms. Love. She needs a good friend right now. The first time Kara ever saw this man was on Sunday, but we'll get to that later. Ms. Love, do you know Sylvie Vaughn?"

"Well, yes, of course."

"Do you know many of Sylvie and Josh Vaughn's friends?"

"Wait a minute, did you show Sylvie his photo? Does she know him?"

Sherlock said, "Yes, I showed Mrs. Vaughn his photo, and she said she'd never seen him before. I understand you weren't at Mr. Vaughn's birthday party nine months ago?"

Love gave a rude snort. "I remember that party. I wasn't about to go, and I remember I told Kara she shouldn't, either, but she said Sylvie begged her to come so she'd have her own special friend there to support her. Support her, ha! Besides, Josh is a pig. You couldn't pay me to get near him."

Sherlock cast a wider net. "Sounds like you don't much care for Sylvie Vaughn. Or the pig."

"The pig is a pig and doesn't try to hide it, but Sylvie's a phony who lucked into a very lucrative business. Look, Agent Sherlock, I'm not bad-mouthing her for the fun of it. I heard her YouTube phenom—*Cycling Madness*—was all another woman's idea, even that cool title, and Sylvie stole it. And no, she can't prove it, nothing was written down. And yes, that woman is a friend of mine, and that's why she told me about it." Sherlock heard a sigh. "I believe her because it fits Sylvie more than not. She's never been at all pleasant to me."

"Does Kara know how you feel?"

There was a slight pause. "Well, no, I never thought it was right to lay that crap on Kara, even after my friend told me what she'd done. I wanted Kara to be free to make her own choices, not to have to pick between us. The thing is, Kara's so wholesome, you know what I mean? She's serious and always wants to see the good in people, and, well, she's very nice. I knew it would hurt her. And Sylvie treated her well, so I left it alone."

Sherlock said slowly, feeling her way, "It seems Kara

and Sylvie met by chance at the gallery where Kara worked in Baltimore, that they hit it off right away?"

Love snorted. "Yeah, that's what Kara told me, and I bought the kismet deal until maybe a month or so after the birthday party, I overheard Sylvie tell one of her satellite friends—you know, one of her social media buddies—that she'd asked this no-style prude who sold her paintings in a third-rate gallery to be on her YouTube fashion show, but she'd turned her down. She laughed, said she'd been relieved. What would you think of a friend who said that?"

Not much. "You didn't tell Kara what you'd overheard?"

"I probably should have, I mean, this was out of Sylvie's mouth, so it wasn't gossip. I'd almost worked myself up to tell her when out of the blue Kara told me she was pregnant. That sidetracked me, to say the least. I asked her who the father was, but she only shook her head, begged me to leave it alone. I wasn't about to pile on by telling her what a two-faced bitch Sylvie was. And when she made up her mind to leave Baltimore, I couldn't see the point, it would only add more misery to her situation. Whatever Sylvie was about, you know, being nice to Kara's face, but talking about her behind her back, she'd be out of Kara's life."

Sherlock said, "This is where I need your help, Ms. Love. Kara was drugged at the party. The father is a man she never saw before, a man who doesn't seem to have been there. Sylvie Vaughn said she didn't know him, and you don't know him, either. Kara never said anything to you about it?"

A moment of silence as Brenda Love took it all in. "No, I spoke to her a couple of days later, at lunch. I remember asking her about the party and was really surprised when she told me she must have drank too much and blacked out. Let me be perfectly clear here, Agent Sherlock. I have never seen Kara drunk. And enough booze to black out? She told me she couldn't remember anything. I should have followed up, but I didn't. I was breaking up with my boyfriend, and all into myself. I'm an idiot."

Sherlock cut that off. "Hindsight is always an amazing thing, so don't beat yourself up. Tell me, was there anyone else you remember in Kara's life around that time? Before the party?"

"Not really. She didn't have a steady boyfriend. She occasionally went out, but nothing serious. She led a quiet life. She was really into her painting, of course, and she's good. Have you seen her landscapes? They're like stepping into a dream, the colors all wreathed in a misty light."

"I haven't had a chance yet to see her work, but I will. Ms. Love, I need you to think back. Can you remember anything unusual that happened to Kara before the party? Any men she might have met, any offer of drugs she told you about?"

A pause, then, "No, I really can't, Agent Sherlock."

"Okay, how about anything that needed medical care, that required she take drugs?"

"No, sorry. Wait, I do remember that a few weeks before the party Kara showed up to lunch with a huge, ugly bruise on her arm. She told me she'd gotten a call from a local university, I don't remember which one, asking her to give them a sample of her blood for a study they were doing. They paid her for it, a one-time blood draw; that was it. Obviously whoever drew her blood messed up. Does that mean anything?"

"It's possible. I'll ask Kara about it."

"I'm flying home tomorrow, Agent Sherlock. I don't have to be back to work until next week. Do you think I could come down to Washington and be with Kara? I haven't seen her in a couple of months. Do you think it would help?"

"Yes," Sherlock said, "I think it would, but call Kara, see what she thinks." Sherlock left Brenda Love to her latte.

She called Agent Butler, filled her in.

When she'd finished, Butler said, "This depresses me, Sherlock. I thought Vaughn was funny, straightforward. Maybe Brenda Love was jealous, made it up, maybe exaggerated?"

"No, I don't think so. But the fact is, Connie, even though I was suspicious of her, I liked Vaughn, too."

"But still you put that GPS tracker on her car."

"Yes." Sherlock added, "A couple of weeks ago I interviewed a talented up-and-coming sculptor, and I really liked her, too, believed her."

"It turned out she wasn't what she seemed?"

"No, not at all what she seemed. I made a vow I'd always err on the side of caution after that."

"Bolt—Agent Haller—was sure Alex Moody was

taken for ransom until he heard John Doe was the baby's father, and someone tried to murder him last night. He's coming around to the idea that unlike most of our kidnapping cases, this one isn't about money, or custody, it's about something else entirely. None of us on the CARD team has ever dealt with anything so crazy convoluted as this."

Sherlock paused a moment. "Connie, this is my gut talking, but not entirely. Somehow I can't help but feel Kara could also be in danger. It's possible the hospital will try to discharge her soon. If they do, maybe the person or people behind the kidnapping will make some kind of contact with her. I'm not sure, but I'd feel better if Agent Haller stays with her at her house. Brenda Love could stay with her, too. "

"Sounds right to me. Bolt and I will discuss it with our supervisor, see what he thinks, and we'll get back to you."

"Where has Sylvie Vaughn been since we left her yesterday?"

"Pretty regular stuff, nothing strange—the grocery store, a small studio on Cline Street where she films her YouTube show *Cycling Madness*, her yoga class at Bay Watch Fitness Center, and last, she met her husband for dinner at Papa Leoni's in the Inner Harbor."

"Nothing suspicious in the Vaughns' financial records so far, or their phone records. Not as useful now that anyone can buy a burner phone to use. We'll both keep checking, okay?"

Sherlock got up from her desk to update Dillon,

saw through the big glass window that he was working on MAX, probably researching the mystery drug
Dr. Wordsworth said they found in John Doe's blood,
seeing what MAX could find in one of the compound
libraries.

She knew Kara's number by heart and punched it
in. She caught Kara sitting with John Doe, talking to
him again, Kara told her.

"Has Brenda called you back, Kara?"

"Yes. She's changed her flight to Dulles. I want to
see her, but I'm a mess. I hope she'll understand."

"She will. She's very upset about the whole thing.
Keep her close, Kara. Can you tell me about the big
bruise Brenda said you had on your arm a few weeks
before you got pregnant? You gave some blood for a
study of some kind?"

"She remembered that? Yes, a woman called me
from the University of Maryland, told me their genetics department was conducting a study in population genetics, something about how various athletes
are distributed in different ethnic groups around the
country. I was picked at random and offered two hundred dollars to give a sample of my blood. It was only
for one time, and so I agreed. I swear, though, it was
the first time the guy had ever drawn blood. It was brutal. I ended up with a big bruise for a week. Why?"

"Filling in blanks, that's all. Kara, can you describe
the man who drew your blood?"

"Goodness, why, for heaven's sake?"

"Indulge me."

"Well, I remember he was a big guy, in his thirties, and as I said, he wasn't good at it. He suggested he come by the gallery where I worked at quitting time and if I liked, he could draw my blood there. I agreed, seemed easier than going to a lab somewhere. He introduced himself, but I don't remember his name. He gave me two one-hundred-dollar bills and left. And that was it, I never heard another word from anyone at the university."

"Do you think you could give an artist a good description of the man?"

"Yes, but why not let me draw him?"

"Excellent. Kara, stay strong. How are you feeling?"

"Still trying to come to grips with the fact that the man whose hand I'm holding right this moment, this stranger I'm telling my life story to, is Alex's father. I asked Dr. Wordsworth if she believed he could hear me. She said she spoke nonstop to her own mother when she was still unconscious after surgery and when her mother woke up, she smiled and remarked on what a talker she was." Kara laughed. "Dr. Wordsworth also says he's still getting better and to keep talking; he'll be waking up soon. It's all so crazy, isn't it?"

Sherlock said, "It's only crazy until it makes sense." She decided she wouldn't tell Kara about Sylvie Vaughn, either, not yet. It wouldn't serve any purpose. Brenda Love would be there the next day, someone Kara was close to, to help keep her spirits up, maybe help her sort through all of this.

39

Jack climbed into Cam's Miata outside the Satterleigh Condominium complex, fastened his seat belt. "I'd call this a bust. The manager told me Ms. Cortina Alvarez is traveling, always traveling. This time, it's Milan and Florence for the Latin princess, where, he said, she owns houses. She isn't due back for three weeks." He asked without much hope, "Did you have any better luck?"

Cam fastened her own seat belt, opened all the windows, slipped on her dark sunglasses, and turned to face him. "Her next-door neighbor told me the same thing. 'Always on the go, that's Cortina,'" she said. "She recognized her passport photo, though, even with the spiked hair and Goth makeup."

"At least she does live here, sometimes," Jack said. "I already called Savich. He wants us to meet Ruth and Ollie at that Alexandria warehouse where they captured Manta Ray. The FBI field office has already been all over it looking for the stash he robbed from the bank, but Savich wants us to go in with a fresh eye, turn it over again ourselves. He believes something's still got to be there. Wherever that Robinson choppered Manta Ray and the woman with him yesterday afternoon can't be all that far away. And Manta Ray and whoever that helicopter took him to probably wants it back. Otherwise why go to all the trouble of breaking him out? Hey, why aren't you wearing your sling?"

Cam pressed the start button and the Miata roared to life. "I'm good to go, Jack, don't worry. Let's say Dillon is right; let's say the reason they broke Manta Ray out was to get whatever he stashed from the bank robbery. If he doesn't want to give it up, someone might be pulling his tonsils out through his nose right now."

"Maybe, but Manta Ray is a pretty smart man. I'd put my money on his thinking of a way to come out of this alive. With Jacobson out of the picture, he might. In any case, there's a chance someone's going to be headed back there looking to find that stash."

Cam banged her fist on the steering wheel, and winced. "With our luck today, he's probably already come and gone."

"So how long to get us there, Cam? I see your arm still hurts, you want me to drive?"

Cam had already turned the corner. She stuck her flasher on the roof of her Miata, gave him a huge grin. "Nah, this is nothing. I wanted to be a race car driver until I was nearly twelve." She gunned the Miata, swerving around cars that didn't melt away in front of her. Even traffic on the Francis Scott Key Bridge hugged the sides as she roared past them, screeching into a hard right turn onto Franklin Boulevard.

Jack was grinning like a maniac and he wasn't even in the driver's seat. He loved speed, loved the adrenaline rush, could feel the roaring of the blood through his veins and wondered if Cam felt the same way. Her wavy blond hair was whipping about her head, and he saw she was whistling. He felt very good at that moment; he felt energized. He sat back and enjoyed it. Seven minutes later, Cam pulled the Miata up on a curb half a block from the abandoned warehouse district where they'd first found Manta Ray lying with a dirty torn sheet pressed to his bleeding side.

"That was well done, Wittier; I'm impressed. You want to race with me sometime?"

Cam's adrenaline level was still soaring upward. "I'll have you know that was official business. If Savich was right about Manta Ray coming back here, we had to get here fast."

"Sure, believe what you need to believe." He gave her a big grin as he climbed out of the Miata and looked around. He saw a desolate hardscrabble landscape with abandoned parking lots fronting a dozen dilapidated warehouses and loading docks, their windows broken out, probably for decades. Nests made of cardboard boxes were huddled around the warehouses, to give shelter from the wind. He saw half a dozen homeless people sitting on warehouse stoops, their backs against building walls, paying them no attention.

"It's this one," Cam said, pointing to a warehouse that looked on the edge of collapsing in on itself. Cam pulled off her sunglasses as they made their way into the

dim interior of a large empty single-story space. The air
smelled like dead rodents and rotted food. They both
snapped on nitrile gloves and started going through
every corner of the ramshackle space where Manta
Ray had picked to hide. They banged on floorboards
that hadn't already been ripped up, checked every crev-
ice behind the busted-up wallboard. They didn't find
Manta Ray's stash, or any trace he'd ever been there.
They stood in the middle of the vast space and tried to
look at it with fresh eyes. But their fresh eyes didn't see
anything, either.

As they walked out of the warehouse, none of the
homeless people paid them any mind, most kept their
heads down, not wanting to draw attention to themselves. But one man was singing "Take Me Home,
Country Roads." He looked at them and smiled. Jack
and Cam trotted over to him, both ignoring the other
eyes suddenly watching their every move. The man was
leaning back against some broken-down cardboard
boxes propped against the side of a warehouse. He had
an old filthy towel draped over his head, wore a ragged
hula shirt open to a dirty T-shirt. They couldn't tell if
he was fifty or eighty. Jack went down on his haunches
beside him, got a whiff of something very ripe. He took
a hundred-dollar bill out of his wallet. "This is yours if
you can tell me anything about this man." He called up
Manta Ray's photo on his cell.

"It's not enough," came a phlegmy old voice. "Double or nothing."

"What? You from Las Vegas? All right." Jack pulled

out a second hundred, his last. "You've emptied the bank. Tell me."

His bloodshot eyes focused on Cam. "You sure are pretty. I had a girl once who was pretty as you. I wonder sometimes what happened to her. I guess she isn't so young anymore. I sure ain't."

"Thank you. Sir, this is really important. Have you seen him? He's a seriously bad man, a criminal. We believe he might be coming back here."

"I know who he is, missy. It's that Manta Ray character. Sally over there"—he flapped a veiny hand toward a head of matted red hair hunkered down in a ragged bundle of blankets inside a cardboard box some twelve feet away—"I call her Dancin' Sally. She used to be a stripper. She saw him first, told me while we were sharing a nice half bottle of bourbon that this here Manta Ray was about the cutest boy she'd ever seen. She said he was so bad hurt, he'd probably bite the big one."

He waved a gnarled hand. "Then I saw him. He was dragging himself around, moaning and carrying on." He looked at the photo again, turned his head, and spit. "Don't see it myself. He looked like another vicious mongrel to me. I haven't seen him back here since all the cops took him away. I don't remember when that was, a long time ago, maybe. Last year?"

"A long time ago," Cam said. "So, you haven't seen him? Maybe this morning?"

"Nary a glimpse. So he survived. I wondered, so did Sally. He get away from you guys? You're cops, right?"

"Yes, we're cops," Jack said. "You haven't seen anyone you don't know drive up here this morning? Or maybe late last night?"

"Nope, just my usual neighbors, and the dealers meetin' up with their fancy buyers, the putzes. All of 'em belong in jail, you ask me." He turned his head away and coughed.

Cam felt a hand on her shoulder, looked up to see Agent Ruth Noble. She hadn't heard Ruth; she'd come up so quietly. "Let me, Cam." Ruth fell to her knees beside the old man. "Hello, Dougie," she said, and gave him a Kleenex, waited until he'd wiped his mouth.

40

"Wow, that you, Ruth? You're looking happy. What? Haven't seen you in a couple of weeks. Or maybe longer. I can't remember. How's Dix and the boys?"

"They're well, thank you." She placed her fingers against the pulse in his dirty neck, counted, then nodded. "You told me you were going to stop the booze, Dougie."

"Yeah, well, a man's weak, ain't he? That's what Sally always says."

"All of us are weak, Dougie. I heard you tell my friend you haven't seen Manta Ray come around either last night or this morning?"

"That's right."

Ruth thought a moment. "Okay, then, have you seen anything odd, anything unexpected, since the police took Manta Ray away? Something that made you pay attention? Something that surprised you?"

"Well, yes, Ruth, all of us had a really big surprise, ended up with dirt in my hair until I pulled my towel over my head."

"What did you see?" Jack was bending down close. "Why didn't you tell me?"

Dougie cocked his head, said to Ruth, "Don't know why he's so pissed off, neither of these two kid cops asked me about nothin' else but Manta Ray."

Ruth pulled out a twenty-dollar bill. "Spill it, Dougie. No, no more, you've already fleeced us enough."

He gave her a cunning look, but Ruth shook her head, stared at him, and waited. He said in his scratchy smoker's voice, "Well, all right, if you're going to be a hard-ass. A fancy white helicopter came right down here early this morning, at first light. I couldn't believe my eyes. The sucker landed right over there." When he shifted to point, the towel fell away from his dirty grizzled gray hair. "It ain't all that big a place for a heli-copter, but it set itself down nice and smooth, right there in front of that warehouse. Didn't bother to turn off those noisy blades, either; they kept whirling and kicking up dirt.

"I couldn't believe it, Ruth, I mean I hadn't seen no helicopter ever land around here. The noise woke every-body up, scattered dust something fierce, like I said. Is that strange enough for you?" Dougie rearranged the threadbare dingy gray towel with a faded *Marriott* printed on it over his head. "If it was bigger, I could tie it under my chin, you know, if that chopper comes back and stirs up the dirt."

Ruth smiled at him, her hand still on his arm. "You're doing good. Tell me more, Dougie."

"No one got out of the helicopter, but then I heard

this guy shout, he was using a bullhorn, I guess, 'cause it was loud—he shouted for Humbug to get over there, quick. And sure enough, I look up and see Humbug staring down at the helicopter from out of his third-floor window, and he shouts back that he's coming and waves. I don't know how they could have heard him, what with those blades whirling around so fast, sounded like a war down here they was so loud, and enough dirt was kicking up to blind you. Got in my hair, right? Humbug had to bend over, cover his face with his hands and run, the dirt was so thick, like one of those African siroccos, got all over all of us. He trotted over to that helicopter and I couldn't believe what he did—he climbed right in, and after a while he climbed back out again and the helicopter lifted right straight up. That's why I'm wearing a towel, in case it comes back, I don't want no more sand on my head." And again, he patted the towel on his head.

"That's smart, Dougie," Ruth said, her voice patient. "But you didn't see Manta Ray?"

"No siree, Ruth, only heard that bullhorn voice." He looked up at Jack. "Can I keep the bucks?"

"Sure," Jack said, and stuck out his hand. "Dougie, I'm Jack and this is Cam. Was Humbug carrying anything when he ran to the helicopter?"

"Yeah, it was one of them leather carryalls, brown I think. Don't know where he got it, why he had it, and why he took it to that helicopter. Don't know nothing more, Ruth, not a blessed thing."

Cam said, "Is Humbug in that warehouse right now?"

"Nope, not yet, but Hummer'll be back. He always comes back."

"What can you tell us about him?"

Dougie looked from Jack to Cam. "You guys cop partners?"

"We are right now," Cam said.

"If you weren't so pretty, missy, I'd say you drive the bus, but I don't know. This guy, he's all tough-looking, hard—" He shook his head, as if getting his brain back on track, and gave them a smile, showing surprisingly white teeth.

"Come on, Dougie," Cam said, "tell us about Humbug."

"Yeah, well his name's really Hummer, calls himself Major Hummer, doesn't like us calling him Humbug. He sometimes lives here, sometimes goes back to that other world out there, but four, six months later, he's back again, babbling about all the jerks and cheats out there trying to kill him. Then he needs a drink and disappears into his room in the warehouse."

Cam interrupted him, she was so excited. "Dougie, did you say Hummer is his real name?"

"Sure, he's Hummer. He says Humbug means he's supposed to hate Christmas, only he doesn't, not really. He gave me this towel around Christmas, I think." Dougie smoothed it over his ears, shook his head, gave Cam a sweet smile. "You know what else? Humbug is always rantin' how if only the Feds had let him and his men loose he could have won that first shoot-out with Saddam in Iraq. He wouldn't of stopped, nope, he'd have marched his ass to Baghdad and wiped out those damned terrorists, not let that Saddam fellow wiggle his way out of it like he did. Sometimes he gets so worked up he don't make much sense, but sometimes—" He shook his head again, brought himself back. "I guess all I know about that war was it was a long time ago. Long time."

Dougie's towel had slipped again. This time, Ruth smoothed it back around his head.

"Ruth, it's funny, you know? Here Humbug fought in the U.S. military and he's Irish. Isn't that strange? I mean, why would he give a crap about terrorists hurting the United States? But I guess we've got all sorts over there throwing bombs at each other. It beats me how anybody knows who the good guys are."

"Irish," Ruth repeated. She leaned down and gave Dougie a big hug, then smiled really big up at Cam and Jack. "Humbug is Irish. Sounds to me Manta Ray may have found a friend the day he was shot."

Jack said, "Or maybe they already knew each other and that's why Manta Ray came here in the first place. Dougie, which warehouse does Humbug live in?"

Dougie pointed an unsteady finger toward a tall skinny building some twenty yards away. "That's the oldest place around here. Everyone except Humbug thinks it's too dangerous. Like I said, he's on the third floor when he's here, lived there for a long time now, on and off, don't know how long, maybe a year."

Ruth tucked another twenty-dollar bill into Dougie's collar, told him to stop drinking and buy some food.

"Ruth? I forgot to tell you, I think the guy on the bullhorn was Irish, too, he parlayed in this thick brogue. It coulda been fake, but who knows?"

"Thank you, Dougie." She rose, grinned at Cam and Jack. "Time for us to pay a visit to Humbug's crib."

Jack and Cam shook Dougie's hand and walked with Ruth past a half-dozen cardboard dwellings. Ruth said, "Most of all the homeless in this neighborhood prefer living outside rather than in any of the abandoned buildings, only bitter cold will drive them inside. They hate the rats and they're afraid the floors will collapse on them. Do you know I didn't know Humbug's name was Hummer?" She shook her head at herself. "I must be slipping."

Jack looked up at the decrepit warehouse. "The government spends so much money, why hasn't this place seen a dime of it?"

Cam said, "Sooner or later, it'll be made into condos. I wonder where Dougie and Sally and all the others will go?"

41

After they negotiated three floors of rotting stairs, they found Major Hummer's crib quickly, the only place on the third floor that looked occupied. It was actually a small room with no door, its walls broken down to their bare wood frames, its two broken-out windows facing the front of the warehouse covered with cardboard thumb-tacked over them. Most of the space was stuffed six feet high with decades of newspapers.

"So Humbug's a hoarder," Cam said as she carefully stepped around a stack of *Washington Posts* from 1993. "This isn't going to be easy."

Ruth pointed. "See that pile of blankets on those newspapers in the corner? That's where he slept. I wonder if he kept Manta Ray's carryall under his bed?"

She'd dug nearly to the bottom of that stack of newspapers when she blinked, called out, "Hey, what's this?"

Cam and Jack made their way over to her, watched her carefully unfold a 2003 *Washington Post* want-ads section. She held up a bracelet. Diamonds spilled through her fingers, sparkling even in the dim light.

"Looks like Humbug went through Manta Ray's goodie bag and lifted a souvenir. Or maybe this was his reward."

Jack took the diamond bracelet from Ruth, tossed it back and forth, watching the diamonds gleam and sparkle. "Pretty small diamonds, but a lot of them. Maybe high five figures?"

"Tell you in a minute." Cam took out her cell phone, pulled up a set of photos with descriptions beneath them. "Ah, here we go. These inventory photos of the goods stolen from the safe-deposit boxes show this piece belonging to Mr. Horace Goodman, a big shot at the Stronach Group. They're a holding company with real estate investments all over the country, including Pimlico in Baltimore, home of the Preakness Stakes. It says this bauble was insured for sixty thousand dollars."

Jack said, "Mrs. Horace Goodman will be a happy camper when she gets it back."

"Or whoever," Ruth said, cynical to the bone.

Cam said, "Do you think Hummer knew the bracelet was from a robbery? Do you think he ever opened the leather carryall?"

"If he wasn't tripping in outer space the whole time, how could he *not* look?" Jack straightened, looked around him. "I wonder what he thought when he heard Manta Ray calling to him, looked out that window to see a helicopter waiting for him."

"Relieved? Happy?" Ruth said. "I'll bet you Manta Ray convinced him they were best mates. Talked him into holding the loot."

"Good bet." Jack handed around his cell, showed them a photograph. "Here he is, Major Patrick Sean Hummer, the photo taken in 2001, only a week after 9/11." They looked at a soldier with buzz-cut graying hair and sharp brown eyes, focused and filled with intelligence. Jack scrolled down. "He was divorced in the early nineties, two kids, a boy and a girl, given over to his ex-wife. They're about our age now, Cam. The photo was taken before he simply disappeared, went AWOL. That's still how he's listed, so he wasn't ever found—that is, if anyone bothered to look for him."

"A life lost, simply thrown away," Cam said, "by us." And she kicked at a pile of *Washington Posts*.

Ruth slipped the diamond bracelet into a small plastic evidence bag. "I almost wish we could leave it here for him. We owe men like him more than a jail cell. Do you guys mind if we keep his name to ourselves?"

Jack said, "I don't understand the question, Ruth. How would we know his name?"

42

Liam shouted into the bullhorn, "Major Hummer!"

Elena stared disbelieving when a man appeared out of a third-floor window in the warehouse and started waving wildly back at them. A moment later, a lanky man in a dirty white T-shirt and dusty jeans tucked inside military boots dashed from the warehouse toward them, a leather carryall under his arm.

Elena was shaking her head back and forth. "I can't believe this. You actually left your stash with a homeless man? Look at him, he's crazy."

"Major Hummer's not homeless; he told me he lives in a cozy apartment on the third floor. Crazy? Nah, the major and I had a nice chat about Ireland, and Derry, and we talked about what it's like to be shot. What I am is an excellent judge of character." He grinned at her, shaking his head. "Especially useful when there's no other choice." Liam said to Henley, "Don't lift off until I tell you to. We're going to have ourselves a little reunion first." He was still grinning as he grabbed Major Hummer's arm and pulled him into the helicopter. "Hello, mate. Long time no see. You're looking fit."

Major Hummer tossed the carryall to Liam, and without thought, buckled himself in. It had been years since he was in a helicopter, but he remembered, and it felt good. He leaned over and hugged Liam. "You look even better, all clean and sharp, Manta Ray. I really didn't think you'd make it, but here you are. The FBI came back after they carried you out, like you told me they would, tore up the warehouse floors, banged on the walls, pulled off plasterboard. They rousted all of us who didn't manage to get away before they showed up. When they came up to my place, you know what I did? When they stood there staring at all my newspapers, I told them they were all in order by date, so whatever date they wanted to see, I could show it to them. You want to know what I did then? I started singing that old song Dougie sings—"Country Roads"—right in their faces. They looked around some, but that was it. I watched them leave from my window, shaking their heads. They weren't happy. Wasn't hard to make them think I was crazy."

"Crazy like a fox," Liam said. "Well done, Major, you're a genius." Liam embraced him. "I knew I could trust you, a countryman and a soldier, knew you'd take care of my stuff for me. You didn't pawn the bracelet I gave you yet, did you? No, I know you didn't, that was the deal we made. When you do pawn it, remember not to take less than fifty thousand, okay?"

Humbug shook his head. "I still have it all safe and sound at my house. I like to look at it at night when I light my candle, watch those diamonds shimmer and shine in the candlelight. It took me a while to get your blood out of the crevices, though." He turned to look at Elena sitting on Manta Ray's other side. He gave her a beatific smile. "You're very pretty. What's your name?"

"I'm Elena. Who are you?"

Humbug's shoulders straightened. "I'm Major Patrick Hummer, United States Army, self-retired, at your service, ma'am." He saluted her. "Some of my neighbors here call me Humbug, a bad joke, really, a play on my name—Hummer." He took in the duct tape at her wrists and ankles.

"Why'd Manta Ray tie you up? I mean, look at him, ma'am, a strapping Irishman. Seems to me he'd have to run from women so they don't tackle him. I've never used duct tape to tie anyone up like that. What'd you do?"

"I kept him alive, the idiot," Elena said.

Humbug looked back and forth between them, then frowned. "Well, I guess that's all none of my business. As long as you're not going to hurt her, is that right, Manta Ray?"

"She'll be safe with me, Major, so long as she behaves."

"See now, Elena, you can trust Manta Ray to do what he says. He came back here like he said he would, even after they took him away in an ambulance. He was lying there, all bloody and moaning, and I tried to help him. You know what? No matter how bad he felt, he still talked to me. And he gave me a bracelet that's worth more than anything I've ever owned. He's a man you can trust, a man who keeps his word." Humbug beamed at Liam. "You're the sort of man who comes back."

"You knew I would," Liam said. He opened the carryall, saw everything was untouched, and marveled at Hummer's lack of curiosity. He picked up the metal box, about the size of a flattened bread box, still locked. It was true, he was usually a good judge of character, he'd had to be to survive, and he hadn't been wrong about Major Hummer. Odd, but he'd simply had no doubts. Then the sirens had wailed, coming closer and closer, and he'd made sure Major Hummer was well away from him before the FBI burst in.

"So you haven't been out in the world since the FBI took me away? You haven't spoken to anyone about me?"

"Nope. I didn't feel like going anywhere, too many eyes and ears out there, all of them looking at me, maybe calling the military police on me. They'd take me away for what I did."

"Understood, but nobody's looking anymore, Major. It's ancient history." Liam knew he had nothing to fear from this man, no reason not to let him go. He surprised himself, honestly felt sorry Hummer was broken, even more surprised he wished he could help him. At least he had the bracelet. "Thank you, Major, for everything you've done for me. You can go ahead and climb out now, and you take care of yourself." He hugged him, whispered in his ear, "Wait a second, I have something else for you."

He said to Henley, "Give me your wallet." Henley hoisted an eyebrow but gave Liam his wallet without comment. Liam pulled out a fifty-dollar bill and shoved it in the major's pocket. "Try a bottle of Krug, it's my favorite. And, Major, thank you."

Major Hummer gave him a wave and jumped out of the helicopter. They watched him run, bent down, his hand over his mouth and nose as the helicopter lifted off and stirred up dust.

Elena looked at Major Hummer until the helicopter swung to the south. She said, "You took a huge risk."

"Did you look at him, really look?"

Slowly, she nodded. "You're right. I wonder what happened to him." She glanced at the metal box on Liam's lap but said nothing.

"I'm taking a much bigger risk now, dealing with your boss. After that, I'll have my freedom and enough money to do whatever I please for the rest of my life."

"Where are you going to go?"

He gave her his beautiful smile. "Wouldn't be very bright to tell you, now would it? Somewhere nobody's looking for me, and that's most of this big beautiful earth. But you know, just between you and me, I've been thinking about miles and miles of sand dunes. Hey, how about Morocco?"

She said, "I've been there, most of it's a hellhole, nothing but heat and desert and camel stink. And those clothes the women have to wear—" She broke off.

Liam said, "Where would you go, girl?"

"Fiji."

Liam gave her the once-over. "You would look great in a bikini. I have to say I agree with Major Hummer."

"About what, you Irish beggar?"

He leaned over and lightly bit her earlobe. "You are pretty."

She whooshed out her breath, and he felt the warmth feather against his skin before she jerked back.

"Now, now, love, I know you want to kill me, but it isn't going to happen. Sit still and be good."

She was angry, frustrated at her own impotence. He said, "You know what's in the box, don't you?"

She said nothing.

"I'd guess it's leverage, for blackmail. But you know something, lass? I don't frigging care the first thing about it." He thought it amusing that he'd had a hand in frustrating Petrov for over a month. Now it was nearly over.

Liam leaned over, brushed his knuckles against her cheek, and started singing "Molly Malone," his grandda's favorite song, in a fine baritone. " 'In Dublin's fair city, where the girls are so pretty, I first set my eyes on sweet Molly Malone—' "

Elena closed her eyes, reminded herself Sergei would let her kill him as soon as he had the chance.

43

Henley settled the helicopter once again on its pad on the barren stretch of land off the Potomac, turned off the rotors, and started his checklist. Liam said, "Good job, mate. Are you going to get reimbursed for the fifty bucks?"

Henley shook his head. "Consider it my contribution to Major Hummer's welfare, Mr. Hennessey. Is Krug champagne really that good?"

"The ambrosia of the gods; give it a try." Liam lifted Elena out of the helicopter and stomped his feet in the shoes Abram had given him. They were too big for him, which was good, since there was a thick bandage wrapped around his heel. The shoes were white patent leather, made him feel like Elvis. Best yet, they didn't hurt his heel.

"My turn," he said to Henley, and hoisted Elena up into his arms. "Don't move or I'll drop you on your head. Then who knows what I'll do?"

The area looked deserted once again, but Liam knew Petrov would be prepared for him this time. He'd be safe only until he delivered the metal box to him, and then he'd have only Elena and the gun to her head to keep him alive. Good thing for him Petrov held her in high affection. A slight breeze rustled the oak leaves as he walked behind Henley, his every sense alert for any movement. He sniffed the air, recalling the odd citrus smell Abram had worn, but there was nothing.

Petrov and Abram were waiting for him on the porch, both men standing quietly, watching them approach, Petrov's eyes on the metal box in his hand. Petrov had to know Liam could shoot him where he stood, a bullet to his forehead.

Liam wasn't invited into the house this time.

"Give Elena to Henley, Mr. Hennessey, then place the box on the porch."

Liam eased her down and stood her against Henley. He never took his eyes off Petrov as he placed the metal box at the edge of the porch. He stepped back, waved the Walther. "Now the four million dollars, Mr. Petrov."

Petrov picked up a bulging satchel from behind him and laid it next to the metal box, stepped back.

"Ralph, ease Elena onto the ground and fetch the satchel," Liam said. Henley did as he was told.

"Now open the satchel, count the money out loud."

Petrov made a disgusted sound.

When Henley finished counting, he looked a bit shell-shocked. "I've never seen so much cash before. It's correct, four million."

"Take a couple of hundred for your efforts," Liam

said, and watched Ralph peel off two hundred-dollar bills. "Now pick up Elena."

Liam waved the Walther at the metal box. "It's all yours, Mr. Petrov. You want to check it?"

Abram picked up the box and handed it to Petrov. Petrov studied the box a moment, looking for any signs it had been broken into. Liam smiled. "Not a scratch on it."

Petrov pulled a small key out of his pants pocket and opened it, studied the contents, gently closed the box. "No curiosity, Mr. Hennessey?"

"Mr. Petrov, the box doesn't interest me. It never did. It was a job, nothing more."

"I have to admit I'm surprised the box was where you left it. The FBI did an extensive search."

"They surely did, but don't you see? I'm smarter than the FBI."

"He had a homeless man keep the carryall for him," Elena said.

A black eyebrow shot up, matching his dramatic widow's peak perfectly.

Liam shrugged. "You have your box. I wish you luck with your blackmail. It's past time I leave now. I'll be taking Elena with me again. I'll send her back with Ralph once we land where I tell him to."

Petrov frowned. "You have your money; you have the helicopter. There is no reason to take Elena."

Liam shrugged again. "I've always believed in redundancies, Mr. Petrov. One never knows what might happen to a helicopter or what might happen on the way to a helicopter. I know you have more affection for Elena than you do for Ralph and me, so it's safer that way."

Abram gave a low growl, took a step forward.

"Control your dog, Mr. Petrov."

Petrov shook his head at Abram, and Liam gave them both the same salute Major Hummer had given Elena.

"No need to worry. Elena will come back to you safe." Liam laughed. "If she wants to come back to you, of course."

It wasn't long before Liam was staring out the helicopter window at the Potomac below. He would miss the city, particularly the lights at night, and all the countless marble monuments, a beautiful sight really. But still, it wasn't Belfast. Liam remembered the pounding excitement of besting an enemy or a mark. Thinking about it still made his blood pump fast and hard. No, there was nothing like Belfast in the bad old days.

Elena said, "All I want is to get back home and take a shower."

Liam looked at her, smiled. "Maybe where we're going we can shower together."

She turned to look at him. "In your dreams. You look like a clown in Abram's white shoes."

He leaned over, lightly rubbed the Walther's muzzle over her smooth cheek. She didn't move. He admired that. He drew back, smiled at her. "You have guts, *moy golub*," he said.

"I wonder if I will have time to kill you and exactly how I'll do it."

Liam laughed.

Ralph's voice came over Liam's headphones. "Where do you want me to go, Mr. Hennessey?"

"Do you have a full tank of gas, Ralph?"

"Nearly."

"Fly north, mate, I'll tell you when to drop me off."

44

Dr. Emanuel Hicks, FBI psychologist and huge Beatles fan, stood when Savich and Sherlock walked into his office behind a pale-faced young man. He had dark smudges beneath pale blue eyes that held no hope. He looked ready to climb in a coffin and pull the lid down. Dr. Hicks had seen the same look in the terminally ill. He wore jeans, a white shirt, and an old dark-brown hoodie. So this was Saxon Hainny, the twenty-four-year-old brilliant young grad student in computer science at George Washington and the son of the eminent Eric Hainny, the president's chief of staff. Dr. Hicks thought the young man would have looked quite handsome if the life hadn't been leached out of him.

"Mr. Hainny," Dr. Hicks said, and shook the young man's limp hand. It felt nearly boneless. "Thank you for coming."

Saxon slowly nodded. "Agent Savich told me you could help me remember." He looked down at his sneakers. "I don't understand how, since everything is a blank."

Dr. Hicks waved to a comfortable armchair. "Please sit down, Mr. Hainny, and I'll explain to you what we're going to do."

Saxon Hainny shot a look at Savich, who smiled and said easily, "Saxon, I would trust Dr. Hicks with my life. You told us you wanted to know the truth. None of us believes what happened to you the night of Mia Prevost's murder has been simply wiped out of your memory." He lightly laid his hand on Saxon's arm. "It's time to have some faith."

Saxon studied Dr. Hicks, a man his father's age, but unlike his father, Dr. Hicks was thin as a pole, his wire-rimmed glasses set over intense dark eyes. "I can't see how that's possible, sir. I mean, I told the police and I told Agent Savich I've tried to remember, but there's nothing at all. I don't think your waving a silver coin in front of my eyes will make any difference." His voice caught; his eyes went blank. Savich knew he was thinking about Mia Prevost.

Dr. Hicks gently pushed him down onto the chair. "Mr. Hainny, have you ever been hypnotized before?"

"No, sir. I've always thought it was fake."

Dr. Hicks smiled. "We'll see." He pulled an old-fashioned round gold watch from his pocket. "This was my father's watch, given to him by his father. It's an old friend, nothing more really than something for you to look at. All I ask you to do is sit back and relax."

A slight smile lit up that haggard face for a moment. "If you're going to try to dig into my subconscious, you can call me Saxon."

"Thank you. I want you to relax, Saxon, simply look at the watch, focus on it. Very good. Now empty your active mind as much as you can, and pay attention only to the watch. Think about how many daylight savings times this old watch has seen, never knew when we lost an hour, not like the new ones that do it all for you. Look at the shine on that old gold finish, how it picks up the light. You can see yourself in the gold, if you try. That's right, Saxon, look at it and think about time melting away, an hour here, an hour there, until time means nothing."

He continued speaking, more nonsense than not, then lowered the watch and slipped it back into his pocket. He nodded to Savich and Sherlock, rose. "He's a very intelligent young man, focused enough to go under like a dream. He's ready for you to question him now."

Savich sat down in a chair, pulled it closer, and lightly laid his hand on Saxon's arm. "Saxon, tell me about Mia Prevost. How did you meet?"

A real smile appeared at a memory all of them knew would stay with the young man until he died. "I was in a graduate seminar when a beautiful girl wandered into the room. There were six of us guys in the class and every eye was fastened on her. She blushed, apologized, and left. After class, she was sitting outside in the hallway reading. I'll never forget what she said, 'Here I thought that was a class on deviant behavior. To me gigabytes sound like a vampire with huge teeth. Who knew?' She laughed and asked me if she could buy me a cup of coffee. She was so pretty, so kind, she made everything easy for me. I didn't feel clumsy around her, and when I couldn't think of anything to say or stumbled around, she'd laugh and pat my hand and tell me I was so good-looking I didn't have to talk, girls wouldn't care. My mom always called me her beautiful boy, but who believes their mom?" He paused, then his face lit up again. "Our first dinner together was at McDonald's. We had so much fun. We talked and talked. She told me one night she couldn't believe how she felt that first time she saw me. She told me she was falling in love with me." His voice caught. A tear slowly slid down his cheek.

"And you, Saxon?"

"I told her it was the first time in my life I knew what it was like to have another person make me so happy my skin felt too tight. I told her I loved her from the start, the way she laughed and teased me about my white socks, the way she listened to me. I told her I wanted to give her the world." He paused, said with such sadness it broke your heart, "I had so little time with her, and then some monster killed her."

"Saxon, what did your father think of Mia?"

"He told me she was the most beautiful girl he'd ever seen and he wanted my secret." Saxon gave a small smile before his face went slack. "My dad and I have had dinner together twice a week since I was thirteen and my mom left. He's used to people fawning all over him because of who he is, but Mia didn't fawn. She was herself, showed interest in him like she did with everybody." Again, he paused. "I don't know what my father really thought of her. I guess I was afraid to ask him. More than that, I really didn't care, Mia was all that was important to me, no matter what anyone else thought."

"Did you ever meet her parents?"

"Mia said they lived in Oregon, but she was planning on seeing them in the fall. We were planning to go together."

"Did you sleep together?"

Saxon nodded, gulped. "I was sort of scared in the beginning. I didn't want to be a klutz, but again, she made it so easy, so natural, told me to relax and we'd learn everything together. And we did."

"Did she ask you questions about your dad?"

"Well, yes, everybody does. And Mia was interested in him, sure."

"Do you remember telling her anything your dad had told you, say about policy issues the president had discussed with him, how he felt about it, things like that?"

"Yes, of course. My dad is President Gilbert's right hand, but he's still my dad. We exchange opinions; he likes that. But he has an ironclad rule: if I ask him about anything classified or maybe embarrassing to the president, he laughs it off, shakes his head. That means I shouldn't go there.

"I remember that happened with Mia once. She asked my dad what he thought of Putin's invasion of the Ukraine. He smiled, said he couldn't talk about it. She took no offense. I remember she apologized."

"Mia told you she was raised in Oregon?"

"A small town near Ashland. Something like Bolton. Her dad was a Baptist preacher, her mom a housewife. She was an only child." His throat seemed to clog and he swallowed, tears sheened his eyes. "She said her folks were great, that they always encouraged her, paid attention to her. Maybe that's why she was so sweet and such a beautiful person."

"Think back to the night Mia died, Saxon."

Saxon began shaking his head, back and forth, his breathing came faster.

"No, it's all right, Saxon. Breathe slowly, relax, that's right. Tell me about that night."

"It was our six-week anniversary and I wanted everything to be perfect."

"When you picked up Mia at her apartment, what was she wearing?"

"An amazing black dress, short and elegant. It had almost no back. She had a beautiful back. And high heels. She came to my nose. I remember she laughed and kissed me right outside the restaurant with a half-dozen people around, said it was hard to compete with me I was so handsome."

He swallowed. "She fixed my tie before we went in."

"Where did you go?"

"Luigi's in Alexandria. My dad loves their risotto, told me if I ever wanted to impress someone, it was the place to go. He and I went there sometimes. I ordered spaghetti and meatballs."

"What did Mia order?"

"Some sort of weird salad and a small antipasto we shared. She wasn't a big eater."

"What did you order to drink?"

He frowned. "I think Mia asked me if I'd ever had a cosmopolitan and I said no, I'm not much of a drinker—she knew that—except for a little wine sometimes. She told me she wanted me to try one, said it would make our time later more fun." He blushed, actually blushed. "She meant sex, you know."

"Yes, I know," Savich said. "You ordered a cosmopolitan."

"Yes. I liked the taste, and she was right. It loosened everything up, made what I wanted to say come out easier. I laughed a lot, with the second one. And then she wanted to leave, go to her apartment, said we were going to have a fantastic time." He stopped, ran his tongue over his lips. "And then it simply stops, I don't remember anything more. I woke up the next morning in my own bed in my apartment."

"I want you to picture you and Mia leaving the restaurant, asking the valet to fetch your Toyota."

He slowly nodded. "Yes, I see him, a really young kid, with acne scars. He stared at Mia, but I was used to that, all the guys did. He brought the car around, and I helped Mia into it. We were laughing. I don't know why, everything seemed so funny. I was driving, and she put her hand on my leg and started talking about what we were going to do in her bedroom."

"You drove to her apartment in Carlan Heights."

He nodded. "She lives"—he swallowed—"lived, on

the third floor. Usually we take the elevator, but that night she wanted to climb the stairs, and we kissed all the way to her apartment door." He paused, his face lighting with the memories. Then his face tightened, and he swallowed hard.

Savich squeezed his arm. "It's okay, Saxon. You're walking down the hall, kissing, laughing, and then you're facing her front door. What color is it?"

"It's red."

"Did you unlock the door?"

"No, she did. She did it while she was kissing me, and the door opened, and she grabbed my tie and pulled me into the apartment. I nearly stumbled. I remember now. I was getting woozy and I guessed it was the cosmopolitans, but I was so happy. Well, tired, too, I guess."

"Did you tell Mia you were woozy?"

"Yes. She laughed, said that was part of the fun, it didn't matter. And she started taking off my shirt and pulled me to her bedroom."

"Did you make love?"

45

Saxon licked his lips again, frowned, and slowly shook his head. "No, I felt weird, not drunk weird, I know what that feels like, but her bedroom was spinning and there were three of her and her laughter was too loud and I wanted to throw up and sleep at the same time. I don't remember anything after that, really, it's all gone—"

Sherlock lightly laid her hand on Savich's shoulder, and he moved back. She leaned in close, took a leap. "Saxon, do you remember me?"

"Yes, you're Agent Sherlock. You have beautiful hair."

"Thank you. Now, Saxon, I want you to look at Mia. Really look at her. You feel rotten, you're dizzy, but you still see her clearly. Do you see anyone else?"

He blinked, shook his head. "I don't know—wait, yes, there is someone. I don't know where he came from, but he's there, in her bedroom, standing behind her. He has his hand on her arm and he's turning her around to face him."

"What does he look like?"

"I can't see him clearly. All I can think about is throwing up."

"Forget your nausea, your dizziness, Saxon. You aren't feeling that now. You feel fine. Picture the man. Focus on him. Do you see him?"

"Yes, I can see him, but he's blurry."

"Describe him to me."

"He's older, in his forties, I guess. And he has this weird widow's peak, you know, his hair sort of spears forward, then he's bald on either side of it."

Sherlock took a shot. "That's good. Saxon, don't look away from him. Watch him. Is he talking? What is he saying? No, don't shake your head. Focus. Listen. Can you hear him now?"

"Okay, yes."

"Good. What is he saying to Mia?"

"He's asking her why I'm not under, asking her how she could screw it up. Why she hadn't done what she was told."

"Does he sound angry?"

"Yes, but not screaming anger, more like ice-cold anger, the kind my dad used on my mom that makes you shrivel up. That's why she left, I think."

"Okay, I understand. What did Mia say?"

"She said to give her a minute and I'd be out and he could take all the photos he wanted." He frowned. "I don't understand. Why was this man there? Why was Mia talking about photos?"

"Don't worry about that now. Think back. What happened next?"

Saxon fell silent. Sherlock knew he was trying to remember but she wasn't surprised when he shook his head. After a few more questions and rephrasings, Sherlock guessed he'd fallen unconscious then, too deep for memories or impressions.

"When you woke up the next morning, you were in your own bed?"

"Yes."

"What were you wearing?"

"I still had my pants on, even my shoes and socks, but my tie and shirt and my undershirt were gone. I couldn't find them. I felt really bad, a killer headache. I tried to remember how I got home from Mia's, what happened, but everything was—blank."

"Did you call Mia?"

"I did, half a dozen times, but her cell phone went to message. Then a friend came over—Ollie Ash. He was my roommate in college. He wanted to go to breakfast, tell me about the AI program he was working on, but I didn't want to, I felt too bad.

"Ollie said I should go take a shower and some aspirin. I felt a little bit better after that, but I was worried. I knew something was wrong. While I was dressing, I heard the news on the TV from the living room." He stopped dead, then whispered, "The newslady was talking about a woman's murder, and she gave the address, Mia's address. I remember thinking, how can she possibly be saying those things?"

"I came running out of the bedroom. I'd told Ollie I was seeing an amazing girl, but I hadn't told him her name. I stood there, not wanting to believe it, but that newslady went on about her, kept showing her picture."

"You said Ollie didn't know about Mia. What do you mean?"

"Only my dad knew about her."

"Why was that? Was keeping secret her decision?"

"Yes, I wanted to shout it to the world, to all my friends, but she said there was an ex-boyfriend and she didn't want him to know she'd found someone she really liked so quickly after she'd booted him out. She said she didn't trust him, he had a bad temper and was still mad at her. I offered to speak to him, but she wouldn't tell me his name. So I agreed, and we kept it quiet, except for meeting my dad. She was really happy to meet my dad. I remember she said meeting people high up in politics would help her with her deviant-personality course. I laughed."

"Go back now, Saxon. Your dad called you that morning, right? Before you could do anything?"

"No, he showed up at my apartment, told Ollie we were leaving, and took me home with him. I couldn't process it—that Mia was dead. It made no sense. Dad held me, and I cried, but Mia was still dead. I told him I couldn't remember anything and my shirt and undershirt were missing, and for all I knew I was the one who killed her, but he said no, that wasn't possible. I could never kill anyone. It sounded to him like I'd passed out from drinking too much. Someone else must have murdered her. But who? Why?"

Saxon's hand was a fist on the chair arm. Sherlock

laid her hand over his fist, smoothed out his fingers. "Listen to me now, Saxon. The man who killed her, he was the man you saw behind her, the man with the widow's peak. And we will find him."

She looked at Dillon, raised an eyebrow.

Savich had no more questions, shook his head. Dr. Hicks said quietly, "This is a great deal for him to take in." He leaned over Saxon and said in his soothing voice, "Saxon, you will wake up on the count of three. You will open your eyes and you will remember everything. You will understand it was Mia who drugged you. You will also know that Agents Savich and Sherlock will find this man. You will feel better now that you understand what happened; you will feel more at peace. One, two, three—"

Saxon Hainny opened his eyes, blinked a couple of times, and turned to Sherlock. She saw a moment of hope, then suddenly, devastation at the truth of what and who Mia Prevost was. He stared down at his clenched hands, whispered, "Mia and that man wanted to take pictures of us. But why?"

Savich said, "We don't know yet, exactly, but there are a few things we need to think through together, Saxon. From what you remember, it's obvious you didn't pass out from drinking too much that night. You were drugged."

"But I can't imagine how that could have happened. As I told you, I was with Mia. You mean you think Mia drugged me?"

"No one else could have, Saxon. Then she took you

to that man in her apartment, where she believed he was going to take pictures of you after you passed out. What she thought the plan was after that, we don't know yet, but she certainly didn't plan on getting herself murdered. They might have fought over something, but it's more likely killing her was part of the plan all along, the part she didn't know.

"You said your shirt and undershirt were missing. Detective Raven said nothing about finding your clothes at the scene. Did you tell him about them?"

"My dad told me not to mention it, he said it would sound suspicious."

Savich supposed Hainny hadn't told him about the missing shirt and undershirt for the same reason. He said, "Then it seems that after the man killed her, he took your clothes to link you to her murder. You're your father's son, Saxon, and he's a man with power and money. The man had to know your father would protect you, pay them if he had to."

Saxon raised dazed eyes to Savich's face. "She never loved me, did she? She was using me all along, like some chess pawn to sacrifice." He lowered his face in his hands. "But I loved her; I really loved her."

Savich said, "I'm very sorry, Saxon. You're an intelligent man, but you're not the first man who's had to face betrayal. At least now you know the truth, you know what it is you have to deal with."

"Me? Intelligent? That's funny, Agent Savich. The woman I loved played me like a fish on her line."

"You loved Mia; you trusted her. You were not responsible for who she was or what she did. Saxon, you didn't kill Mia, and you did nothing wrong. And you know what? I think in the end you'll recover, you'll do fine. You can trust we will find the man who killed her."

Saxon gave an ugly laugh, shook his head. "I can't imagine my future now."

Sherlock said, her voice emotionless, "Then consider your father's future."

He looked like she'd slapped him. "My dad—what will happen to him? Is that man going to blackmail us? Use me to ruin my father? It is my fault, all my fault."

Savich took his hand, pulled him to his feet. He put his palms on Saxon's shoulders. "Listen, Saxon, Mia's murder is not your fault. Now, I'm making you a promise. We're going to fix this as best we can, all right?"

"I don't know you. But my dad—" He looked into Savich's eyes. "You know what? I don't care what she did to me, I don't care if everything she did was fake, she shouldn't have died for it. I want to kill that man myself."

Get in line. Sherlock said, "Trust me, Saxon, we're going to find him and we're going to finish him." She took both his arms in her hands. "If we don't finish him, I'll help you buy the gun."

Saxon Hainny heard no doubt in her voice.

46

On the way back to the Hoover Building from Quantico, Sherlock's black briefcase honked three times in three different registers. She grinned. "My new ringtone, Larry, Curly, and Moe Duck." She pulled out her cell. "Sherlock here." She paused, listened, then, "At last Sylvie Vaughn is up to something that doesn't involve yoga or dry cleaning. Yes, I've got the attachment, thanks. You've already found out a lot about these people. We're headed to the CAU now."

"What was that all about?"

"That was Connie Butler, CARD team. That GPS tracker I put on Vaughn's car—we've been monitoring where she goes. It hadn't led to much more than grocery stores and gas stations, but she drove her Jaguar out to a really posh area a little while ago, in Anne Arundel County. She stopped at one of the big enclosed compounds, called the Willows, entered through the private gate. Connie said the property is owned by Mr. Beau Breckenridge Maddox, the founder of Gen-Core Technologies."

Savich gave the Porsche a nudge with his foot and they leaped forward past a classic black Corvette. The woman driver gave him a huge grin and a thumbs-up.

"Yeah, yeah, stop your baby flirting with that cold-hearted Corvette and listen to what Connie sent me. B. B. Maddox is seventy-eight years old now, retired from the leadership of Gen-Core Technologies for the past fifteen years. The current CEO is his only child, Lister Evelyn Maddox. I wonder why he saddled his son with such weird names. Lister is pushing fifty, married twice, divorced twice, no children. Up until fifteen years ago, the father, B.B., was a mover and shaker in the industry and a big social animal, but then overnight, he became a recluse. He never leaves his home now, sees hardly anyone. There are rumors he has some sort of debilitating illness, like a stroke, or dementia."

She looked up. "There's lots more here, but the question is, why would Sylvie Vaughn, a women's fashion blogger and YouTube phenom, visit the reclusive founder of Gen-Core Technologies?"

"Should I get MAX involved?"

"Maybe later, yes. Let me see what we've got here first." She hunkered down and worked until Savich pulled into the FBI garage. He took her hand, pulled her in for a quick kiss. "I remember the name Gen-Core Technologies now from my research on the drug John Doe was given—one of their subsidiaries is a smaller pharmaceutical, Badecker-Ziotec. We'll put them at the top of our list, find out if they ever did research on a drug in the same chemical class as sirolimus."

Sherlock nodded. "Dillon, I keep wondering where all this is headed. And how is John Doe involved? It gets curiouser and curiouser."

47

MAX found a small cabin near Lake Ginger in western Maryland, the owner listed as Renée Altman, Mrs. Bowler's maiden name. Savich sat back, shook his head. "Do you really think you're safe hunkered down out of state, Mr. Bowler?"

He called in Ruth and Ollie. "I think MAX may have found Bowler," he said, and gave them the GPS coordinates of the Lake Ginger cabin under Mrs. Bowler's maiden name. "I think Bowler's the linchpin, so it's important to keep him alive if you find him there. Lake Ginger's a forty-five-minute drive. Keep me informed, and don't forget, Bowler's got a gun and he's already killed once, doesn't matter that it was in self-defense. He's used it now and he'll use it again, so take care."

Savich could feel the electricity in the air as Ollie and Ruth grabbed their FBI jackets and left the unit. Now he could focus on finding the helicopter. He walked over to Agent Lucy McKnight's desk, leaned down, and looked at her monitor. She was studying video feeds.

Lucy said, "I've checked out the owners of all the Robinson R66 helicopters registered in the D.C. area, verified they're all legitimate. That left local air shuttles and helicopter charter services. Most of them have a Robinson R66 in their fleet, and most of those wanted to see a warrant if I wanted information about any flight plans filed for locations near the Daniel Boone National Forest yesterday. I told them in confidence the man who may have been picked up by one of their helicopters was an escaped murderer and lives were at stake." Lucy grinned up at him. "Turns out I talk a good game. It also turns out none of them had any flight plans for trips outside the D.C. area.

"Of course the pilot could be on someone else's payroll besides the charter service and covered up the trip, so I asked them to lend us their security video feeds. This is Beleen Air, flies out of Manassas Regional Airport, near the Dulles corridor. They have three white Robinson R66s in their fleet of nine helicopters. Unlike the others I've looked at, Beleen is really security-conscious—good quality recordings, and they keep the security videos for six weeks.

"I think we hit pay dirt, Dillon. We know the tail number on our Robinson was fake when it picked up Manta Ray and his buddies, and that means the pilot had to change it back again without anyone seeing him do it. So I've been comparing tail numbers from all their videos, morning to evening when all the helicopters were returned, hoping at some point to find a discrepancy. I think I've found it."

Lucy panned a row of seven helicopters lined up on their helipads, zoomed in on one of the tail numbers—N43785X. "That was yesterday morning. Now look at what it was last night when it first landed back from a rental to"—she read from the copy of the flight manifest—"Leesburg, Virginia." It took a moment to forward the video, but they saw the Robinson setting back down at 5:05 the previous evening, only its tail number was now N38257X. Lucy grinned up at Jack and Cam, now crowding in. "N38257X— that's the tail number you guys saw yesterday at the national forest, right?"

Jack Cabot leaned down and kissed her on the mouth. "Indeed it is, at least the N382 part. Lucy, you're brilliant."

Lucy looked at him upside down, grinned. "Best not do that again, my husband might haul you off to the gym for a bit of friendly pounding."

Cam laughed, leaned down, and kissed Lucy herself.

Savich said, "They either didn't have time to change it, or they didn't bother, since they were planning to use it again this morning and thought no one would notice. Lucy, is the helicopter there right now?"

Lucy punched up the current video, scanned. "Nope, it's gone."

Savich said, "Cam, you and Jack get out to Manassas Regional Airport and find out who's been flying this particular helicopter and where he is now. And if you can, get passenger names, anything you can find out. Hair-on-fire time, people, things are finally coming together."

His cell sang out Skyler's "Punched Out." The ID was blocked. He turned back to his office. "Savich."

"Agent Savich, this is Eric Hainny. I've spoken to my son. He told me he'd been hypnotized this morning."

"That's right. And we found out quite a bit." He waited to hear relief, perhaps a thank-you from Hainny.

But that didn't happen. Hainny's voice was controlled, but cold as an ice floe. "I allowed you to speak to my son even though I didn't think anything would come from it. I did not authorize this complete invasion of his rights. You have exceeded your boundaries, Agent."

Savich felt a punch of surprise. He said slowly, "I do not understand why you are angry, Mr. Hainny. Saxon realizes the truth of what happened to him now. He knows Mia Prevost was using him, that the man who paid her to use him, the man who murdered her, was there with them that night, looking down at Saxon sick and nearly unconscious on the bed after Mia drugged him. We have proved he did not kill Mia Prevost, perhaps not in a way admissible in court, but at least to him. I think Metro's investigation will be focused where it should be by that hypnosis as well.

"Let me remind you, Mr. Hainny, Saxon is an adult who made his own decision. I came to you as a courtesy. You will have to explain your anger to me."

Savich had to move his cell from his ear. "There was never any solid proof against Saxon in the first place!

What he remembered is something I suspected all along, and if at some point he had to know, I could have told him in my own way. What you have done, Agent Savich, as a result of finding your so-called truth, is to destroy him. He's out of his mind with grief, and now I fear for his sanity after what you did to *help* him. Did it occur to you his not knowing was better for his mental and emotional stability, better that he never find out the woman he loved was betraying him, using him? That is why I never pushed the idea with him because it was better to let him live with some happy memories, not risk destroying him with this ugliness."

Savich said, "Mr. Hainny, your son could have been indicted. We saved him, and you, from not only a possible murder trial but a political scandal that could harm the president."

"A trial? That wouldn't have ever happened; there was no proof. He was safe, as well as the president."

"Saxon wasn't safe from his own doubts, from his own demons." Savich paused a moment, then: "Saxon told me he couldn't deal with not knowing, with the guilt that he might somehow be responsible for her murder. Now that he knows, Saxon has a chance to work through what happened to him. It will take time, but he will endure. He will heal, Mr. Hainny."

Savich heard angry breathing, but Hainny said nothing. *Well, that didn't work.*

"Mr. Hainny, Saxon gave his consent because he wanted the truth, if we could uncover it. Did he tell you he gave us an excellent description of the man who murdered Mia Prevost? He is distinctive-looking. We are looking for his features now in our criminal database. If we are not able to find him there, we have other avenues to pursue. I have no doubt we will find him. And then we will know why he did this to Saxon."

"You're dreaming, Agent Savich, trying to convince me and yourself that what you did will bring my son some benefit. After all, we're not talking about your son, are we? What is Saxon to you? Merely a means to an end.

"You exceeded your boundaries, Agent Savich, and with the wrong man. I will inform the director about your callous, irresponsible behavior, and we will see how you deal with the consequences." Hainny hung up on him.

Savich stared at his cell phone. He wished Sherlock was with him, but she was up to her earlobes in finding out all she could about B. B. Maddox. Then he heard her voice in his mind. *Dillon, why is Eric Hainny so upset?*

48

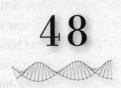

LAKE GINGER, MARYLAND
WEDNESDAY AFTERNOON

The afternoon was a humid scorcher, only a slight breeze off the lake to stir the maple leaves. Agent Ollie Hamish lowered the binoculars and handed them to Ruth. "I don't see any movement of any kind, no vehicles near the house. It looks like no one's home."

Ruth looked through the binoculars at an old A-frame cabin near the water, its wood weathered to a muddy brown. There was one main floor and an upstairs loft that peaked sharply. Ivy billowed out of hanging baskets and crept up the sides of the cabin nearly to the windows. An ancient rocker stood on the narrow front porch, adding a bit of charm. The thick tree cover was cleared in a twelve-foot perimeter around the cabin and down to the water, and a twenty-foot rock path led from the front steps to the dock. The place was private, the closest neighbor a hundred yards away. Ruth wondered how much land the Bowlers had to own to keep it that way. She whispered, "It looks like an old painting, everything frozen in time." Even the small winding lake was still, the water motionless, a flat gray, everything quiet in the heavy air. "Or like that cabin in the woods where Hansel and Gretel nearly came to a bad end."

"Don't make me think about ovens," Ollie said. "It's too hot."

Ruth felt the sweat pooling beneath her shirt. She said more to herself than to Ollie as she scanned the lakeside with the binoculars, "He could have heard us, I suppose. He could be hiding behind the trees. Or under the bed. Or loading his gun to blow our heads off."

"Or in the water hunkered under that boat dock, if he wants to be dramatic. Ruth, there's no boat, so maybe he's out on the water catching his dinner."

"We don't even know if he has a boat." She lowered the binoculars. "There's no reason for him to be afraid of us, Ollie. We're here to save him."

Ollie's eyebrow went up. "Help save his skin, maybe. But he knows we're going to throw his butt in jail."

"Which is exactly where he belongs. Don't forget what Dillon said, he's already killed once, so we can't think of him as a harmless civilian. I know in my gut he's here. Let's go get him."

She and Ollie stopped at the edge of the forest and studied the cabin up close for any sign of Bowler, or anyone else. They saw no sign of life.

"Let's give him a chance to end this," Ruth said. At Ollie's nod, she cupped her mouth and shouted, "Mr. Bowler, it's Agents Noble and Hamish. We spoke to you Monday in your office. I was in the garage in Alexandria later on Monday afternoon when you managed to kill the man hired to murder you. It was self-defense, so you don't have to worry about any charges being brought against you."

Nothing.

She tried again. "Mr. Bowler, whoever hired you to broker the deal with Manta Ray, he won't stop, he'll keep coming until you're dead. Your best chance to survive is to throw your gun out the front door and come out, your hands behind your head. We'll take you back to Washington and keep you safe. You're a smart man. You know once you tell us what you know, he'll have no more reason to kill you."

Well, except he'd be mightily pissed.

There was still no answer.

They drew their Glocks, racked the slides, and quietly circled around to the back of the A-frame cabin. There were two high windows on the second-floor loft. Mr. Bowler wasn't staring down at them.

Ruth whispered, "What if Dillon's wrong? What if Bowler never came here?"

Ollie smiled and pointed down at the freshly crushed grass. "Someone was here, got to be Bowler. He wasn't taking any chances, probably parked his car some distance beyond the edge of the trees. If he's not here now, he'll be coming back."

They walked around to the front of the cabin, pressed themselves against either side of the door. Ollie reached out his arm, knocked. "Mr. Bowler, FBI!"

They heard nothing, then a sort of mumbling. Ollie kicked the door and it crashed inward. They burst in,

Ollie high, Ruth low, and saw Bowler tied to a chair facing them, a sock stuffed in his mouth, making guttural noises. He looked terrified.

A man's deep voice, thick with a slow Southern accent, said calmly from the small kitchen, "Either of you special agents move and you're both dead. I don't want to kill you, but I will if I have to. Do not turn; keep your eyes on Mr. Bowler. Now, slowly drop your Glocks."

Ruth and Ollie dropped their Glocks, both guns hitting the wood floor like cannon shots.

"Excellent," the man said, stepping out now from behind the kitchen partition. "Both of you get facedown on the floor, hands behind your heads."

Bowler managed to spit out the sock. "He's going to kill all of us! You have to do something!"

"Shut up, Bowler. Down, both of you. Now!"

Ruth lay on her stomach, watched Ollie start to go down on his knees. He stumbled on a table leg, grabbed his leg, and yelped. Ruth twisted onto her side to face the man, jerked her Kahr P380 from her ankle holster, and fired. He flinched but fired back, missing Ruth, the bullet thudding into a sofa back. She rolled behind a ratty old recliner and the man kept firing, at Ollie now, and one bullet hit him squarely in the chest as he dove behind the sofa. Ruth's heart flipped when he went sprawling backward to the floor.

Ruth fired again, but he'd ducked behind the bar dividing the kitchen from the living room. She stilled, waited until he finally reared up and fired two more rounds. More bullets hit the recliner. Ruth came up on her knees, fired two more shots, and struck him center mass before he could get off another round. The man stared at her a moment, silent, and fell heavily to his knees, then tipped over onto his side, his gun flying out of his hand to the linoleum floor. Ruth ran over to kick the gun out of his reach, then rushed to Ollie's side. He lay on his back, taking light shallow breaths, holding his chest. He cocked an eye open. "Give me a minute, Ruth. I'm okay, but you know a bullet at this range packs quite a punch. Thank you, Kevlar."

Ruth said a silent prayer of thanks he hadn't shot Ollie in the head.

Bowler called out, "You killed him?"

Ruth patted Ollie's arm, got up, and walked to the kitchen to kneel beside the man. She pressed her fingers against the pulse in his neck. There wasn't one. His chest was soaked with blood, now dripping into a pool around him. His eyes were open, staring up at her in mute surprise. Soon his eyes would begin to dull. She felt the shock of violent death, forced herself to breathe deeply, until her heart began to slow. She checked the man's pants pocket, pulled out his wallet. No ID, only three one-hundred-dollar bills.

"Yes, he's dead," she said over her shoulder. "He was a professional, like the man who tried to kill you Monday." She stood, locked her shaking legs, took out her cell phone, punched video, and said, "Unidentified white male, midforties, brown and brown, medium height, medium weight, seriously receding hairline. He has a cell phone, a burner, no incoming or outgoing numbers show on it, probably to be used only once, when the job was done." She panned the entire area, identified Bowler and Ollie, and satisfied, punched in Dillon's number. When he answered, she told him the situation, sent him the video she'd just made. She knew the Washington Field Office was closest and they'd be there within the hour.

Savich was silent, then: "I've got your video. I'll get this man through facial recognition. He'll be in the system." He paused. "Ruth, you and Ollie did well. Now squeeze all the juice out of Bowler you can before the crime scene people arrive."

Ruth saw Ollie rubbing his chest, nearly back together. She started untying Mr. Bowler. He was breathing hard, still terrified. She crossed her arms, looked down at him, said in a disgusted voice, "You had to know the man who hired you wouldn't stop after the miss Monday, and he didn't. You're a great big loose end, Mr. Bowler. You do realize that now, don't you? He found you quickly, as we did, which tells you what a crappy plan it was to hide out here." Ruth leaned over, right in his face. "Do you finally understand, you moron? He wants you dead. Because of what you know, what you might tell us about him. Are you ready to come into the light—that's us—or do you want to repeat this scenario until you're dead? The boss man you're trying to cover for seems to have an unlimited supply of killers to send at you."

Bowler moaned, shook his head back and forth. "But I don't know anything."

"If we hadn't come, our friend over there in the kitchen would have shoved your dead body into a landfill, or better yet, concretized your shoes with you in them and dumped you in the middle of Lake Ginger."

49

Bowler raised his head to face them. "He wanted to know what I told the FBI when you agents came to my office. I should never have called the emergency number they left me, never told them anything about it. Yes, all right, I did broker a deal between Manta Ray and, well, certain people, but I did nothing more. I'm a lawyer, my livelihood depends on keeping confidence with my clients, keeping my mouth shut. I wouldn't have ever said anything to the authorities. How could they not know that?" Bowler swallowed. "Would you please untie my ankles, Agent Noble?"

She leaned down, untied him. "Don't move."

She turned. "Ollie?"

Ollie had hauled himself up to sit on the sofa. He was still rubbing his chest.

"You've probably got a cracked rib, so go slow and easy."

"I'm okay." He forced himself to stand. He looked at the dead man lying on the kitchen linoleum, then over at Bowler, who was rubbing feeling back into his hands and feet. "How long was that man here before we arrived, Mr. Bowler?"

Bowler stared at him. "I still can't believe you're alive. I saw him shoot you in the heart. You fell on your back, and I thought you were dead."

"The wonder of Kevlar. How long, Mr. Bowler?"

Bowler glanced over at the dead man, then quickly looked back at Ruth. "I was eating some cereal when he snuck in on me about a half hour ago, tied me up. Then he sat down, drank my last two beers, and told me he'd kill me slowly and then go after Magda and Renée if I didn't tell him exactly what I'd told the FBI. He never stopped smiling when he told me what he would do to them."

Ollie looked him over. "He had half an hour, but you don't look like you've been harmed. Why are you still alive?"

Bowler gave an ugly laugh that wasn't a laugh at all. "I'm a lawyer, Agent Hamish. I can talk, and so I did. I told him the truth, at great length. I told him I didn't know who his boss was, I didn't know much of anything at all. My role was the middleman, so what could I have told the FBI that his own people hadn't told me? He kept asking me what I knew about the man who'd hired me, about what Manta Ray had told me. I knew he was going to kill me in the end, like that man in the garage Monday, and I knew there was nothing more I could do for my wife and daughter. And then I heard you shout, Agent Noble. He stuffed that sock in my mouth and told me to keep quiet."

Bowler began crying, tears running down his cheeks. "I thought I was going to die for sure. I still can't feel my feet."

"Get up, Mr. Bowler," Ruth said. "Stomp your feet and walk. If you try to run, I will hurt you, do you understand me?"

"Yes, yes, I understand." He hiccupped. "Thank you, really, you saved my life." He began to stomp his feet as he hiccupped.

Ruth said, "We have the same questions, Mr. Bowler. Who hired you to meet with Manta Ray in prison and broker his escape?"

"Listen, you've got to believe me, he never told me his name and I never saw him. I spoke to him only one time on the phone, at the beginning when he first called with the offer."

Ollie said, "Obviously he knows you don't have his name. But he must believe there's something you know about him that would help us to identify him. Yes, I can see from your face that you do know something. What is it?"

"All right, but I don't know if it'll be helpful." Bowler drew a deep breath. "I'm almost certain he's Russian. I've had Russian clients before and I know the accent. I'd say he was educated in England, sounded like an upper-class Brit, but still he had this slight Russian accent." Bowler shrugged. "But there have to be lots of men around who sound like him. My hearing his voice and recognizing he was Russian, that's no reason to kill me."

Enough to sign your death warrant. Russian—Ruth couldn't wait to tell Dillon.

She said, "Tell us about the first phone call. What

did the man say to you? Be as exact as you can, Mr. Bowler."

"He told me about Manta Ray—Liam Hennessey's his real name—that he was going to be tried for robbing a bank and for murder. I'd heard about the case already. He told me Manta Ray had something that belonged to him, something important and he wanted it back. Manta Ray would know what it was, and he would give Manta Ray two million dollars and arrange to set him free if Manta Ray agreed to return it to him. But it had to be done quickly, so I had to tell Manta Ray to accept a plea bargain right away, which he did. I assumed it was something Manta Ray had robbed from the bank, but neither of them told me what it was. I realized the deal went through when they broke Manta Ray out on his way to federal prison a couple of days ago. That's pretty much all I know." Bowler's eyes went again to the dead man. "I told him what I told you, but he kept smiling and telling me in that slow Southern drawl of his to say something he didn't know or he was going to have to hurt me. I knew he was getting ready to kill me. I could tell by his eyes. I've never talked so much in my life."

Ollie said, "How did you communicate with this man—okay, let's call him the Russian—after that first phone call?"

"It was simple, really. Both of us had passwords to a single account. He'd write an email, save it as a draft and I would log in, read the email in the drafts folder and then delete it. I'd write a response, save it to drafts."

"Give me the password," Ollie said.

"There is no way to retrieve it," Bowler said. "You know there's no way."

Ruth said, "What is the password?"

"Mac and cheese," Bowler said.

Ruth shook her head at him. "Why didn't you simply tell us all this Monday at your office, Mr. Bowler? We could have saved all the drama and you could have prevented two attempts to kill you." *And us, you putz.*

She saw Bowler couldn't take his eyes off the dead man in the kitchen and the blood, black and viscous around him. He shuddered, shook his head. "I knew you couldn't prove anything, and I had to hang tough. I never thought— Well, I was wrong."

Ruth wanted to kick him. "You've defended some very bad people over the years, you know how they think. The Russian, you're telling me you never even gave it a thought?"

Ollie started laughing. "It was all about money, Ruth. How much did he pay you, Mr. Bowler?"

He gave them an earnest-lawyer look. Ruth almost smiled.

"Yes, there was the money, I won't deny that, but as I told you, I've had several Russian clients, and this man, this Russian, he knew a great deal about some of the, ah, services I'd performed for them. I could take the money he offered or he could make those services known and ruin the firm with what he knew."

Bowler ran his tongue over his cracked lips. "I got the first half of the money right away. I was to receive the second half after he'd gotten Manta Ray free. It was a lot of money—five hundred thousand dollars—and all I had to do was be the go-between.

"But everything happened so fast. You were at my office and I knew you didn't believe me, but where would you find any proof?"

Ollie said, "Mr. Bowler, of course we were on your doorstep right away. You were the only one who visited Manta Ray in prison in Richmond. It was obvious after Manta Ray escaped we'd come calling."

He shrugged. "Yes, but again, you couldn't prove I'd had anything to do with Manta Ray's escape. Listen, I only wanted to get the other half of the money he owed me and put it all behind me, so I wrote the Russian a draft email using our system, but there was no reply. I called the number he gave me for emergencies. I didn't speak to him, but the man I talked to said he worked for the boss, and he agreed to bring the money to the Bilbo Baggins restaurant in Alexandria."

Ruth said, her eyebrow raised, "And naturally you believed him? He'd walk in with a bag of money? A cashier's check?"

Bowler stuck out his chin. "The whole deal, it was straightforward, part of our agreement. Why shouldn't I believe him? I waited for him, but he didn't come. I didn't know you were following me, Agent Noble."

"That's good to know. Did you call the number again? Ask what was happening?"

"Yes, but there was no answer. I wanted to get home, see what Renée thought we should do. I nearly ran to my car. I passed an older couple in the garage and then

I heard the old man getting hit and moaning, and I knew I was next. I had my gun with me and I ducked behind a car when the lights went out. I heard you calling out to me, Agent Noble, and then the lights came back on and there he was, his back to me. I shot him and ran out the rear garage exit and into a motel down the street. I knew I couldn't go home, they would be waiting, so I came here. I called Renée, told her and Magda to hunker down and make arrangements for us to leave Washington for a while."

Ollie said, "Where is the gun you used in the garage yesterday?"

"No, please don't take it. It's all I've got."

"Where is it?"

Bowler pointed to a telephone book that lay on top of a rough-hewn coffee table. It wasn't a phone book, it was a hollowed-out box. Ollie called out, "A SIG Sauer P238. Where'd you get it, Mr. Bowler?"

"At a gun show in Baltimore maybe twenty years ago." He swiped his hand over his cheeks to wipe away the tears. "A criminal I defended didn't like the sentence the judge handed down and he tried to kill me. I bought the little SIG then. I never leave home without it." He looked down a moment, then said, "I don't suppose I can talk you out of taking me back to Washington?"

The assassin's burner rang.

Ollie and Ruth exchanged looks.

Ollie picked up the cell. "Hello?"

50

BELEEN AIR
MANASSAS REGIONAL AIRPORT
WEDNESDAY AFTERNOON

Ms. Mindy Fuller checked the schedule on the company computer in front of her, then looked up at Cam and Jack. "Agents, I haven't heard from Ralph Henley, but that's not unusual. He's with a client he normally flies. He left early this morning before I came in, entered their destination today as Richmond, a scheduled return at two o'clock." Mindy checked the schedule, frowned. "He should have been here an hour ago. He has another client scheduled at seven o'clock for an evening tour of Washington."

Cam said, "Show us his flight manifest, please."

"I don't have it. Ralph always keeps his own book with him." She pointed to the computer. "All I have is his schedule and destinations."

Jack leaned closer. "What was his schedule yesterday?"

"He was with one of his usual clients, his destination Leesburg, Virginia, arriving back here late. It says he clocked out at ten o'clock last night."

"What is his client's name, Ms. Fuller?"

She looked nervous. "A moment, please." She dialed an extension, waited, then asked in a near-whisper, "The FBI agents are asking for a client's name."

She listened, slowly nodded. "This is highly unusual, but Bob says to give you whatever you want. And he's asked to speak to you. The client's name is Alvarez, Cortina Alvarez."

"The address?" Cam asked.

"The Satterleigh Condominiums, 2378 Rutherford Avenue Southwest."

Cam and Jack traded a look and followed Mindy behind the service counter to Bob Jensen's small office. Jensen was one of two owners of Beleen Air, in business for thirty years. He was an older man, laugh lines around his mouth, but he wasn't laughing now. After they showed him their creds, he told them he'd already spoken with Special Agent Lucy McKnight. "I understand we're dealing with criminals here, and believe me, I want no part of it. Of course I'll tell you everything I can."

But Mr. Jensen had never met Cortina Alvarez, had occasionally seen a woman and others climbing into the helicopter, but they never came in. Ralph collected the payment for each trip for them, always in cash. Yes, that was unusual, but everyone was free to pay in whatever manner they wished. He had no other contact names. As for Ralph Henley, he'd been on the payroll since 2008, above suspicion until now. He was conscientious, you could count on him, and it wasn't like him to be late.

They told him about the fake tail number and Henley's actual destination yesterday, the Daniel Boone National Forest.

Mr. Jensen stared at them. "You're telling me Ralph is working for this Cortina Alvarez woman, filing false flight plans? He flew one of my helicopters to the national forest? Why? Is he transporting drugs? Drug dealers?" Jensen spurted out a string of robust curses. "I'm going to take him apart when he gets back."

"No need, Mr. Jensen," Jack said. "We suspect he's been doing worse than transporting drugs. Agent Wittier and I will deal with Mr. Henley. We'll remain here until he lands."

Cam and Jack were waiting in Cam's Miata when Bob Jensen came running out of the building an hour later, waving his hands at them, obviously upset. They were out of the car in an instant, met him halfway. Jack grabbed his arm. "Mr. Jensen, what is it?"

Jensen swallowed convulsively, blurted out, "The helicopter Ralph was flying, it was reported down in a wooded area in Maryland. Eyewitnesses said it exploded in midair. I don't know anything more, I can't find anyone who knows anything or who will talk to me."

Cam was already on her cell. Two calls later, she was speaking to the rescue crew on the ground at the crash site. When she punched off her cell, she cupped Mr. Jensen's hand. "A witness saw the helicopter explode in flight. They're guessing it was a powerful bomb, from how far the wreckage is strewn over the woods. They're still searching for victims on the ground."

Jensen swallowed hard, his Adam's apple bobbing up and down. "As I told you, Ralph was scheduled to fly Ms. Cortina Alvarez today, but I don't know for sure if she was his passenger. Do you think she was on board with him?"

"We don't know yet, Mr. Jensen. But we believe the wanted criminal we've been looking for was on board with Ralph this morning. We'll call you as soon as we have anything definite. I'm very sorry, sir."

51

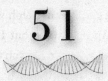

THE WILLOWS
HOME OF B. B. MADDOX
BALTIMORE, MARYLAND
WEDNESDAY AFTERNOON

"You failed again, Quince."

Quince hated that tone of voice, disappointed and condemning at the same time, and something more, a promise of punishment. It made the hair on the back of his neck stir. Quince always hated coming here, hated the monstrosity of a house that was a cold museum to him, two of its rooms pretending to be in some ancient English house. Even the air smelled old, closed in, stale. But Dr. Maddox had ordered him to come here and not to his big office at Gen-Core, so he'd had no choice.

He cleared his throat. "Yes, but it wasn't my fault."

"Your failure the first time wasn't your fault, either? It could have been done so fast and easy and clean, Quince, before you even left the hospital on Monday."

"But I told you, sir, they'd placed a police guard on Enigma Two's room. I don't know why. What was I supposed to do, kill the guard, too?"

"If you hadn't panicked, if you'd been smart enough to cause a diversion—well, it's over and done with. I am not unreasonable, Quince, I'd already forgiven you your failure to kill him on Monday morning, but Monday night? I even gave you a workable plan to divert the guard. Everything should have gone smoothly. According to Burley, there wasn't even a guard there when you arrived, he'd been pulled off duty, and Enigma Two was without protection. All you had to do was slip into his hospital room and inject the potassium chloride into his IV."

Quince had been an idiot to confide in Burley, but she'd commiserated with him, and he'd poured it all out. And then she'd gone running to Dr. Maddox the minute his back was turned. Didn't Dr. Maddox know by now that Quince would never lie to him, just as Quince had never lied to his father? Or was Dr. Maddox torturing him for his own amusement?

He wondered if Burley had told Dr. Maddox the exact truth or colored what had happened to make him look worse. "Sir, that woman, Kara Moody, was there, sitting next to him, holding his hand, talking to him. I couldn't understand why she was even there. He attacked her on Sunday—"

The cold, precise voice interrupted him. "So why didn't you kill her, too, Quince? You're strong enough. You could have quickly snapped her neck. Why didn't you?"

"I thought you might have further use for her." That was the truth as far as it went. Quince wasn't about to admit he hadn't thought of killing her, then everything had happened too fast, all of it unexpected.

Quince watched Dr. Maddox's worry beads glide smoothly through his fingers, faster now, which meant he was getting agitated. "Sir, she saw me, picked up the water pitcher and threw it at me, then she flung herself over him and screamed her head off and she wouldn't stop. I could hear people running toward the room. I had no choice but to get out of there before security came. You wouldn't have wanted me to get caught or to have to kill any police." Why didn't Dr. Maddox see he'd behaved exactly as the professional he was, given the circumstances.

He listened to the worry beads clack in the silent stale air. He could think of nothing else to say. He didn't move, waited, barely breathing.

Lister slowly nodded. "You may think Burley really dislikes you, Quince, but she doesn't. She knows she owes me her complete loyalty. She knows what would happen to her if she failed to keep me informed, just as I expect you to keep me informed about the results of her assignments. Now you've left nothing out, either, and that is very wise of you."

Lister waved his hand toward an uncomfortable high-backed chair covered in green brocade. "That isn't why I asked you here today in any case. Stop standing there like a stick, Quince. Sit down."

Quince sat down carefully on the edge of a chair that looked fragile and ancient. Or was it a reproduction?

The silence lengthened. Dr. Maddox paced the long living room, the worry beads threading through his fingers, faster now.

Quince eyed the man who'd taken control from his father, B. B. Maddox, a man Quince still loved, though he spent most of his time upstairs now in a wheelchair, his eyes blank as a slate, in that ridiculous bedroom. He remembered the long ago afternoon B.B. had approached Quince when he'd been only eighteen years old and fresh out of juvie for stealing cars for a chop shop on Culver Street. He'd taken Quince's skinny shoulders between his large hands and said, "I hear from Detective Lancey that you've got a brain. Is that true?"

Quince remembered he'd been terrified but determined not to show it. He didn't know who this rich man was and he wasn't about to show weakness, that way led to bullies with knives and piles of hate at your door, so up went his chin. "I'm bright as the sun, that's what my mother always told me before she died."

The large man had studied his face, slowly nodded. "Your name is Jubilee Quince, an excellent name. What I'm going to offer you is the chance for a different life. Do you want to try it on for size?"

Quince had never regretted taking B.B. up on his offer. He'd always done whatever B.B. had asked him to do until that day fifteen years ago, when everything changed. He looked at B.B.'s son, Lister, as brilliant as the old man was, maybe more so, given what he'd accomplished, not only for his father, but for Quince as well. Out of habit, he looked into the gilt mirror hanging on the wallpapered wall beside the fireplace. He studied his reflection, raised an eyebrow, then smiled at it. He still marveled but was finally coming to accept that the young man he saw in the mirror was who he was now, who he'd become again. And all of it was thanks to this man with his fricking worry beads who liked to scare the crap out of him.

He said into the deadening silence that underlay the clacking worry beads, "Sir, has the adjustment you made brought any benefit to your father?"

"No," Lister said. "Hannah told me there's been no change at all." He resumed his pacing, said over his shoulder, "There is no longer a way to eliminate Enigma Two. He's very well protected now that the FBI knows he's under active threat. All we can hope is he sinks deep into the coma and never wakes up. Or if he does wake up, we can hope he won't remember much of what happened to him, or if he does, no one will take him seriously, since they all believe he's a madman."

Quince said, "But, sir, I did try to kill him, and they know that. Surely they'd listen to him if he woke up."

Quince saw Dr. Maddox didn't want to hear this. He'd already constructed his theory and he would stick to it. He waved his worry beads at Quince. "This is what concerns me, Quince. If Enigma Two does wake up, he may remember where he was kept. Since he escaped from the Annex, he would be able to take them there. We can't risk it. I want you and Burley to drive to the Annex right away. Take a Gen-Core delivery van, it won't be missed. Remove all the servers, the pheresis units, everything medical that can't be explained. Put all the finished drugs and the frozen plasma stores into the portable freezers and pack them all into my powered storage unit. Then I want you to burn down the Annex. And, Quince, use that magnificent brain my father assured me you have, make it look like an accident, a faulty gas main, whatever. Call me when it's done."

Lister watched Quince walk from the living room. He waited until he reached the door and called out, "Quince, there will be no more failures, do you understand?"

Quince nodded. Lister listened to his footsteps across the large entrance hall, heard him close the front door behind him.

Lister slid his worry beads in his pocket. It was time to check on Ella Peters and Alex Moody, Enigma Three. He trusted Ella implicitly, as his father had, but he hadn't expected he'd have to call on her services quite so soon. They'd planned to leave the baby with his mother so long as Enigma Two remained a useful subject, but his escape had upended that careful plan. Now Ella was dealing with a newborn, by herself. A pity he wouldn't have the mother to use as his next research subject. She would have been Enigma Three, not her baby, until the child grew large enough to join her as a research subject. He'd wanted to wait until both mother and baby were home, on their own, before acting. Enigma Two's escape had changed everything. Lister knew the FBI was deeply involved. They didn't have his brilliance, but he wasn't a blind fool, he knew they were good at what they did. He didn't see how they would find him, though, unless Enigma Two came out of his coma and told them, which meant he had to get ready.

Lister sighed, turned at the top of the wide staircase, and walked down the long hallway toward the south wing. Another long hallway led him past guest rooms, a music room, a movie room, until he reached the old nursery, and he prayed, his whispered words echoing in the empty hallway, *Let Enigma Two never wake up. Make this incredible child my crowning achievement.*

Lister knocked on the nursery door. He heard Ella's soft-soled shoes after a moment coming quietly to the door. She eased it open, saw him, smiled, and quickly put her fingers to her lips. "Alex is sleeping. Come look at him, Lister, he's beautiful, a perfect child."

"Don't be sentimental, Ella. He will be our perfect subject, combining the genetic strengths of Enigma One and Enigma Two. He is my father's best hope, the best hope for all of us."

She walked to the crib, looked down at the sleeping baby, lightly touched a fingertip to his thick black hair. Lister frowned at the besotted look on her homely face. What Ella saw was a baby she thought beautiful. What Lister saw was a triumph, the culmination of all his research, all his efforts, all his experiments. Alex Moody would show him how to save his father and then how to save himself.

He said more to himself than to Ella, "I wish we could have waited until he was older, taken both him and his mother. Now we must care for him ourselves until he is old enough to begin running our tests."

She turned toward him, her back pressed against the crib, as if protecting the baby. Her voice was sharp. "Lister, Alex is far too young for you to be considering any tests, anything that would hurt him."

He put out his hands. "Yes, Ella, of course he is. I assure you I do not wish to torture him. I want to protect him and nurture him as much as you do, perhaps more so. I've spent a great deal of time and money finding his mother, assuring her pregnancy, and I found her only because she's a cousin of our first subject, Enigma One." He shook his head. "You remember how surprised and pleased I was when I found they shared the same structural variant, the same DNA inversion I found in his genome near the HLA gene complex on chromosome six."

Ella usually didn't understand his talk about genomes, most of it was gobbledygook to her, but she knew enough to be impressed. She said, "Well, it was a shame that Enigma One died. You told me what an excellent subject he was."

"Yes, he was drug-resistant and a strong responder, almost as strong as Enigma Two. And now, Ella, this baby is my finest creation. He combines both of their genetic gifts. His value to me will be incalculable, worth far more than Gen-Core itself." He added, his voice low, heartfelt, "Don't ever forget, Ella, this is the child who will save my father."

Ella looked at the sleeping baby. "But you don't

know yet, Lister, how he'll do, whether he really will tolerate your drug."

"He will, I know he will."

Ella listened to the baby sucking on his tiny fingers. Enigma Three. No, she couldn't, wouldn't, call him that ridiculous name. His name was Alex Moody, and he was a helpless baby, not a test subject, not yet. It wasn't fair to expect him to carry the weight of all that hope on his shoulders. He shouldn't have to carry anything. Then she thought of B.B. and sighed.

52

The conference room sounded with the clatter of computer keys, the occasional comment and halfhearted curse. Water bottles, coffee cups, and a plate with half a Danish hanging off the edge sat in the middle of the long table surrounded by CAU agents. Ruth and Ollie were working through passports of Russian citizens who'd entered the United States and also made frequent trips to England. Ollie was going through photos of Russians with British and international driver's licenses. Jack was looking at surveillance videos of the entrances to the chancery of the Russian Embassy on Wisconsin NW, and Cam, to the Russian Consulate on Tunlaw Road NW. Savich was on MAX, scouring old English private school records for Russian students from twenty and thirty years ago, cross-matching the names with recent American visa applications. They were looking for a Russian in his forties with a pale complexion, who may have been in the Washington area six weeks ago. It was tedious work that took intense focus.

An occasional chair scraped back to allow a stretch or a bathroom break. Savich called a ten-minute time-out when pizza arrived.

They'd been at it for three hours, found several Russian middle-aged men who could fit Saxon Hainny's description of him, but there was always something not quite right—the height, the weight, the widow's peak not dramatic enough, the background, the record of recent travel.

It was seven o'clock in the evening and everyone was tired, their nerves jangled from too much coffee. They were taking their first bites of pizza when Ollie shouted, "Look at this! Everything fits, finally. Come look!"

Chairs scraped back in unison and everyone crowded in behind Ollie to look at the passport photo on his computer screen. "Look at him, he fits Saxon Hainny's description. Look at that widow's peak."

Energy flashed in the room, everyone on alert as Savich read out, "Sergei Petrov, age forty-six, five foot eleven, one hundred seventy pounds, resides in Moscow, but a frequent visitor to the U.S., mainly Washington and New York. He last entered the United States eight weeks ago. Listed as a businessman, the purpose of his visit listed as pleasure and business. Does he have a local address, Ollie?"

Ollie typed madly, pulled up a Google map, and raised his head. "He's listed at 1701 Arcturus Road, Alexandria, but it's really south of the city, in a rich private area, right on the Potomac."

Savich said, "All we need is verification by our eye witness, Saxon Hainny"—Savich rubbed his hands together, gave them all a blazing smile—"and we can go get him. Ollie, print out Petrov's photo. Everyone, get started on a dossier of Mr. Widow's Peak. I'm calling Saxon in."

Computer keys were clacking again when Savich punched off his cell. He looked around the table. "Saxon will be here in a few minutes. Ollie, you said when you answered the burner cell, you spoke to a man with a thick Russian accent?"

"Yes, his accent was so heavy I was tempted to say *da*, but I stuck to mimicking the dead man's voice, said as little as I could. If he knew I wasn't the dead guy, he didn't let on. He said to be sure to bury the burner with Bowler's body somewhere neither would be found. He ended the call telling me the other half of my money would be mailed to my P.O. box. Then he hung up."

Jack said, "So Petrov believes he's safe; he's cut all the loose threads, killed both the pilot and Bowler. But guys, who is Cortina Alvarez?"

Cam grinned. "Maybe we'll find her on the same passenger manifest as Petrov's to and from Moscow."

There were forty-seven women on the passenger manifest of Aeroflot 104, leaving Moscow in the morning and arriving at Dulles in the early afternoon. None of them were named Cortina Alvarez, but one of them— Elena Orlov—listed Petrov's address in Moscow.

"That's it; that nails it," Cam said.

Ollie read out, "Elena Orlov is thirty-four, five feet

six inches, one hundred twenty-five pounds, purpose of visit listed as business. She matches Kim Harbinger's description of the second person with Manta Ray at the national forest."

Savich looked up from MAX's screen. "The CIA's file on Sergei Petrov lists him as an officer of the Transvolga Group, an investment firm that's a partial subsidiary of Bank Rossiya. And would you look at this—the second largest shareholder of the Transvolga Group is Boris Petrov, Sergei's father." Savich scrolled another minute on MAX, then: "The Bank Rossiya was pegged by the Treasury Department as providing material support to Russian officials, meaning they serve as personal investment bankers for all the millions of dollars the kleptocrats steal from the Russian people—including senior officers of the Russian Federation, and Putin himself."

Cam cocked her head. "So father and son are important Russian bankers. How does that fit in?"

"Another moment, Cam," Savich said, still typing. He sat back. "Boris Petrov, Sergei's father, was included along with dozens of other Russians in the sanctions the Treasury Department issued under the president's executive orders of 2014 and 2015. You remember, the sanctions have been in place since Russia annexed Crimea and sent its military into eastern Ukraine last year. The people under the sanctions can't do business in the United States, can't access financial markets, had billions of dollars of their assets frozen. As a result, the Russian economy fell into a recession, the ruble and stock market dropped, and there was massive capital flight from the country. More than two thousand millionaires left Russia. The individuals sanctioned aren't even allowed to travel to the U.S. or to Europe."

Cam said, "You're saying Sergei's father was sanctioned?"

Savich nodded. "Big-time. More than one hundred million dollars of his personal investments are frozen, and the Transvolga Group lost much more—they were put virtually out of business. That includes a great deal of money belonging to very powerful Russian officials."

Ruth said, "So we've sanctioned the bankers who invest a lot of the communist big wigs' money and put a big dent in Putin's pocketbook."

Savich nodded. "I've got to think some powerful Russians are very angry at the Petrovs for not protecting them. And now Sergei Petrov is in the country because his father can't be. The question is what he's up to."

Jack called out, "Here's something on Elena Orlov. Her father is a mid-level manager at—guess where—the Transvolga Group in Moscow. She's an only child, educated in Switzerland, where she became proficient in four languages, then returned to Russia. She entered the Military Educational and Scientific Center, but dropped out after a year. She's been on Sergei Petrov's staff for ten years, listed as his bodyguard. According to her file, she's also his lover."

Ollie looked at her photo, said under his breath,

"She's very beautiful, puts a new twist on the concept of bodyguard."

Ruth punched him. "Ollie, pay attention. The man you spoke to on the burner phone with the thick Russian accent, I wonder if he could be one of Petrov's muscle. There could be more of them."

Jack said, "And I'll bet we find some of his flunkies with him at the Arcturus address on the Potomac."

Ruth gave herself a head slap. "I just realized. That name Detective Ben Raven found in Mia Prevost's address book—Cortina Alvarez, a woman who doesn't really exist. That's it, isn't it? Cortina and Elena are the same woman. Now she may be dead along with the pilot in that helicopter crash today. But how does it all fit together?"

Shirley, the CAU secretary, stuck her head in the conference room. "Dillon, Mr. Saxon Hainny is here to see you."

Savich rose, picked up the photo of Petrov that Ollie had printed out. "I'll be back as soon as Saxon tells us it's Petrov for sure."

Savich quietly closed his office door. Saxon was sitting in front of his desk, his hands clasped between his legs, staring down at his scruffy sneakers. He still looked beaten down, folded in on himself.

"Thank you for coming, Saxon." Savich handed him the black-and-white copy of Petrov's passport photo. "Is this the man you saw standing behind Mia Prevost the night she was murdered?"

Saxon seemed to stop breathing. He stared at the

photo and back at Savich. "Yes, those are his eyes, I remember them, staring at me and talking to her, to Mia. It was like I was nothing at all. And his hair, see how it looks like a sharp spear on his forehead? Yes, that's him."

"You're absolutely certain?"

"Yes, Agent Savich. It's him." There was life in his face, at least for the moment, the deadly pallor gone, his eyes no longer deadened with pain. "How did you find him?"

"You gave us an excellent description of him, Saxon. We found him on an inbound flight to Washington from Moscow. If you'd never remembered seeing him, it would have been very difficult." He laid his hand on the young man's shoulder. "Now that you've confirmed his identity, we can bring him in."

"What's his name?"

"Sergei Petrov. He and his father are personal investment bankers to Putin and some other Russian plutocrats."

Saxon looked blank. "He's a banker? But why would a banker want to set me up for Mia's murder?" Saxon began to laugh. "He hired Mia to get close to my father, didn't he?"

Savich said nothing, only watched him. Saxon's face leached of color again. "It was never me, was it? Mia was supposed to get close to my father, maybe hack his computer?"

"Yes."

"But wait, didn't Petrov know my dad would never

tell anyone anything that could hurt President Gilbert or the United States? He never talked about anything remotely sensitive to either me or my mother. It was always 'off the table.' As for hacking his computer, I know my dad keeps everything important at the White House, and his personal laptop has some pretty high-tech safeguards I installed myself. I didn't even build in a trapdoor for myself. No one could get into that computer."

Saxon licked his dry lips, said slowly, so much pain in his voice Savich winced, "My missing shirt and T-shirt." He raised his eyes to Savich's face. "They were covered with Mia's blood, weren't they? And he took them."

Slowly Savich nodded. He looked down at his watch. He had to hurry.

53

Sherlock looked down at Kara Moody's rendering of the man who'd drawn her blood a year before. Mid-fifties with longish unkempt gray hair with a comb-over topping it off. He had a sharp chin and a large nose, but still there was something familiar about him, something that nagged at her. She'd never seen him before, had she? She kept studying the man's face, and it struck her. She called up the photo of the man they'd videoed helping to kidnap Alex Moody from the hospital and put it beside Kara's sketch of the older man who'd drawn her blood. "Look, Kara. Compare these. Don't these two men look very similar to you?"

Kara glanced down at the photos, shook her head. "Oh, no. Look at them, Sherlock, the man who drew my blood could be his father. I gave him the look of a mad scientist, with all that grizzled gray hair. The young one looks, well, fit, in his prime."

"Bear with me, Kara. Study them."

Kara studied the photo and her drawing, frowned, then slowly raised her head. "Okay, they do look a bit alike, Sherlock, despite the obvious age difference. But look, the older guy's comb-over doesn't hide the fact he's going bald, and the kidnapper had thick brown hair. It is close to the same color, I guess. And look, the younger man's jaw is more square, no jowls yet, and that's because he's at least twenty years younger than the guy who drew my blood. He was in his fifties if he was a day. Maybe good cosmetic surgery could shave off ten years or so, but not this much."

All good points, but Sherlock was still bothered. "Kara, look only at the eyes, look at how similar they are. Do you think you could have drawn in the younger man's eyes without meaning to?"

Sherlock watched Kara cock her head as she studied her work. "Okay, their eyes do have the same almond shape, the sort of upward tilt at the corners. And the distance between the eyes looks about the same. I don't think I could have drawn the younger man's eyes on him. Sherlock, the man I sketched is definitely the man I remember drew my blood, not the man at the hospital. You showed me his picture, but only for a moment." She sat back. "All right, there are similarities, I grant you that. But what could that mean?"

"I don't know, it could be they're related. If we identify one, we may find the other."

"Why did you have me sketch the man who drew my blood?"

"I called the genetics department at the University of Maryland. They haven't conducted any kind of study like the one described to you. In fact, they didn't have your name as a test subject on any study they'd ever done. The whole incident sounded strange to me, but no stranger than anything else that's happened to you. And I wondered if that blood draw had anything to do with your pregnancy or with John Doe, or with Alex's kidnapping."

She squeezed Kara and rose. "You did good, Kara, keep the faith, okay?" Sherlock smiled. "I can't wait to meet your friend, Ms. Love."

"Bless her, she'll be arriving tomorrow. I imagine she'll want to see Alex's father. I'm glad the hospital is afraid to kick me out. They're moving a bed into his room so I can stay with him tonight. Maybe they'll bring in a second cot for Brenda tomorrow."

Sherlock didn't doubt the hospital would gladly give Kara use of a limo if she asked for it. She smiled. "Good, Brenda can tell him stories about you." Sherlock rolled up Kara's drawing, gave her a hug, and left her to walk back to John Doe's room.

Her cell squawked only Curly Duck, and she had to shake her head. What had Dillon done with Moe and Larry Duck? Were they going to take turns? She nodded to Ray Hunter, the maternity-floor security guard as she answered. "Connie, what do you have?"

"Are you leaning against a wall so you don't fall over?"

"What is it? What have you got?"

"It's about Sylvie Vaughn. I did a background check on her. She was born Sylvie Fox, thirty-five years ago, in Baltimore. Her mother is listed as Hannah Fox. I did a background check on Sylvie's mother and found out Hannah Fox's address is the Willows, home of B. B. Maddox. I made some calls, found out she's his longtime lover and for the past fifteen years, his live-in caregiver."

Sherlock sighed. "That gives Sylvie a reason to go to the Willows, to see her mother."

"Yeah, but listen to this. We had the video of the dark blue Toyota SUV that picked up the man and woman who took Alex from the hospital on Parker Street. Bolt had stayed all over that. We never did spot them on any of the cameras on I-95, so Bolt started checking businesses on the side roads that run parallel to I-95. He spotted the SUV on a security video pulling into a taqueria, where there are no cameras, and that's where they made the transfer, because five minutes later a white delivery van with the same driver pulled back out into traffic. Bolt went right back to the I-95 video recordings, spotted the van exiting from I-85 in Anne Arundel County, not far from the Willows. What kind of coincidence could that be? We have a CSI team at the taqueria now going over the blue Toyota SUV, looking for the kidnappers' fingerprints. We already know the car was stolen. I gotta say Bolt and the tech teams working with him were high-fiving and guzzling down their drink of choice, Mountain Dew."

Sherlock whooshed out a breath. "Connie, tell me Bolt was able to follow the van right up to their front door."

Connie laughed. "Afraid not, but never fear, grasshopper. We couldn't see the license plate on the commercial van, but on a hunch I checked out all the vehicles registered as being owned by Gen-Core Technologies. They own six of that same model, all white."

"Connie, if Dillon ever falls down on the job, will you marry me? I think it's time we meet Mr. B. B. Maddox and his family and have a little chat. I'll meet you at the Willows in forty minutes. We've got a double-pronged approach going here, Connie. Dillon is on his way to Baltimore, to the university. He'll let us know what he discovers."

54

OUTSIDE THE WILLOWS
BALTIMORE, MARYLAND
WEDNESDAY LATE AFTERNOON

Sherlock opened the passenger door of her stalwart Volvo, and Connie Butler slid in. Their cars were parked at the south end of the stone-walled compound called the Willows. "Sylvie Vaughn's still inside," Connie said, and looked down at her iWatch. "Over two hours now. Bolt called to say he's headed back to Baltimore to interview Josh Vaughn at his investment firm. Then he's going back to his list of the others at the party." She paused a moment. "Not many people know it, but Bolt's own baby son was kidnapped out of a hospital. That was before there were guards and cameras everywhere. He and his wife were very young, didn't have a dime, and had to mortgage their lives to get their son back, which thankfully they did. It's why he has a fire in his belly, why he's in the CARD unit, and why he'll do everything he can to get Alex Moody back."

Sherlock nodded. "If they were young and didn't have any money, why would kidnappers target their baby for ransom?"

"Bolt's in-laws were very wealthy, but they'd disowned their daughter when she went against their wishes and married him, a poor boy from a working-class background. The kidnappers hadn't realized the Bolts' in-laws wouldn't pay them a dime. The FBI agents working the case were shocked when the kidnappers believed them and lowered the ransom. They were never caught. But what's important is that David Haller, Bolt's son, is a happy sixteen-year-old boy, at home with his folks."

"I was wondering why you're in CARD, Connie."

Connie Butler shook her head. "The idea that anyone could steal a child, it makes me rabid. I'll tell you my own story some other time. You ready to roll?"

Sherlock drove the Volvo to the closed gates of the Willows and pressed the intercom button, both she and Connie well aware of the cameras pointed at their faces. They held up their creds to the lens.

There was a full minute of empty silence, then a man's voice said, "Agents Sherlock and Butler, you may park in front of the house."

"Don't you love such efficiency?" The gates slowly swung open, and Sherlock drove the Volvo through.

Connie said, "Those gates—I doubt a tank could bust through, that's really high-grade steel. And these walls. Looks like they want to keep out the walking dead."

"And other assorted riffraff."

They drove down a wide graveled drive circling a vast well-tended lawn shaded by three huge oak trees, flower beds around each of them. The central core of the three-story dark redbrick house was flanked by two brick wings, with large formal English gardens on either side. Sherlock had read the house was built to resemble Restoration House in Kent, England, and pulled up a photo of it.

"Wowza. Connie, it does look like that old house in Kent. Do you feel like you've been transported to jolly old England?"

"It's amazing, all right. Look at the gardens and that lawn, Sherlock. They must have an army of gardeners."

"Speaking of an army," Sherlock said, looking around, "I wonder how many security guards Dr. Maddox employs."

"I guess we're about to find out."

Sherlock parked the Volvo in front of the entrance. They saw Sylvie Vaughn's Jaguar parked outside a six-port garage some twenty feet away, set next to the north wing of the house. All the bays were closed. An old green Mercedes sedan was parked next to it.

They walked up flagstone steps to a front door that looked strong enough to withstand a battering ram. Connie said as Sherlock thwacked the lion's head knocker, "The article I read said two of the rooms are exact replicas of their counterparts in Restoration House. It took nearly fifteen years because of all the portraits that had to be copied. B. B. Maddox doesn't have any worries about money."

The front door wasn't opened by a butler or a maid, but by a slender middle-aged man wearing a slouchy cardigan and chinos. He had longish straight blond hair threaded with white, and eyes as light a blue as

Sherlock's, his covered with black-framed thick glasses. He was tall, but his shoulders were a bit slumped, as if he spent too much time hunched over at a desk or a computer. They recognized Dr. Lister Maddox, son of the founder of Gen-Core Technologies, B. B. Maddox. Oddly, he had worry beads in his hands, and was sliding them smoothly through his fingers.

"I take it you are the two FBI agents Cargill said were requesting entrance."

"That's right," Sherlock said, stepped forward, gave him her patented sunny smile, and introduced herself and Connie. They handed him their creds.

He took the creds and studied them even as he continued to block the front door. He handed them back. "May I ask what this is all about, Agents?"

"That would depend on who you are, sir," Sherlock said.

"I am Dr. Lister Maddox. I am in charge of this house."

Connie said in a precise schoolteacher voice, "But this home belongs to Dr. B. B. Maddox, doesn't it? Why isn't he in charge?"

Maddox blinked, took a step back, then straightened to block the door again. "Our family's affairs are none of your business. Why are you here? What do you want?"

Sherlock said, "Are you Dr. B. B. Maddox's son?"

"I am."

"We would like to speak to your father, Dr. Maddox, then to Sylvie Vaughn and her mother, Hannah Fox."

The worry beads began threading more quickly through his long thin fingers. His blue eyes behind thick lenses were cold. "That won't be possible, ladies."

"Agents," Connie said. "You're too young to be so forgetful of titles, Dr. Maddox. Perhaps your pharmaceutical subsidiary, Badecker-Ziotec, could offer their help to you to improve your short-term memory."

His head jerked back as if she'd slapped him.

A man's hard voice said from behind him, "Dr. Maddox, is there something you'd like me to do?"

Maddox never turned. "No, it's all right, Cargill. The ladies—excuse me, the *special agents*—wish to speak to my father, and of course that isn't possible."

The man nodded but remained standing where he was, his arms over his chest, watchful. Sherlock saw the bulge in his jacket. He was carrying. Why would Maddox need armed security?

Connie continued in her full schoolmarm mode, "Dr. Maddox, we have only a few questions for your father. It won't take long."

"I told you it isn't possible. His ill health precludes it. I would like you both to leave now. If you have questions for me, you can contact our lawyers."

Sherlock jumped in. They needed to question him, not have him kick them out and sic his lawyers on them. "Dr. Maddox, actually it's not necessary we speak with your father. After all, you've been the CEO of Gen-Core Technologies since your father stepped down fifteen years ago, and, as you say, you are the master of this exquisite home. We would be grateful, sir, if you could spend a couple of minutes with us and answer the questions we were going to ask your father." She'd really laid it on with a trowel, but at least it gave him another option, a chance to reconsider. She watched his desire to know why they were there and what they knew overcome his annoyance, until finally, he nodded. "Very well, I have a few minutes before I have to be in a meeting. Come this way." Lister led them through a time portal into a wealthy seventeenth-century salon.

He walked to the middle of the room and turned to face them, his arms outspread. "Since you are interested in my home, I'll tell you that it began when my father traced our lineage back to Henry Clerke, a rich lawyer in the early sixteen hundreds. Clerke joined two houses together to create Restoration House in Rochester, Kent. My father fancies he lived a past life in that house. He's visited many times over the years, and indeed, is a close friend of the current owner. His bedroom—the King's Bedchamber—and this room, are exact replicas. The rest of the house is quite modern. You are correct: the house is my father's. He conceived and built it." He paused, waiting for what? Praise? Applause?

Sherlock obliged him. "A fascinating story, Dr. Maddox."

Connie pointed to the portraits covering the walls. "Are these people any relation to you, Dr. Maddox?"

"I believe Mr. Clerke simply bought many of the original portraits to fill the walls of Restoration House, so no one knows who they are. My father never concerned himself with finding out. It was enough for him that they were in Restoration House for them to be here as well." He waved a hand toward a gilt chair. "It won't break, go ahead, sit down and ask your questions." He looked down at his watch.

The chair was surprisingly comfortable. Sherlock said, "Dr. Maddox, on Monday afternoon a baby was stolen from the maternity ward of Washington Memorial Hospital. His name is Alex Moody. One of the cars the kidnappers used was traced to this neighborhood. A white delivery van. We've learned that your company, Gen-Core Technologies, owns six such white vans."

Lister blinked at her, the worry beads stilled in his hands. "Many companies use vans, Agent Sherlock. Why would you come here to point that out?"

Connie said, "We know you're not directly involved with managing all your company's vans, Dr. Maddox. This is a large property, and it's possible one of the vans might be kept here. Would you mind if we looked around, perhaps checked your garage?"

"Don't be absurd. Of course you may not go traipsing around my property."

Sherlock said, "Perhaps then we can get your permission to check your fleet of white vans at Gen-Core, see if one is missing?"

"Not without a warrant, Agent. If you are concerned one of our vans was used illegally, I'll have to contact our lawyers, let them start an internal investigation."

Connie pulled up photos of the man and woman who'd kidnapped Alex Moody from the hospital. "Do you know either of these people, Dr. Maddox?"

Lister felt his heart kettledrum. Of course they'd have photos of Burley and Quince from the hospital videos, but Quince had assured him they'd been very careful changing vehicles, so how had they spotted the white van? He forced himself to look at the two photos on the agent's cell phone. He shook his head. "Sorry, I've never seen either of these people in my life."

Sherlock watched the worry beads quicken between his fingers. She smiled. "Dr. Maddox, we've discovered an interesting coincidence. Sylvie Vaughn is the daughter of one of your employees, Hannah Fox. Ms. Vaughn is also one of Kara Moody's best friends, the mother of the stolen baby. We saw Ms. Vaughn's car outside. We'd like to speak with her and her mother."

Lister said, "I fear that you will get neither of your wishes. As I told you, my father isn't well and cannot be disturbed. Sylvie is out on the boat with her mother." He looked down at a thin Piaget watch yet a second time. "They won't be back for several hours. Sylvie always takes her to the Inner Harbor, for dinner at Marvin's."

Sherlock pulled up a photo of John Doe. "Tell me if you know this man."

He shook his head and looked bored, but the worry beads gave him away, threading faster and faster through his fingers. "I'm sorry, Agent, I've never seen this man in my life, either. Who is he?"

"Did you hear about the crazy man who burst into a house in Georgetown on Sunday?"

"Of course not. I have no interest in local news in Washington, D.C."

"This is that man. He's currently in a coma at Washington Memorial Hospital."

Connie picked it up. "Someone tried to murder him Monday night. We're asking you about him because it turns out he's closely connected to Kara Moody as well. He's her baby's father. Would you know anything about it, Dr. Maddox?"

"Look, Agents, I've been patient, I've listened to your questions, tried to remain civil. I do not see why you would think we would allow a white van you're looking for into the Willows. I do not know why you would believe I've met any of those people. I want you to leave now. I will be calling my lawyers. I'm sure they'll want any further communication to go through them."

He turned and walked straight out of the seventeenth-century salon, across the modern entrance hall, directly to the front door. He opened it, and stood aside, waiting like a doorman for them to leave.

"Thank you for your time, Dr. Maddox," Sherlock said as she walked past him.

Lister didn't say anything. He nodded to Cargill, who hurried to follow them through the front door.

He waited until they'd left, then said, "Cargill, you will never allow those two agents in again."

"No sir," Cargill said. He wanted to ask what he should do if they returned with a warrant, but knew enough to keep his mouth shut.

55

Savich parked the Porsche in the visitor's slot right in front of the main entrance to Badecker-Ziotec. It sat on the far edge of the Gen-Core Technologies main campus, three modern utilitarian glass-and-steel buildings, none of them with the architectural prestige of the Gen-Core Technologies headquarters a quarter-mile distant. He walked into a utilitarian space that held one tall fake palm tree and a large curving counter with two women seated behind it, working on computers. One of the women whose name tag identified her as Millicent Flowers looked up and smiled at him.

"You're FBI Agent Savich?"

He nodded, handed her his creds.

She rose, handed back his creds. "I'm Millicent Flowers. Follow me, Agent Savich. I'll take you to Dr. Zyon."

They got off on the second floor and walked down a wide sterile hallway to a door with an embossed plaque:

DIRECTOR OF RESEARCH. She knocked, waited, knocked again.

Savich heard a man's annoyed huff from inside. Ms. Flowers said, "He's not really rude, just off exploring another part of the universe." She gave him a big smile. The door opened and an older rotund man not taller than five foot four stood in front of Savich, glaring up at him. He looked like he'd just gotten out of bed, with wrinkled clothes and bedhead hair. He wore thick-lensed glasses with no frames and he was frowning ferociously. "Am I supposed to know you?"

Ms. Flowers said before Savich could introduce himself, "Dr. Zyon, you remember, Special Agent Savich of the FBI is here to speak to you? We discussed it. You agreed."

Savich stuck out his hand. "A pleasure to meet you, sir. Thank you for taking the time to speak to me."

Zyon wore no rings on his small plump hands. Savich saw the pads of his fingers were scarred from burns, perhaps from chemicals. Had one of his experiments gone awry?

Zyon left him in the doorway, walked to the middle of an office that held an ancient desk covered with state-of-the-art computer equipment, a single desk chair, and a simple metal chair for visitors. Zyon was evidently a man with no time or desire for meetings or visitors. Savich saw a half-dozen diplomas, awards, commendations on the walls, and a photo taken with Zyon standing next to President Clinton. He looked puffed up and quite pleased with himself, and a foot shorter. So he had a little vanity, good to know.

Zyon stopped in front of his desk, turned, and looked Savich up and down. "You're big. I always wanted to be as big as you but it never happened. If I agreed to talk to you then I guess I don't have a choice, so come in, come in. Flowers, you can go away."

Millicent Flowers gave Savich another warm smile, Dr. Zyon a tolerant nod, and left them to it.

"I won't waste your time, Dr. Zyon. I'm here because your CEO confirmed your company conducted research on drugs similar to sirolimus."

"Sirolimus? Yes, we did, about three years ago. But it was a wasted investment, never got to human testing. I don't suppose you know sirolimus was first called rapamycin when it was discovered on Rapa Nui—Easter Island as it's more commonly called. That's where they found a bacterium that produces it."

"Yes, I read that."

Dr. Zyon eyed him with some interest. "It was developed as an antifungal agent at first, which is how that bacterium uses it, but nowadays it's used mostly as an immunosuppressive to prevent organ rejection."

"Dr. Zyon, I really need to know what work you did on that drug, and why."

Zyon crossed his arms and cocked his head to one side. "Tell me why the FBI wants to know about a drug that prevents organ rejection."

"I will, but humor me, Doctor."

Savich had sparked his interest, he saw it. Dr. Zyon

looked thoughtful. "I recall Dr. Lister Maddox, our founder's son, asked us to synthesize about a dozen chemical variants of rapamycin—congeners, we call them—in the hope we would find one that was less toxic, or bind it with a broader class of cellular receptors. I remember Dr. Maddox was particularly interested in the effects of those compounds on tissue aging."

"And what did you find?"

"Some of the congeners showed promising results in our tissue cultures. They rejuvenated muscle and fat cells, some of the aging, senescent cells in the cultures died off, and even stem cell function improved. But when we moved on to testing laboratory mice, we had to quit."

"Why?"

"It's not a big mystery. The congeners we tested proved too toxic, particularly to the nervous system and bone marrow. We stopped then because there's only so far a pharmaceutical company can venture into basic research like that. We survive by developing drugs we can sell, and being old isn't a reimbursable medical condition. None of the insurance companies are set to pay for any such drug, and so extended work in an area like anti-aging isn't in our financial interest. Even Dr. Maddox had to agree."

Dr. Zyon paused and waved his plump hands. "Time to pay up, Agent Savich. What is this all about? I don't understand your interest in these anti-aging experiments. Aren't you young enough already?"

"Dr. Zyon, I asked you about this class of drugs

because there's a young man in a coma right now at Washington Memorial Hospital. They don't understand why he's in a coma, but they did find a drug in his bloodstream that's similar to sirolimus, but not known to them. Can you tell me how that drug could have ended up in his bloodstream?"

Dr. Zyon shook his head. "No, no, that's impossible. You would have to verify the drug in the young man's system is indeed one of the compounds we actually developed here."

"And if it were verified?"

"It would mean someone stole it from us, or at least stole the information about how to synthesize that particular compound. And then that someone gave it to the young man illegally."

"Doctor, let's say someone did steal your drug, how would they use it? What kind of testing would they do? You said you abandoned your research because the drugs were too toxic?"

"Since you've already put ethics aside, I have to say it depends on what they're hoping to accomplish. I suppose they would give the drug in various doses to test subjects, evaluate them for toxicity and whether the drug is having the effects they're hoping for. They might search for subjects who seem to tolerate the drug better, for whatever reason, and focus on that group for further study. Eventually they might give the drug in combination with others known to have a similar or synergistic effect. I have to say, the thought of anyone doing such a thing turns my stomach."

Mine as well, Doctor, believe me. "Would these test subjects have to have a great many blood draws, enough to leave scars?"

"Possibly. Pharmaceutical research requires a great deal of blood testing, yes, often on a schedule after each dose is given. Even sizable volumes of plasma can be taken for harvesting, for testing, or for the immuno-globins or other proteins in the plasma that can be put to therapeutic use. Tell me why you ask."

"Our John Doe—the man in the coma—has scars like that on his arms."

Dr. Zyon stared at him. "I really don't know what to say, Agent Savich. I will immediately begin a careful search of our computer records and our drug library for any evidence of tampering or unauthorized access. It sounds impossible." Zyon shook his head. "I presume we will speak again?"

Savich smiled at the man he knew he could come to like, shook his hand. "You've given me a great deal to think about already, Dr. Zyon. Thank you for your time." He walked to the door, turned back when Dr. Zyon said from behind him, "Agent Savich, everything you've told me is very disturbing. Can you tell me what you think has happened?"

"I'll let you know when I've confirmed what I think, Dr. Zyon."

When Savich stepped out of the elevator at the lobby, the two women at the counter were yelling.

"There's a fire at the Annex!"

Savich ran out the door and toward billowing

flames a hundred yards away. Sirens sounded in the distance. People were standing in small groups outside their buildings, staring. Savich saw a man and a woman in a white van driving slowly away, looking back at the fire. Savich stared at the driver, saw the face he'd seen on the hospital video, the face of Alex Moody's kidnapper. The man looked back, met Savich's eyes, and gunned the van. Savich drew his Glock and raced after it.

Savich aimed at the back tires and fired six rounds. The driver's-side back tire exploded. The van swerved and hit a wire fence, tore through, and shot into a shallow water-filled ditch outside the compound. The van teetered, then landed back on its four tires. The rear doors flew open and Savich saw what looked like a freezer and medical equipment fall out the back. The man and woman burst out of the van, both of them carrying guns, and fired at him. It was the woman from the hospital video. Savich dove behind a can labeled REFUSE, flattened himself, and fired back. He heard them yelling to each other, saw them running away from him, and from the van. He could have chased them but he had more important things to do. He called the Baltimore Field Office, spoke to SAC Jake Murphy. The local agents would find them. He dusted himself off, pulled out his cell, and called Sherlock.

56

THE WILLOWS
WEDNESDAY LATE AFTERNOON

Sherlock and Connie were standing by Sherlock's Volvo when her cell rang. Sherlock held up a finger and listened to Dillon. When she punched off, she pumped her fist. "That's it! We've got him!" She told Connie everything Dillon had found out from Dr. Zyon, and about Alex Moody's kidnappers burning the Annex and the van they abandoned.

"Dillon believes Maddox held John Doe against his will in the Annex, used him as a test subject, and today he ordered the two kidnappers to burn the Annex and destroy what evidence he could. Luckily, all the research equipment and drugs they removed were in the van when they ran from Dillon. He's on his way here now."

The two agents stared at each other. Sherlock said, "We could wait, Connie, as Dillon suggested, but Alex Moody could be in that house. If Maddox finds out what's happened, who knows what he'd do? Alex could be in imminent danger."

Connie nodded, pulled her Glock, racked the slide. They raced back to the house.

Sherlock pounded on the door. "FBI! Open up. Now!"

They heard the security guard, Cargill, call out, "No, Dr. Maddox instructed me not to admit you. Call the Gen-Core Technologies lawyers, get an appointment!"

Sherlock was nearly ready to put her fist through the door.

"Things have changed, Cargill. We have a legal right to enter. An FBI backup team is on its way. We don't want to enter forcibly, but we will, if we have to. Open the door!"

Sherlock heard Lister Maddox's voice, and then the door opened. Cargill stood there, tense, white-faced, his hand near the gun on his belt.

Connie got in his face. "Stand down, Cargill, take out your weapon and put it on the floor, then step back."

Cargill looked back at Dr. Lister Maddox, standing on the bottom stair of the lavish staircase, one hand clutching the railing, the other his worry beads. He shouted, "Why did you come back? This is an outrage! There's nothing for you here!"

Sherlock aimed her Glock at Maddox. "We'll discuss that in a moment, Dr. Maddox, but first tell Cargill to take out his weapon and put it on the floor."

"Very well, there's no need for you to have your gun aimed at me or him. We're not criminals. Cargill, do as she said."

Cargill pulled a Beretta off his belt clip, leaned down, and placed it carefully on the entrance hall tile.

Connie picked up the Beretta, put it in her jacket pocket.

Sherlock said, "Dr. Maddox, you need to tell us now—is there anyone else in the house?"

"Well, of course. My father and his nurse, Hannah Fox, are upstairs in his bedroom. There may be a housekeeper or two. I'm not sure if they've left for the day."

Sherlock said, "You said earlier that Hannah Fox and Sylvie Vaughn were out on your boat."

Lister shrugged. "I didn't want you bothering them."

Connie said, "Cargill, are there any other security guards in the house or on the grounds?"

"No, ma'am, Agent."

Sherlock slipped her Glock back into its belt clip. She walked to where Dr. Maddox stood unmoving, except for his worry beads. "We have news, Dr. Maddox. The man and woman you hired to kidnap Alex Moody from the hospital were stopped in a white van, fleeing a building called the Annex after they set fire to it." He didn't need to know they weren't in custody yet, they would be soon enough. "The FBI found some interesting medical equipment and a freezer that fell out of the back of the van. I'm sure you know exactly what was in that van, Dr. Maddox, given what an agent who interviewed Dr. Zyon at Badecker-Ziotec was told about the research you ordered them to do three years ago on compounds that affect aging. Dr. Maddox, we're expecting a warrant any minute. We believe there are more people in the house, in particular, that missing baby, Alex Moody."

"That is ridiculous."

Sherlock continued, "Dr. Maddox, you can either speak to us here, or you can contact your lawyer to meet you at the Hoover Building in Washington."

Lister froze. Then he shook his head. "I can't imagine why you think I would burn down my own building, and a useful one at that. If the Annex is burning, I should see to it, but of course you won't let me do that, will you? As for Zyon, he doesn't know much, hardly anything about my research or my results, and that means you don't, either."

Sherlock plowed on, ignoring him. "You'd be surprised, Doctor. We know the man who drew Kara Moody's blood more than nine months ago looks amazingly like the same man who kidnapped Alex Moody on Monday, though he looks fifteen years younger. Would you like to see a sketch Kara Moody made of the man who drew her blood and compare it to the photo of the man at the hospital? Can you tell me I'm wrong?"

Lister stared at the young woman with glorious red hair and eyes as blue as the summer sky, eyes that were boring into him, condemning him. Kara Moody had remembered Quince well enough from nearly a year ago to draw him? He'd never considered anyone would make that connection. He looked straight at Sherlock and smiled, and for once, his worry beads stilled. "Agent, I have no idea what you're talking about. I resent your barging in here once again and throwing around your absurd accusations. I want you to leave."

Sherlock said over him, "I told you we're not going anywhere, Dr. Maddox. As I said, Alex Moody's kidnapper looks at least fifteen years younger than the man from about ten months ago. Does that mean you succeeded in your research? Managed to turn back the clock for him by fifteen years? That would be quite an accomplishment." She paused a moment, then said, "Dr. Zyon must be a genius."

Lister leaped to the bait. "Zyon, a genius? That's a joke, that posing bore gave up, said we shouldn't go on, that it was impossible, the compounds were too toxic, the cost too high. I had to continue the experiments on my own. I was the one who made the discoveries, not he!" He was panting hard. It took him a moment to realize what he'd admitted. He straightened, pulled his shoulders back, and thrust his chin up, now the man in charge, the leader. "There is nothing wrong with my doing research, Agents. I have worked for a laudable goal. You are police officers, you reduce everything to prosaic black-and-white. You are being shortsighted, ignoring what you have seen with your own eyes. Open your minds, consider possibilities you never dreamed of, consider the amazing results standing before your very eyes."

Sherlock said, "Dr. Maddox, I do appreciate what you've accomplished, it seems remarkable. Perhaps you'll tell us who else you've experimented on?" Sherlock waited a beat, then turned to Cargill. "How old are you?"

Cargill looked at Lister. "Sir?"

Lister waved his hand. "Tell her, she can find out your age easily enough."

"I'm fifty-seven."

She wouldn't have believed him, but Sherlock had seen Kara's drawing and she'd seen the kidnapper. "You look about thirty-five."

"Yes," Cargill said, throwing back his head. "I owe the man I am now to Dr. Maddox."

Connie said, "Dr. Maddox, why haven't you given yourself any of your magic drugs? You look every one of your fifty years."

"Don't be ridiculous. It's too early, I must perfect the treatments first. I'm the only one who understands the drugs and how to use them safely. If any problems develop with the test subjects, I'm the only one to fix them. The entire project depends on my staying healthy."

Cargill was staring at Maddox. "Dr. Maddox, I never thought of Quince and me as your *test subjects* before. Is that what we are? Like lab mice?"

"Cargill, I've rolled back time for you and Quince, extended your life by at least fifteen years. You're not stupid, you knew there were risks. You should be grateful."

So Quince was the name of the kidnapper? Suddenly, it came to her in a flash. Sherlock said, "We want to speak to your father, Dr. Maddox."

"No! You have no reason to bother him. I told you, he is too ill for visitors, much less law officers who would browbeat him. He wouldn't understand in any case. Look, I realize this is all quite unusual, seeing Cargill, it is no doubt a shock to you. I'm perfectly willing to discuss my research with you. I will go with you to your Hoover Building. We will join my lawyers there, and I will tell you what it all means. But leave my father alone."

"He's seventy-eight years old," Sherlock said slowly. "I presume you've given him your drugs as well, like Cargill and Quince, isn't that right?"

Lister said nothing.

"Of course you have. So why can't we see him? Or did your experiments on him go wrong? Did you put him in a coma, like the young man at the hospital?"

Lister Maddox leaned back against the wall, his shoulder touching a picture frame. He was frantically working his worry beads, weaving them through the fingers of both hands. It was a mesmerizing sight. "Of course not. You don't understand."

"Then explain it to me. Make me understand."

He remained silent. Sherlock realized they were still standing in the entrance hall, but that was fine with her until the others arrived. Push him, she thought, keep pushing him. "Tell me what I don't understand, Dr. Maddox."

"I'm a scientist, Agent. I didn't expect to reverse my father's illness, but still, I had to try. I failed."

"What went wrong, Dr. Maddox? What happened to your father? Why can't we see him?"

It seemed to Sherlock he was going to burst into tears. He looked defeated. He waved his hand, his worry beads swinging. "Very well, why not? It seems I can't stop you. When you do meet him, you'll see I've treated him as well, that I've managed to restore much of his muscle mass, fat, and bone, but for my father, simply restoring him to a man of fifty years old again wasn't my ultimate goal. Some fifteen years ago my father suffered a catastrophic neurologic event that smashed his brain like a hammer. It left him an empty husk, a man who isn't even aware of what I've done for him, what I'm still trying to do." Lister paused, his face twisted. "When I show him his reflection in a mirror, he doesn't even know it, doesn't even realize it's a mirror! I had so hoped my treatment would eventually restore and heal his injured brain tissue, bring back that wonderful mind of his." He swallowed, looked at Sherlock with pain-filled eyes. "But it appears I've failed him; I've failed my father."

The entrance hall was silent until the worry beads started clacking again.

Sherlock didn't turn when she heard footsteps near the front door open behind her, she knew it was Dillon. She kept her focus on Dr. Maddox. "So, to be clear, Dr. Maddox, you admit you've given a number of human subjects your experimental drugs, without any oversight or approval, without any review of their safety? Do you consider that ethical?"

Lister straightened again, barely glancing at Savich, outrage pouring off him. "You break into my house, and then you expect me to listen to you condemn what I've accomplished? Outside review? Come now,

Agents, don't tell me you're surprised I've tried to avoid that kind of interference. Do you think I would let those faceless idiots at the FDA dictate whether my father dies, how long it will take before all of us standing here will die, because I was afraid to flout some of their rules? And this is the same bureaucracy happy to let charlatans and hucksters peddle every kind of worthless snake oil to the desperate and dying, who will pay them anything to live just a little longer. The FDA scoff at them, yes, but they continue to let the scam artists rob people with their outlandish claims that their magical herbs, their absurd apricot pits, their pseudoscience diets will cure them of their diseases, extend their lives. Those are the people you should prosecute, those are the people you should arrest, Agents, those liars, not me!

"Most of our important medical advances were discovered outside the bounds of accepted constraints. It was Quince's and Cargill's choice to take the treatments, they gave me their permission. And so I moved forward, and I've succeeded, given these two men fifteen years of life! Can you begin to imagine what that means? Fifteen more healthy years they wouldn't have had!"

Sherlock said, "And when they stop taking your magic pills? What will happen to them?"

"I assume they'll simply resume natural aging."

Cargill said, "Dr. Maddox, you told me I'd stay young forever!"

"With the treatments, of course. But without it? I don't know—how could I?" He drew himself up. "I know I'll probably have to answer to the authorities for breaking their rules. So be it; I am prepared for that."

Sherlock said, "Tell us about your fountain of youth, Dr. Maddox." She paused, added, "And tell us what you're prepared to answer for."

Lister Maddox nodded, obviously pleased to be asked these questions. "The sought-after fountain of youth. People have tried to slow aging since the beginning of recorded history. The Taoists may have been the first to strive for immortality by following their magical diets and leading what they termed tranquil lives. They invented acupuncture and tai chi to help them, and those are still with us today.

"You want to know why I have succeeded? In short, the genomic revolution, Agent. We age because our bodies have evolved to keep us alive and vigorous long enough to reproduce and nurture our young. Sooner or later, our cells stop dividing, become senescent, or die. We suffer dwindling strength, disease, debility. Since the beginning of time, we've had no choice but to submit to our own decay even though we fight it every step of the way.

"We only recently started to see aging as a genomic illness, like cancer, activated by genomic pathways. It is our master regulatory genes that set the aging clock back to zero when each of us is born, the same genes that build and repair us. I've been lucky enough to stumble onto a small part of that programming and alert enough to appreciate what I've found. Imagine curing all the diseases of aging, all the tortures of frailty.

Imagine the joy you'd feel at being rejuvenated! Talk to Cargill, see how he feels and you will hear wonder in his voice. And yet you stand there proposing to stop me?"

Savich said, "Dr. Maddox, the rules are there to protect all of us from people who value the answers they seek more than they care about who they might hurt to get them. Consider the Nazi human experimentation. Undoubtedly, they justified their every action. And you, I notice you seem to be carefully avoiding talking about the crimes you've committed to develop your treatments." Savich counted off on his fingers. "You haven't mentioned your attempted murder of the young man in the hospital, or your kidnapping Kara Moody's baby for some reason we still don't understand. Tell us, what did you do to that young man lying in a coma? Can you show us his consent to be your test subject? Or did you kidnap him as well? Please do not throw out that old chestnut that the ends justify the means."

"I did only what I had to do."

Connie said, her voice vibrating with anger, "And kidnapping Alex Moody, a one-day-old baby? How does he fit in with your grand philosophizing? Were you planning on using him as a test subject as well?"

He said nothing.

Sherlock said, "It's past time we see your father now, Dr. Maddox. We can wait for the warrant to arrive, but I see little point. Do you?"

57

A woman yelled, "Lister! Help me!"

Sherlock looked up at the landing to see an older woman doing her best to support a man who was mumbling to himself, waving his arms, trying to pull free of her.

"Lister, B.B. woke up. He raised his head when he heard the shouting, and he actually turned his head to the bedroom door. He started struggling to get up." She wrapped her arms around him and said in a voice filled with wonder, "He looked at me, Lister, and said, 'Help me, Hannah.' I think he's trying to get to you."

Lister seemed unable to move. He simply stared at the man and woman above him.

Sherlock said, "Is that your father, Dr. Maddox? Is that Dr. B. B. Maddox?"

Lister shouted over his shoulder as he ran up the stairs, "Yes, it's my father! It's worked, it's worked! Hannah, it worked!"

B. B. Maddox managed to pull free of Hannah and stagger toward the stairs to his son, leaning heavily against the wall to keep him steady.

Lister couldn't believe what he was seeing. His father looked confused, but there was cognizance in his eyes, awareness of what was around him. Lister's heart leaped. It wasn't that his father couldn't walk, with help, thanks to Hannah's incessant exercises, massages, and stretching, and to Cargill's holding him up and walking with him every morning. But that flicker of light, that awareness, was it real?

Lister was so elated he was dizzy. He reached his father, pulled him against him. "Father? You're here? You're really here?" He stopped short when he heard his father's once-dominating voice say slowly, as if finding words was difficult, "All these voices, who are these people?"

Lister caught his father as he sagged against him. "It's all right, sir. You're here, with me. These people don't matter, ignore them."

His father pulled back and stared down at him. He cocked his head, a gesture from long ago. "What's happened to you, Lister? You look old."

"I have aged, Father, fifteen years. Let me help you back upstairs, and I'll tell you everything. Don't worry about the agents, it's a misunderstanding. I'll clear it all up, don't worry."

B.B. said, "I'm hungry."

Hannah said from behind him in her soothing voice, "I can get you some of your favorite poached salmon, B.B., how would that be?"

He looked back at her, frowned. "Hannah? Why do you look so old?" He looked down uncertainly at Sherlock and Connie and Savich, showed no recognition of Cargill. His mouth worked, but only a moan came out. He collapsed into his son's arms. Savich let Cargill run up the stairs and the three of them lifted B. B. Maddox and carried him down the hall, his head resting on his son's arms.

Savich, Sherlock, and Connie followed slowly. Connie paused a moment, to look into an antique gold-framed mirror. "I wonder if he'd be even more surprised to see himself now, if he looked."

Savich said, "I'll keep an eye on them, Sherlock, you and Connie go find Alex Moody."

Sherlock and Connie walked down the long corridor, looking into guest rooms, a movie room, a gym. They heard a mewling sound and looked up to see a door open and a woman standing there, a baby in her arms.

Sherlock said, "We're FBI. Is that Alex Moody?"

The woman looked back and forth between them, slowly nodded. "I'm very glad you're here. I'm Ella Peters. Dr. Maddox is having me take care of the baby. He wanted me to hide him in the laundry, pretend I was a housekeeper, but I couldn't do that. When I heard your voices, I knew help was here."

Sherlock took the baby from the woman's arms. She looked down at the perfect little face and blurry blue eyes looking back at her. He was sucking on his fingers. "Is he well?"

"Of course," Ella said, patting his head. "He's perfect. I'm a nurse."

Sherlock smiled down at him. "It's good to see you again, Alex. Your mama's going to be very happy."

Sherlock and Connie turned at the sound of Dr. Lister Maddox's voice. "Take him back to the nursery, Ella! What are you doing?"

"His name is Alex, Dr. Maddox, and he's not staying here, not with you. He belongs with his mother."

Lister took a step forward, stopped, and sagged against the hallway wall. "You betray me, Ella? You betray my father?" Tears sheened his eyes. "He's gone again, my father is gone." He waved his hand toward Sherlock and the baby. "I suppose you will take him, like everything else."

"Dr. Maddox, we have the baby now, and we have Ella and the others to tell us everything we need to know. And we'll soon find Sylvie Vaughn. Isn't it time for you to admit to us what you've done, for you to help us put some lives together? Who is the young man in the hospital? Where is his family?"

He only shook his head, said nothing.

Ella said, "His name is Arthur Childers. I did my best for him as well. And there was another one before him, another subject. Dr. Maddox called him Enigma One. His name was Thomas Denham. He died."

"You stupid woman! After all I've accomplished! My work must continue, it must go on!"

Connie said, "Cut the crap, Dr. Maddox. You used those men like lab rats. This nightmare is over, and you are going to jail. I pray for a very long time."

"How can you be so blind? You've seen Cargill!

You've seen my seventy-eight-year-old father. Why can't you understand I had to use human subjects?"

Sherlock gave the baby to Connie, pulled flex-cuffs from her belt, walked over to Lister, and jerked his arms behind his back.

"But the baby! Someone must study him! He could hold the answer for all of us!"

Sherlock fastened the flex-cuffs around his wrists. "I thank the Lord none of that will ever be up to you again."

58

**SERGEI PETROV'S HOUSE
SOUTH OF ALEXANDRIA
WEDNESDAY NIGHT**

A half-moon shone on the Potomac, and wind-whipped waves slapped against the wooden dock, rocking the yacht gently at its moorings. It was a pity about the half-moon and the bright clear sky with its stunning display of stars, but there was nothing to be done about it.

Jack and Cam huddled down near the water with five of the FBI SWAT team out of the Washington Field Office, at the edge of the woods looking at Petrov's house. Ruth and Ollie were already with the other half of the team in the trees at the back of the house. The SWAT team's standard-issue earpieces and the microphones in their shoulder pouches were dialed into the CAU comms units at their wrists. They saw bright lights shining from the living room and the master bedroom, and Ruth had reported lights in the first-floor back bedroom.

They all wore black from head to toe, their faces blackened. Cam and Jack wore black caps pulled low, Kevlar beneath their FBI jackets, the SWAT team wore their military-issue bulletproof vests, camouflage helmets, and night-vision goggles. They all carried H&K MP5s that could be set to full automatic for thirty-three rapid rounds, and extra ammunition on their belts. Cam and Jack carried their FBI-issue Glocks as well, and the SWAT team their preferred Springfield .45s. Several of the SWAT team carried crowbars and lightweight battering rams to breach the front door.

As they moved quietly into position, Cam whispered to Jack, "I feel seriously underdressed next to these guys."

He whispered back, "They've got to be ready for battle, an ambush, anything. We can move faster if need be."

SWAT team leader Luke Palmer set up a parabolic mic facing the house and they listened for voices, hoping to count and place everyone inside. They heard only the sound of a single man's footsteps in the living room.

Jack looked down at his watch, said low into his comm, "Ruth, is everyone in place?"

"Yes, we're ready."

At Luke's nod, Jack raised the SWAT team bullhorn. "This is the FBI. Sergei Petrov, come out now with your hands over your head. The house is surrounded, there's no way out."

They heard a shout, and someone running, then another man's loud voice, but they couldn't understand his words. He was speaking Russian.

"I make two men," Luke whispered. "They're running, getting weapons together." He said into his microphone, "Launch tear gas grenades." The launchers fired in unison from both the front and back of the house. They heard the sounds of breaking glass as the grenades crashed through the windows. The lights went out, they heard more shouting, and then the obscenely loud crack of weapons on full automatic aimed at their positions. They heard more automatic fire from the back of the house, loud and clean on their comms.

Luke said, "Open fire," into his comms, and the SWAT team, most of them flat on their bellies, opened up a deafening barrage of fire louder than anything Jack had heard since Afghanistan. It smashed the glass doors and windows, peppering the walls with flying dust and bullet holes. There was a brief lull while most of the team shoved in new magazines. Jack said, "Luke, keep laying down fire, I'll take two of your men to the north side of the house where the house plans show only one window, see if we can't end this." He said into his comms, "Ruth, give us sixty seconds to get their attention away from you, then see if you can close in on the house from your position."

"Sixty seconds."

Jack and two SWAT members loped through the trees to the north and sprinted across the open clearing at the side of the house. Jack realized all the heavy gunfire was coming from the front of the house after the SWAT team's first barrage. "Ruth," he whispered into his comms, "both men are in front firing at us, but be careful entering the house, there could be booby traps."

"Approaching the kitchen, moving forward."

Jack went down to his knees, crawled to the big shattered picture window, felt the hit of tear gas floating out from the living room. He rose and emptied his H&K through the smoke.

He heard Ruth's voice come through his comms, "We're in through the kitchen."

Bullets flew at Jack through the smoke. He flattened himself against the foundation, reared up, and threw a flash bang through the living room window, shielding himself as best he could from the deafening noise and the blinding flash of light. He heard yelling, someone running. He shouted into his comms, "They're moving toward the back of the house." He waved the SWAT team forward. They kicked in the bullet-ridden front door and broke through into the entrance hall. The living room was filled with smoke from the flash bang and the tear gas. They all froze in place, listening, heard only the breathing of the agents beside them. Then they heard Ruth and the SWAT agents moving toward them from the rear of the house. Jack talked to them through the comms until Ruth, Ollie, and their team came bursting through the closed door at the back of the entrance hall.

"They're gone," Jack said. "But where?"

Suddenly there was gunfire. They heard a yell from the other side of the house. Someone was hit.

They ran out of the front door, saw Petrov burst into the woods at the side of the house, running all out toward the yacht. Was there an escape route not on the house plans?

Jack heard a SWAT team member on the comm. "Target number two is down. He was carrying a machine gun. We're clear here."

Jack took off after Petrov, only vaguely aware of shouting and running footsteps behind him. He saw Petrov again on the wooden dock, unlooping a mooring line from its iron cleat and jumping up onto the deck. Petrov heard Jack running toward him, jerked around, and fired off a half-dozen rounds from a handgun. Jack dove to the ground, felt the shock of a bullet slap high into his right arm. He fired back, saw Petrov flinch when a bullet hit his thigh, but he didn't slow. He limped into the pilot house and the big engine roared to life. The yacht began to pull away from the dock.

Jack ran onto the dock, heard footsteps behind him, but didn't turn. He dropped his H&K, took a flying leap, and grabbed the deck railing. His arm screamed with pain, and he tried to pull himself up, but he couldn't, he could hardly hold on. He saw Petrov in the pilot house, steering out, and then he heard Cam yelling, saw her leap up to the yacht railing near the bow.

"Hold on, Jack." She pulled herself onboard, then braced her feet against a cleat and pulled him up. He fell on his belly on deck. She jerked around, saw Petrov standing in the pilot house doorway, aiming his Beretta at them as he clumsily tried to tie a towel tightly around his bleeding leg.

He stared at her. "You're as ferocious as Elena."

"Elena? You mean Elena Orlov? Your bodyguard? Your lover?"

He looked startled.

"You really do look like a vampire in the moonlight," Cam said. "I could suggest using a tanning bed occasionally, might help keep people from trying to stake you."

"Shut up. From this distance I could kill you both before either of you could aim your weapons. I won't if you don't give me any more trouble. I will set you both off on one of the small islands down the river. But first, drop your Glocks. Now."

Jack came up onto his knees, pulled his Glock off its waist clip, and dropped it on the wooden deck in front of him. Cam followed suit, dropped her Glock beside his.

Petrov said to Jack, "You're bleeding on my yacht. Wrap up your arm."

Cam shrugged out of her FBI jacket, pulled the black T-shirt covering her Kevlar vest off over her head, and shrugged back into her jacket. She went down on her knees and tied the shirt tight around Jack's arm. She whispered against his ear, "It'll be okay, Jack."

"Shut up and move away from him." Petrov waved the Beretta. He looked back to see the SWAT team standing on the boat dock staring after them. He smiled.

59

"We killed your man," Jack said. "He was too loyal for his own good, staying back to let you escape."

"Abram was with me since I was a boy and he a young man of twenty." He pointed his Beretta at Cam's chest. "I told you to move away from him."

Cam took two steps back to lean against the railing. From the lights moving along the shoreline, she could tell they were picking up speed, heading south. She said, "It was one of our agents who spoke to Abram on the burner phone you provided your assassin at Ginger Lake. Keeping him alive helped us find you." As she spoke, she flicked her comms unit to transmit. Now Ruth and Ollie and the SWAT team would hear everything. She waved her hand toward the pilot house. "You put it on autopilot, heading south."

"Of course, there's no need to adjust the course this time of night."

Jack said, "Did you put the boat under Elena Orlov's name, that is, Cortina Alvarez's name?"

Petrov said nothing, grimaced as he tightened the towel around his leg.

Jack's arm pulsed with pain, but he ignored it. "Listen to me, Petrov. You're a banker, not a trained KGB agent. You've got no more assassins waiting in the wings for your orders. You've got to realize there's no way you're going to get out of here. The Coast Guard will be along soon."

"It's not the KGB, you fool. The KGB no longer exists."

"Oh yeah, new name, same thugs."

Petrov moved his Beretta back and forth between Jack and Cam. "You will now tell me how you found me. How you know about Elena and Cortina."

Cam gave him a wide smile. "We're special agents for the Federal Bureau of Investigation. We've got really good brains, plus you're on our turf."

Petrov actually sneered. "You idiot woman, you're nothing compared to Putin's GRU and FSB."

Jack laughed. "I've got to admit you did a fine job of freeing Manta Ray on Monday. But look here, Petrov"—he snapped his fingers—"it's only Wednesday night and we found you already."

Petrov winced at the pain in his leg, knew it hadn't stopped bleeding. He touched his hand to the towel, pressed it in. He saw Cam move and immediately straightened. "Don't you take another step! If you move again, I will kill you. Now, I won't ask either of you again. How did you find me and Elena?"

But Cam hadn't moved, scarcely breathed, she'd only leaned a bit toward Jack, away from him. She didn't want him to hear the low-level feedback coming from her comms. She said, "Come now, Sergei, it wasn't that difficult. Elena flew to Washington with you on Aeroflot 104 from Moscow, she wasn't hard to find at all. She's listed as your employee, your bodyguard. It made sense you would use her to rent a safe-deposit box as Cortina Alvarez. You sure weren't about to use your own name. And why waste that near-perfect legend you had created for her?"

His forehead furrowed, not in pain, but something he remembered he didn't like. Then he shook his head. He looked back south over the water.

Cam said, "Elena wasn't at your house, only Abram. Where is she, Sergei? Was she with your pilot when you blew up the helicopter?"

"I won't tell you again, shut up."

Jack said, "I'll bet she was in the helicopter. She became one last loose thread to you, didn't she, Sergei? You killed not only your pilot, you killed your lover. Anyone else in the helicopter?"

Cam said, "I don't suppose Manta Ray was in that copter with them?"

"Shut up, both of you. You haven't explained anything. How did you find me?"

Cam said, "A young man named Saxon Hainny. Under hypnosis, Saxon saw you clearly standing with Mia Prevost as he lay in a stupor on the bed, before you murdered her."

"That's impossible! He was unconscious, I checked him myself."

"Sorry, Sergei," Jack said. "He wasn't unconscious,

and as Agent Wittier told you, he remembered everything under hypnosis. He saw you, described you. That hair you have, that widow's peak, it's very distinctive. And that white, white skin of yours, like a vampire. By the way, the towel around your leg is getting soaked with blood, the pressure isn't working. That isn't going to turn out well for you."

Still, Petrov kept looking south. Cam knew he wasn't looking for any islands, he was planning to kill them and dump them overboard, as soon as he was out far enough. She looked at the wave caps shining and sparkling in the moonlight and felt a punch of fear. She clamped it down.

"Jack's right, Sergei. You're going to bleed out before you can find medical help."

He didn't answer, looked back between her and Jack at the frothing water churned up by the yacht's engine.

She said, "Want to tell us why you murdered Mia Prevost?"

Petrov shook his head. "She was a tool, nothing more. I'm tired of talking. Shut up."

Cam said, "Sergei, face it, you've failed. It's all over. You, your daddy, and Transvolga are all beyond help. You'll never get out of American waters."

He trained the Beretta on her. Both Jack and Cam knew it was crunch time. "Help him up. You can both go over the rail now or I will shoot you and throw you over myself."

"What's this?" Jack said. "And here I thought you were going to set us down on a nice deserted island."

"Do it!"

Cam dropped to her knees beside Jack, leaned in close to help him rise, whispered, "Distract him."

"What did you say?"

"I told him he had to stand."

Jack got slowly to his feet, his right hand clutching his left arm. He groaned and stumbled back against the yacht railing. Cam leaned toward him to grab him, whipped out her ankle piece, and fired, center mass.

The bullet struck Petrov high in the chest. The force of the bullet sent him back into the pilot house. Still he managed to fire two more rounds at them as they dove behind a teak storage box on the deck. One of the bullets slammed into the box, but it was sturdy enough to stop the bullet from going through.

"Give it up, Sergei!" Jack yelled.

He came out of the pilot house, blood streaming down his leg, blood staining his chest, heaving with pain, with the loss of everything he saw as his by right. He didn't stop, couldn't stop. He fired at them, but the Beretta was empty. He pulled another magazine out of his pants pocket, shoved it in with bloody fingers.

Cam shouted, "Drop the gun or I'll put a bullet through your throat."

He yelled something in Russian, raised the Beretta.

Cam shot him in the throat.

60

Savich parked his Porsche in the circular driveway in front of Eric Hainny's home on Kentfield Lane. The white, two-story colonial was set back from the road like most of the other houses in a quiet cul-de-sac, bordered by a thick copse of maple and oak trees. The half-moon still shone down on the neatly mowed grass, bordered by banks of petunias, impatiens, and flowers Savich didn't recognize.

Savich rang the doorbell, waited, and rang again. He finally heard footsteps, a man's mumbling voice. He looked into the camera above his head, knew he was being studied. He called out, "Mr. Hainny, it's Agent Dillon Savich. Please open the door."

He heard Hainny disarm the security system, unlock the dead bolt, and slowly pull open the heavy front door. Hainny looked like a different man without his Ralph Lauren suit and Italian loafers. He wore an ancient red flannel robe, belted at his ample waist, and old black slippers worn down at the heels. His graying hair was messed, and gray whiskers sprouted on his cheeks. He looked ten years older than he had yesterday at Rock Creek Park. He got in Savich's face, snarled, "It's after midnight. Why are you here? It isn't about Saxon, is it? He's all right?"

"Yes, Saxon is fine. I'm here to end it, Mr. Hainny."

"End what?" Hainny looked at him blankly, took a step forward to block him. "I don't know what this is all about but I do know you are overstepping your bounds again, Agent Savich. You shouldn't be here in the dead of night, you shouldn't ever be at my home without my invitation. You will not come in unless you tell me right now what you're doing here, and it better be good."

"Sergei Petrov is dead."

Hainny froze, blinked rapidly, then said carefully, "And why is that important? I don't know a Sergei Petrov. Why would I care if he's dead? I can't imagine what you think his death has to do with me." He straightened his shoulders, getting himself in control again, the chief of staff to the president once more. "I think you should leave now, Agent Savich. I'll be speaking to the director in the morning and I will tell him of your inexplicable, highly inappropriate behavior." Hainny stepped back to shut the door.

Savich held out a metal box. "I was going to give this to Saxon, but I realized it would be better if you had it."

Hainny stared at the box, licked his lips. He stuck out his right hand, then drew it back, shrugged. "A metal box? What is that?"

"It's exactly what you're praying it is—the manufactured proof that Saxon murdered Mia Prevost. Agents found it in Petrov's desk. Of course, you already know all about the contents, Mr. Hainny. I'm sure Petrov called you today, probably gloated since once again, thanks to Manta Ray, he had the box back in his hands."

Hainny grew very still. He said very slowly, "I don't know what you're talking about, Agent Savich." He held out his hand. "Give it to me and I will look at the contents in my own time. Now I want you to get off my property."

"Mr. Hainny, you are a good liar, you have to be, given your position, but you know as well as I that the contents of this box were being used to blackmail you. The Russians call it *kompromat*—compromising material they use on each other and, of course, on foreigners, to control them. With you, Petrov succeeded, and he would have continued to, if he still had control of the box. And if he were still alive, of course.

"I'm here at your home, Mr. Hainny, out of courtesy to you. I did not want to have to march into the White House to arrest you. It's time to end this, sir. It is time for you to speak to me honestly, either here or at the Hoover Building."

Hainny turned and walked down the wide entrance hall, his slippers slapping on the floor, to the last door on the right. He disappeared inside, flipped on the light switch. Savich followed him into a long narrow room, with floor-to-ceiling bookshelves reaching up into shadows. A dark brown sofa sat in front of a dark stone fireplace, and a large mahogany desk dominated the other end of the room. The window behind the desk was covered with heavy, closed draperies. It was a dark room, a room with no color, perfectly suited to Hainny. Savich could picture him hunkering down in this silent, brooding room, weaving his plans in the shadows, deciding how and when to use secrets he had no right to know without compunction to get what he wanted.

Hainny walked to the sideboard, poured himself a glass of whiskey, drank it down, and slowly turned to stare, not at Savich, but at the small, gun-metal steel box he held. "Well, what's in the box?"

"Saxon's bloody shirt and T-shirt, several letters from Mia Prevost to Cortina Alvarez, a supposed friend of hers, detailing how Saxon's behavior had changed, how he was becoming violent, ranting at her, trying to cut her off from her friends, that she was afraid of him, and didn't know what to do. And of course the pièce de résistance—the knife used to kill her, her dried blood still on the blade, Saxon's fingerprints no doubt on the handle. In short, more evidence than a prosecutor would need to convict Saxon of murder and send him to prison for life. And naturally, destroy your career as well."

"There is no such person as Cortina Alvarez!" Finally, a spark of rage.

Savich nodded. "Of course there isn't. It's a near-perfect legend created for Sergei Petrov's bodyguard and longtime lover, Elena Orlov. Are you ready to tell me your side of it now, Mr. Hainny? Ready to tell me the truth?"

Hainny poured himself more whiskey, then walked slowly, like an old man, to the dark brown sofa. He sat down, motioned Savich to sit beside him. He said nothing for a very long time. He sipped at his whiskey, raised the glass to study it. "This is Glenfiddich, not the most expensive, but it's my favorite. My father introduced me to it on my eighteenth birthday, as I did Saxon." He laughed. "Saxon hates it." He paused, rolled the glass around between his palms. "Petrov called me the day after Mia Prevost was murdered, told me he'd done me a favor and taken away all the evidence that Saxon had murdered Mia Prevost from her apartment, as you said, more than enough to send Saxon to prison for life. He sent me photographs of the bloody shirt and T-shirt, the letters, and the knife. He said he'd hide them from the police if I cooperated with him—that was the word he used, *cooperated*. I asked him what he wanted and he told me what he wanted wasn't beyond someone in my position, someone with my abilities and reach. He even assured me it was nothing treasonous. He was going to ask me to do only what was necessary to keep my beloved son from prison. And now he was sure I had the motivation I needed." Hainny fell silent.

Savich waited for him to continue, but he didn't, merely rolled the glass of whiskey in his palms. "Mr. Hainny, we know his father, Boris Petrov, and his Transvolga investment firm were sanctioned by presidential executive order and lost hundreds of millions of dollars, and that most of what was left was frozen. That's what he wanted of you, wasn't it? To arrange to overturn that order, and, in return, he would give you the evidence against Saxon, the evidence in this box."

Hainny drew a deep breath. "I don't know how you found out about it, and so quickly, but yes, that's what he wanted. As you know, these sanctions were retaliation for the Russian invasion of Crimea and the Ukraine. They worked admirably. Not only did they cause great damage to the Russian economy, they drained billions of dollars, bringing capital investment to a standstill. Of course, the sanctions levied against specific individuals, their banks and financial assets, were designed to hit Putin directly in his pocketbook, to pressure him to withdraw from Crimea and the Ukraine. Will Putin withdraw? Or at least keep a lid on the hostilities?" Hainny shrugged. "Things are very bad in Russia but only time will tell.

"When Petrov told me he wanted the sanctions removed from his father and the Transvolga Group, that he wanted billions of dollars unfrozen, I told him I didn't have that power, he should have picked a rank-ing official in the Treasury Department. They were the ones who set the sanctions, they would be the ones to remove them. And technically, that's true. But he laughed at me. He said my talents are well-known and that I had one week to make progress on lifting the sanctions or my son would find himself on trial for murder."

He fell silent again, then said in surprise, "Petrov is Russian, but do you know, he's perfectly fluent, speaks with a British accent? And now he's dead." He raised his whiskey and toasted Savich. "Will you tell me what happened?"

"When FBI agents went to his home to arrest him, he and another man opened fire. They were both killed. Mr. Hainny, you said Petrov gave you a week. You could have called us then, but you didn't. Did you arrange anything on Petrov's behalf?"

"No, I didn't consider that an option at first. Actually he called me a couple of days later for a progress report and I lied to him, told him I'd spoken to the undersecretary for financial intelligence, that a review was under way, but it would take more time. I believed I could handle the—situation—myself and I almost succeeded, until everything went sideways." He drew a deep breath. "But of course you already know what happened."

Savich said, "You acted, you hired Manta Ray to steal the safe-deposit box from the Second National Bank of Alexandria. How did you know the evidence against Saxon was there?"

"Petrov would have preferred to stay anonymous, but of course he couldn't, he had to give me his father's name and the name of his firm if I was going to act on the sanctions. It was easy for me to find out that Petrov's son was in the United States. The father couldn't be, naturally, since the sanctions banned him from traveling here or to Europe."

Hainny rolled the whiskey glass around between his palms out of habit. "I realized Mia Prevost had been working for Petrov, that it had all been a setup. I decided I wouldn't tell Saxon. I'm a man with considerable power, Agent Savich, and I used some of it to neutralize this man. I knew he wouldn't have the items at his house, he'd have to know I could locate that quickly enough, and of course I did. He has no ties to the Russian Embassy, so he couldn't use their premises to hide the blackmail items.

"I decided a bank deposit box was an intelligent choice, perhaps one it would be hard to trace to him. But if so, which bank? I had an analyst whose name I cannot tell you investigate Sergei Petrov, his activities, his connections. He found Elena Orlov for me quickly, Petrov's closest contact. He even unearthed the name Cortina Alvarez, the alias she uses when it suits her. A search of her bank records showed me she had opened a safe-deposit box at her bank, the Second National Bank of Alexandria, the day after Mia Prevost was murdered. I didn't know for sure, but that safe-deposit box seemed the only way forward.

"I hired Liam Hennessey through an intermediary, an acquaintance from twenty years back, a man far enough removed so he wouldn't be linked to me. I paid him fifty thousand dollars to remove Cortina Alvarez's safe-deposit box and five other boxes around it, to confuse the issue. That's when it all went sideways.

"As you know, Hennessey's partner—a man he hired without telling my intermediary—killed a bank teller, and Hennessey got himself shot and ended up caught in a deserted warehouse in Alexandria. It was a tragedy, that poor woman murdered, and it was my fault, I was culpable." He raised incredibly weary eyes to Savich's face. "I was prepared to admit everything to President Gilbert when the FBI reported they couldn't find the contents of the safe-deposit boxes, that somehow Liam Hennessey, even grievously wounded, had managed to hide them before the FBI found him. Perhaps if he'd died or didn't tell them, there was still a chance for Saxon." He gave a laugh. "And for me."

"When Hennessey survived, I didn't dare contact him to arrange a deal for the whereabouts of Cortina Alvarez's safe-deposit box. I would have had to borrow a great deal of money, and it might have exposed me. When it came down to it, it didn't matter because Petrov outbid me. I'm sure he offered this criminal more than I ever could have, and he managed to pull off an amazing escape for him.

"You're right about Petrov calling me today. He said I had cost him a great deal of trouble and money, but no more. He gave me seventy-two hours to get the sanctions lifted from his father and the Transvolga Group or he would give all the evidence against Saxon to the police. He told me I'd end up in jail also, next to my son. I was a murderer, after all. Petrov has— had—a very ugly laugh.

"I will be honest with you, Agent Savich. I hadn't decided what I would do tomorrow. I like to think I would have confessed all of it to the president, but it was tempting to try to get those sanctions lifted from Petrov Senior and his company. And now you've made that moot.

"I cannot tell you how very sorry I am that bank teller was killed. I never intended—" He shook his head. "I know that I am legally guilty of murder, I know I have lost everything, my position with the president, my freedom. If you will allow me, Agent Savich, I would like to tell President Gilbert in the morning."

Savich nodded.

"What will you do with the box?"

"I've given it a lot of thought, Mr. Hainny. The man who murdered Mia Prevost is dead, so he can't be prosecuted for that crime. I would prefer to destroy it, put all of this mess as far behind Saxon as I can, but if you are brought to trial for your part in the murder of that bank teller, then it would be considered evidence. I intend to keep the box until a determination is made about your future. I will not tell Detective Raven about the plot against you, or about the box. The murder of Mia Prevost will officially remain unsolved, I see no way around that. In the end, she did have justice. I will explain what happened to Saxon, if you would like me to."

"I will speak to Saxon. I'm his father. He'll hate me, Agent Savich, and who could blame him? I lied to him and left him nothing but my shame to face."

A tear slowly fell down his cheek. "At least my son will be safe."

"Mr. Hainny, don't underestimate your son. He might choose to stand with you."

Savich rose and walked to the study door, turned and asked, "Could you have gotten those sanctions lifted?"

Hainny laughed. "Very probably. You wouldn't believe what I can get done in this town."

61

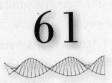

SAVICH HOUSE
GEORGETOWN
THURSDAY EVENING

Savich looked around his living room at the agents he and Sherlock had invited to their house for an evening to decompress and chow down pizza and Sherlock's amazing apple pie. It was still bubbling it was so hot, and the smell of cinnamon filled the air. No one broke the reverent silence as Sherlock carefully cut the slices the same size and divvied up the entire pie, sliding a slice onto each waiting plate. She said, smiling, "This has been quite a wild ride for all of us, guys, so sit back and enjoy. I've got to remember to wash the pan and put it away tonight so Sean doesn't see it. He wouldn't let up until I made another one." She lifted her own plate and breathed in the wonderful smell before she settled into her chair.

There were occasional moans of pleasure, and finally, the scraping of forks on empty plates. Cam looked at her empty pie plate, sighed, and set it on the coffee table. She started up again, telling the CARD agents about the melee at Sergei Petrov's house the previous night, lightly patting Jack's wounded arm for effect, and waving her own right arm to show she no longer needed a sling. "The boy here was the only casualty. He and I agree we can both handle getting small nicks from time to time."

Jack said, "That's right, Wittier. You and I, we've covered a lot of territory since Monday, first our memorable hike into the Daniel Boone National Forest and finally that shoot-out on the Potomac with Petrov last night. Quite a ride." He nodded to Ruth and Ollie, raised his beer bottle, and toasted everyone. "Here's to small nicks."

Sherlock began stacking the empty plates. "And Eric Hainny, chief of staff to the president, was at the root of it all. I find I feel sorry for him, even though the one time I met him, I wanted to smack him in the chops. He's had to resign and now he'll probably be indicted for the bank teller's murder."

Ollie said, "And it was all set into motion by Petrov. I wonder if Hainny ever considered killing him."

"I wouldn't doubt it," Savich said, "but the fact is, he's not a killer, despite what happened at the bank. He did what he did to save his son, the single most important person to him in the world, and the rest of the world be damned."

Sherlock said, "That's why I feel sorry for him, Dillon. I know I'd sign over the galaxy to keep Sean safe, as I bet all of you would for your kids."

There was no disagreement.

Cam poured herself another cup of coffee. "And Sherlock, what you and Connie and Bolt have been through. I understand this Dr. Maddox wanted people with a specific DNA, but I don't understand what he was looking for."

Sherlock said, "Near as we understand for now from his records, Maddox looked through the DNA of laboratory mice first, identified the few that could tolerate his drug, discovered how they were genetically different. Then he looked through the thousands of genomes housed at Gen-Core to find the people with the same variant of the human gene, and he found Thomas Denham, his first victim, or as Dr. Maddox would insist, his first test subject. He only lived three months. Dr. Maddox went looking again and found another, more useful, variant, and he kidnapped Dr. Arthur Childers, his second victim, and put him under lock and key. He's the young man still in a coma at Washington Memorial. Both Enigma One and Enigma Two, as Maddox labeled Denham and Childers, metabolized the drug differently from everyone else, and the metabolites in their blood, and in their plasma, were no longer toxic. So he took plasma regularly from Arthur Childers while giving him the drug, and it's that plasma he gave to others, and to his father, along with whatever else he thought might be helpful. When he impregnated Kara Moody with Arthur Childers's sperm, he was trying to combine both those genetic variants in one person, trying to create someone who could tolerate his drug without any toxicity at all.

"And that someone was Alex Moody, or Enigma Three, his wonder source."

Connie said, "It appalls me to think what he would have done to that baby." She took Bolt's hand. "But it didn't happen."

Bolt said, "When you think about it, DNA is a big part of what makes each of us unique, right? Scary to think Kara Moody and Arthur Childers were victimized because of their DNA."

Sherlock said, "It makes me worry for the rest of us. There might not be many lunatics like Lister Maddox out there, but what about all the businesses and governments that might want to make use of our DNA information? The abuses could be endless. We could be denied insurance, a good credit rating, certain jobs, for example. They could even use our DNA to predict how to advertise to us."

Bolt took a sip of Savich's sinfully rich coffee and sighed. "Savich, your coffee is as good as Sherlock's pie. You're right, Sherlock, and more and more people are getting their DNA tested, to evaluate their health risks or find out where their families are from. It's getting cheaper and faster all the time. I was tempted myself, but when I picture Lister Maddox in my mind, I'm not so sure anymore."

Ruth said, "I'm sure they have guidelines, some precautions in place, but we all know computers can be hacked."

Jack sat forward in his chair, put down his coffee cup, and clasped his hands between his knees. "I find it amazing we might be able to extend life by slowing or reversing aging with some kind of medical procedures, or even a simple pill. To think of living, say, two hundred years, now that's mind-blowing."

Savich said, "Sherlock and I were talking about that earlier, about mortality, and what it means, and we find we disagree. I guess I come down on the side of things as they are. Most everything we human beings value, everything we call wisdom and experience, is a consequence of our being mortal and knowing it. We are granted a finite number of years and everything we strive for is shaped by the inevitable fact of death.

"Everyone whose words you've read who came before us, all those thoughts you've shared, all of them lived knowing their lives would end. I wonder what the world would be like where no one died except by accident?" He paused, smiled. "I wonder if after a while, we'd all get bored."

"Accident or murder," Ruth said. "We've got to keep our jobs."

Cam said, "I don't think that would be good news for the planet. We'd all have longer to keep destroying it, and there would be more and more of us to do just that."

Jack said, "Living as long as, say, vampires. Now there's a thought."

Savich said, "Even most of the vampires you read about, they all say they see everything happen over and over, and people being people, or vampires, the same things would drive them, millennium after millennium: Greed, war, love, repeating itself into eternity."

Jack said, "Yeah, sounds like term limits would be

better. But seriously, what about the effects on society? Especially if only the rich could afford the magic pill? What would happen to everyone else? The possible consequences are inconceivable."

Sherlock said, "Back up, guys. Forget forever, say if we could all live a couple of hundred years. Don't forget we now live twice as long as people who lived two hundred years ago, and we seem to be managing. I think it would be incredibly exciting. Think of what we could make of ourselves, learn about ourselves and the world, the time we'd have to recognize and right our mistakes, travel new roads, goodness, we could travel the universe, all of this if only our own mortality didn't hover over our shoulders. I hope, Cam, we'd gain enough wisdom not to continue trashing the planet. Oh, and I think of the video games Sean could come up with if he had two hundred years." She grinned. "I asked MAX to tell me about what he thought and he gave me geneticist Francis Collins's quote that 'one man's longevity is another man's immortality.'"

Cam said, "If I were a vampire, I'd set Dr. Maddox the noble goal of working on changing my diet."

Connie grinned, shook her head at Cam. "Whatever way you lean on the mortality versus the immortality issue, one thing makes me very happy. Kara has her baby back."

Bolt said, "Amen to that." He looked down at his watch, jumped up. "Speaking of time, I just ran out. I promised my wife I'd be home by ten. Now I'm in trouble. It's possible I'd need all of Sherlock's extra years to make it up to her."

Connie rose with him. "I wonder, with two hundred years, how all our marriages would fare? Only one husband or wife for the duration, until death do us part at the end of the millennium? Bolt, I'll check with your wife, see what she thinks about that."

When Savich and Sherlock came back into the living room after showing out the CARD agents, Jack said, "Savich, I heard you saying you need to hit the gym, it's been four days and your body's yelling at you. I'll go with you, do some lower body."

Cam rolled her eyes at him. "Don't be an idiot. You can't use that arm for at least a week, doctor's orders. There's no such thing as only lower body, all of you would be involved. It should be weeks before you work out." She turned to Savich. "You say your bod is yelling at you after only four days? Mine is saying, 'Leave me alone to nap and grow fat cells' and contemplate a new vampire diet, say peanut butter being the primary food source."

Ollie laughed, pointed his licked fork at Jack. "My recommendation is three months, Jack, and make sure your will is in order if you're planning on going hand to hand with him. He shows no mercy. I learned my lesson a long time ago."

"My will? Savich is that scary? Okay, then, if he is, I should make some changes. After evaluating Agent Wittier in close quarters for the past three days, I've decided to leave her my most valuable possession."

She cocked her head at him, sending a thick hank of wavy blond hair listing over her left eye. "You've been evaluating me? Okay, Cabot. I'll bite. What is your most valuable possession?"

"My dog Cropper. He's hanging out right now with my brother in New York State—in White Plains. I'll need your muscle to help me liberate him from my brother's wife and three boys. You can drive the get-away car."

She pictured it, smiled. "Do you know, I'd like to have a dog. I've traveled so much since I've been out of the academy, I never thought it would be fair to have a pet. But now I'm settled here in Washington, why not? Cropper, that's a good name. What is he?"

"Purebred mongrel. Got him when he was a puppy at the pound."

"How big is he?"

"You need a king-size bed and ear plugs. He snores."

"Okay," Cam said, "I'll take him."

"Since this is in my will, you might not get him until his golden years."

Ruth said, "Now that Cropper's taken care of, Sherlock, I don't suppose there's one tiny piece of apple pie left, maybe hidden in the kitchen?"

Jack said, "If you're hiding some, Sherlock, I need it more than Ruth. To get my strength back. Here's another idea—leave this goombah and come live with me. I'll provide the apples and the oven and endless praise."

Cam looked at Jack. "Nah, you can forget Sherlock.

If we had two hundred years, she'd sign up for all of them with Dillon."

"I might," Sherlock said, and waggled her eyebrows. "I'll give it a lot of thought, let you know." She leaned over and patted Cam's shoulder. "You know, Cam, I'm thinking you should be our guest tonight at Hotel Savich, or maybe Hotel Savich and Infirmary. You can have the guest room, and Jack can sleep in Sean's room and talk sports until our boy conks out. Sorry, but there'll be no stopping Astro from licking your face."

Jack said, "Not a problem, Sean and I can talk basketball. Believe me, I'm used to Cropper's big tongue." He arched an eyebrow at Cam. "Maybe if Sean wakes me up with a snort or two, I could check in to see how well Wittier's sleeping, maybe spoon her, make her feel all safe and warm."

Sherlock watched Cam smiling as she punched Jack on his uninjured arm. If Sherlock had to guess, she'd say Cam thought spooning with Jack could be a fine idea.

She said, "Cam, would you like another glass of wine since you're not driving tonight?"

Sherlock handed her a glass of chardonnay, watched her chug it down, keeping one eye on Jack, a bit of appalled comprehension on her face. Sherlock looked over at Dillon, who was eyeing the two of them. He could thank her later for that very smooth move. He did want Jack to transfer out of the New York Field Office and come to Washington. And after tonight, who knew? Dillon might get his wish.

After Ruth and Ollie left, Savich walked Astro to his favorite oak tree down the block. It was clear and warm, a beautiful night, the stars vivid in the sky. His neighbors' lights were going off, one after the other. It had been a long, nonstop week for both him and Sherlock and all the agents visiting them tonight. He looked forward to relaxing and playing with Sean over the weekend, trying to put their world back into place, life back into perspective. When Astro finished with his oak tree of choice, he gave a little bark and a hop, raised his head for Savich to praise him, which he did. Satisfied, Astro pranced back to the Savich driveway.

Two hours later, Hotel Savich was quiet, all the lights out. Both Sean and Astro were snuggled together and sound asleep. Jack lay on his back in Sean's room on a single bed, his feet hanging off the end, his head pillowed in his arms. He got up, looked down at Sean, listened to him snort a couple of times, petted Astro's head, and made his way quietly to the guest room.

He opened the door, looked over at the bed, and smiled. He didn't know what had taken him so long to decide about Cam Wittier. It was time to try his hand at spooning.

EPILOGUE

ARTHUR CHILDERS'S HOSPITAL ROOM
WASHINGTON MEMORIAL HOSPITAL
WASHINGTON, D.C.
FRIDAY MORNING

Alex slept pressed against Kara's heart, his fist in his mouth. "I'm glad you're asleep," she whispered, kissing his forehead, "because the milk truck is empty." She smiled hugely, rocking him.

Kara laid her sleeping baby into his bassinet, and walked back to sit beside Arthur and started talking, so used to speaking to him she didn't even think about it. "They told me your name is Arthur Childers. I still can't get my brain around everything that's happened since you burst into my house last Sunday, a crazy man I'd never seen before in my life. Can you believe what's happened? Well, of course you can't, you haven't even been here. But it's over now, Arthur. You're safe, and Alex is safe. Everything will be all right as soon as you heal up, as soon as you wake up. The marks on your skin are fading, and Dr. Wordsworth says you're getting better every day.

"Sherlock says you're thirty-eight, and it's that fountain of youth drug that makes you look younger than I am. I told you I have your whole bio now. Agent Sherlock uploaded it to my tablet. You're a scientist, you work at NASA, officially still on a sabbatical to work with scientists at the Sondheim Institute in Stockholm, but of course you never showed up."

She paused a moment, turned to look back toward Alex. "Imagine that, Alex, your daddy is a rocket scientist. Maybe he was working on a spaceship to Mars." She turned back, lightly touched her fingertips to Arthur's cheek, squeezed his hand. "You realize I don't blame you for any of what happened. You didn't inject your sperm into my cervix, that was Dr. Lister Maddox. As for Sylvie, I have to admit I really was a gullible fool. I fell for her instant friendship-kismet deal right away. I'm still angry at what she did, and I hope they put her in jail. As for Dr. Maddox, I hope they shove him in a black hole somewhere, forever. Yet isn't it amazing what came out of an evil man's plans? We got Alex. And we got each other."

She squeezed his hand. "Sherlock told me your wife died in an automobile accident five years ago, and you don't have any children. I'm very sorry about that, but now you have a son. I can't imagine what your parents will say when they see you again. Sherlock said she's contacting them today, and when you wake up, you and I can talk to them together. It will be difficult, trying to explain to them what happened to you. We'll see what Sherlock recommends."

His breathing stayed smooth and even.

"I hope you never remember too much about what

happened to you. I really don't understand it all, but I do know it all has to do with your genome and mine, and ours being somehow special.

"Did you understand what he was doing to you? Or did he keep you drugged to your gills the whole time you were his test subject, his prisoner? I have a hard time not wanting to kill him, Arthur, shoot him dead for what he did to you, and what he planned to do to Alex and me. I am so grateful you managed to escape him and come to me. To us."

She lightly squeezed his hand, warm, alive. "It's good to have everyone gone, to have some silence again. Are you tired of hearing my voice? Do you want me to stop? Sorry, not going to happen.

"Arthur, five days have passed and my life has changed so much. When you wake up, you'll see that yours has changed as well, and for the better. I pray you'll give Alex and me a chance."

She heard Alex sucking on his fingers, the only sound in the silence.

"I like your name. Arthur Childers, well, Dr. Arthur Childers. Do you have a nickname, like Art or Artie? I think I prefer Arthur, it's a good name, a solid name." Kara leaned close, whispered against his cheek, "Arthur, it's really time for you to wake up and meet your son."

He lay so quiet, so very quiet, and he breathed slowly and steadily. She got up and picked up Alex, burped him, and snuggled him against her. She rocked him, sat down again. "Arthur, everyone wants you to wake up. There are questions only you can answer."

Kara fell silent. She was out of words. She leaned close, lightly kissed his slack mouth. "Arthur, it's time for you to wake up before I become permanently hoarse from talking so much. I think I've told you about every minute of my life, all my twenty-seven years. I hope you won't think I'm stupid. You know I'm an artist, not a scientist."

Alex gave a little shudder.

"What are you dreaming about, sweetheart?" She held him close, kept rocking him. He was deeply asleep. She carried him to his bassinet and tucked him in once more, then returned to her vigil beside Arthur Childers's bed. She felt exhaustion hit her like a hammer. She fell asleep holding his hand.

She awoke slowly, aware of a man's voice very close to her. "You're—Kara." He spoke slowly, his voice slurred.

She raised her head and looked into beautiful eyes as green as moss. He smiled at her.

"Hello, Arthur. I'm glad you're back. Would you like to meet your son?"

"My son—Alex."

EPILOGUE

Hannah gently wiped the smear of lentil soup off his mouth, offered another spoonful, pressing down on his lower lip. He took the soup in, swallowed, turned his head away, and closed his eyes.

"That tasted good, didn't it, Beau? You rest now while I read to you. It's a Hercule Poirot mystery. Remember you always liked Agatha Christie?"

Hannah rose, leaned down, and kissed his forehead, ran her fingers over his beautiful face, lightly stroked her fingers through his thick hair.

He'd been whole for five minutes, not completely whole, but he'd been aware of her and Lister, and he'd spoken. She wouldn't think about what he'd said to her. He hadn't meant it, not really, he simply hadn't understood. If only he'd stayed with them, Hannah could have made him see that people who love each other grow older gently and gradually, with time for them to adjust. He'd been struck with everything at once. He didn't understand why she looked older, that was all.

She didn't know what would happen to him now.

The FBI had sent a doctor to visit him yesterday, a Dr. Wordsworth from Washington Memorial in Washington. The doctor had been amazed at how young he looked, of course. At Hannah's questions, she said that no one could know exactly what would happen now that he wouldn't be receiving any more of Lister's drugs, but she was inclined to agree with Lister that B.B. would probably start aging normally once again. If that was true, Hannah might be dead or infirm before he was a seventy-eight-year-old man again. She wanted to cry. Her beautiful Beau, blank-brained, uncaring, and unaware of anything or anyone, was housed in a beautiful fifty-year-old body. She still remembered his holding her, stroking her hair, making love to her. Better if the drug hadn't brought him back, had given him fifteen more years, only to steal his mind again after such a short time.

She was feeling sorry for herself, for him, for them and what they'd once been together and would never be again. She carried his tray to the hallway and set it on a table and walked to the balcony that overlooked the entrance hall. No sign remained of the havoc of two days before, of what had been the end of all of it. Sylvie had been arrested by the FBI agents. What would happen to her daughter? No one would tell her anything yet. At least they hadn't arrested her, thank heaven, not that she knew that much about what Lister had done or what Sylvie had done. Had Lister paid her money? She prayed with all her might they'd leave her alone, they had to, or who would take care of Beau?

There were no more secrets in this house. Ella, the woman who'd been in charge of the infant Alex Moody, had been taken away with Sylvie. Now it would be only she and the housekeeper and two maids inside, the three gardeners outside, and Berry, who'd so faithfully taken care of Beau's precious yacht for so many years.

She didn't want to think about what Lister had planned to do with the infant he'd kidnapped, it both scared and sickened her. All she knew was Lister needed the infant to test his drugs. For his father. She realized how reprehensible that was, wondered at herself that she hadn't stopped it earlier. It was all a mistake, meant to slay Lister's dragons, not Beau's. Beau hadn't asked for any of it. Would he have if he'd been able? She didn't know, didn't want to know, ever.

Hannah sighed and walked back into the King's Bedchamber. She paused in the doorway, looked at Beau sitting motionless in his wheelchair, his head down, as if he was studying his slippers. There was no use lying to herself, it was time to face the truth. Lister was not coming back with any more drugs, any more promises. Beau was gone forever now. She was all he had, and she'd never leave him, as long as she lived.

She looked around his precious King's Bedchamber. She realized she hated this room. An exact copy of a centuries-old room, faded, pathetic, really. She wanted a soft carpet beneath her feet, not the wide oak planks. She wanted that absurd harpsichord out of here, and those bed hangings, she would burn them. Yes, she would change everything.

Hannah looked toward the Hercule Poirot she'd been going to read to him. No, let him sleep. She walked to the closet and began collecting Beau's clothes. She would donate the lot to charity.

B. B. Maddox opened his eyes, raised his head. He watched Hannah as she took his clothes out of the closet. He thought she seemed tired, noticed how thick she looked around the middle. Why was that? She'd been so slender. He opened his mouth to ask her what she was doing with his clothes, but his head fell against his chest once again, and he slept.

EPILOGUE

THE CLIFFS OF MOHER
WEST COAST OF IRELAND
FRIDAY, SUNSET

"There's no more beautiful spot on this blessed earth," Liam said against Elena's hair. "And glory be, it's stopped raining. Now, girl, get ready for the show."

"You've become a romantic." Elena leaned up, bit his earlobe, and snuggled into him as they watched the huge orange sun slowly sink into the ocean. Tourists and locals alike fell silent, watching the spectacle, and let out a collective gasp when the sun at last disappeared, falling into the ocean. Liam helped Elena to her feet, brushed the dirt off her jeans. He cupped her face in his hands, kissed her cheek, her mouth. "You ready for a pint at the pub and a lively fiddle? This romantic is going to dance a jig with you."

Elena, marveling at the vagaries of fate, put her hand in his. He would have to teach her how to dance an Irish jig.

AUTHOR'S NOTE

Enigma is a work of fiction. Yet in today's laboratories the search for the fountain of youth is no longer shrouded in mysticism and legend as it has been for millennia. As our tools improve and our research continues, we may find ourselves perilously close to James Hilton's Shangri-La, where no one ages, or to Dr. Lister Maddox's nightmare landscape.

Will we eventually take a pill to keep our youth, our health, and live longer? Say, two hundred years? We must always be careful what we wish for.

Turn the page for an exclusive look at

PARADOX

by CATHERINE COULTER

Available now from Gallery Books!

PROLOGUE

Wake up, wake up. Something's not right. Sherlock's eyes snapped open. She was instantly awake, adrenaline surging, but why? She didn't move, listened. There—three beeps coming from the security monitor beside the bed. She'd never heard them before, but she knew what it meant: the security system was off. The beeps would get louder and louder. Possibilities scurried through her brain, none of them good. Dillon was on his back beside her, stirring now from the noise. She leaned down, whispered, "Dillon, the alarm's off."

He was instantly awake. He heard the beeps and turned off the alarm. "You check on Sean. I'll see what's going on." They'd had this protocol in place since Sean had been born, but this was the first time they'd had to use it.

Savich unlocked the closet safe, handed Sherlock her small ankle Glock and a suppressor. The last thing either of them wanted was for Sean to wake up to a gunshot, terrified. He fitted a suppressor on his own Glock and racked the slide. He prayed for a simple malfunction as he pulled his pants on, but he knew it was unlikely. "Be careful," he whispered against her cheek. He ran down the stairs, and Sherlock, her bare feet whisper-light on the hall carpet, headed to Sean's room. His door was partially open, as it always was at night. She stopped, leaned in to listen, heard him make a little snort in his sleep. He was all right, no need to alarm him.

She heard a soft footfall and her heart seized. Someone had disabled the system and that someone was now in Sean's room. Sherlock slowly pushed the door inward, her heart pounding, her adrenaline spiking even higher. Moonlight poured through the window, silhouetting the man bent over Sean. His head looked distorted—no, he'd pulled a stocking over his face. She ignored the toxic punch of fear, raised her small Glock, and said very quietly, "Get away from him, or I'll blow your head off."

She saw the gun clutched in his gloved hand, a Ka-Bar knife in the other. He jerked up but didn't turn. "I'll shoot him before you can kill me." A young voice, low and hard. And something else. It was fear she heard, she knew it.

"All right, move away from him, and I won't shoot you. Drop the gun and the Ka-Bar and back away."

He slowly turned, but the gun still pointed at Sean. "How did you know I was here?"

"I've got bat ears. Who are you? What do you want?"

He looked undecided, then said, "You try to shoot me and he's dead, you got that?"

She wanted to vomit, she was so scared. *Hold it together, hold it together.* "All right. Get away from him, and I won't shoot you." Again, she saw indecision. "You fire and you'll see, I'll still shoot him!" The man ran six feet to the open window and jumped through a gash in the screen and onto the roof.

Sean jerked up, rubbed his eyes. "Mama? Mama? What's wrong?"

She had to move, had to get him, but she had to soothe Sean. "Everything's all right, sweetie. Don't move." She ran to the window and jumped onto a thick oak branch that nearly touched the house. She saw him below, nearly to the ground now. She didn't have a good shot through the thick leaves and he was juking and jiving from branch to branch, but she fired anyway, missed, the bullet gouging tree bark a foot from his head. He didn't fire back.

He swung from the lowest tree branch six feet to the ground, landed on his side, rolled and ran, not all-out because he was limping. She fired until her magazine was empty, but he was zigging and zagging, the limp even more pronounced now.

He disappeared around the corner of Mr. McPherson's house. She heard McPherson's puppy, Gladys, barking her head off.

Dillon's quiet voice came from behind her. "Sherlock, stay with Sean. I'm going after him."

They heard a car engine fire up. Sherlock grabbed his arm. "We can't get him now. Come back in."

He helped her back through the slit in the screen. He studied her face, ran his hands over her arms, up and down her back. "I called 911. The police will be here soon."

Sherlock cupped his face between her hands. "Dillon, I'm not hurt, I'm fine." But of course she wasn't. Her heart was pounding, fear for Sean pouring off her.

"Mama! Papa!"

Savich quickly slid his Glock into his waistband and grabbed up Sean into his arms, hugged him tight against him. He whispered against his small ear, "Everything's all right, Sean. Don't worry, okay?" He closed his eyes as he rocked his small son.

Sean reared back in his arms and looked over at his mother. Sherlock pressed her own Glock against her leg so he wouldn't see it. "I heard you yell, Mama. Did you have a nightmare? What were those loud popping sounds?"

Her heart still pounded, her adrenaline still pumped wildly, but she could deal with that. She could deal with anything because Sean was all right, the danger was past. She looked at his small beloved face and said a thank-you prayer. She smiled, lightly patted his face. "Like your papa said, sweetie, everything's all right.

The popping sounds, it was probably somebody's car backfiring. Some messed-up car, right? Too loud for our neighborhood. That's what woke up your papa and me." Did her smart son buy that whopper? Or would he realize the popping hadn't happened until she was in his room? Well, she'd lied as clean as she could. Savich brought Sean close again, rocking him, breathing in his sweet child smell until Sean pulled back . He put his hand on his father's cheek, cocked his head.

"There's something wrong, isn't there, Papa? I dreamed I heard a man talking. And Mama, you said something, too, and you sounded angry. And then someone was running to the window. His head was all weird-looking, like a space man, and you were running after him, Mama. I saw you going out the window. It wasn't a dream, was it?"

Savich knew he had no choice. "There was someone here, Sean, but your mama took care of him. He won't be back. Now, it's time for you to go to sleep." While Dillon was speaking to Sean, Sherlock scooped the Ka-Bar off the Winnie the Pooh rug by Sean's bed. She hadn't even seen the man drop it.

"But—" Sean gave a jaw-cracking yawn.

Savich kissed him and tucked him under a single light sheet. He saw Sherlock quietly closing the window over the slit screen. He hoped Sean wouldn't notice it in the morning, but chances were good he would. Savich would have to figure out what to tell him without scaring him. He waited quietly until he heard his son's breathing even into sleep.

He went to Sherlock, saw her give a little shudder of reaction. The words burst out, low and controlled, but Savich heard the thick fear coating every word. "He was standing over Sean, Dillon, a gun in one hand, a Ka-Bar in the other." She swallowed. "He wouldn't tell me who he was. I couldn't shoot him—he said he would kill Sean. He held the gun toward Sean and ran to the window. Was he a pedophile who wanted to steal him? Or someone who wanted to kidnap him for ransom? Or some random crazed lowlife?"

His brain immediately latched onto *pedophile*, a word that scared every parent to his toes. He didn't want to say it aloud, or it would bow him to his knees. He felt violence stir in his gut, rancid and black. He pulled her close, whispered against her curly hair. "No," he said, more to himself than to her, "Whoever he is, he had to believe we're rich because of my grandmother's paintings."

"Well, your Sarah Elliott paintings do make you rich, and a lot of people know it. They also know you'd sell one or all of them in a flash to save Sean."

"No matter who or what he is, we'll get him, I promise you. You saved our boy. Sean's safe. You're my hero."

That brought a hiccupping laugh. "I tried to shoot him, but he got down that tree in a flash." Her breathing hitched. "I wondered why he had both a gun and a Ka-Bar, but he needed the knife to slit the screen. Was he going to kill Sean?"

They held each other, saying nothing now, their eyes on their sleeping son, but only for a moment.

They had to hurry because Metro cops would be here very soon. The last thing they wanted was for Sean to wake up to the police pounding on the door.

While they stood in the open front door, waiting, Savich said, "I asked the dispatcher—it was Jordan Kates—to send them in silent." He kissed her forehead. "They'll be here any minute now. Did anything about him seem familiar to you or strike you as different?"

"It happened so fast—I don't think so. Wait, his voice was young, Dillon, and he moved young, too. Something else: when he told me he could kill Sean even if I shot him, I think I heard fear in his voice. But then again, he hadn't expected any trouble."

"Maybe he'd talked himself into coming after Sean, but he didn't have another plan if he was challenged."

She nodded. "Well, at least we have the knife, for all the good it will do us. He was wearing gloves. Dillon, I went after him, emptied my magazine, but I missed him. I actually missed him—me, can you believe that?"

He loved hearing the outrage in her voice. It meant she was getting back on an even keel. "Even *you* have to miss sometimes. You were terrified for Sean, pumping out adrenaline, and so hyped you could have rocketed yourself to the moon. I hear a car coming. You can fill in the blanks when we tell the police what happened."

"Okay, I've got it together—well, I'm close. Thank heavens we had a plan in place if those three beeps ever sounded, otherwise . . ." She paused, then, her voice shaking. "Without the suppressor, I think Sean would have freaked. Even so, it was loud. So fast, Dillon, it all happened so fast. I wonder why he never fired back at me."

"He knew if he hesitated, turned back to you, you'd nail him."

A Metro squad car pulled into their driveway, cut its lights, and two officers climbed out. "Agent Savich?"

After introductions, Sherlock gave them a quick rundown, then Officers Pattee and Paulette headed out to search the neighborhood. They were back ten minutes later. No sign of their intruder, not that Savich or Sherlock expected them to spot him.

Paulette said, "No lights on in any houses, so the sound of the car engine didn't wake anybody up."

"And no neighbors standing on their porches to tell us anything," said Pattee.

Savich was studying his security system beside the front door. He called, "Come look at this." Both Paulette and Pattee looked over his shoulder to where he pointed.

"That's more wires than the back of my TV," Paulette said.

"Looks untouched to me," Pattee said, leaning in. "But how can that be possible? The guy got into your son's window. It's alarmed, right?"

"Oh yes," Sherlock said.

Dillon said, "I'm thinking we've got a guy with major computer skills."

"You think he disabled the alarm system remotely, using his computer?"

Savich nodded. "To do it, he'd have to be very good,

because I upgraded the system myself. But he succeeded, and now I'll have to figure out how he did that and fix it."

The three men studied the complex mess of wires for another couple of seconds, then Paulette turned to Sherlock. "Could we go inside? You can tell us exactly what happened."

They went into the living room and Officer Paulette switched on a recorder. Sherlock went through it all again, answered their questions, and finished with "I can't tell you what he looked like. He wore a stocking mask, but I do believe he was young, twenty-five at most. When he ran across the yard, I saw he was limping a bit. From the jump? Maybe. I didn't notice a limp when he was in Sean's bedroom." She closed her eyes, pictured him. "It was his left leg."

They asked questions, Sherlock gave more details, and finally Officer Paulette switched off his phone recorder and smiled at her. "You really told him you'd shoot his head off?"

Paulette, no more than twenty-five himself, had a great smile, and Sherlock found herself smiling back as she nodded. "That's what came out of my mouth, yes. Come on, guys, if someone was leaning over your sleeping child, a gun and knife in his hand, what would you say?"

"I don't know if I'd say anything," Pattee said. "I'd probably just shoot him."

"Yeah, sure, Joel," Paulette said, and smacked him on the arm. "That's what you'd want three-year-old

Janet to wake up and see—blood and gore all over her bed."

Pattee pointed. "Yeah, okay, you have a point. I see a dog toy over there. But no wild barking?"

Savich said, "Astro would have brought the house down if he'd been here. But he's in love with a neighbor's new puppy, so our son let him do a sleepover."

Paulette said, "From now on out, I'll bet it'll be the puppy sleeping over here."

"You're right about that," Sherlock said, "and yes, we're going to cut those branches off first thing tomorrow."

Officer Pattee said, "You guys had this plan in place in case something like this happened?"

"Yes," Sherlock said. "It sure paid off tonight."

"Now that's something I'm going to talk about with my wife," Pattee said. "You know, it would have been easier and cheaper for him to snatch your son off the sidewalk or out of a neighbor's yard or from the playground at school."

Sherlock said, "Yes, it would. I hadn't thought of that."

Pattee said, "You said, Agent Sherlock, you heard fear in his voice?"

She nodded.

Paulette said, "Well, he wasn't expecting her to walk in on him with a gun."

Pattee said, "That isn't the point. This doesn't sound like a pro someone hired to kidnap your son for ransom. Those guys have metronomes for hearts, nothing shakes them." No one had to say it, but everybody was thinking it—maybe the guy was a pedophile.

Savich said, "Officers, we'd like to speak to Detective Ben Raven in the morning. Will that be a problem?"

It wasn't a problem. Savich wanted Raven to check for any recent break-ins remotely like this one.

Pattee paused at the front door. "I've got to say something you already know. The guy who tried to take your son? I'll wager he'll keep trying. All his preparations show a big commitment. I'd say he's in for the long haul."

Both Savich and Sherlock hated it but knew he was right. Sherlock said, "At least we have the Ka-Bar. I'll get it to our FBI lab people in the morning."

Paulette said, "You'll let us know when you catch the guy?"

What faith. Sherlock smiled. "Yes, of course we will."

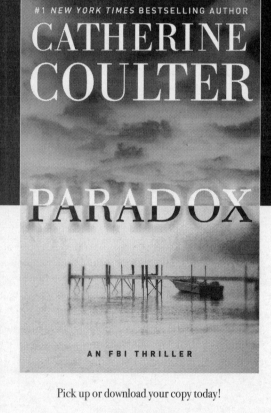